Meet the Newmans

ALSO BY JENNIFER NIVEN

When We Were Monsters
Take Me with You When You Go (with David Levithan)
Breathless
Holding Up the Universe
All the Bright Places
American Blonde
Becoming Clementine
Velva Jean Learns to Fly
Velva Jean Learns to Drive
The Aqua Net Diaries
Ada Blackjack: A True Story of Survival in the Arctic
The Ice Master: The Doomed 1913 Voyage of the Karluk

Meet the Newmans

A Novel

JENNIFER NIVEN

FLATIRON
BOOKS
NEW YORK

MEET THE NEWMANS. Copyright © 2025 by Jennifer Niven. All rights reserved. Printed in the United States of America. For information, address Flatiron Books, 120 Broadway, New York, NY 10271. EU Representative: Macmillan Publishers Ireland Ltd., 1st Floor, The Liffey Trust Centre, 117–126 Sheriff Street Upper, Dublin 1, DO1 YC43.

www.flatironbooks.com

Library of Congress Cataloging-in-Publication Data

Names: Niven, Jennifer, author.
Title: Meet the Newmans : a novel / Jennifer Niven.
Description: First edition. | New York, NY : Flatiron Books, 2026.
Identifiers: LCCN 2025026599 | ISBN 9781250372444 (hardcover) |
    ISBN 9781250442581 (international, sold outside the U.S., subject to rights
    availability) | ISBN 9781250372451 (ebook)
Subjects: LCGFT: Fiction | Domestic fiction | Novels
Classification: LCC PS3614.I94 M44 2026
LC record available at https://lccn.loc.gov/2025026599

Published by arrangement with Flatiron Books.

Our books may be purchased in bulk for specialty retail/wholesale, literacy, corporate/premium, educational, and subscription box use. Please contact MacmillanSpecialMarkets@macmillan.com.

First U.S. Edition: 2026

First International Edition: 2026

10 9 8 7 6 5 4 3 2 1

To Uncle Bill, honorary dad and granddad, who arrived when we needed him most, armed with unconditional love, immeasurable humor, and a whole lot of wisdom. Such as:

"A book should not be so long and big that it has to be hauled around in a wheelbarrow."

"If you are bored writing something, people will most likely be bored reading it."

"You don't want to repeat the same words too often or you'll get on the reader's nerves."

And to the families we choose.

Well, it ain't Ozzie and Harriet.

—Herbert I. "Hi" McDunnough,
Raising Arizona

Prologue

March 20, 1964

The night the world as she knew it ended, Dinah Newman stood at the stove of her Toluca Lake kitchen and stared down at the charred remains of pork chops. She had been doing fine until attempting the pineapple–soy sauce glaze. It had somehow caught fire, leaving the bottom of the pan black and sticky like a catastrophic oil spill. Like the one from last January in which three and a half million gallons flooded the Mississippi River and all the ducks had to be rescued and cleaned.

Dinah removed the skillet from the stovetop, carried it to the trash can, and dumped all of it—pan and contents—in. She was a terrible cook. Usually Flora Klausen, their longtime housekeeper, made dinner, but tonight Dinah had wanted to do it herself. It was a surprise for her husband, Del.

The kitchen was lined with shelves of cookbooks, most of them gifts from Del and their sons or well-meaning fans who assumed Dinah would enjoy reading about the origin of ham loaves or what to serve with creamed eggs or how to congeal a gelatin corned beef without losing its shape. After all, it was incomprehensible that the most famous cook in America, the spokeswoman for Hotpoint appliances and Pyrex kitchenware, couldn't feed her family.

Tonight, though, she had wanted to show her husband she was making an effort, not with dinner but with *them*. Unfortunately, carbonized sweet-sour pork was not going to save her marriage. She would have to come up with something else.

A sound from outside distracted her. The low mosquito buzz of a lawn mower. She stared at the trash can, the ruined pan, and then she tore off her apron and went upstairs.

From her open bedroom window, she watched the neighbor mow his lawn. She could just see him over the wall that surrounded their house. Ted or Tad, she couldn't remember, because he was no one she would ever be attracted to in real life. But here? In the Los Angeles suburbs? Where she had somehow ended up? She imagined marching over to his house, grabbing him by the collar of his polo shirt, pulling him down onto that freshly mown lawn, and riding him like, well, a lawn mower.

Never mind that he had no business mowing the lawn at dusk. For the past week—ever since her forty-second birthday—Dinah had spent each evening standing in this same spot, smoking a clandestine cigarette, watching this same man perform yard work and chores, envisioning the same torrid affair. She would never do it, of course. She'd never had sex in a public place, not unless you counted the back seat of Del's car when they were young and unable to keep their hands off each other, back before the boys came along. Besides, she was married to the only man she'd ever loved, a man she still loved—for better or worse—twenty-three years in.

Yet here she was. And there he was. Ted or Tad. As she imagined joining him on his half-mown lawn, handing him a cool drink, wiping his sweating brow with her hand, rolling across the grass in his arms, their middle-age joints popping and cracking—all she could think was *this single act could blow up everything*.

She could see it. The look of surprise on his face. Followed by the look of pure, animalistic pleasure. Followed by a grainy, blurred photo of the two of them splashed across the front pages of newspapers and gossip rags, taken by a particularly stealthy member of the paparazzi. Tongues wagging across the country, everyone up in arms over the scandal. Del and the boys in disbelief. Everyone in disbelief. Not *Dinah Newman*.

She marveled at the idea. Honestly, it thrilled her. How one move in a different direction—left instead of right, back instead of forward, no instead of yes—could change a life forever.

And then, because the Dinah Newman of today, star of one of the most famous TV shows in America, had more than she'd ever imagined back when she was a kid with skinned knees and a Texas-size imagination, and because the idea of blowing up her entire world was shocking and hilarious, she laughed. There was no one to see her, and so she tossed her head back and cackled. This, her father would have said, was the Shepherd in her, the genes passed down from her mama's side of the family that were responsible for any hint of emotional or mental instability in Dinah. *Your mother's people*, her father had told her ominously, on more than one occasion, *are prone to hysteria*.

The banging of the front door caused her to jump. Her younger son was either just getting home or just going out. These days, there was as much chance of one as the other, and she had long ago stopped trying to keep track. She stubbed the cigarette out and flung it into the bushes below.

"Shep?"

No answer.

She heard footsteps coming up the back stairs and then, from down the hall, a male voice, a one-sided conversation. She wondered who he could be talking to. Her father had been the type to listen in on phone calls, but Dinah had vowed to love her children without interfering. What was easy practice with Guy was trickier with Shep because, at seventeen, he was craftier than his older brother had ever been.

That time they'd found a naked girl in his bed. *You never said I couldn't have an overnight guest*. That time he didn't come home one night and they sat up phoning hospitals and police until Del discovered him in the morning passed out on the lawn. *I was back before curfew. You never specified that I had to come inside.* That time he had gotten into the LSD prescribed for Del by his psychiatrist to help him through a creative impasse. *If you have it in the house and it was prescribed by a doctor, how can it be bad for you?*

This was the kind of thing they had to contend with. Shepherd Newman was the master of loopholes. Guy, four years older, had been easier, was still easier. He had always been the reliable, self-sufficient one, the one they never had to worry about.

Outside, the night went suddenly quiet. The neighbor was sitting on the silent lawn mower looking out toward the street. From her perch in the window, Dinah lit another cigarette, momentarily forgetting about her son.

Why him? the gossip rags would say. *Why Tad? What was it about him that made her blow up her entire life?*

She started to laugh again. From somewhere in her house, another door banged open or closed, and Dinah could just make out the figure of her younger son as he crossed the yard. He disappeared into the darkness, and then, seconds later, there was the revving of an engine, and his motorcycle roared away.

Even though three members of the Newman family lived under the same roof and the fourth member—Guy—lived in the nearby guesthouse, they all led separate lives off camera. Especially Shep, because he was not someone you could fence in. He was seventeen, almost eighteen now, which meant Guy was, what, twenty-two? Was that even possible?

Which meant—she quickly did the math—she hadn't turned forty-two after all. She was forty-*three*. It was a sobering thought, and Dinah's eyes, still wet from laughing, suddenly went bone-dry. She glanced at the slender band of gold on her wrist, the watch Del had bought her on their first anniversary because she almost always ran late. It was nearly eight o'clock.

At 8:30 p.m., twenty million American viewers would gather in front of their television sets and watch the antics of their favorite family. Every Friday night, no matter what was happening in their lives, Dinah and Del watched the show together after dinner. Once upon a time, the boys had joined them.

Now, she sat by herself, one eye on the RCA Victor console TV, the other on the window that faced the driveway. On-screen, the door to the Newman house swung open, and under the announcer's voice— "Eastman Kodak Company and Listerine are happy to invite you to *Meet the Newmans!*"—Del, Dinah, Guy, and Shep emerged, arms linked, beaming at the camera. The music swelled and the episode began, fading in on Dinah—in heels, dress, and signature pearls—as she went about her morning chores.

It was the episode where Del writes a column for the local newspaper and ends up spilling family secrets. It followed a familiar formula, one Del called "the old tried and true." Del unintentionally creates trouble for Guy and Shep and oftentimes himself. Dinah offers advice and homemade meals.

Twenty-eight minutes later, the show came to an end, as it always did, with a song from Shep, and then the credits rolled. *Written by Del Newman. Directed by Del Newman. Produced by Del Newman. Starring Del Newman.* Dinah clicked off the set and padded in bare feet through the empty house, turning lights on as she went because they made her feel less alone.

At ten o'clock, she sat in the living room where she could see the front door. Her second attempt at dinner—baked chicken that was somehow both dry and rubbery—sat on the kitchen table growing cold.

You're ridiculous, she told herself. *Waiting for Del to get home as if the cameras are rolling.* But she continued to sit there, anger glittering off her, until she could feel the heat radiating from her skin and through the top of her head.

She made herself think about why she was so angry in the first place. For starters, he should be here and he wasn't. In the beginning, *Meet the Newmans* had been a family project, a way for the four of them to spend time together. No more long absences from home for Del or Dinah as they flew off to exotic movie locales. But then Del had gotten busier and busier, and the boys had grown up and gotten busier and busier, and meanwhile Dinah had stayed exactly the same. The one Newman who hadn't changed and was now, somehow, expendable.

It was more than that, though. Last year, Del and Dinah had suddenly stopped talking *to* each other and started talking *at* each other. Foolishly, it had taken her by surprise. When Del reached forty-four without a hint of midlife crisis, she had congratulated herself. They'd made it unscathed through one of the trickiest times in marriage.

But three months ago, he had turned forty-five, and with the arrival of new gray hairs came the arrival of a Del she didn't recognize. Her warm, meddlesome husband, always available to them with guidance—even the guidance they didn't ask for—began snapping at her and the boys, retreating into his office over the garage and shutting himself away.

At first, it was a night or two—he fell asleep on the foldout couch opposite his desk. Dinah didn't think anything of it. She was used to going to bed while he was still up and working. And then it was more than a night or two, and then it was a month, and then at some point Del had moved into the office, and they never talked about it. They continued to film the show, to go about their lives as usual. The only change was that—unbeknownst to anyone, even their sons—America's favorite married couple was now sleeping apart. Which was ironic since, before Del and Dinah, every TV married couple slept in separate beds.

So, yes, Dinah was angry. At the very least, her husband should be home when he was expected home. Surely they weren't *that* far gone. She was also angry because waiting like this made her feel stupid. And because, behind the anger, she had a feeling of great anticipation. Not anticipation. Foreboding. Del was never late.

She got up and poured herself a glass of wine. She carried it into the living room as the grandfather clock struck ten thirty. Then eleven.

She peered out the window, moving the curtains aside, even though from down here she couldn't see beyond the wall that encircled the house, the one they'd built to protect Shep—and themselves—from the carloads of girls who drove past day and night, honking and screaming and trying to break in.

She sighed. Checked her watch. Sat back down. Stood back up. Walked outside. Came back in.

When the grandfather clock struck midnight, she telephoned the studio soundstage, but no one answered. She thought of calling Guy in the guesthouse across the lawn, but the windows were dark and she didn't want to alarm him when Del was certain to walk in any minute, whistling, no doubt with a story to tell.

She sat back down, picked up a book, and stared at the page without reading. No one had prepared her for marriage. In movies and fairy tales, the challenge was finding the person you were meant for in this great big world, but once you did, you were guaranteed a happily ever after. No one said, *Oh, that's only the beginning.* Why had no one told her the truth?

The telephone rang, loud and shrill, and she jumped in her chair.

"Dinah," a male voice said, breathing quick and ragged.

"Sydney?"

Sydney Weiss was their executive producer and longtime friend. She couldn't remember a time he had ever phoned this late at night. Her first thought was that something had happened to the boys. A mother's instinct.

"Dinah," Sydney said, "it's Del. There's been an accident."

The Renewal

The New York Times

MARCH 19, 1964

Dear CBS: I've Met the Newmans, Thanks, and They Have Overstayed Their Welcome

by Walter Kerr

For the past twenty years, the real-life Newmans—Del, Dinah, and sons Guy and Shep—have ruled the airwaves as "America's Favorite Family," first on CBS Radio, later on CBS Television. From the start, patriarch Del has been the creative motor behind the show, crafting it around his likable family and the wholesome, humorous situations they find themselves in—Del is locked out of the house in his pajamas! Dinah must give a party on an hour's notice! Guy buys a new car and hides it from his dad! Shep has two dates for the same dance!

What worked in 1952, when the series debuted on TV, doesn't work (at all) in 1964. The situations—unassuming and harmless—remain largely the same as they were twelve years ago. Del still invites us to laugh along with him at himself, while providing a gentle lesson on virtue and doing good by others. Dinah, devoted wife that she is, unfailingly supports this message and her husband. Meanwhile, the boys are polite and clean-cut and never give their parents any real worry.

But—as Bob Dylan sings—the times they are a-changin', and in the aftermath of JFK's assassination, the black-and-white universe of the Newman family comes off as square and outdated. They are a time capsule to a world that perhaps never truly existed except in the minds of entertainment executives.

Newmans has never been revolutionary. Nor has it changed the world for the better. I realize that it's meant to be entertainment, that—one can argue—it's merely an example of what ails us and not the actual problem. But in my opinion, it *is* the problem.

So, CBS, we have come to my plea.

Let Del play himself—the shrewd, hardworking dictator who's sitting atop a hugely prosperous twenty-year business. Let Dinah lose her temper—surely she gets sick and tired of bailing her husband and sons out of trouble. Give Guy *something* to do other than get married, become a dad, follow in his father's footsteps. Let him be funny or jealous of his younger brother's runaway success or both. Unleash Shep.

Or admit that it's time to retire *Meet the Newmans*. Send Del and Dinah off to join Fibber McGee and Molly, Jim and Margaret Anderson, Ward and June Cleaver and all others who came before and have since—wisely—faded to a warm memory of a simpler time. While you're at it, put the long-suffering Guy out of his misery. Shep can still make records, go on tour, be on TV in another vehicle, as long as it reflects the times he's living in. The kid is too young to be middle-aged.

Just please—keep the Newmans as we know them out of our homes. Let America's weariest family disappear into obscurity where they belong.

ONE

MARCH 19, 1964

Twenty-four hours earlier

T he telegram arrived as Del was leaving for the day. It was delivered by Larry, the security guard, who had taken posses-
sion of it from Sharon in reception. All his life, Del had made
friends easily and with everyone. CBS Television City was no excep-
tion. He not only knew the names of the people who worked there,
he knew their families. It was one of the many things everyone loved
about him.

"Caught you just in time," Larry said as he handed Del the envelope. "What's for dinner tonight? Let me guess. Beef stroganoff? No,
no—beef Wellington."

The guard rubbed his hands together as if awaiting a much-
anticipated gift. He had a happy marriage of his own. A nice house, a
loving family. He didn't envy Del those things. What he did envy was
the legendary culinary skill of Dinah Newman, America's preeminent
housewife. He and his own wife divided the cooking duties equally,
which meant they ate a lot of cold cuts and sandwiches.

"A surprise," Del said and flashed the smile he'd been flashing
since he was a kid, the one that was as natural to him as breathing. He
didn't mention that he ate steak almost every night, that their housekeeper, not Dinah, cooked it exactly as he liked it—medium rare with
just a hint of salt and pepper.

Del certainly hadn't married Dinah for her cooking. He'd fallen for her laugh, for the way she challenged him and spoke her mind and forced him to lighten up whenever he took himself too seriously—which, unfortunately, was often. He'd fallen for her ambition and get-up-and-go, her enormous dreams for the future, and her unshakable optimism.

Outside in the parking lot, he slid the telegram inside his jacket pocket, where it remained unopened during the ride home. It pressed against his chest, thrumming like it had a heartbeat of its own.

Later that night, after dinner, Del and Dinah went up to their bedroom, where she sat at her vanity and applied cold cream to her face and he removed his tie and jacket, careful that the telegram didn't slip out and onto the floor. He hung the jacket in his closet—his clothes still lived in here even if he did not—and changed into the old burgundy sweater he'd had since college, back when he played football at the University of Southern California. He liked to say he had left a part of his heart on the field of the Los Angeles Coliseum.

"What should we expect in tomorrow's meeting?" Dinah asked, leaning into the mirror. She was, as the magazines observed, still a looker. Long legs, blond hair she'd always worn short, pert nose, blue eyes that turned green or gray depending on what color she was wearing. Rosy cheeks and porcelain skin, more girl next door than vamp. She had freckles year-round that lately she had stopped hiding under a layer of powder because she thought they made her look younger. *A real dish* was how Del described her whenever he recounted the story of how they met and fell in love. *Then and now.*

He sat on the bed and removed his shoes. "I don't know much except that Aubrey wants to see us." James T. Aubrey being the president of CBS Television. "I assume he wants to discuss the new contract." He instilled his voice with a confidence he didn't feel.

When they'd signed the twelve-year contract with CBS, time had stretched before them limitlessly. A twelve-year contract was unheard of back then, a testament to Del's shrewd negotiation skills, business savvy, and charm. Now, one month away from the end of their twelfth season, renewal was heavy on the minds of all four Newmans. Heavier on the mind of Del, who—unbeknownst to the other three—had not managed their money as well as he could have.

From the beginning, he had taken complete control of the show—producing, directing, editing, acting, writing, and handling their income. He knew he had been a headache for CBS and their sponsors. Taking five days to film each episode instead of three. Not allowing a studio audience to attend the taping. Paying an Oscar-winning cinematographer to shoot the episodes like a movie, using expensive 60 mm film because it looked brighter and sharper and held up better. The network had only relented because *Meet the Newmans* brought in thirty-five million viewers each week.

Recently, though, the ratings had fallen. Last week, out of the 108 TV shows in the prime-time schedule, they had finished forty-seventh. *Forty. Seventh.* Worse, they had been beaten by *Flipper*, *Lassie*, and *My Favorite Martian*. Del couldn't believe it. A dolphin, a collie, and a man from outer space. This was what America wanted to see over the warmhearted adventures of a loving family played by an actual real-life family.

"How much should we worry?" Dinah asked.

She didn't know about the money situation. The boys' trusts were largely intact, but the primary accounts, the ones the four of them drew their living from, had somehow dwindled. They weren't exactly *empty*, but the amount in each was just so much lower than he'd expected. He had discovered it three months ago. It was the thing—unbeknownst to his wife—that had inspired his midlife crisis.

Not that the Newmans lived a lavish lifestyle. They were too busy working to take expensive vacations. His car and Shep's had both been gifts from automobile companies. And sure, he had purchased a left-driving Bentley S2 Continental because it was a limited edition—one of only forty-nine produced between 1960 and 1962. And he owned a

1931 Rolls-Royce Phantom I, as well as a 1964 Rolls-Royce Phantom V. There was a Porsche 550 racing car that only had about two thousand miles on it, a Ferrari 500 Superfast that he didn't trust himself to drive, and a luxury 1961 Facel Vega Excellence imported from France before the company shuttered for good. This was what happened when you grew up without anything, walking everywhere, barely enough food on the table—you made up for it in big and small ways.

Which was why it wasn't just cars. There were the other collections, if you could call them that—the colonial coins and the modernist art. Ephemera from Arctic and Antarctic expeditions circa 1900 because in his heart Del fancied himself an explorer. Leather-bound first editions, which were housed in a special glass case in one of their two dens. And unique musical instruments, such as an uilleann pipe, a glass harmonica—like the one invented by Ben Franklin in 1761—and a Theremin.

Then, of course, he had bailed out employees and, in some cases, their families on more than one occasion. That time one of the lighting grips had fallen from a ladder—not even at the studio but at home, installing a window—and hadn't been able to work for five months. That time Wendy from craft services needed a new car because her boyfriend totaled hers. Hell, he'd even paid for college for a few of their children. Things he had done without a second thought because these people were as good as family.

He was also in the habit of paying off the press when one or the other of his sons—Shep, most often—broke the morals clause. And, okay, there were the "news" reporters—the ones he kept on the payroll, ensuring that the public would only ever see good, wholesome articles about Del, Dinah, Guy, and Shep. But that could hardly be called an extravagance. The reporters in his back pocket were, in his eyes, bodyguards for the Newman reputation. You couldn't let your guard down, not even for a second, when there were gossip rags like *Confidential* sniffing around, dishing dirt, destroying careers, not caring whose lives they ruined.

"How much should we worry about the contract?" Dinah repeated, turning away from the mirror to stare at him. The cold cream made her look like his great-aunt Ruth.

"Not at all," he told her. There was no sense alarming her. He was worried enough for the both of them. "For all we know, he just wants to talk about the wedding." CBS was making a meal of the forthcoming TV wedding between Guy and Eileen Weld, who played his on-screen love interest. "Well," he said. "I need to work on the script."

"Try to get some sleep." She kissed him good night, his beautiful wife, barely meeting his lips. Their lips hadn't properly met in a year or two, possibly longer.

When Dinah disappeared into the bathroom, he slipped the telegram out of his jacket and walked downstairs. In the kitchen, he poured himself a fresh cup of coffee, and then he retreated to his office. At his desk, he ran his hands across the smooth, cool wood. This was where he worked early in the morning and in the evening after they wrapped. The desk was one of the first things he had bought with the money they made from their radio show, the one that had preceded the move to television, and was a symbol of all he had done and all he had yet to do.

For a few seconds, he let himself gaze around the room at the framed photos on the walls, the ones that spanned two decades, reflecting their radio and television careers and, before that, the movies he and Dinah had starred in both separately and together, as well as his days as a popular crooner.

Del was known in the business as a powerhouse. A force of nature. He had the ability to remember the various cogs and wheels, the inner workings of the very complicated, very intricate clock that made each day run. He thrived on the daily schedule of show, atmosphere, people, every single fucking demand that he had assigned himself when they began this journey.

But for a man who'd always taken the stairs two at a time, who could manage the moods and expectations of the people in his life at the same time he could manage a stable of actors, a crew of forty, and a network, he was suddenly feeling his age.

He took a sip of coffee—he still had hours of work to do—and opened the telegram.

I need to see you.

There was no signature, but it didn't need one. He knew instantly who it was from.

After so many years of silence, five short words.

He had been careful not to reveal his home address. But, of course, he was easily found at the studio. With a jolt, he wondered whether it had been delivered in person or by courier. The idea of being so easily reached, even at the studio where there was a reception desk and security guards you had to go through, left him feeling winded.

His instinct was to tear up the message and throw it away and pretend it never existed. But this wasn't like the extortionist he'd paid last year when Shep was photographed smoking marijuana. This was personal.

His latest script lay on the desk beside the telegram. The episode title was "Del Changes History." He stared at it for a long time. Once upon a time, he believed that he had, that he would. But sitting here, at forty-five, the past suddenly back and reaching for him, he wasn't so sure.

TWO

MARCH 20, 1964

Fifteen hours earlier

They shot *Meet the Newmans* out of CBS Television City, on the other side of the hill. From their wide, tree-lined street in Toluca Lake—*a community of dignity, charm, and hospitality*—Dinah drove the same route she had been driving five days a week for the past twelve years. She turned onto the narrow ribbon of Laurel Canyon and aimed the car up the hill into the blue sky.

The car had been Del's idea—a 1962 gold Chevrolet Impala he had purchased for her fortieth. Toluca Lake had been his idea too. Dinah had yearned for the beach—Malibu, Santa Monica, the Palisades. She wanted to be able to see the ocean even if she never had time to wade in it. She needed a horizon, something Shep had inherited from her. But Del said Toluca Lake was cheaper. They could get a bigger house and more land. Dinah didn't want more land. She wanted the Pacific, even if it was the wrong ocean on the wrong coast, the beaches too wide and enormous, the sand hard-packed and brown compared to her gentle North Carolina beaches with their soft white dunes.

Once she reached the top of the hill, she considered turning right onto Mulholland Drive instead of continuing straight across the road and down the other side. Del sometimes took winding, twisting Mulholland, with its views of the city and the ocean beyond. The boys liked to drive it, much too fast, but her way was safer. Guy once knew a girl—this was four or five years ago now—who had driven off the side, plummeting to her death.

Dinah continued straight because that's what she always did. In the aftermath of Kennedy's assassination four months ago, she told herself there was a comfort in doing the same things she always had. What America needed, what its people needed to heal was a sense of order and stability and routine. And so she would go through this day like every other day, wearing the same clothes or a version of them, reciting the same lines or a version of them, wrestling with the same on-screen family situations or a version of them, playing herself or a version of her. Just about everything in her life was something she could do in her sleep.

Except that this morning, for the first time in a very long time, she was breaking the routine. She had an appointment that she had not mentioned to Del or her sons.

Dr. Berke's office was on a quiet tree-lined street in Beverly Hills, a good three miles from CBS, which meant it was a safe enough distance from the studio and all who worked there. Dr. Berke was their private physician, the one all four Newmans went to because he understood the need for discretion when you were America's most famous family.

When Dinah reached the doors of his office, the doctor himself unlocked it and escorted her back to the exam room. As promised, he was the only one there. Dinah settled herself onto the examination table and looked at him expectantly, as if he was the one who had called her. He was a slight, balding man with a mustache and glasses. She liked his face. In her opinion, he was handsomer than the neighbor, even though there was a virility to Ted/Tad and his lawn mower that ignited something in her.

"So tell me what's going on," he said now.

"There's a numbness," she replied, no need to beat around the bush. She glanced at her watch again. "In my hands. And my neck. And my right shin. It started a few weeks ago."

It had spread quickly, like wildfire. She pictured her body as a forest, trees being felled as the fire blazed a path. One of those controlled burns that returns nutrients to the soil, not devastating enough to kill *everything*, but enough to cause damage.

"At first," she continued, "it was more of a prickling in my fingers, as if I'd been sitting on them and they just fell asleep. I've still got some feeling. They aren't all the way numb." She heard the hopeful note in her voice. She had tested the numb places with a sewing needle, enough to register that she could still feel pain.

Dr. Berke's face remained neutral. "Are you under any stress?"

"No," she told him. "The show is doing well. Del is doing well. The boys are doing well."

My life is perfect.

"My life is perfect," she said aloud. Perhaps because actually, if she were being completely honest, it didn't feel perfect. It felt like a great, yawning void somewhere in the very pit of her. It felt like the hunger she had experienced during both pregnancies combined, when she had eaten her weight in ice cream and Little Debbie's Swiss Rolls.

But Dinah wasn't about to say any of this to Dr. Berke, even though he was staring at her as if he didn't believe what she was telling him, not about the numbness but about her life. *Why shouldn't he believe me?* she thought. Any woman would be happy to trade places with her. She knew this to be fact because of the letters that arrived each week in care of the studio. While her sons received mountains of mail from adoring girls, Dinah received recipe letters, as she called them. In them, her fans praised her homemaking skills, her mothering skills, her obvious success as a wife, and requested copies of her dress patterns and directions for her famous sour cream cinnamon coffee cake, the one she always baked for Del and the boys on the show. (In reality it showed up ready-made from a local grocery store.)

They also wrote to ask her for advice. *I don't know how to talk to my daughter. My children hate me. How do I fix my marriage? I've just discovered my child is pregnant / is drinking / has dropped out of school—what do*

I do? I dream of running away from my kids, my husband, and my entire life. I worry that I'm depressed, and nothing seems to help. Why do I cry when nothing is wrong? What can I do to make my husband love me like Del loves you?

On and on. So many women in need of help.

"I have everything I've ever wanted," she said, making it clear to Dr. Berke and herself that she meant what she was saying. "Besides, it's not just the numbness. I'm more tired than usual. And I can be in the air-conditioned studio and all of a sudden it's as if I'm standing under the set lights because it's so hot." She laughed a little too high, a little too loud. "*So* hot."

"How old are you?"

"Forty-two." She didn't bother correcting herself.

"How old was your mother when she went through the change of life?"

"I'm sorry?"

"The change of life. Menopause."

She narrowed her eyes at him. "Meno . . ."

"Fortunately, medical science is so much more advanced now. Gone are the days when we believed it was a sign of madness, a death knell to femininity. We no longer lock women away in asylums like we did in Victorian times."

"Well, that is fortunate." *A death knell to femininity.* She didn't know how long she could hold her smile. Any longer and it was in danger of cracking her face in half.

"Yes. It absolutely is." He waited, as if giving her the chance to confess that, actually, come to think of it, she believed she *was* entering the change of life, that she had noticed a rapid loss of femininity and frequent onsets of mania. When she didn't, he said, "I think, while I have you here, I'd like to conduct an exam. Check your vitals. Make sure there's nothing serious going on."

At this, her heart fluttered. Even as she'd been going numb, limb after limb starting to atrophy, it hadn't occurred to her that there might be a serious reason for it. Cancer, multiple sclerosis, Lou Gehrig's disease, a brain tumor. Dinah liked to think of herself as practical and grounded, not someone prone to worrying without cause, but she felt the ground suddenly shift.

The doctor took her blood pressure and temperature, listened to her heart, felt the lymph nodes in her neck, looked down her throat and in her ears and up her nose, and then he drew blood, filling three small, clear vials. While he did all of these things, he asked her about Del, about the boys.

"Guy's good," she said distractedly. *Polio, stroke, Parkinson's disease.* "He's happy." At least she thought he was happy. She tried to remember the last time she'd asked him or the last time she'd been over to the guesthouse, which he shared with his friend Kelly Faber. Buddies since high school, Guy and Kelly were now working actors who were busy with friends and girls, and Dinah didn't like to intrude.

"And Shep," she added brightly. "Shep is great." *Thank god for Shep.* Except for the fact that he would *not* be going to college, because, as he explained, it was a waste of time, seeing how he was already more successful than most kids his age, and music—not school—was the thing he loved. The news had sent Del into a deep depression.

"And Del," she said, somewhat faintly, thinking of their separate bedrooms. She held up her hands, the gesture limp and unenthusiastic. "You know Del."

"Yes," the doctor replied, frowning. "It's been a while since I've seen him. I should get him in here soon, make sure he's taking care of himself."

As Dr. Berke scribbled a few notes into Dinah's chart, she rebuttoned her blouse and picked up her purse. Then he promised to phone her with the test results. In the meantime, she was to make sure she was sleeping and eating properly—no skipping meals. And if the numbness grew worse, she was to come back and see him.

As Dinah walked briskly from his office to her car, her long dancer's legs found their rhythm without her telling them to, the slight sashay that was her trademark. A human metronome. *The charm of Dinah Newman*, a journalist had once written, *is that she is just sexy enough for men to take notice but not too sexy that it alienates women.*

She would drive to the studio and find her husband before the meeting with Aubrey so that he could tell her their game plan. Del always had a plan. And in doing so, he would be letting her know that all was okay. She was okay. They were okay. It wasn't the same as telling him about the numbness that made her seek out Dr. Berke, but it would be a kind of reassurance just the same. And she needed as much of that as she could get. Del had that kind of authority. If he told you everything was going to be all right, you believed him.

16

The Newman Boys:
Which One Will You Choose?

Guy and Shep Newman grew up together, but they couldn't be more different. On the one hand, there's Guy. All of twenty, blond and broad-shouldered. Confident. Cheerful. Keeps his cool. On the other hand, there's Shep. Just sixteen, tall and dark, impulsive, passionate, and moody. (He also happens to be a rock 'n' roll star.) One takes after their mother, the other after their dad. But how do you decide which brother is for you? We're here to help!

Guy may play the serious big brother on TV, but he's actually the extrovert of his family and has a terrific sense of humor.

Shep is a heartbreaker, often going steady with five girls at once! But he dreams of the day he'll meet the right girl so he can settle down.

Guy loves to cook, a talent he inherited from his mom. His favorite dish is Swedish meatballs, with Baked Alaska for dessert. He's very international!

Shep has always been a picky eater. If he could, he would eat hamburgers, potato chips, and oatmeal cookies at every meal. Just don't ask him to eat his vegetables!

Guy often reads three books a week when he's not surfing, fencing, or racing dirt bikes. He's also a trained trapeze artist!

Shep loves to play music and write songs, scribbling them on the backs of envelopes, record jackets, and one time Guy's homework!

Guy wears British Sterling aftershave, the same one favored by his dad. With notes of sandalwood, mint, and Italian bergamot, it's a sophisticated and refined scent for a gentleman.

Shep prefers to smell like his pomade of choice—either Royal

Crown (cinnamon, leather) or Black & White (fresh coconut). The same brands used by Johnny Cash and Elvis Presley!

Guy loves girls who are smart and well mannered and like to have fun. His ideal woman is his close friend Shelley Fabares, who stars as Mary Stone on *The Donna Reed Show*.

Shep loves girls who are independent and carefree and speak their minds, but we hear he also has a thing for Jayne Mansfield.

A date with **Guy** would find the two of you snuggled on the couch watching a football game (he was a Division I quarterback!) or riding horses on the beach at sunset.

While a date with **Shep** would be all-night dancing at a club followed by a motorcycle ride down the Pacific Coast Highway, ending with a passionate kiss.

Both boys bring their mother flowers, praise her clothes, and notice her new hairdos. Both are courteous, respectful, and heed their father's guidance. Which just goes to show you can't go wrong with either of them!

THREE

MARCH 20, 1964

Fourteen hours earlier

Across the hills, high up in a neighboring canyon, Juliet Dunne rolled out of bed, regretting yet another life decision. She gathered her clothes without glancing back at the long, naked body sprawled face down on the bed. The Musician was messy, beautiful, and wounded at his core like she was. Right now, in the bright light of the California morning, she hated him for it.

Thankfully, she'd driven herself, following him up here because she had a code of rules she lived by, one of the biggest being *Never get yourself trapped*, which meant always being able to drive away at a moment's notice. This was especially important with him.

He was the famous lead singer of a very famous band. When he was here in LA, he lived on Wonderland, perched in the hills above Sunset Boulevard. The name made her think of Alice and the White Rabbit and the Red Queen and *Off with her head*. They had found the little house together and lived there together, once upon a time.

She felt dirty for some reason, though she wasn't sure why. She'd chosen to come here. Driven herself, for god's sake. She'd been a willing participant, knowing full well what would happen if she saw him again. But the memory of it was like a smudge she couldn't wipe away.

Outside, it was chilly, and she was barefoot, in too much of a hurry to pull on her boots. The grass was cool and damp, and then the gravel, which stabbed the tender spots of her feet.

She backed her VW Beetle out of the driveway down to the dusty road below and paused there, engine idling. She gazed up past the bungalow and the trees to the sky. That goddamn wide-open blue sky. It was one reason she'd come here from the Midwest, where the sky was gray five months of the year. Everyone thought she'd followed a man out here or, worse, followed her dreams, which had always been too big for her small Indiana town. But that blue sky up there was the real reason. She hadn't anticipated the smog that settled over the city like a thick brown fog on either side of the Santa Monica Mountains.

Up here on Laurel Canyon, though, she was above it. She rolled the windows down and breathed it in—the lush sweetness of jasmine and honeysuckle—and as she did, the carnal wickedness of the night before faded, rising off her skin like a mist and vanishing into the morning. *Poof.* She lit a cigarette, inhaled, fluttered her eyes closed.

It was that first inhale that did it for her—the burning sensation hitting her lungs. After that, nothing was as good. The same was true of men. That first touch, first kiss, first lay. Nothing was ever as good. Except with him. He was the only man she'd ever met who could hold her attention. Juliet opened her eyes and blotted out the cigarette in the ashtray.

If she stopped at home, she would be late to the office, and as one of only two female reporters at the *Los Angeles Times*, she couldn't afford to be anything less than punctual. The male reporters, most of them, seemed to expect histrionics and drama from her simply because she was a woman. Like they were eager for it so they could say, *There it is; we knew it was only a matter of time.*

She pulled over on Hollywood Boulevard and swiped at the mascara under her brown eyes, running fingers through her hair, which was the color of wheat and fell lank and heavy around her shoulders except for her fringe, which just brushed her eyelashes. She found the stub of a lipstick in the bottom of her purse, dabbed a little on her cheeks and then her lips. She reached for the enormous sunglasses that nearly covered her face. Thankfully, she'd changed after work yesterday and carried an emergency pair of pumps in the trunk. It would do. She would do.

The *Los Angeles Times* lived in a large art deco building at the corner of First and Spring. Juliet's high heels clicked against the marble floor of the lobby as she walked to the elevators. Even now, three years in, she felt proud to work here. More than the blue sky, the *Times* was the reason she had come to LA, filled with idealism and big ideas.

She had started in the dungeon of a mail room—*Help Wanted: female*, the classified ad had read. *Good figure, aptitude helpful. Some typing.* The only advertised reporter jobs had been for men. From the mail room, she'd worked her way upstairs to the all-female typing pool, and then to the research desk as a fact-checker. With each promotion, whispers followed her—she must have slept her way up the ladder.

Last year, she'd finally been promoted to the Lifestyle desk, formerly known as the Woman's Page—an outdated concept created three decades ago by newspapers hoping to attract more female readers. Gloria Steinem argued that issues impacting women should appear on the front pages, so now they had Lifestyle. A section that offered etiquette, housekeeping tips, beauty tips, marital and parenting guidance, celebrity news, advice columns, recipe exchanges. And, most recently, a chance to talk about political issues relating to "the fairer sex." Even so, there was still relatively little being written about women at the *LA Times*. And most of the Lifestyle writers were men.

In spite of this and in spite of the whispers, in spite of the fact that she was required to wear lipstick, dresses, nylon hose, and three-inch heels, and in spite of the antiquated views of almost every man who worked there, Juliet loved the newsroom. The furious clacking of keys and clamor of voices. The cigarette smoke that hovered like smog over the heads of the men hard at work. The constant flurry of activity, particularly when there was a deadline or a big news story. The reporters sitting behind enormous wooden desks like captains of industry. An ashtray and telephone on every surface. Overflowing wastebaskets beneath. Grooves in the floor from the constant rolling of chair wheels. The smell of ink. The high windows and polished floors. The slant of the light in the morning and again in the late afternoon.

The only other female journalist, Paula Goodman, sat on the outskirts at her own smaller desk. She had been at the *Times* for seven years, worked exclusively on the Local News page, and made it clear on Juliet's first day that they were not, nor would they ever be, allies. No one whispered about Paula, who didn't wear makeup and didn't socialize and rarely ever smiled.

By the end of the year, Juliet planned to be working at the National News desk, which would make her the first woman on the paper to do so. Charlie Murdock, one of the News editors, had told her on her first day, *No skirt has ever written for News, and no skirt ever will.* Which was why she hadn't told anyone about her plans. Instead, she kept them tight inside her, an eternal flame that was hers and hers alone.

When she wasn't writing fluff pieces for the Lifestyle section—*Textured stockings are in this season!*—she was shadowing Nick Mitchell, a senior editor and one of only three Black reporters on staff.

Around the office, she was "Mitchell's girl," because you belonged to the man you worked under, and most everyone assumed you were sleeping with him too. The only one who didn't call her this was Nick himself. He'd set down rules when he first started working at the *Times*—if anyone called him *boy*, he wasn't going to answer. He told Juliet in no uncertain terms, "You aren't my girl, you're my colleague. And I don't expect you to respond when they call you that."

Nick frequently reported on the civil rights movement, but he also reported on crime. He had—Juliet quickly learned—a preternatural obsession with the whys of homocide, which stemmed from his own mother's unsolved murder a decade earlier.

Now, on this Friday morning, Juliet nursed her first cup of coffee, relishing every bitter drop. She drank it black like the men did because she knew she was under scrutiny, and even something as innocuous as how she took her coffee mattered. She helped herself to a second cup and then dove into Nick's latest copy.

The story was about an armed robbery on Skid Row. A homeless man had been killed when he tried to protect a woman and her children. The Minnesota driver's license found on his body stated that he was Vincent Morrow, fifty-seven years old. Juliet couldn't let these details sink in, because she had to focus on the words themselves, the layout, the mechanics, most particularly the punctuation—Nick was a terrible punctuator. Later, when she was home, she would think about it. Only then.

Someone walked by, singing the familiar lines of a familiar song. " 'Juliet, sleeping. In my bed. In my head. She's Juliet, sleeping.' " A fat stack of pages was dropped onto her desk. The other reporters seemed to forget she'd been promoted, treating her as if she were still in the typing pool.

"I need that by the end of the day," said Charlie Murdock, late thirties, hair starting to recede, waistline starting to expand, ego larger than all of downtown.

He swaggered off, returning to the song as he did. From across the room, the sound of someone else humming along. Juliet didn't look up. If she looked up every time some idiot sang these lines at her, she would have a crick in her neck a mile wide.

It was a famous song written and sung by a famous man—a man she had once stupidly loved, perhaps still loved, a man who currently sprawled naked across a bed up on Wonderland, right where she'd left him. The song was about her.

What was worse, there had been a news story last year. The news story that haunted her. The *Daily Mirror*, the *Daily Express*, *The Sun*, the *Evening Standard*—the British tabloid rags gleefully reported the drug bust of the Musician and his bandmates.

It was the first of January. The boys were at their estate out in Surrey, most of them tripping on acid. Juliet had stopped by, found the Musician, and gone off with him to one of the guest rooms. When there was the sound of a car outside, of someone ringing away at the bell, Juliet wrapped herself in a fur skin rug, the first thing she could find to cover up, and opened the door. She'd expected to find one of the other girlfriends. Instead, she found the police.

There was an arrest and a trial, but she was the thing everyone remembered. Juliet Dunne, the Musician's girlfriend. The Girl in the Fur Skin Rug. It was the lowest moment of her life. In that instant, she became everything she detested. A token. A trophy. A groupie. A girl in a long line of girls. And now an international joke. If she was going to live her life with a label, she wanted it to be one of her choosing.

A towering figure dropped onto her desk, nearly overturning her coffee mug. Boyd Hartley, managing editor, hands folded serenely on one leg.

"Where are you with *Meet the Newmans*?" Hartley always launched right in as if the two of you had been in the middle of a conversation. He was referring to her latest assignment, one that came directly on the heels of a piece she'd written on the proliferation of women's bowling leagues in the southland.

"I was thinking," she said, carefully relocating her mug to the other side of her desk. Her instinct, always, was to call him *sir*, but the newsroom was an informal, if frenetic, place, men frequently shouting across the room at one another, tapping cigarette ash onto the floor when they were deep in a story or deadline, unable to take the time to use an ashtray. "There's a story I'd like to do on the Pill. It's the most popular form of reversible birth control, some 2.3 million women are using it, yet it can only be prescribed to married women with the authorization of their husbands. There's this woman. Sixty-four years old. Estelle Griswold . . ."

Hartley held up a hand, a signal that she was about to be cut off.

She spoke faster. "The LAPD's abortion squad has been operating for thirteen years. Five detectives and a lieutenant. They go under-cover to bust abortion rings. Women are forced to testify against the doctors who, in many cases, saved their lives." Birth control was the subject she was most passionate about—women owning the rights to their own bodies—but she always had other ideas at the ready when Hartley's attention lapsed as it was doing now. "Or maybe a piece on the Reproductive Biology Research Foundation in—"

"Juliet—"

"I could talk to Betty Friedan. She's working on a sequel to *The Feminine Mystique*—"

"Juliet, enough."

It was Boyd Hartley who had conducted her initial interview when she first applied to the *LA Times*. He'd been editor of the Woman's Page then, and when he asked why she wanted to write, she'd told him, *There's power in words. They're important. Not just to tell stories but to tell the truth about the world around us.*

She had said more, all of it unrehearsed, impassioned, and from the heart.

To his credit, Boyd Hartley had listened to every bit of it. Then he said to her, *Do you think you can be objective? A reporter's job, after all, is to tell both sides of the story.*

She had been honest. *Yes. And no. Do I want to put myself in the shoes of a misogynist who mistreats women or a bigot who marches with the Klan? No. I believe most people who hurt people are hurt themselves. I can have empathy. But I also believe that there are people in this world who don't deserve to tell their side of the story.*

He didn't speak for a long time, and she thought she'd lost him. But finally, he'd nodded, rapped the desk once with his knuckles, and said, *I agree. I promise I will never ask you to do that.*

Now, three years later, sitting on her desk, Boyd Hartley regarded her like he'd regarded her then.

"I think for now," he began, "it's best if you write the Dinah Newman piece. Have you had the interview?"

Juliet sank a little. "I'm meeting her this evening. At her house."

Meet the Newmans was one of those interchangeable family situation comedies left over from the 1950s, square and outdated. All the women as interchangeable as the shows themselves. Aproned saints who puttered about their shiny kitchens and had nothing but patience and love—and the occasional word of sweetly delivered advice—for their families. Juliet had grown up watching it. She had seen every goddamn episode.

Hartley nodded. "Good," he said. "Excellent."

"Walter Kerr just skewered them in *The New York Times*. He thinks they're irrelevant."

"And what does Juliet Dunne think?"

She didn't answer, because she both agreed and disagreed with Kerr. Instead, she blinked up at Hartley. *Smile but not too broadly, lest he think you're too eager to please. Look serious but not too serious so he doesn't think you're a bitch or, worse, a shrew.* It was exhausting, having to constantly control one's face.

He nodded then and rapped the desk once—just as he had three years ago—and left her. She watched as he strolled back to his office, a graceful reed of a man with a full head of white hair. When the description of her in a fur rug made headlines last year, he hadn't batted an eye. Hadn't even mentioned it. She had been terrified of being fired, but that was another thing about Hartley—he was, at his core, unconventional. He oversaw one of the busiest news desks in the country, but he ambled everywhere like an old-time movie cowboy.

During the hour-long editorial meeting, Juliet took the notes because Marcia, the stenographer, was out sick. Afterward, she met her friend Renee at the Xerox machine so that she could make copies of the notes for every man in the office. She would deliver them, desk by desk, and these men—her colleagues—would say, *Thanks, sweetheart* or *Thanks, babe*, if they even said thank you at all.

As the copier began to hum and whir, Juliet asked Renee if she'd ever watched *Meet the Newmans*. At twenty-five, Renee Otero was still in the typing pool. If she was envious of Juliet for moving up and out, she had never let on.

She whistled. "That big brother is handsome. You know, in that way your family doctor is handsome or, like, your friend's dad. He has a . . . solidness." She sighed. Renee loved solid men, especially Gregory Peck and Sidney Poitier. Her mother was Black, her father Cuban, and Renee had grown up in San Diego. She was just over six feet tall and—as if her height didn't make her stand out enough—always dressed in bright colors, outfits she designed and made herself. Today, she was wearing a yellow sleeveless minidress, fuchsia seamed stockings, and cherry-red pumps. Tied around her neck in a jaunty knot was a scarf swirled with orange and pink flowers. "Is that what Hartley has you on?"

Juliet nodded.

"At least it isn't the Beverly Hills Women's Club," Renee said. "You're moving up in the world."

But as Juliet plucked the paper from the copier and collated it, one stack after another, some fifty in all, she thought, *I am meant for more.*

FOUR

MARCH 20, 1964

Thirteen hours earlier

S hep Newman turned south on La Cienega from Sunset Boulevard, his motorcycle airborne for three glorious, hair-raising
seconds as he flew down the hill. He felt alive, the way he did
whenever he played music to a crowd of thirty thousand screaming
fans or alone in his room, just him and his guitar.

He wished he could always live in flight. The closest he came was
touring with his band, standing onstage with his guitar and a microphone. He had played hundreds of places in hundreds of cities over
the past two years, and he was blown away by the frenzy that he, Shepherd Newman, inspired. The thousands of crying, screaming fans,
most of them female. So many fans that the concert venues gave him
police protection. And not just in the States, where *Meet the Newmans*
was broadcast—abroad too.

But then, inevitably, Shep would return home to the house he grew
up in, missing chunks of hair, shirts in tatters, ears still ringing from
the feverish screams of *Shep, Shep, Shep,* to parents who saw him as
what he was—a teenager. They made sure he did his chores and studied
his scripts and shaved his sideburns and said, "Yes, sir," "Yes, ma'am."
If he stayed out all night, returning home the next day smelling of
booze and women, they took his car away.

It made him feel alone. Like some strange hybrid man-boy creature. The three people who knew and loved him most couldn't begin to understand what it was like out there. He would lie in bed examining the teeth marks from overzealous fans, wondering if he had dreamed that other life.

His favorite book was Jack Kerouac's *On the Road*, which he'd first read when he was ten. It traveled with him across the country where, on tour buses and in hotel rooms, he opened it again and again to chapter 3 and skimmed the lines that captured his own feelings, words he had memorized long ago:

I was far away from home, haunted and tired with travel, in a cheap hotel room I'd never seen, hearing the hiss of steam outside, and the creak of the old wood of the hotel, and footsteps upstairs, and all the sad sounds, and I looked at the cracked high ceiling and really didn't know who I was for about fifteen strange seconds. I wasn't scared; I was just somebody else, some stranger, and my whole life was a haunted life, the life of a ghost.

He touched down to earth now with a jolt. He had spent the night at the recording studio laying down tracks for the new album and, after two hours of sleep, awakened in his childhood bed feeling hungover, brooding, and frustrated. The brooding meant there was a song itching to come out of him. Whenever he woke up staring at the ceiling and wondering what it all meant, he knew there was something in him that needed writing down.

The frustration came from the fact that his life wasn't his own. From the moment Shep gazed into the cameras—on Friday, December 14, 1962—and sang his first song for TV audiences, Del sensed Something Big. He wasted no time negotiating a lucrative deal for his son at CBS Records, with the result that CBS now owned Shep Newman—both on television and on vinyl—for at least as long as the TV contract lasted. He had nine thousand fan clubs across the country, received upward of twelve thousand fan letters a week. In addition to album covers, his likeness graced comic books, paper dolls, posters, T-shirts, and magazines.

Yet his only source of income was a weekly ten-dollar allowance. The hundreds of thousands of dollars a year he earned from *Meet the Newmans* and his records went directly into a trust that he couldn't access until he turned twenty-one.

For now, he stood where he was told to stand, delivered the words he was told to say, sang what he was told to sing. Critics wrote him off as a vapid teen idol who relied on his good looks. Shep knew he was more than that, but in his darkest moments, it didn't matter. He was nothing more than a prop, a ventriloquist's dummy, with Del and CBS pulling the strings.

Worst of all, the girls he met swooned before he even spoke because he was *Shep Newman*. They thought they knew him because he was beamed into their living rooms each week as himself and because they listened to his records and read articles about the kinds of girls he liked. But they didn't know him at all.

Eileen Weld was different, though. She had been hired at the end of last year to play Guy's steady girlfriend, now Guy's fiancée, on the show. Shep had hit on her because she smelled good and had a great smile and because whenever his dad was directing her, she stood with her feet planted, hands on hips, brow furrowed like a general. When she told Shep she wasn't interested, he'd felt an unexpected flush of disappointment. But then she came to set the next morning and cracked a raunchy joke and said, "Don't let things be weird between us, Shep Newman. I think you'll see that I'm a pretty good friend."

The joke's on you, he'd thought. Aside from his guitarist, Tommy Hutchins, Shep didn't have friends.

But every morning, Eileen showed up for work and talked to him, and before he knew it, he started getting to set on time just so he could see her. On breaks, the two of them would sneak into the neighboring soundstages, climbing up to the rafters to watch rehearsals for *The Red Skelton Show* and *The Defenders*. They sometimes ate lunch in the prop room—amid towering statues and fake trees and various piles of furniture—at an old diner set that had been used in an episode of *Alfred Hitchcock Presents*. In the evenings, if they finished at the same time, they would sit outside in the parking lot and watch the sun set over the hills.

Shep waited to grow bored of being with Eileen, waited to run out of things to talk to her about, but it hadn't happened. Instead of having *less* to talk about, they seemed to have more, and he found himself storing up moments throughout each day to share with her the next time he saw her. Maybe the best, scariest thing of all, she saw through his bullshit and swagger and recognized what it really was—a protective shell.

Which was why, last night, he'd rung up Lorrie Cabot, the girl he'd been seeing off and on since January, and told her he wanted to end things. This was going to be a whole new leaf for him. No more overlapping of girls, no more stringing them along, which for Shep meant disappearing. From now on, there was only one girl for him, even if she didn't know it yet.

But then Lorrie had said, "I'm pregnant. Eight weeks. It's yours. I don't expect you to marry me, but I wanted you to know. I was going to tell you this weekend, but then you called to break up with me."

When he didn't respond, she'd told him she was going to keep it, which meant she wouldn't be able to work at the Whisky a Go Go, where she danced in a cage, once she started to show.

There was a morals clause in the *Newmans* contract dictating what was suitable and unsuitable behavior for two growing boys in the public spotlight. When Guy and Shep first started going out with girls, Del and Dinah had lectured them on being careful, especially around female fans. No compromising positions. No behavior unbefitting of a role model. Del had drilled it through their heads that if they screwed up, it wasn't just themselves they were hurting. They'd be putting forty people and their families out of work.

Shep pushed the motorcycle faster, wanting to see what it could do. He usually only opened it up on deserted canyon roads, but he couldn't hold it in. Not even when he heard the wail of a siren.

He glanced in the side mirror and saw the police car behind him. He was used to fleeing the girls who chased him, but now his adrenaline raced the way it always did when he defied the law and, by extension, his father. Del, Dinah, Guy, Lorrie, CBS, the record label, his unborn child. He was outrunning them all.

FIVE

MARCH 20, 1964

Thirteen hours earlier

CBS Television City was famed for its state-of-the-art layout. Four soundstages, each totaling sixteen thousand square feet, each with seats for 250 audience members. Rehearsal halls built above them—long, drafty rooms equipped with tables and chairs and plenty of empty space. The main corridor running the length of the building, as wide as a freeway, with ceilings that vaulted skyward. A carpenter shop, paint shop, and prop storage at one end. And— hidden away beneath the parking lot—the machine and camera maintenance shops.

In the makeup room of soundstage 33, Guy Newman watched as Linda, the makeup artist, covered the most recent outbreak of pimples on his forehead. He had grown into a handsome young man with a dimple in his chin that was his alone, but part of him would always be the awkward teenager who was self-conscious of his weight and the acne that flared as he hit puberty.

He was usually grateful for Linda, who was mostly silent as she worked, so that he could sit in her chair and recite his lines in his head. Unlike Shep, he'd never been comfortable on camera. Each week, he studied the script and made sure to hit his marks, while his little brother showed up shamelessly unprepared and hid cue cards around the set—inside a cookie jar, a magazine, the refrigerator, the backs of doors.

Right now, though, Guy was having trouble concentrating. This morning, he'd arrived early, as he always did, only to learn that James T. Aubrey wanted to meet with him. In the show's twelve-year history, Guy had never seen the inside of Aubrey's office. He knew enough to know that he wasn't going there to be congratulated.

To make matters worse, Jim Flachek, one of his father's production assistants, had handed him a message from the night before: *6:14 p.m. Zeke at NBC returning your call. He says no directing jobs right now, but will let you know if that changes.*

Guy had known Zeke since high school. The two of them had played football together, and after graduation, Zeke had gone right into the business, landing a job at NBC Radio before moving on to television, while Guy—at his father's insistence—enrolled in prelaw and later law school at USC just like his television self. Fans of the show congratulated him on pursuing such a fine, upstanding profession. His parents must be so proud. America was so proud. Look at what a role model he was. Guy never had the heart to tell them he wasn't actually a lawyer, and—what's more—he'd dropped out of law school with two more years to go. Something Del didn't yet know.

The note didn't say who had taken the message, most likely Sharon at the front desk. The only thing Guy could hope was that his father hadn't seen it.

When you grew up in front of thirty million people, it was hard to have and keep something of your own. When Guy discovered surfing, his dad wrote it into the show. When he tried martial arts, wrestling, football, those were written into the show too. Just like Shep's music, every interest Guy ever developed was borrowed and given to his on-screen self, including the more outlandish ones—fencing, boxing, dirt bike racing, the flying trapeze. He had attempted whittling, juggling, scuba diving, model building, rock climbing, playing the trombone. Even his friends on the show were his friends in real life: Clint, Trent, and Howie, who played Clint, Trent, and Howie, his fraternity brothers.

One by one, he gave them up—not the friends but the interests. The last had been directing, his biggest dream of all, although he had tried to avoid it for as long as he could. It was a dream that Del refused to take seriously in spite of the fact that, over the past twelve months, Guy had done everything he could to show his dad how serious he was. Adding film classes to his already full schedule, shadowing Del on set, and then—finally—asking him flat out to give him a chance.

Three weeks ago, it had happened. Del said yes.

On the morning of, Guy had stood on the set of their television living room and addressed the crew, tearfully thanking his father—only to have Del second-guess everything he did. He hovered, he criticized, he overruled his son's direction. Guy finished the day's shoot, walked into his dressing room, and put his fist through the wall. And then he drove downtown to the USC campus and withdrew from school.

The next morning, Del took back the reins. They hadn't talked about it since, because what was the use? Guy wasn't just Guy. He was one-quarter of a much greater thing. So much of his life was pretend. A natural leader who wasn't allowed to lead, because the family already had one. He wasn't even allowed to love the person he loved, not publicly, at least. His family still believed Kelly Faber was his roommate. *Always be aware of your public image.* Which, in the case of Guy and Kelly, meant pretending to be friends, nothing more, because that was the way it worked in 1964, all the more when you were famous.

At twenty-two, he detested that other self. He sometimes wished they would let him die a fiery on-screen death, putting him and real-life Guy out of their misery. Just as Walter Kerr had recommended in *The New York Times*.

Linda dabbed at his forehead, where he was now perspiring. Guy was suddenly aware of his breathing, which was coming in strangled gasps. It was as if an elephant were sitting on his chest, crushing his lungs.

"Here," Linda said from a long way off. She handed him something. A paper bag stamped with the word *Avon*. "Breathe."

He put his mouth to the mouth of the bag and did what he was told, because, after all, that was what he did best. He closed his eyes, the world narrowing to the sound of his breath, the feel of the bag in his hands, the distant noise of Linda rummaging for something.

"Here," she said again. She held out a glass of water and a yellow pill. "Valium. It helps with anxiety."

He took it without question, even though Guy, unlike Shep, didn't dabble in drugs, because he was as straightlaced and boring as his on-screen self. Linda continued to dab at his forehead, first with cotton balls, then with a cloth. Gradually, he felt his pulse, his breathing start to regulate.

"So," she said in a moment, "what's our fact of the day?"

Since he was a kid, Guy had always been interested in little-known facts simply because, in contrast to his parents and brother, he felt little known.

He expected his voice to come out a croak, but it sounded surprisingly normal as he told her, "The world's oldest living tree is out in Wheeler Peak, Nevada. It's close to five thousand years old, which means it was alive when they were building the pyramids."

Linda tilted his chin and applied another layer of pancake makeup.

"A *Pinus longaeva*—a Great Basin bristlecone pine. Nicknamed Prometheus for the god who gave fire to humans. The forest service keeps its exact location secret to protect it. I'd like to visit it one day. See it for myself."

When she stepped back, finished, he observed his reflection. While he had inherited Del's broad smile and broad shoulders, his own hair was a dark blond, his eyes a forest green. When Shep had first started growing taller and better looking and more popular, Guy went through a dark phase, constantly comparing himself and coming up short. He liked to joke that his younger brother might be better looking and more talented, but at least he'd never be born first. Guy's role as oldest son was the one thing his family couldn't take from him.

He said, "Well, Linda, you've done the impossible. You've made me look like Shep Newman's brother."

In spite of the fact that she was nearly forty years old and had been married for ten years, she blushed. Part of Guy's charm was that he was chivalrous and self-deprecating but not in a way that made you feel sorry for him.

The office of James T. Aubrey, on the other side of the building, had the feel of an old-fashioned cigar club: dark wood and leather and air that smelled of smoke, even though there was none to be seen. An enormous desk the size of an airplane wing filled half of the room.

Del and Dinah perched together on the sofa across from Aubrey, who had been working as president of CBS Television Network since December 1959. He lounged in a chair that was purposely higher and bigger than the low sofa, which was too small for two grown people. Another man was present, seated in a hard-backed chair, the executive in charge of West Coast television production for Listerine. An identical hard-backed chair sat conspicuously empty. A curvaceous young woman with dark red hair served coffee and took a seat in a corner, out of the way. She plucked a pencil from behind her ear and waited for the meeting to begin.

"Where's Mr. Kodak?" Del asked, staring at the empty chair. Once upon a time, they'd been funded by a single sponsor per season, but as the ratings began to decline, advertisers had become, in Sydney Weiss's words, squirrely. This was why Kodak and Listerine now split the cost of *Meet the Newmans* between them.

"Gone," Aubrey said. A rakish man of forty-five with thick, dark hair, he was handsome and polished, with Ivy League manners, and could have been a television star himself except for the hard, cutting smile that failed to meet his eyes. They didn't call him the Smiling

Cobra for nothing. He had fired people—not just any people but important people who made the network a lot of money—on the spot, for no reason, without explanation, and with just two words: *You're through.* Lucille Ball abhorred him so much she dealt exclusively with Bill Paley, president and chairman of CBS. But Del preferred to deal with Aubrey directly, man to man.

"Gone?" repeated Del. "Gone where?" He had visions of Mr. Kodak on vacation in the South of France or Mexico.

"Kodak has bowed out."

"What do you mean Kodak has bowed out? We aren't finished with the season." Del stared at Aubrey, at Mr. Listerine.

"Let me get right to the point," Aubrey said. Beyond him, the secretary touched the end of her pencil to her tongue and began to write. "The *New York Times* piece was bad."

Del didn't know Walter Kerr, the author of that piece, but he knew of him. The man famously hated the films and television and books he reviewed, a fact that didn't make Del feel any better. He wasn't one to dwell on bad reviews—he wouldn't be where he was today if he had. But this one stung. It was so scathing, so personal, as if Kerr had some kind of vendetta.

Del said, "Surely a single article doesn't warrant jumping ship before the season is over."

"A single article? No." Aubrey snapped his fingers, and the secretary leaped up to fetch him something from his desk. A piece of paper. From which he read, "'What handsome TV star is rumored to be keeping company with a good-looking movie cowboy? And when we say, 'keeping company,' we mean more than dinners and date nights. Once photographed around town double dating with gorgeous young actresses, they've lately ditched the girls and gone stag. With each other. These young men, claims our source, also enjoy sleepovers, although you won't hear it from them. We wonder what the TV star's famous daddy has to say about this.'" Aubrey let the paper drift to the floor. "Well, 'Daddy'? What *do* you have to say?"

"That's outrageous," Del said. "Guy and Kelly are just friends."

Kelly Faber was Guy's roommate, a rugged young film actor riding high from his latest picture, a hit western starring John Wayne, James Coburn, and Natalie Wood. Del himself had lived with a buddy when he first struck out on his own. No one ever thought to question whether they were *lovers*.

"They've been buddies since high school," he told Aubrey. "They played football together."

Beside him, Dinah recrossed her legs and gave a little cough.

"Which is exactly," Aubrey said, "what I told *Confidential* when I paid them off."

Confidential. Of course.

"But you understand why I don't like seeing articles like this. Because articles like this lead to headlines like 'America's Favorite Big Brother Prefers Boys,' and that leads to viewers running away. They don't tune in to *Meet the Newmans* to see Gil get it on with his friend Howie—"

"Guy," Del corrected, but Aubrey wasn't listening.

"They tune in for good family values. And as I told Raymond Burr, they won't just be running away from your show. They'll be wondering if Rob Petrie and Jethro Bodine are homosexuals too."

The mention of Raymond Burr was a warning. Burr, the star of *Perry Mason*, the network's long-running legal drama. Burr, who had created not one but two fictional dead wives and one fictional dead son to cover up the fact that he lived with a man. When, a couple of years earlier, Burr was photographed kissing a drag queen, Aubrey had paid off *Confidential* to kill the story.

Del knew Raymond Burr. He liked Raymond Burr. But Guy had nothing in common with that man.

"So what does this mean for the two remaining episodes?" Del asked, purposely steering back to the show.

Aubrey waved as if he were swatting a fly. "Kodak's on the hook for the next episode, but their contract gives them the option to walk away before the finale. Which they're doing. Kerr isn't wrong about the show. *Your* show. Your ratings are in the toilet. I know you're hoping for renewal, but frankly, you'd be better off hoping for Jayne Mansfield to fall from the sky, through the ceiling, and onto your lap." There was a tutting sound from Mr. Listerine. "In other words, it doesn't look good. I don't have to remind you—or maybe I do—that CBS is America's number one television network. Since I've been president, our profits have risen from twenty-five million to forty-nine million. *Twenty-five million to forty-nine fucking million.*"

Mr. Listerine nodded, suitably impressed.

"You're slow and you're expensive," Aubrey continued. "It takes you five goddamn days to film one episode. Everyone else does it in two or three. Your sponsors—*sponsor*"—he pointed at Mr. Listerine— "is spending ninety thousand dollars per show."

"Nothing is expensive if it shows up on the screen," Del said, flashing a smile at the room. This quote by Cecil B. DeMille was one of his favorites. While guarded about his childhood, even with Dinah, this much was known—Del's parents, long dead, had run their own theater in his small California hometown, and he had learned as early as seven that much of a show's value was in its stage production.

"It's expensive when no one's goddamn watching," barked Aubrey.

"*Meet the Newmans* is frequently in the top twenty." Del's own voice was barbed with irritation. He was starting to perspire along the collar of his shirt, and he felt bottled and explosive, like a soft drink that had been shaken to death.

"You used to be in the top fucking five," Aubrey said. "You want to know what the top five is now? *The Beverly Hillbillies. The Dick Van Dyke Show*, *Petticoat Junction*, *The Andy Griffith Show.*"

Aubrey himself had brought *Hillbillies*, *Junction*, and *Griffith* to the network. Del thought of it as the dumbing down of America. He had made a living on feel-good humor that was relatable. Real situations that he found funny and that he and Dinah and the boys had lived through. But Aubrey seemed to have a Midas touch when it came to predicting what audiences wanted, here in 1964, which apparently was dolphins, collies, Martians, and bumpkins.

"You forgot *Bonanza*," Del added helpfully. He couldn't resist. The western had aired on NBC for the past five years, but it was always vying for number one and consistently beat out *Gunsmoke*, which belonged to CBS.

Aubrey locked eyes with him. The two men were of similar size. Both tall and broad-shouldered. But right now, sunk onto the low couch, Del's shoulders were up to his ears, his knees practically in his face.

"Except for *one*," Aubrey said, his tone frigid, "the top fifteen shows are from this network. And yours isn't one of them. America wants broads, bosoms, and fun. They want dramas with at least three fights per episode."

Aubrey gestured to the secretary, who rose quickly from her seat and pulled a cigar from a box on his desk. She sliced off the end, offering it to him along with a light, her hand shaking slightly. Del wondered where she had worked before this and who she'd pissed off to be placed here. Aubrey puffed on the cigar for a moment and then blew a single smoke ring, a perfect O.

"Let me explain something. Twenty-two million babies were born between 1946 and 1951, and now those babies are teenagers hungry for a culture of their own. They represent the largest goddamn portion of the general population, and it's time to give them what they want."

His eyes glinted at them, the small, shining eyes of an animal.

"So here's what we're going to do. You've got two good-looking sons who receive a bounty of mail every week from our female viewers, the very demographic we're trying to win." He winked at the remaining sponsor. "It's the ladies who drive the advertising. They may not have money, but they sure do spend it." He laughed. Mr. Listerine laughed too. Aubrey dropped his smile and pointed the cigar at Del and Dinah. "In these last two episodes, you're going to focus solely on Gil and Shep."

"Guy," Dinah said. "His name is Guy."

Aubrey looked at her just long enough for his eyes to move down her legs and then back up again. "I think," he continued to Del, "even with the upcoming TV wedding, we can all agree big brother is less interesting than little brother. So we make him more interesting."

He once again snapped his fingers in the secretary's direction. She once again jumped to her feet. This time, she opened the door to the office and Guy appeared with Eileen Weld, their faces blank with confusion.

There was a shuffling as Del offered Eileen his seat, and he and Guy arranged themselves on opposite arms of the sofa. Whatever Aubrey was up to, Del didn't like it. The boys—much less secondary cast members like Eileen Weld—were never included in these meetings.

"We were just discussing the wedding," Aubrey told the young people. "We're going to marry you off on the show *and* marry you off in real life. Presto chango. No more rumors." He glanced at Mr. Listerine, who nodded vigorously before craning his neck around toward his secretary. "Are you getting this down?"

"'And marry you off in real life,'" she read back.

"Right. Kill two birds and all that."

"Wait," Eileen said. "I'm sorry. What?" She looked from Aubrey to Guy to Del perched above her, to Aubrey again, her dark ponytail swinging back and forth. At nineteen, she was long-limbed and fresh-faced, with a smattering of freckles across her nose and cheeks and a smile as frequent and bright as California sunshine. But she wasn't smiling now.

"Who decided this?" Guy stared at his father as if he already knew. "Just in case anyone's forgotten, Eileen and I aren't characters in a script. We're actual people with actual lives. . . ."

"And actual feelings," Eileen finished.

"And actual feelings," Guy repeated, then fell quiet when he saw the look Del was giving him.

"Kelly Faber moves out," continued Aubrey, waving his hand, cigar ash scattering like dust. "Eileen moves in. The audience is happy. Which means I'm happy. Which means CBS is happy. Which brings me to son number two. Now, no offense to Gil here, but the real focus is Shep. The girls fucking love him. And they'd love to fuck him. I assume you've heard of the Beatles."

The four boys from Liverpool had arrived in the States last month, appearing on *The Ed Sullivan Show*—filmed out of CBS-TV's Studio 50 in New York City—in front of seventy-three million viewers. The press was calling the nationwide frenzy "Beatlemania."

"Of course I've heard of the Beatles," Del sniffed.

Aubrey jabbed the cigar in his direction. "They've got the top five songs in the country. You know who's number six? Your son. Which means he's literally the only one able to touch them right now. Have him sing his lines. Have him stare into the goddamn camera, right into the hearts and panties of every female viewer. Just make sure he's singing."

"What about us?" Del gestured at himself and at Dinah. "What are we supposed to do?"

"Retire," Aubrey said simply.

"Retire?" Del snapped, much too loudly. "We're not even fifty and you're—what—suggesting we become . . ." How did Walter Kerr phrase it? "'A warm memory of a simpler time'?"

He had a bizarre urge to drop onto the floor and start doing one-armed push-ups. But Aubrey wasn't looking at him. His eyes were narrowed at a spot somewhere above their heads.

"We tell viewers Del and Dinah have moved to Florida. Gil and Eileen, our newlyweds, move into the house with Shep, so if the show comes back next season, we don't have to pay for new sets."

"And the title still works," offered Mr. Listerine.

"Exactly," said Aubrey.

"*Florida?*" Del spat. "The viewers care about all the Newmans, not just Guy and Shep. They care about Del and Dinah too."

The planes of Aubrey's face suddenly shifted, a set being struck, leaving the raw bare bones of it. "Which viewers are you talking about? The ones who used to watch you back in 1959? Because the ones I'm concerned with are the actual viewers who are actually watching the show. They care about Shep Newman. And they care about Gil."

Del jumped to his feet, standing to his full impressive height. "His name is *Guy. G-U-Y.*" From the opposite arm of the sofa, Guy seemed to fold into himself. "How goddamn hard is that to remember?"

Dinah laid her hand on Del's arm. A gesture that held all their years of marriage, the years that bound them, that had given them a short-hand, the ability to talk without talking. The gesture said, *Cooler heads prevail. Keep yours. I'll keep mine. We are smarter than this man. He needs us more than we need him.* Del shook her arm off and stood glaring at Aubrey.

"I'm tossing you a life preserver," Aubrey said. "We are tossing you a life preserver." Lest Del and Dinah think for a second that the sponsor was on their side. "Television is making the move to color. If *Meet the Newmans* is going to make it to season thirteen, it needs to prove that it's worth the extra cost to transition. But here you are, in the middle of the north fucking Atlantic, an iceberg-size hole in your hull, and you still think you're going to swim to safety." He turned in his chair. "When's the finale supposed to air?"

The secretary and Mr. Listerine answered at the same time, "April twenty-fourth."

Aubrey squinted at the ceiling as if he could see it there—the entirety of his glorious kingdom and his own magnificent legacy. "Marry them on it. Make it an event. Make it the biggest goddamn wedding since Grace Kelly and the prince of Monaco. Make it . . ." A light bulb went off in Aubrey's brain. He clapped his hands and sprang to his feet. "Make it live."

"The episode?" Del's voice was faint.

"No, the tango. Yes, the episode. We film it live. That way, America gets to watch as it happens. No man left behind."

"Brilliant," agreed Mr. Listerine. "Viewers will eat it up."

But Aubrey was focused on the Newmans. "I'm giving you till April twenty-fourth to turn this ship around." The terrible smile was back. "That finale had better be a goddamn ratings *bonanza*." He aimed the word at Del. "But first you'd better get out there and find another sponsor."

"That's okay," Del said with forced optimism. "There are any number of sponsors who would love to finance the show."

Aubrey emitted one loud, perfunctory snort.

And with that, it was clear the meeting was finished.

As the three Newmans and Eileen reached the door and freedom, Aubrey called out to them from his desk, from behind a cloud of smoke. "And, folks? Lest you forget. I'm the fucking iceberg."

SIX

MARCH 20, 1964

Twelve hours earlier

S hep pulled into the CBS lot, around the side near the entrance labeled *Artists*. As he shut off the engine, he saw the black-and-white squad car drive up to the guard gate. He watched as the guard waved it through. As the car parked outside the main doors of the building. As two uniformed officers climbed out.

"Is that about you?"

He turned to see Eileen, a book in her hand, staring up at him from the concrete wall that encircled the studio like a moat. Her eyes were the most remarkable thing about her—large and iridescent, the color of amber—and right now, they were flashing in a way that meant she was angry.

"Probably," he told her.

He knew he should run, but running from the parking lot meant running from Eileen. So instead, he rose from the bike and dropped onto the wall beside her. "What's wrong?" he asked.

"Nothing." Her voice bristled. "Other than the fact that marriage is antiquated and stupid." She opened the book where she had marked it with a finger and began to read. "'I still had this idea that there was a whole world of marvelous golden people somewhere.'"

As she read, he watched her, the way her eyelids fluttered as her eyes moved across the page, the way she sat with her legs to one side as if she were riding sidesaddle.

He reached for a cigarette, even though he did his best not to smoke where Del might see him. The old man would burst a blood vessel if he caught him. Shep actually didn't love smoking. It was something he did only because it would piss off his dad, like riding a motorcycle—which he did love—and sleeping with girls—which he loved even more. Now that there was a baby coming, he wondered if suddenly these things would need to stop, if he would have to start wearing suits and complaining about how the weather affected his joints.

"'Sort of heroic super-people, all of them beautiful and witty and calm and kind, and I always imagined that when I did find them I'd suddenly know that I belonged among them, that I was one of them, that I'd been meant to be one of them all along.'" Eileen slammed the book closed and looked at him, a challenge.

Shep took his time. Nodded. Asked, "What's it about?"

"The fact that we're all unavoidably, irrevocably alone."

"Fun."

"Yet we think we can fool nature by saying, 'I do,' as if that's all it takes. As if that fixes everything."

"What a bunch of assholes," he said in agreement.

Her eyes fell on the cigarette. "You're smoking."

"It's been a morning." And an evening. And a whole fucking life.

"It's always a morning with you," she said, but she didn't sound as hostile now.

He exhaled, careful to do it away from her—Guy wasn't the only gentleman in the family. There was so much being said between them that wasn't being said aloud. It was enough, Shep thought, to be here with her, a reminder that, despite the chaos and noise of the world, there was peace to be found in the company of someone else.

He began to sing softly, a tune that always made her laugh. "'Lydia, oh, Lydia, say, have you met Lydia? Oh, Lydia the Tattooed Lady.'"

It was a number from an old Marx Brothers picture. He sang it loud and bawdy, not at all like himself, and waggled his eyebrows, à la Groucho, at her. Cheering her meant cheering himself, and he felt his own anger and fear loosen a little.

Then, like an exhalation of breath on a cold day, he could see the rest of her anger dissipate. She began to hum, then to sing along, their voices soaring across the parking lot.

"'She can give you a view of the world in tattoo, if you step up and tell her where. . . . With a view of Niagara that nobody has, and on a clear day you can see Alcatraz.'"

Eileen was maybe the one person he didn't have to put on a show for, and no matter what happened—if he never kissed her or went to bed with her—he wanted her in his life. He wondered if she'd still want to be in it once he told her about the baby.

"Did you know the 'Beat' in 'Beat Generation' comes from 'beaten down'?" he asked when they finished singing. "Jack Kerouac was talking to the writer John Clellon Holmes—this was back during the Cold War—and he said, 'This is really a beat generation.' Meaning 'lost and desperate to believe in something.'"

"That could describe us. Or any generation, really, even our parents'."

"Kerouac was a believer in the truth of the heart. I gave the book to Guy once because I thought, hey, this is as good a way as any for him to get to know me. But he never read it. He said it needed an editor." He heard the bitterness in his voice. "Guy missed the whole point of Kerouac, which is first thought, best thought. Old Jack believes revision is just a form of lying."

"As actors, we revise all the time."

"And you could say we're professional liars."

From behind him, there was a noise.

It was his father, looking furious, emerging from the side entrance with a checkbook in his hand. From the front of the building, there was the sound of car doors slamming. Shep watched as the police drove away. As his dad grumbled toward him.

Something about Del was off. The expensive suit was there, yes, but the way it fell was different. His entire person—both the suit and the man inside it—looked windblown and distracted. Rattled, even. This, in turn, rattled Shep, so much so that he forgot to hide the cigarette.

Jesus.

Shep's first thought was that Del must be dying. Instinctively, he glanced over his shoulder for Guy, even though, as brothers went, they hadn't been close for years. They were so drastically different, and then Shep's star had exploded and Kelly had come along and taken his place as Guy's best friend. But if he was about to receive life-altering news, he'd prefer it if Guy were there.

"Shepherd Newman," his father began. Never a good sign. Shep took the opportunity to stub out the cigarette, holding it in his palm so that his dad would see he wasn't, on top of everything else, a litterbug. "Goddammit."

Shep considered deflecting and asking his dad just what the hell was going on with *him*. But if it really was something serious, he didn't want to find out here in the parking lot of CBS.

Del said, "I have just written a very large check to the LAPD for reckless driving."

"It was about time someone fined them," Shep quipped, knowing Del hated when he did this. He was not a fan of one-liners unless he came up with them himself.

"I'll be deducting the amount of that check from your salary."

"Yes, sir." It wasn't as if Shep ever saw his money, so what did he care what went into it or came out of it?

"Young lady," Del said to Eileen, as if only just noticing her.

"Sir," she said and leaped up, scrambling toward the stage door. Before disappearing inside, she turned and waggled an eyebrow, Groucho-style, in a way that made Shep laugh.

Del said, "This isn't funny. The police aren't funny."

"Some police are funny. . . ."

"God. Dammit."

"Sorry." As if in front of the camera, Shep adjusted his expression to Serious Face. Thanks to his mom, he knew that his dad had once been like him—quietly rebellious, burning to make his own way. Apparently, he just didn't like to remember it. Shep also knew—thanks to his own insightful nature—that while Del loved both his sons, he found it easier to love Guy. Not for who he was but for the simple fact that Guy had not eclipsed Del's own success.

"Believe it or not," Del said, "you're not going to be Shep Newman forever."

"Uh . . ." Shep's expression changed to Bemused Face. About-to-Make-a-Joke Face.

"Not this version of Shep Newman," Del snapped. "Fame is fleeting and ephemeral, and so is money. Show business should be considered a means to an end. Nothing more."

Shep didn't bother pointing out that Del's entire life and career revolved around show business, that show business was—as far as he could tell—synonymous with Del Newman and vice versa.

"One day, you're going to wish you'd gone to college. You've got a brilliant mind, even if you don't always use it. Which is why I've taken the liberty of enrolling you at UCLA."

It was a conversation they'd been having ad nauseam since Shep turned seventeen. But this was the first he was hearing about his father *enrolling him*.

"I think you've got me mixed up with Guy," Shep said. His brother's acceptance letter to USC had appeared the week before he graduated high school. The next thing you knew, he was commuting to campus and reading Glanville Williams's *Learning the Law* for fun.

"It's your choice," Del said, more for the sake of the woman walking past on the way to her car—wide grin, fluttering eyes—than for his son.

Shep couldn't help but laugh again. Who was Del fooling? Nothing in Shep's life was his choice. He was owned by his dad and CBS. Owned and produced. He was a copyright. A commodity, an unexpected gold mine that had sprung organically from the television show. Whichever direction he looked, he couldn't see a way out. It was true that he was untroubled, even lazy about most things, but music he took seriously. Music was his refuge. He longed to put out an album that would earn not just listeners and fans but respect, with the kind of sound he yearned, more and more, to play—searing and soulful and electric, not even *of* the times but ahead of it. Songs that meant something, that would make people spontaneously combust just by listening to them.

"Okay, Pop. Whatever you say." He would no more be going to college than he would be opening a doughnut shop and learning to yodel.

"Good. Then we're done discussing it."

The fuck we are, Shep thought but didn't say, because Del always had to have the last word. Father and son strode into the building, not speaking, together but separate. As far as either was concerned, they were a country—if not a world—apart.

Guy Newman and Kelly Faber:
Bachelors on the Loose

Guy Newman and his younger brother **Shep** are two of the undisputed kings of television. Although fame rests lightly on Guy's rugged shoulders, his throne room is a lonely place. A year ago, he was engaged to marry pretty young starlet **Shelley Fabares**, who stars as Mary Stone on *The Donna Reed Show*. But today, he is a bachelor on the loose.

The reasons for his breakup from Shelley continue to remain a mystery. For now, Guy seems to have settled into comfortable bachelorhood with his best friend and roommate, **Kelly Faber**. If Faber's name sounds familiar, it's because you've seen him on the big screen in hit films *Deadwood* and *Down by the Old Mill*, or maybe you recognize his handsome face from the magazines, where he was—until recently—photographed with girlfriend **Natalie Wood**.

When Guy and Kelly aren't out on the town, they're enjoying a cozy life in the Newman family guesthouse, which they've turned into a real bachelors' paradise. The boys often entertain—frequent guests include **Howie Sherman** and **Clint McClean** from *Meet the Newmans*, Faber's *Deadwood* costar **Troy Donahue**, as well as brother Shep and a revolving door of beauties.

The Newman-Faber house is famous for good food, good drinks, and good fun. When the boys aren't throwing parties, they love cooking, sports, and exercise. You can often catch sight of them going for a jog on the beach or a swim in the ocean. Guy loves to surf, while Kelly prefers to lie on the sand. Guy boxes, Kelly lifts weights. Guy rides motorcycles, Kelly prefers fast cars.

But here's one thing these bachelor boys can agree on—girls!

SEVEN

MARCH 20, 1964

Eight hours earlier

For the first time in *Meet the Newmans'* long history, they were in danger of running behind. Dinah stood beneath the lights burning down on their artificial grass backyard and watched her husband stride back and forth, a thin line of sweat at his hairline, his smile fixed and tight, barking directions at his sons. Guy, stiff as a wooden puppet, anger bubbling beneath the calm exterior, and Shep, ad-libbing for laughs. It was 5:00 p.m., and she had lost all feeling in her right arm.

The supporting cast lingered on set as they always did, even though they weren't needed in this scene—Eileen Weld, Howie Sherman, Clint McClean, Artie Fordham, and Peggy Livingston, who played Artie's wife and Dinah's best friend. Just beyond the too-green plastic grass, 250 seats sat empty in the theater, the overhead monitors blank and silent. Later, in the editing room, Del would layer in a laugh track.

There was the scent of lilacs as Peggy fell in beside Dinah. "You look like you ate some bad salmon."

She was the closest thing Dinah had to a best friend in real life. Just one more thing the show had given her that she wouldn't have otherwise—friends, family dinners, sons who got along with each other, who told her where they were going and what they were doing, everyone under one roof, situations that resolved themselves neatly in thirty minutes or less, a husband to crawl into bed with at the end of the day.

"I'm fine," Dinah told her. For a second, she considered saying, *I feel peckish and hungry but not in a food sort of way. Like there's a great hollow place inside me wanting to be filled. I feel restless. So restless I barely sleep. And I'm slowly going numb. I don't know what this is or why it's happening. But it's been coming on for a while, like a bad cold. And I don't know if I can ignore it any longer.*

She smiled.

Peggy looked skeptical. Her on-screen character was a lovable ditz, but in real life, she was one of the few women Dinah knew who had not only gone to college but earned an advanced degree. Peggy had her master's in mathematics from Pepperdine.

"Well, okay," she said. "But do me a favor and avoid seafood for a while. There's a crab pâté on the craft services table that looks suspicious."

Del yelled, "Action!" and Guy and Shep began to throw the football. Three lines of dialogue, simple choreography. In. Out. Then this day would be over and they could go home and temporarily forget James T. Aubrey and *Confidential* and maybe have a good strong drink.

As Dinah watched her boys—Guy more at home now with the football in his hand, Shep trying to keep pace with him, just like when he was little—she let herself breathe for the first time since early morning, and her mind wandered, as it often did lately, to the teenage girl from North Carolina who had come west at sixteen to make her living. Was this what she'd envisioned for herself when she was taking dance classes and going to high school back home, living in a cramped house with two brothers, an exhausted mother, and a father who worked long hours before he disappeared and left them for someone else? When she was on the train from there to here, the country stretched out before her, full of possibility?

It was both more than she'd ever imagined and less.

Once upon a time, she had been Dinah Garfinkle, which she had quickly changed to Dinah Shepherd in honor of the parent she loved more than anything. She had hung out at the Cotton Club, smoking, drinking cocktails, dancing with dashing foreign men. She had dyed her crisp blond hair blonder and starred in pictures alongside Cary Grant and James Stewart and Frank Sinatra. She had once dated band leader Artie Shaw. She had been engaged, for Christ's sake, to a Brazilian stunt pilot. But then Del Newman roared into her life like a freight train, and that was it. Not for the first time, she wondered what her life would have been if she, like her old pal Ginger Rogers, had stayed at RKO instead of choosing Del and having children.

Where would she be right now?

The scene came to a sudden halt, Del's frustrated voice climbing to the rafters, the boys starting to bicker. The two of them had once been inseparable, back when they were eight and twelve. Now they barely tolerated each other.

The bickering continued in spite of Del, and then they turned on him.

"Come on, old man," Shep said to his father. Dark-haired and lanky, still growing into his body, he was the tallest of the Newmans, taller even than Del, something she knew irritated her husband. His eyes underneath the long lashes were a smoky violet gray. It was what most people noticed first. Sometimes his beauty startled her. He looked so unlike any of the rest of them, and she wondered where he'd come from.

"Why don't you join the game?" Shep crowed, an edge to the sarcasm. "Unless you need to sit down."

Del prided himself on the fact that he'd always done his own stunts, the occasional pratfall or tumble. He was forty-five now, with one bad knee and a trick back, but he still insisted on keeping up with his sons.

"Yeah, Pop," Guy said. *Pop.* A name he only ever called his dad on-screen. "Don't let Walter Kerr get the last word." Guy, like Shep, knew exactly what buttons to push.

As Del strode onto the grass, Dinah watched from the sidelines, a bad feeling crawling up her spine. When he felt he had something to prove, he was like a dog with a bone—not just any dog but a rabid one.

"Del," she called from the edge of their plastic, too-green yard. "Del," she said again, louder this time. She thought about James T. Aubrey watching on the television in his office behind a cloud of cigar smoke. Aubrey, who thought Del was old and irrelevant.

She watched as Del called, "Action," and father and sons positioned themselves on the artificial grass. Her heart began to knock so fast and loud that she could feel it outside of her chest.

Guy pitched the ball to Shep, and Del intercepted. Till the end of her life, Dinah would never forget the look on his face—the genuine, unadulterated surprise and glee that managed in that moment to transcend the anger. The joy as he started to run, ball tucked into the crook of his arm.

A shout from the playing field. Guy and Shep chased their father. The two of them leaped into the air, a synchronized ballet of movement and force, and crashed into him.

The three of them hit the ground hard.

For a moment, there was nothing but silence.

Then the cameraman rushed forward, then Artie, then others. Dinah felt her legs carry her through the crowd, until she was there, standing overhead, looking down at her husband.

He lay on the artificial grass for a good thirty seconds, eyes closed, Guy bent over him, fingers on the pulse of his neck. After a long, breathless moment, Guy looked up and nodded to no one and everyone. Yes, there was a pulse. Yes, he was still with us. Dinah drew in a breath and knelt beside him, laying a hand on Del's head like she was checking for a fever.

"Del," she said, her voice froggy. "Del."

His eyelids fluttered, and her heart started to beat again. And then he opened his eyes and looked at her.

"I'm okay," he said, his voice faint.

He got to his feet, shaking off the outstretched hands of his wife.

He wobbled and then righted himself, straightening to his full height. Sweat was dripping down his face, his neck, his back.

Then, because he was Del Newman after all, he managed to direct his megawatt smile, the one he was known for, at everyone on the set and in the wings. Playing to the very back row, just as he had learned to do.

He cleared his throat and called, "Cut."

An eruption of applause, and Del bowed. For a split second, his smile wavered and he looked like he was going to vomit up his lunch.

He met Dinah's eyes, still concerned, and then—after only a slight delay—she beamed her own megawatt smile in the direction of her sons and, just beyond them, those who worked on the show, their second family.

As her heart swelled, she tried to remember what it was her mother used to say. *You will never be younger than you are right now.* She wanted to freeze the moment like they were watching it play back in the editing room. It was perfect. They were perfect. Not outdated or obsolete but hopeful, vibrant, timeless. And like no one who would ever retire to Florida.

EIGHT

MARCH 20, 1964

Six hours earlier

Dinah found Del sitting on the couch in his dressing room, script on the seat beside him, ice pack pressed to his head, another on his knee. His eyes were far away, and he was staring into the middle distance. She had heard it called that once. It was a phrase that intrigued her. *The middle distance.* Where was the middle distance, exactly? And what, if anything, lived there?

A long time ago, when she and Del were first married, they had lain in bed, limbs intertwined, her head on his chest, and she had posed questions along similar lines. If Del thought she was odd, that her brain was wired in strange ways, he never said so. Instead, he pondered the question and together they discussed it with all the seriousness of politics. It was one of the things she loved most about him—not just his acceptance of her but his acceptance of things out of the ordinary. He could always see possibility.

"I'm on my way home," she said. "I have that interview with the *Times*. The journalist is coming to the house."

He blinked but otherwise didn't move. In this light, the threads of silver in his dark brown hair and the faint lines around his eyes were more pronounced. He had smoked a long time ago, but only briefly, so the corners of his mouth were unlined. It was the reason she'd given up smoking herself, back when they married. Sheer vanity.

"Del?"

It wasn't the silver hair or wrinkles that made him look older. It was the way he held himself, leaning forward, back slightly hunched, arms resting on knees, as if he was trying to catch his breath. Unlike so many men of his generation, he had always worn a wedding ring, and now he twisted it, over and over, as if it was a switch he was trying to click on.

She crossed the pale blue carpet the studio had installed—at Del's request—last summer and dug through her purse until she found the aspirin. She handed him three and a glass of water from his vanity. He took them from her and continued to sit there, looking at once cross and vacant.

"I'm going to stand here until you swallow them," she said.

"Do you want to check under my tongue?" he snapped, meeting her eyes. His were a different blue from hers. Less cornflower, more navy.

"If that's what it takes," she said. Del was stubborn, but so was she. She wouldn't snap back, because she knew her husband well enough to know he was angry at himself and feeling helpless and probably old, which was something he hated feeling, especially on the heels of the morning's meeting. She tilted her head to the side and waited. He took the damn pills.

She sat down beside him, picked up the script, and set it on her lap. Watched him carefully. Guy had gotten a concussion once in high school, and she knew the signs to look for.

Del said, "It's all going to come down to the last episode."

"So I've heard."

"We've got one episode of the regular season. And then the finale. The *live* finale. If we can find anyone to pay for it." He cast a miserable eye on the script. "Two episodes, Di. That's it. Two episodes of a twelve-year run."

"I was thinking we might approach General Foods. Or Corning—with all the kitchen products they manufacture, they might be interested in sponsoring—"

"I'm going to see Mr. Kodak. Persuade them to come back."

But what if they don't? she thought. For the first time, she could see the end of *Meet the Newmans*. Taste was shifting. The world was changing. The medium of television was changing. Color was coming. She told herself Del knew the business better than she did. He knew most of these executives by name. There had been that time, halfway through the sixth season, when they lost Quaker Oats, and Del had gotten on a plane and flown to Chicago, where they were headquartered. Before he even touched back down again in LA, they had signed on for the next two years.

"I thought we were changing history," Del said in a moment. "But we're not. There's nothing revolutionary about what we're doing. Aubrey's right. Malcolm X. Kennedy. Muhammad Ali. LBJ and his war on poverty. They're *actually* changing history. When I was a kid, you know who I idolized? Will Rogers. He went from cowhand to home-spun philosopher. He became the nation's most popular public speaker, newspaper columnist, author, and movie star. He's still the most quoted man of the twentieth century."

"Sure, so far." Dinah kept her tone purposely light.

"The aviation industry wouldn't be what it is today if not for him. He gave his fortune to charities. . . ."

"So let's start giving away our money."

"He never forgot where he came from. He was true to his roots, true to himself. And look at the impact he made. He used to say, 'You've got to go out on a limb sometimes because that's where the fruit is.'"

"Where's this coming from? Aubrey?"

He sighed. "I don't know." He stared off toward the middle distance again. "I guess I thought what we were doing was more important than it actually is."

"A person can change history in big and small ways." She nudged his shoulder with her own. "You can't take on every fight. But you can still make a difference. I know for a fact that you impact people in ways you don't realize. The crew. Their families. The viewers. Maybe someone watches an episode and sees one of us doing a good deed. That inspires them to go out into the world and be a little kinder."

He continued to gaze off and away, but she thought from his stillness that he was listening.

"My mother always said to make the world lovelier than how you found it. Isn't that what we've tried to do?"

Her mom could always—no matter what else was happening around them, no matter what she herself was going through—make Dinah feel better. In that moment, she missed her fiercely.

When Del didn't answer, she said, "We're Newmans. We don't back down and we don't give up. We give them something to talk about."

He met her eye, gave her the faintest smile. She could see it there behind the anguish—gratitude. Love. She reached out her pinkie and felt a sense of relief as he linked it with his. It was something they'd done for years. A reminder that they were in this together. That no matter what, they had each other and all would be well.

She felt something wash over her. Love for this man who'd been with her from the start, or at least since she was eighteen and he was twenty. The music they'd made. The movies they'd starred in. The radio shows that led to the radio series that led to the TV series. When they first met, Dinah had the feeling of being taken by the hand and pulled along, like she was a kite caught in a strong wind. It was exhilarating and heady, the sensation of flying. But sometimes it left her motion sick. In those days, they were almost like one person.

It had been a while since she felt that way and since she'd experienced that sudden rush of love. But right now, her pinkie hooked with his, the warmth of him cutting through her own numbness, Dinah felt a kind of motion sickness. It had been easier when they were filming movies together. The project would be intense but short-lived, and they would come back to each other afterward. She thought about how the boys didn't need her like they used to. How Del didn't need her like he used to. The four of them like individual planets in the same solar system. She wondered when that had begun.

After a few seconds, he said, "We're getting old."

"Speak for yourself."

"You, Daisy, will be young forever." His old nickname for her, one she hadn't heard in a long time. She was used to him singing it out when he was teasing her or whispering it when it was just the two of them in their bed, but right now, the name sounded sad on his lips.

"That's just as bad," she said, smoothing the script pages absently. "Can you imagine being young forever? How exhausting that would be?"

For some reason, they laughed. Two war veterans. Comrades once again.

And then he said softly, "I don't know who I am without this show. I think I may be in the midst of a midlife crisis." The words sounded private, like a secret thought.

Dinah took his hand.

"You existed before *Meet the Newmans*," she said, "and you'll exist after it's over."

But as she sat there, her hand linked with his, neither of them capable of feeling anything other than a kind of distant, foreboding loss, she wondered if this was true for any of them.

DECEMBER 1962

The Secrets to a Happy Marriage

by Dinah Newman

Dinah Newman, star of Meet the Newmans *(Fridays at 8:30 p.m. on CBS), has one of the most enviable and admired marriages in real life and on TV. She and Del Newman don't just play husband and wife, they* are *husband and wife. They wed twenty-one years ago and have been inspiring other young marrieds ever since. When we asked Dinah her secrets for wedded bliss, she was only too happy to share.*

1. Remember to smile
Even if you're feeling frazzled and overwhelmed, it's important to greet your husband with a shiny demeanor. Put yourself in his shoes. After a long day at the office, which would you rather come home to—a grumpy wife who complains to you about the housework or a wife who is freshly dressed, perfumed, and wearing a bright smile? No one likes a sourpuss!

2. Take care of yourself
By this, I mean always look impeccable. Find the style that suits you best—be it dresses or slacks—and show off that figure! Invest in rouge and mascara and a weekly trip to the beauty parlor. If he doesn't buy you perfume, buy some for yourself, and make sure to dab it on before you greet him at the door.

3. Take care of him
Instead of joining your local Women's Club or investing time in the PTA, take a course in Swedish massage so that you can help him unwind after a stressful day at work.

4. Listen to him

Your husband is a busy man who has a lot on his mind. It's true that marriages are built on communication and trust, but they are also built on your ability to listen. Don't chatter away at him about nonsense when he has something important on his mind. Honor his wish for silence or, if he engages you, lend a sympathetic ear.

5. Become Betty Crocker

Don't just be a can opener! The food you serve your husband and family should be fresh, digestible, warm, appetizing, and clearly cooked with love. Likewise, the table you set should be beautiful and welcoming.

6. Don't be a nag

This goes hand in hand with listening and smiling. If your husband has forgotten to take out the trash or if the lawn *still* needs mowing, don't badger him. All he will hear is his own mother. Simply wait for him to remember or, if worse comes to worst, do it yourself!

7. Shed those nasty habits

If you must smoke, do so in private, so as not to offend or embarrass your husband. A lady never smokes in an elevator or on the street. If you must smoke, always carry your own cigarettes, because no man wants a wife who's always borrowing theirs.

8. Remember who's in charge

While I do have my own opinions and a busy career, at the end of the day, I know who rules the house. My husband always has the final word, and I wouldn't have it any other way.

9. Wear pink underwear

The lacier the better! Pretty undergarments not only please him, they have the added benefit of making you feel feminine. And they can add a little oomph to your walk, even if they are tastefully hidden beneath your clothes!

NINE

MARCH 20, 1964

Five hours earlier

T he Newman home sat back from the street overlooking a thick, green lawn. Unlike most of the neighboring houses, it was largely hidden behind a high brick wall. Juliet tried the gate at the entrance, and it swung open, making her wonder if it—like the family itself—was only for show. Once inside, she stood on the walkway, bag over her shoulder, studying the house as she would a stranger.

It was a generous Cape Cod painted a sunny yellow, with a sloping roof, high, wide windows, and a glossy red door the color of a ripe tomato. It was large and lovely but not ostentatious. Along the stone path and around the entrance, snapdragons, pansies, and primroses bloomed in Technicolor, and twin king palms stood like sentries on either end of the house itself. It was the house, she realized now, that they showed at the start of each episode, and she was suddenly overcome with an intense feeling of déjà vu. Their very own home played their TV home, just like the Newmans played themselves. The whole thing was as bizarre as it was revolutionary. What sort of people would volunteer for such a life?

Juliet considered getting back into the car and driving away. She had done interviews like this before with celebrities—going to the home, being welcomed by staff, asking all the standard questions, hearing all the standard answers, then being shown the door as soon as the allotted time was up. Knowing she, Juliet, had made no impression, that the star was already on to the next thing. Interviews like this were a waste of her talents.

But then the red door swung open and Dinah Newman stood there. It took Juliet a second to register the shining blond hair, the sparkling blue eyes, the faint sprinkling of freckles, the bright smile. In her experience, this was a first. Usually, the door was answered by an assistant or manager or housekeeper.

"Juliet Dunne?" Dinah extended a hand. "Dinah Newman. Won't you come in?" She stepped aside, opening the door wide enough to welcome an entire cavalcade of reporters. "I thought we'd sit on the sunporch since we still have some daylight."

Dinah wore a blue dress, the color of an autumn sky, with a belt and three-quarter-length sleeves. The pearl necklace was absent, but otherwise, she looked exactly like what she was—America's most beloved wife and mother.

"Mrs. Newman?" a voice said. A woman in a sensible housedress appeared. She was in her late fifties, large and broad, with a thick accent that, if Juliet had to guess, came from somewhere cold and mountainous—Germany, Scandinavia.

"Juliet," Dinah said. "This is Flora Klausen. She's been with us since Shep was a baby."

Flora nodded at Juliet, no trace of a smile. Her hair was a faded brown, pulled back into a neat bun.

"Should I serve refreshments?" Flora asked. And again, the contrast—the formality of this woman compared to the informality of her employer.

"No thank you, Flora. We'll help ourselves."

Housekeepers were often the confidential informants of Juliet's profession. She thought briefly of what it would be like if she, like her colleagues, were to press money into this woman's hand and grill her for the real story behind the story. But that was the sordid side of reporting, the side she couldn't bear. The one side she'd been subjected to herself. Besides, today she had an agenda.

Dinah led Juliet from the entryway through a spacious living room. Here Juliet glimpsed the second floor, which overlooked the room below from an L-shaped catwalk.

"Technically," Dinah said, "I was the one who found Flora. She was the sister-in-law of a hairdresser I used to go to, back in the early days. Anyway, she was new to the country and needed work, and I hired her, sight unseen. In a way, we've grown up together in this business, in this town."

Dinah crossed the dining room into a sunlit kitchen, the same cheery yellow as the home's exterior, and then through an enclosed walkway that looked out on a courtyard and gardens. These were rooms Juliet had seen before. She felt as familiar with them as she did with her own apartment. Whether it was done for her benefit or whether this was the way the Newmans lived, Juliet had to admit it was comfortable and welcoming. Unlike most celebrity homes, it felt as if people actually lived here.

"But from the start," Dinah continued, "it was clear that Flora merely tolerated the boys and me. It's my husband she adores. I'm 'Mrs. Newman,' no matter how many times I've asked her to call me Dinah. Guy is Arving, which means 'heir.' Shep is Fratz, 'little devil.' But Del is just Del."

They entered a light-filled sunroom, glassed in like a terrarium, that overlooked Toluca Lake itself, where a sailboat glided across the water. On the opposite bank, large homes rose, the mountains behind them.

"I'm sorry about the front gate," Dinah said. "It's a fairly new addition. Too many girls were ringing the bell asking for Shep and camping out on our lawn." She laughed. "Actually, they were climbing up the trellises and trying to break in. It got a little scary. Not for Shep, who's used to it, but for the rest of us."

She shook her head and smiled apologetically, as if Juliet might view the wall as a personal affront. Then Dinah offered her a seat in an overstuffed wicker chair and sat opposite her in its twin.

"That must be a kind of whiplash," Juliet said as she settled herself. "To be so young and still live at home but have that kind of fame. It must be hard for his older brother to have to stand back and watch from the sidelines."

She pulled out a tape recorder and the notebook she always carried, the one that was half-filled with scribble from other assignments, other interviews just like this one. A pitcher of water sat next to a pot of something—coffee, Juliet guessed, given that it was March. It always surprised her that cool weather existed here.

"Guy has his own life and his own projects," Dinah said easily. "There's never been any jealousy between the boys, not even when they were sharing a room." She gave a laugh, one that sounded practiced. "You know, they were the best of buddies till Guy turned thirteen and started wanting his independence." She sighed at the memory.

"And now?" Juliet said.

"Oh, and now too, of course. Anyway. I've been looking forward to this."

Her voice, in person, was warm, as if she might start singing at any moment. For some reason, instead of putting her at ease, this put Juliet on edge.

"I hope traffic wasn't too awful coming over the hill. At least, I assume you came over the hill. The *Times* offices are, if I remember, downtown?"

"They are." Juliet smiled politely. "Traffic was fine."

Dinah poured them coffee in china teacups, the rims and saucers decorated with delicate yellow roses, and then sat back again, folding her hands in her lap. Unlike Juliet, Dinah was beautiful in a classical, nonthreatening way. Before she had cooled it with the Musician, Juliet had made the mistake of dating him publicly. The incident with the fur rug aside, she quickly found out what strangers thought of her. Women spat at her in the street, and the tabloids described her as "doe-eyed and sulky, like a courtesan from the sixteenth century." It was largely because of this and because of the way men had always treated her, like a commodity, that she enjoyed fucking with them. Leaning into their vision of her while proving herself to be the smartest person in any room.

Dinah, on the other hand, was warm. Likable.

Juliet didn't know any women like this. She personally wasn't like this. Renee and her other friends weren't like this. To Juliet, who was sitting there in last night's clothes and makeup, the smell of sex still on her skin, Dinah Newman seemed like a mythical creature. Juliet wondered how men had treated her when she was twenty-six, if she had been dismissed because of her looks, misjudged and underestimated.

"Shep still lives at home," Dinah was saying, "but you would never know it." She laughed again. "And Guy lives in the guesthouse, but he might as well be in Santa Barbara for how much we actually see him."

"Do you miss them? Your sons?" Juliet asked. Damn, the coffee was good.

"I do," Dinah said, almost far away. And then she shook her head and laughed again. "And I don't. I mean, we're a very close family, so we have lots of time together, probably more than most families. And I have so much on my own plate. I mean, there's my philanthropic work, and I try to respond to every fan letter that comes in. And there's my cooking and baking, of course. Which I love."

Juliet made a mental note to circle back to that later as Dinah asked how long she'd been with the newspaper. She was still fiddling with the recorder, which wasn't always reliable. So far, she hadn't been able to convince Boyd Hartley to give her a new one. "A little over three years," she replied, simultaneously proud and uncomfortable. She waited for Dinah to ask—as her father always did—why she hadn't gotten any further than the Lifestyle desk in all that time.

Instead, Dinah said, "Have you always written?"

The question surprised her. It wasn't the reaction she'd been expecting: The people she interviewed almost never showed much interest in her.

"I've always loved writing," she said, which didn't exactly answer the question. "My mom claims she liked to write when she was my age. Not that I've read anything of hers. I'm pretty sure she tossed it all."

It was impossible for Juliet to picture her mother before she was her mother, to imagine she'd had a life before. Roberta Shaeffer had attended one year of college at Indiana University before getting pregnant with Juliet, her only child. Forty-four now, Juliet's mother was still pretty and slim because she worked hard to be pretty and slim. Her clothes were always nicely pressed, even the dresses she had worn past their prime. Years ago, before Juliet left home, Roberta had written to Dinah Newman, and Dinah had written her back. The framed letter was proudly displayed on the wall of their kitchen.

"'Whether you succeed or not is irrelevant, there is no such thing. Making your unknown known is the important thing.' Georgia O'Keeffe." Dinah smiled, a little sadly, and Juliet realized the sadness was in honor of her mother and the words she'd thrown away.

"Do you mind if we start?" Juliet asked briskly.

"I thought we already had." Dinah's own tone was breezy. "Of course. Yes."

Juliet pressed Record. She scanned her notes. *What do you love most about working with your husband? What are your sons like in real life? What is your favorite recipe to cook for your family? What advice do you have for mothers of today?*

She flipped to a blank page, her pulse quickening, and said, "You're a workingwoman. You are one of the stars of a show that's seen by millions of people every week. You've appeared on that show for the past twelve years. And yet the image you portray is one of the happy homemaker, both on the show and in interviews. Also in the guest articles you've written for women's magazines. What do you have to say to your female viewers and to the readers of this piece who think of you as being one of them?"

"I *am* one of them." Dinah shrugged. Her answer felt automatic, delivered without effort or thought. For some reason, this irked Juliet, who, sitting across from this woman, felt rumpled and insignificant.

"No," Juliet said simply. "You're not. Lucille Ball is married to a Cuban bandleader, but that doesn't mean she's Lucy Ricardo, who lives in a small apartment next door to the Mertzes. She's famous. She's rich. So are you."

"You're right," Dinah said. "I'm not one of them. But I also am. It's an interesting position to be in the middle, and by that I mean yes, I am a workingwoman who also happens to be a wife and a mother, on-screen and off. I play both roles. And I play them pretty much round the clock."

"There's an argument to be made, though, that you're trying to have it both ways. You and the writers on the show. I believe your husband writes most of the episodes himself?"

"Yes. He actually writes all the episodes himself."

Juliet waited for more—the history of Del Newman demanding and then winning total creative control at the studio, his creative process and methodology. But Dinah simply sat there, waiting for the next question.

Juliet switched tactics. "Before *Meet the Newmans*, you were a successful singer and motion picture star. You were once quoted as saying . . ." She flipped through her notepad until she found the lines she'd copied down. "This is from *Photoplay*. You said, 'My dream is to be an entertainer first. A wife and mother second, someday a very long time from now.'" She looked up. "Yet you were married less than a year after saying that. And you had your first child not long after."

"Are you asking why I chose to become a wife and mother?" Finally, there it was, subtle but there just the same. Dinah's hackles were up, leaving Juliet feeling strangely triumphant.

She set the notebook on the coffee table next to the recorder. Dinah's eyes followed the movement, then found Juliet's again.

"My mom," Juliet said, "is a housewife. She didn't have the luxury of a contract with CBS. There are other women out there who grew up being told that the only dream—if you can call it that, if they were fortunate enough to have the luxury of dreaming at all—the only dream they were allowed to have was marriage and motherhood. To care for the home, and bathe the children, and cook the dinner. You came to Hollywood when you were a teenager because, presumably, you wanted something more for yourself—"

"Not that there's anything wrong with wanting marriage and children," Dinah interjected. "When your mother and I were growing up, it was almost biologically dictated."

"But a woman should know she has options."

Juliet felt the familiar anger rising in her, the anger that had been there ever since she was old enough to understand that her own mother felt like she'd never been given a choice. Without complaint, she scrubbed the house and cooked the dinners and tried unsuccessfully to please Juliet's father, who oversaw the largest dairy in southeastern Indiana. Her father would praise her, like a puppy he was house training, and her mother would beam, and Juliet's younger self would sit, her eyes on the television screen, and imagine a world in which her mom would tell her dad to make his own damn supper.

Dinah said, "I'm not trying to tell women they don't have options—"

"You're just showing them by example what a woman should be. Think of the women trying to live up to you. In your beautiful house. With your beautiful husband and your beautiful sons. But no one can, it's impossible, whether they have money or don't have money, regardless of the color of their skin. This is 1964, not 1954, but the lifestyle you're perpetuating on the show is like something out of a bygone era. Season five, episode seventeen, Guy coaches baseball down at the local park. But what happens when his best player is a girl? The entire family works to dissuade her from playing on the premise that girls shouldn't play baseball."

Juliet didn't need to consult her notes. She knew the show by heart.

"Season nine, episode three. You—Dinah—decide to buy a hat shop with your friend Peggy. You work well together. You have a knack for business. The shop is constantly filled with customers. But your husbands are having to cook their own meals, launder their own clothes. Guy and Shep are forced to eat at the local malt shop. So Del and Artie trick Dinah and Peggy into giving up the business and staying home again." Juliet took a breath. "As women, we're fit to raise children, entrusted to keep them alive, but we can't be entrusted with a credit account of our own. We can't serve on a jury or fight in the military or take legal action against anyone who sexually harasses us in the workplace. We can't open bank accounts. We can't legally get an abortion or access the morning-after pill. And if our husbands want sex, we are lawfully obligated to give it to them regardless of how we feel. You wrote in *Ladies' Home Journal* that the husband rules the house."

"Yes." Dinah sat motionless.

"Do you actually believe that?"

"I suppose I must, since I wrote it."

Juliet studied her. Her parents were still married. Juliet's father still worked at the dairy. The year Juliet moved to California, she'd changed her name from Juliet Shaeffer to Juliet Dunne, after Irene Dunne, her favorite actress. It was her way of shedding her father and reinventing herself.

"Many women would argue with you," she told Dinah. "Including myself. Many would say your views are outdated. That you're out of touch."

She blamed all of it—her father's sense of entitlement, her mother's aloneness—on the Newmans. Specifically, on Dinah Newman, who, as a woman, should have done better by the women of her generation.

For the first time since they sat down, Dinah opened her mouth, but nothing came out.

"Have you heard of *The Feminine Mystique*?"

Juliet opened her bag and dug out a book. She thumped it onto the table between them. She suddenly felt a swell of anger at this immaculate woman sitting here in her immaculate house. Anger on behalf of her mother, who had never finished college, who had never realized her dreams. Whatever they had once been. Who lived her small life within the walls of her small house in her small town and pretended that was enough.

"Betty Friedan writes about the problem that has no name. That's what she calls it. The pervasive unhappiness of women confined to the home. Women forced to live vicariously through husbands and children because they have no lives of their own. She knows. She was a homemaker before she wrote it. The housewife syndrome. Have you heard of it? Otherwise known as *angry woman syndrome*? Psychiatrists are labeling it a mental disorder. A 'disturbed' behavior. They're diagnosing American housewives who have these episodes of madness or hysteria, saying it's all due to their role as homemakers."

Dinah leaned forward and snapped off the recorder. "Did I do something to you personally?"

The question took Juliet by surprise. "No . . . I mean . . ."

"Because it feels like I did. It feels as if you came here today to blindside me into saying something I'd regret. Either I hate my life and I'm suffering in silent misery, trapped in some sort of antiquated cage of my own making or my husband's making or the making of the studio, or I love my life and the woman I am on television is the woman I think every woman should be. Which honestly would be a pretty arrogant way to feel. But either way, I'm recklessly leading all of womankind down a path of servitude and submission. Is that about right?"

"Not exactly, but the world does not believe in women. And you aren't helping change anyone's mind."

The thing that had ended Juliet's relationship with the Musician—more so than that fucking fur skin rug—was that she had lost herself. She became *his* girlfriend, *his* muse. Until, after a while, it was as if she stopped existing.

"What would you say if you were me?" Dinah asked. "What would you do? Burn the apron? Refuse to make the dinner?"

"I . . ." Juliet struggled to regain her footing. "Twenty-two percent of all marriages end in divorce. One in four mothers works outside the home. Before he died, President Kennedy published a report that women earn fifty-nine cents per every dollar men earn. The Equal Pay Act of 1963 protects against wage discrimination based on sex. Do you get paid the same as your husband and sons?"

"What kind of question is that?"

"A fair one. I suppose there's the argument that your husband should earn more, based on his role as producer, director, writer, but you should earn at least as much as your sons, if not more. Preferably more." Juliet was on a roll again, her heart pumping with adrenaline. She couldn't rein herself in if she tried. "I wonder what you would get paid if you were in your husband's shoes, in charge of the show."

Dinah sat back, as if all the air had left her. "I know without you reminding me that I'm famous and I'm rich. But that doesn't mean I don't have my own problems."

Juliet sat back too. She was being the kind of reporter she detested. A bully. She hadn't meant for the conversation to go this way, but she was suddenly so unspeakably mad both at herself and at Dinah.

"You and I," Dinah said quietly, "are separated by two generations, or at least two decades. You'll forgive me if I'm not as up to speed as you would like me to be. I can only try my best and do my best and tell you how it was for me when I was your age coming up in the business. I didn't create sexism, and if you think I further it by playing the part I play on television—which, I'll remind you, *is* a part—I can only say I'm sorry. But I won't apologize for my husband or the show—or for me."

She stood then, regal as a queen. She didn't seem flustered anymore. She seemed Amazonian, as if she'd walked off the pages of a Wonder Woman comic. Without a word, she turned and marched out of the room.

Juliet waited for Dinah to come back. Surely she would come back. But there was only the distinct sound of footsteps tapping away.

Shit. Juliet scrambled to gather tape recorder, pencil, notebook, the extra cassettes she always brought just in case an interview ran long. She swore as she dropped everything and had to start over again.

Finally, bag on her shoulder, she navigated her way through the house until she reached the entryway. Dinah stood beside the open front door.

A slight breeze crossed the threshold, ruffling Juliet's hair. She brushed the fringe out of her eyes and searched for something to say, profound and memorable parting words. But she suddenly felt speechless, so she merely stepped out into the night.

"Now I have a question for you," Dinah said.

Juliet turned.

"When you were dating the rock 'n' roll star, when he wrote that song about you and everyone in the press said you were just arm candy, just another silly groupie who gave away her heart and her body to a man who didn't deserve it, how did it make you feel?"

Juliet opened her mouth, but nothing came out.

"I do my research too." Dinah smiled, but this time, it didn't reach her eyes. "I'm guessing you were and are so much more than the way you were portrayed. I was raised to believe we shouldn't rush to judgment and we shouldn't judge others based on what we think we know about them. Because really, we're only giving ourselves away when we do."

And with that, Dinah closed the door with a soft but distinct *click*, leaving Juliet standing, alone and speechless, on the stone path.

TEN

MARCH 20, 1964

Five minutes earlier

Del Newman headed west toward the Pacific Ocean instead of north toward the hills. Traffic was surprisingly light for a Friday, and he drove faster than usual because his wife was expecting him.

Turn around, he told himself. *Go home.*

But he kept speeding in the opposite direction. Mr. Kodak had been busy and impatient, the meeting quick and brutal. *I'm afraid it doesn't make financial sense for Kodak to continue sponsoring* Meet the Newmans. *We wish you well.* Like that, Del had been dismissed. As if the show hadn't once netted the company millions of dollars. As if the two men were strangers and hadn't worked together for the past three years.

Del fished through the glove compartment, not sure what he was looking for, and came up with a pack of Camels he assumed belonged to Shep. He'd yell at him about it later. Or what the hell, maybe he'd astonish everyone and let it slide.

Left hand on the wheel, he tapped a cigarette out with the right. He held the end of it to the car lighter and inhaled deeply, the taste sweet and bitter on his tongue. For a moment, it was like no time had passed and he was twenty years old again, his whole life waiting for him.

Then his hand started to shake. His head felt like it was shaking too, somewhere deep inside, like a piece of it had broken off and was rattling around loose, leaving him off balance and off-kilter and slightly breathless. All his life, he'd been able to see the future mapped out. He always knew what needed to come next. But he had no idea where they went from here.

He switched on the radio, cranking it up to drown out his rattling brain and the voice inside him that was chanting, *Turn around, go home, turn around, go home.* He hummed along with the music, and then the song ended and another one began. *The number six song in the country*, said the disc jockey.

The singer's voice was smooth and self-possessed and older than his years, as if he were standing outside in the middle of a storm, calm and steady. Del knew every word, of course, and so he sang along. He needed to keep himself awake, to stop the ringing in his ears. His head felt too heavy.

The farther west he went, the cooler the air grew. It smelled faintly of salt. He closed his eyes just for a few seconds and let the thought of the ocean and the vast horizon wash over him. He rolled down the window, listening for the waves. He could keep going, use up this tank of gas and then fill it up again and continue down the road. He opened his eyes. Closed them. Opened them. Closed them.

For some reason, he thought of something Guy had told him once, a long time ago. If the earth's gravity were to reverse, the gases that make up the atmosphere would float off into space, leaving everyone on earth—those who hadn't floated off with the gases—without oxygen, unable to breathe. Guy found comfort in facts the way other people found comfort in dogs or a soft blanket. He had, since he was a child, explained to his parents how things worked as if he alone understood. Del had listened as best he could, but honestly, there were so *many* facts, and Guy was so long-winded when delivering them—

they had nicknamed him "the Professor"—that there was no way he could remember all of it.

The car drifted into another lane. A horn blared, and Del jerked the wheel.

In less than five minutes, the earth's gravity would reverse, and their lives—Dinah's, Del's, Guy's, and Shep's—would spin off into the unknown, leaving them all without oxygen. Even as he struggled for air, Del Newman would think fleetingly of what Guy had told him all those years ago and wish that he had listened.

Right now, though, he had the feeling of floating, as if time were slowing down and he was filled with helium. As his younger son serenaded him from the radio, with a voice far better than his own, Del was carried upward until he was above the clouds, able to see the entire city spread out beneath him. If he squinted, he could just make out the lights of CBS, and beyond it the hills, and just beyond that the lights of the valley. Somewhere out there, down there, were Dinah and Guy and Shep, the people he loved most in this world.

By the time he remembered to hold the wheel, to open his eyes and watch the road, his car was barreling toward the palm tree. The only thing he had time to do was cover his face and take his foot off the gas.

The last thing he saw was Dinah. And then everything went black.

The Rewrite

Five weeks before the final episode

ELEVEN

The night of the accident

*D*inah, *there's been an accident. There's been an accident. It's Del. Del. Del.* She heard the words over and over as she raced to St. John's Hospital in Santa Monica, foot pressed against the gas pedal, running every red light.

Sydney Weiss was waiting for her outside the emergency room. He was a small, neat man who wore small, neat suits, but this was the extent of his smallness. His voice, usually booming, was hushed as he swept Dinah out of the way of the doors before she could charge inside.

"He's hanging on. He's in surgery." He consulted his watch, which shone against his narrow wrist. "He's registered under the name Roger Thornhill."

One of Del's many aliases, used on rotation with others—Dr. Barnaby Fulton, Jim Blandings, John Robie, all Cary Grant film characters—when booking hotel rooms or cars or making reservations.

"Has anyone recognized him?" she asked.

"I don't know." Sydney's face suddenly folded. She had known this man for almost twenty-five years, had actually dated him briefly before she'd met Del, and had never seen him look like this. "Dinah," he said, "he's pretty banged up."

"What happened? Did he . . . He didn't hit anyone?"

"He crashed into a tree."

She couldn't wrap her mind around any of it. Del wasn't a teetotaler, but he wasn't a lush either. He was a good driver. A safe driver, even when he drove too fast. "He wasn't drinking . . ." Her voice trailed off.

"I don't think so," Sydney replied. "I mean, this is Del."

"How did you . . ."

"I have a friend in the Santa Monica Police Department. He called me after he called the ambulance. He knew we wouldn't want this getting out."

Which meant this man, this policeman, was on the payroll. That's how Sydney referred to it whenever he talked about his contacts, the ones who knew how—when needed—to help them out of a jam. Same with Del's stable of reporters, the ones given special access to the Newmans in exchange for approval over anything they wrote and published. *They're on the payroll.*

"What was he doing here?" she said, and what she meant was *way the hell out here.* Santa Monica was miles in the wrong direction from CBS and Toluca Lake. She couldn't imagine what on earth would bring Del out this way when he was expected home.

"I assumed he had an appointment or an errand to run."

"No. He didn't. I mean not that I . . . I just don't . . . Syd, I just can't . . ."

Her brain scrambled back across the day. The meeting with Aubrey. The mood on set. The tension in the air, in all of them. Del being tackled by his sons. Del lying flat on his back. Del retreating to his dressing room, staring into the middle distance.

"A concussion," she said. "Earlier today, we were filming. There was a game of football. Del and the boys. He was knocked out for a second. I mean, that could be it, couldn't it?"

At the mention of the boys, Sydney frowned. "Where are they right now?"

"Shep is out." She could never be sure where. The recording studio possibly or, even more possibly, with a girl, at a party, with more than one girl at a party, with more than one girl at more than one party. She didn't like to think about it. "He was still out when you called. At the recording studio, maybe." A mother could hope. "And Guy, the windows were dark—at his house, I mean . . ."

"Good. That's good." The emergency room doors opened and closed as people came and went. "The boys being here, it's too risky. Someone will recognize them. Then if they see you . . ." He shook his head again. "We need to get in front of this."

"In front of what?" Dinah felt hopelessly behind, everything in slow motion.

"This." Sydney waved his arms. It made him look ridiculous, less like the Jack Russell terrier they always compared him to and more like a flightless bird trying desperately to take off. "Surgery. The accident. All of it. We don't want the press finding out."

"No," Dinah said, remembering herself. "No. We don't."

"Is there any way I can convince you to stay out here?"

She glanced around at the awning they stood under, the path that led to the street, the enormous building looming over them, the lights of the waiting room just beyond.

"Syd, he's my husband."

Her voice was firm. Resolute. It sounded stronger than she felt. For the first time, she was aware of the tears that burned the backs of her eyelids. They were right there, waiting to spill out of her onto the sidewalk and the street beyond.

"Okay," Sydney said, and he patted her arm. "Okay. Just follow my lead." As if she didn't know the protocol by now. Situation plus member of Newman family equals the need for discretion. "Do you have a hat? Dark glasses? Some sort of disguise?"

"Because I always travel with one?" Her words were biting. But she dug into her bag, the one she'd picked up without thinking in her hurry to leave the house. She found a scarf. Tied it over her head, pulling it forward to shade her face. It was the best she could do.

Sydney surveyed her. Sighed. "Let me do the talking. Keep your head down."

And then Dinah followed him through the doors and into the hospital.

They sat in a corner of the waiting room, Dinah with her back to everyone. Sydney darted about, bringing them coffee, stepping outside to smoke a cigarette, to make a phone call, hovering nearby the check-in desk and the doors that led—where? To the emergency room itself? The ICU? Surgery?

She pictured her husband back there right now, on a table, opened up, his insides exposed, fighting for his life. Sydney hadn't told her enough. *Was* he fighting for his life? It was bad. She knew it was bad. Felt it was bad, deep in her own skin and blood and bone. It was as if she were the one who'd had the breath knocked out of her, not the other way around.

She checked her watch. Somehow, an hour had passed. She crossed and then recrossed her legs, flipped through a magazine without reading it. Every time the door to the emergency room opened, she strained to listen for her name—Mrs. Thornhill. Sydney hissed at her to be still, but being still was impossible.

She found a line of pay phones inside the doors to the emergency room lobby. When there was no answer at her home, she called the guesthouse. Kelly picked up on the first ring.

"It's Dinah," she said over his greeting. "Is Guy there?"

She heard muffled voices, and then her son was on the phone. "Mom?"

She asked if Shep was with him, and when he said no, he hadn't seen him, she told him about the accident.

"Where are you? Which hospital? Are you at Cedars? Did you speak to the doctor? What are they saying? What the hell even happened? I don't know. . . . She hasn't told me." He was talking both to her and to Kelly. "Have Syd ask for the doctor, Mom. I'll find out what's going on. . . . Some sort of accident. . . ." All his words ran together. He sounded out of breath, not like Guy at all. "You've just suffered a trauma. You need someone with you."

For a second, she thought he was saying this to Kelly.

"I can't let you do that," she said. "The emergency room is crowded. There are people everywhere. Your father wouldn't want you here, not like this, not with all these prying eyes." But Guy wasn't listening, and so she spoke louder and sharper than she usually did. "Guy," she said, "you are not a doctor. You are my son. I don't need you here. Not right now."

The line went quiet as she knew it would. Guy's entire purpose in life was to be the support that bolstered them—his parents, his brother—and she had just shut him down. Dinah, barely able to hold herself upright, wished for Del, who could smooth away hurt feelings as quickly as he could cause them.

Then, because she'd already come this far, she added, "And please. Please tell Shep to stay away."

"Yeah," Guy said, and she could hear the sarcasm. "God forbid. Then we'd really have a scene." The line clicked as he hung up.

She stood there wondering how well you could ever know your children, these people you raised, strangers when they were born, strangers still by the time they flew the nest. They were babies and then toddlers and then raucous little boys. They were acne-ridden, lanky teens, all elbows and angles. And then—suddenly—their voices were deep and they were taller than their mother. Each stage was like a different person, some new imposter who took the place of the child she'd loved previously. Which meant that she felt at once at home with her sons and at odds with them. They were men now, not her little boys anymore. They had belonged to her—if they'd ever belonged to her at all—for such a short time.

She stepped outside the doors to catch her breath. The air seemed cleaner here than it was in the valley. She let it fill her nose and throat and lungs and imagined it filtering out every germ and heartache.

A man stood on the curb smoking, a woman next to him, cigarette dangling by her side.

"Excuse me," Dinah said to the woman. "Do you have another?"

The woman's eyes widened, clearly recognizing her, but she didn't say anything. She nudged the man, who offered Dinah the package. She slid one out and leaned in for a light. She shouldn't be doing this in public where anyone could see her. Del would have a coronary if he knew.

Del.

She inhaled. Exhaled. Closed her eyes. Breathed.

For several minutes, she stood beside the two strangers, not talking.

And then she retied the scarf so that it hid her face and reentered the waiting room.

TWELVE

The night of the accident

G uy hung up the phone and began to pace. He should go to the hospital anyway. He needed to know more than what his mom was telling him. His father had been in a car accident. But he had no idea what that meant. Also, his mom needed him. Sure, Sydney was there, good in a crisis, but not *comforting* in a crisis. There was a difference.

He dressed quickly, and when he walked out the front door, Kelly was waiting in his Buick. "What are you doing?" Guy asked.

"I'm driving you."

Guy hesitated, conditioned to think how it would look—the two of them, showing up in the middle of the night together, disheveled, as if they'd just stumbled out of bed.

"Look here," Kelly said from the car. "There's a place and a time for keeping up appearances, and this ain't it. Get in."

As they drove over the hill and west toward the ocean, Guy tried to picture his infallible father lying in a hospital. But because he didn't yet know how bad the accident was, his mind drifted back to the argument he and Kelly had been having when Dinah called.

They're making me marry Eileen. On the show. And off. On live TV.

They can't force you to marry someone, not in real life.

But they can cancel your show and out you to the world if you don't.

And, while they're at it, they can make sure the man you live with also loses his career.

There were so many cautionary tales. William Haines, a popular leading man and box office star from the 1920s, was given an ultimatum: your boyfriend or your career. Haines chose the boyfriend and, at the age of thirty-three, retired from acting. Then take Rock Hudson, one of the biggest movie stars in the world. Just a few years ago, Hudson's agent, Henry Willson, had sacrificed another, less popular actor on his roster—Tab Hunter—when *Confidential* threatened to print something about Hudson and his boyfriend.

Everyone knew someone who'd been affected by the Lavender Scare. It wasn't just about protecting one's film or television career. Even people outside of Hollywood had seen what could happen if someone were to live what the US government considered "a deviant life." Public ostracism. Prison. Or worse.

"What are you going to do?" Kelly asked now, and for a moment Guy thought he meant *What are you going to do about your father?* But then he realized he was talking about Eileen and the sham marriage because that was the kind of infuriating thing Kelly did—read Guy like a book.

"I don't know," Guy said.

Acting was what they did on-screen, and it was also what Guy and Kelly had to do off-screen. Jack Warner himself had told Kelly, "Don't be queer even if you are," and Warner Bros. had fabricated a romance between their rising new star and his costar Natalie Wood. The two of them posed for photos and went out on the town, and everyone was happy. Not that Guy and Kelly didn't hold out hope that things would change. As of two years ago, at least, gay sex was no longer a felony in every US state. So, you know, progress.

"Don't worry about me in this," Kelly told him, one hand on the steering wheel, the other resting on Guy's leg.

"Too late. I'm always going to worry about you."

"Look here." Times like this, Kelly leaned into his hayseed roots, the Kansas City upbringing that had come before his family's move to California. "The sad truth of it is, you and me, we've somehow landed in 1964, which means for now, until something changes, that's the way it is. I love your big, self-righteous heart, but we gotta be realistic. That doesn't mean we give up. It just means me doing a picture with Natalie Wood has got nothing to do with me loving you. And if the studio said to me, you've got to marry her to keep making movies . . ."

He didn't finish the thought. Three years ago, when their friendship had grown into something more, Guy and Kelly sat down and talked about the risks—personally and professionally. It was Kelly's idea to come up with a ritual that would help ground them, a way to cut through the commotion. Which was why, for the past year, rain or shine, they made time for a weekly midnight swim, just the two of them. They would bypass the main house for its lush backyard, where they stripped off their clothes and slid into the pool, whispering—so as not to alert Guy's parents—as they floated beneath the stars.

Now Guy felt for the gold band on the ring finger of his right hand. He rubbed it with his thumb the way he did throughout the day. It was a wonder it wasn't worn to nothing by now. They'd gotten the rings— different styles and different colors—last year as a symbol of their love. Gold for Guy, silver for Kelly, wearing them on the right hand just to be safe. Even though Hollywood was a small town, and most everyone knew or at least suspected who was gay, there was still this ruse to uphold for the moviegoers and television viewers, most of whom resided in the middle of the country. For this reason, he and Kelly could never have their photo taken together, and when they went out—which was rare—they had to bring dates or, at the very least, a third man, so it looked as if they were just bachelors on the town or three fellas engaged in a business meeting.

Guy had dated girls—some the studio had set him up with, others he'd asked out on his own. He and Kelly had even double-dated a few times back in school. But no one made more sense to him than Kelly Faber, unless it was Guy Newman *with* Kelly Faber, the man he loved.

Miles away, Shep—always the last to know—picked up Eileen at the Hollywood Studio Club, where she boarded with a widowed chaperone named Mrs. Dennis and a bevy of other girls, all of them working or hoping to work in the entertainment industry. It was late—the only time he was free to record—and well after curfew, so Eileen shimmied down the trellis from her second-floor room and ran across the grass to the alley where Shep waited on his motorcycle.

They flew across LA, the streets largely empty because LA—unlike New York—went to bed at a reasonable hour. While there was life to be found here after midnight, it was, at its heart, an industry town, with early-morning call times.

Eileen hated curfews. To her, a curfew was just one more rule, and life was already filled with them. Rules were the main reason she wasn't interested in marriage. Most of her friends back home in Mississippi were on the hunt for a husband, but Eileen had never seen the appeal. She believed that being a wife meant the end of a woman's freedom, and—like she'd told Shep—she *didn't* believe that saying "I do" equaled happiness. She was so sick of being asked in interviews when she was going to find a man and settle down.

By marrying Guy in name only, she would be putting an end to the questions and the pressure. And she wouldn't risk giving away her heart or her independence. Besides, she was an actress, and this was just another role, one that could very well launch her career. She had always been good at convincing herself to do things she shouldn't do. Even if somewhere inside her something said, *No, don't, you'll end up regretting this*.

She wrapped her arms around Shep's waist and nestled into his back, enjoying the wind on her face and in her hair and against her bare legs. What the two of them had was platonic, which meant she was free to hold on to him without him twisting it into something it wasn't. His life was complicated and so was hers, and she didn't want complicated—in spite of the fact that he looked at the world with both cynicism and wonder, a combination she happened to share and had never found in another human being. She imagined them doing things like this—late-night motorcycle rides—even after she had married his brother. And yet something was keeping her from telling Shep about Aubrey's plan.

Too soon, they pulled up to the Master Recorders building on Fairfax Avenue. Where a figure stood outside. It was a girl with short blond hair, pacing back and forth, chewing on a fingernail. Shep took his time getting off the bike, and Eileen wondered if this was Marianne the waitress or Astrid the surfer or Rita the model.

"Are you goddamn kidding me?" the girl said. Her eyes flew to Eileen, then back to Shep. Beneath the girl's coat, something shimmered—sequins that caught the light from the sign above the door.

Lorrie, Eileen thought. *The dancer.*

"We literally broke up *last* night, and you show up with her?" She stared at Eileen now. Gave her the once-over.

Eileen was not a girl who enjoyed drama or conflict. The last thing she wanted to be was in the middle of something. She had grown up with three older brothers who settled arguments by pummeling each other. From them, she'd learned to be direct in her relationships, but she didn't always trust other women to do the same.

"*Her*," Eileen said, "is leaving."

She cast a withering glance at Shep as she walked past him and Lorrie and kept going until she was inside the building. Once there, she wasn't sure what to do except stand and fume. Here she stood, in the empty lobby of a recording studio in the wee hours of the damn night with no way to get home. She'd broken curfew for this.

It was what she got for befriending Shep Newman and his massive ego. In that moment, she could think of a lot worse things than being married to his brother, who was reliable and kind and didn't bounce from girl to girl.

Outside, Shep said to Lorrie, "What're you doing here?" She was dressed for work, which was where she should have been.

"We need to talk about what to do, and I knew you wouldn't want me showing up at CBS."

He stared at her, at the building, at her. It was a conversation, he knew, that was inevitable. Like a stone, he dropped onto the curb, because there wasn't anywhere else to sit. Lorrie sat down several inches away from him and hugged her coat tight around her, her bare knees pressed together, feet splayed out wide.

The breeze blew, ruffling their hair. The air suddenly filled with the smell of night-blooming jasmine, which was—Shep realized—the lingering scent of Eileen on his jacket. The premise of a song came to him, a missed connection. A girl who had almost meant something. A love story ended before it began.

She was just out of reach
And the rain came, and the rain came

Something about the rain. He liked the sound of the rain coming. It was sad and poetic. And rare in Los Angeles. He would go inside and fiddle with lyrics, see what came out. He did his best writing when he didn't overthink it.

"So," Lorrie said impatiently. "What are we going to do?"

"I don't know."

"You think you're like Teflon. Nothing sticks to you. You think you're so untouchable."

He wanted to tell her that she was being redundant, but it felt mean, especially given the fact that she was carrying his child. He reached into his pocket and pulled out his motorcycle keys and twirled them. All his life, his family had taken care of any problems that came up.

"You're sure," he said instead. It was a question.

"Yes," she snapped.

"Sorry. I just meant . . ." He didn't say what it was he meant.

"I haven't been sleeping with anyone else, if that's what you're asking. Not since I met you."

He wasn't certain he believed this—she'd been seeing him and at least one other guy, a sound engineer at the Whisky, when they first started going out.

"So what are we going to do?" Lorrie repeated.

"God only knows," he said, thinking that right now would be a terrific moment to believe in god. His father didn't. His mother did, at least vaguely. He and his brother hadn't been raised with any sort of religion, even though everyone in America assumed they were good, churchgoing people. Which was funny since their television selves had never—not once—set foot inside a church.

When he didn't say anything more, Lorrie began to talk, telling him what she thought they should do. Get married, of course. She said it like it was obvious. Find a little house all their own. Something in Holmby Hills or Bel Air, a good, safe place to raise the baby and the others to come.

Others.

"It's safe in Burbank too," he said. And a hell of a lot more affordable. He didn't understand why they had to buy their imaginary house in the most expensive area of the city.

She continued talking as if he hadn't interrupted. He could still appear on the show and make records, but touring was out for obvious reasons. She didn't say what those reasons were. When the baby was old enough, it would attend private school, perhaps the Buckley School, whose two campuses were currently being consolidated into one out in Sherman Oaks. Shep and Guy had attended public high school. It had been good enough for the two of them.

When he said this to Lorrie, she stared at him as if he'd suggested shipping the baby off to Vietnam. The pause was long enough for it to occur to him that the money they were spending in their imaginary life was his.

He said, "You know I don't come into my dough until I'm twenty-one." Saying it made him feel hopeful, as if somehow this would delay the baby's arrival for a few more years.

"What?" she said.

"It's in a trust. Our parents put it away for us. So unless we can buy a house in Holmby Hills for ten dollars a week, you're going to need to lower your expectations."

This set her off, and, man, Lorrie could really go off when she wanted to. Shep did what he always did in situations like this—he shut down. He stared at her through sleepy violet eyes framed by the longest lashes anyone had ever seen and played the part of the most attentive listener in the world. All the while, he was thinking about Eileen and the rain. The heartbreak of rain that was already washing her away, out of reach. And he was thinking about the baby that would be here in months, not years, and the fact that the only good he could see in all of this was that his parents would likely kill him before it was born.

THIRTEEN

The night of the accident

The doctor's name was Carson. Dinah had no idea if this was his first or last name. He was a dignified, bespectacled man of fifty with thinning hair and thinning cheeks, as if he barely took time to eat. He stood in a busy corner of the emergency room with Dinah and Sydney and told them, "With certain head injuries, the brain can swell. In Mr. Thornhill's case, this is causing fluid to push against the skull."

Dinah almost asked who this Mr. Thornhill was, but then she remembered Dr. Carson was talking about Del. In spite of the commotion surrounding the three of them, Dinah's own brain felt asleep, as if none of the nerves or neurons were connected.

Dr. Carson continued, face in profile, eyes fixed on Sydney. "To protect the brain from further swelling, I'd like to induce a coma. I'll give him a controlled dose of anesthetic, which will cause him to—in layman's terms—sleep. We will monitor him, monitor his vitals, periodically recheck the swelling in his brain. And when the swelling has decreased, we can discuss bringing him out of the coma."

Now Dinah turned to Sydney, as if for confirmation. The doctor asked if they had any questions. Both of them staring at Sydney and waiting.

Then Syd was talking. He was telling the doctor they wanted to move Del—Mr. Thornhill—home, and the doctor was saying no, absolutely not, he and the hospital staff needed to be able to observe and monitor him twenty-four hours a day.

That was the moment it hit Dinah. That Del, while here, also wasn't here. He was in another world, suspended between sleep and death. *The middle distance*, she thought again.

The men were talking, but she interrupted them. "Is he going to survive this? When he wakes up, will his brain function be the same as it was before the accident? What are the risks of the induced coma? Is there a chance you won't be able to wake him up?" On and on. No one stopped her or told her to take a breath. They waited for her to finish.

When she did, it was Sydney, not the doctor, who spoke first. He took Dinah's hand and said, "He's a tough son of a bitch. Toughest man I know."

And then the doctor said to Sydney, as if Dinah weren't there, "The fact that he doesn't smoke, doesn't drink, those things work in our favor. He's in good health, especially for his age. I'm optimistic about the outcome."

Later, she would play these words over in her mind. *I'm optimistic about the outcome.* They were hopeful but vague. She was thinking about what Del would have done if it were she lying unconscious in this emergency room instead. He, alone, would have known what was best for her because he, alone, knew her better than anyone. She wanted to shake the doctor, force him to tell her what she wanted to hear. *I'm his wife*, she wanted to say. *Talk to me. Look at me.*

Instead, she said, "What if we hired a full-time nurse to care for him and watch over him while he recovers? Could we take him home then?"

There was something in her voice. Dinah heard it there. A steeliness. A resolve. The doctor must have heard it too because he looked at her for the first time.

"I'm afraid we cannot discharge him," he said. "Not now."

"Surely there's something we can do, Doc." Sydney was used to getting his way, to opening his checkbook and making everything possible.

As Dr. Carson and Sydney began to argue, Dinah tried to remember when she'd last eaten. She'd waited for Del so they could have dinner together. But she'd burned the dinner, and he hadn't come home. And now all she wanted was for him to come home, even if Del himself would have no idea where he was. Suddenly, it was imperative. Her life, not just his, depended on it.

"If it's privacy you're worried about," the doctor said finally, "we can arrange a private room—once he's out of emergency, out of the ICU—where he will not be disturbed. This is a town, after all, of people who don't always want their private lives public, and Del Newman is not the first celebrity we've treated."

The doctor's expression, behind black-rimmed glasses, gave nothing away. Of course he had recognized them. There was the matter of money. Could the Thornhills pay? (They were back to being Mr. and Mrs. Thornhill.) Yes, the Thornhills could pay. Where Mr. Thornhill's health was concerned, money was no object.

"We'll take it," Dinah said before Sydney could start haggling. Then she turned to Syd and told him she would be staying the night. She needed him to go to her house and be there for the boys and explain what was happening.

She turned back to Dr. Carson. "I need to see my husband."

Kelly pulled up to the emergency room doors, and Guy bolted out before the car came to a complete stop. He wore dark glasses, a Dodgers cap pulled low, and a trench coat. He strode across what seemed like endless space between the doors and the front desk, aware that he *looked* like someone who was hiding, a bank robber or, worse, a flasher.

As he approached the woman who sat waiting to direct him to his father and answers, he felt a hand on his arm. Before Guy could protest or plant his body the way he once had on the football field—in his entire career as quarterback, he had only been sacked twice—the hand steered him across the room and out the door.

Sydney Weiss was a small man, but he had the grip of a coconut crab, a creature Guy had read about in the complete set of encyclopedias his parents kept in their den. The crab had the strongest grip of any animal and was the largest land-based crustacean on earth—as large as a human torso.

Outside, Guy shook Sydney off. "Where's my father?"

"He's in the ICU."

"Where's Mom?"

"She's with him."

"What the hell is going on?"

Inside the car at the curb, Kelly leaned across the seat and rolled the window down. "What's happening?" he said.

Sydney looked past Guy to Kelly and frowned. He told them about the accident, the suspected concussion, the medically induced coma. No, it wasn't a good idea for Guy to see Del now. No, he couldn't see his mom, because she was deep within the bowels of the hospital surrounded by doctors and nurses and other critical patients.

"Take him home," he said to Kelly. "One of us will call you as soon as we need you."

Guy still wasn't ready to back down. He brushed past Syd, toward the doors, but then, out of the corner of his eye, there was a spark of bright light. Temporarily blinded, he could see something running at them, and even though he couldn't make out exactly what it was— through the dancing spots of his vision, it was merely a large, formless blob—Guy had been around long enough to recognize a camera flash.

The instinct to flee was so ingrained upon him that he didn't think. Without bothering to open the car door, he dove through the open window into the passenger seat like he was diving after a football, one leg waving wildly in space as Kelly sped away.

Dinah curled up beside Del in his bed. His hand was warm and familiar, but the fingers didn't tighten around hers. For a long time, she lay with him, careful not to move, afraid she would accidentally unplug one of the many wires and tubes he was hooked up to.

She did not sleep. Instead, she stared up at the ceiling or at the window just beyond Del's slumbering form. That was how she had to think of it—that he was sleeping of his own volition. He had always been a sound sleeper, which had surprised her the first time they'd shared a bed. Del, like Shep, was electrically charged from sunup to well past sundown, but when the lights went out, so did he.

From time to time, a nurse pulled back the privacy curtain and checked the various machines. At first, Dinah closed her eyes and pretended to be asleep, but as the night wore on, she didn't bother. The nurses gave her apologetic smiles, the corners of their mouths turned down. She wondered how many of these makeshift rooms they visited throughout the night, pulling back curtain after curtain, checking vitals after vitals.

Around 4:00 a.m., the frantic din of the emergency room subsided to a low hum, an absence of noise that she noticed immediately. Dinah slipped off the bed and, carrying her shoes—as if the tapping of her heels would wake her husband, as if waking him was not something she desperately wanted to do—padded in stockinged feet through the curtain and into the space beyond. She asked a passing nurse for directions to the bathroom and then went in search of it.

Once inside, she leaned against the sink and took a breath. For the second time in her life, she had the feeling she might break in half from the weight of everything. The first time was when her mother died, three years earlier.

She closed her eyes and focused on breathing. It was something she had learned to do back then, a way of calming her heart and her head. She stood there for what felt like a century, the sink as support, the only thing keeping her upright. And then she opened her eyes.

No one would recognize her even without the scarf. She could barely recognize herself. She untied it, letting it fall around her neck. She leaned in, pressing fingers to the circles under her eyes, only her fingertips were numb. She turned on the water and splashed her face, over and over, and suddenly, her entire body was heaving and she was sobbing in great, painful gusts that came from someplace deep within her. After her mom's death, she thought she had cried all the tears. But now here were new ones, and they felt just as infinite.

"There, there," a voice said, and a hand was on her back.

The nurse was dark-skinned, in her midforties, several inches shorter than Dinah. They stood like this, Dinah crying, the nurse patting her gently, rubbing little circles between her shoulder blades the way her mom had when she was sick or had a nightmare. At some point, she handed Dinah a towel so she could dry her eyes.

"Your husband is in the very best hands."

"Thank you," Dinah breathed. "Thank you," she repeated, trying to remember if the nurse had said her name.

"Benita Radford-Hill, but everyone calls me Benny."

Benny led Dinah back to Del's room, and before Dinah disappeared behind the curtain, the nurse said, "Talk to him. Some doctors believe that patients in your husband's condition—they can hear you."

Dinah once again slipped off her heels and climbed up next to Del. She settled in beside him and made herself look at him, really look at him. Not the Del she pictured when she thought of him but this middle-aged man lying in this hospital bed. She had always loved his profile—the strong chin, the straight nose. She had a habit of tracing that nose sometimes, but right now, she traced—so, so lightly—the lines around his eyes, the silver in his hair. When had the two of them grown old?

She met Del Newman on *The Columbia Workshop*, an ambitious, highly respected radio program that featured an ensemble cast of knowns and unknowns in dramas crafted by up-and-coming writers. At first, she found him too good-looking, too confident. Like something carved out of a mountainside. In the studio, he had a habit of stepping on her lines. He ad-libbed frequently, eager to get a laugh, and was always offering up notes on the script, something that seemed to irritate the writers as much as it irritated her.

"Kid," he told her one day, "I'd offer to take you out, but I don't think your mother would allow it."

"Listen here, old man," she retorted—even though he was barely two years older than she was—"I make my own rules. Besides, my mama gave up on me long ago."

This was a new Dinah, one that was just starting to blossom. She'd barely shed her North Carolina accent by the time they fell in love and married three months later. And then began the work of getting to know each other. She had lived eighteen years of her life before she knew Del existed, and then he had arrived and that had been that. They had been together ever since.

She leaned into her husband now and said all the things that people say in these situations. How much she needed him. How much the boys needed him. How they were all counting on him.

And then she told him she was scared.

Actually, she was terrified.

For two decades, she had been *Del-and-Dinah*, as if it were her first name. One half—and not the more interesting half—of a matched set. Maybe, *maybe* you could have Del without Dinah. But she couldn't imagine Dinah without Del.

If her husband were here—really here—he would tell her not to fret. In truth, Del worried enough for everyone, which was one reason they relied on him and looked to him to tell them it would all be okay.

Yet she was the girl who came to LA at sixteen with nothing but her dreams and the $235 she'd saved by taking every odd job she could find in her hometown. It was through her own persistence that she'd been able to conquer the Wild, Wild West. If not for herself, she wouldn't have the television career. She wouldn't have the boys. And she wouldn't have Del.

"Wake up," she whispered to him. "Wake up." She said it over and over again, and then she lay her head on the pillow beside his and, for the first time in what seemed like days, closed her eyes and drifted into a fitful, dreamless sleep.

TV GUIDE

Dinah Newman's Holiday Dessert Table

Just in time for the holiday season, America's favorite homemaker, wife, and mother has agreed to share one of her foolproof recipes so that you can feed your family the way she feeds husband Del and sons Guy and Shep.

Hi! I'm Dinah Newman. I receive letters every week from viewers asking me to share my recipes for baked ham with pineapple, glazed pork chops, twice-baked potatoes, and ambrosia salad. But there's one recipe you seem to crave more than others. It's a favorite at the Newman table and was handed down to me from my grandmother. You can serve it anytime of year, but I especially love serving it after our Thanksgiving or Christmas meal.

SOUR CREAM CINNAMON COFFEECAKE

Cake

1½ cups butter or margarine, softened
3 cups sugar
4 eggs
2 teaspoons vanilla extract

2 cups light sour cream
4½ cups flour
4 teaspoons baking powder
1 teaspoon baking soda
1 teaspoon salt

Topping

1 cup chopped nuts
2 teaspoons cinnamon

¼ cup sugar

Directions

1. Cream butter with sugar.

2.   Add eggs and vanilla. Beat until light and fluffy. Blend in light sour cream.

3.   Add remaining ingredients and mix until blended. Spread half of batter in greased 12" × 20" × 2" pan.

4.   Sprinkle topping over batter in pan. Spread remaining batter over topping. Bake at 350 degrees for 40–50 minutes until lightly browned.

5.   Sit back and enjoy the looks on your family's faces as they delight in the very first bite!

(Pick up next week's *TV Guide* for Dinah's Holiday Side Dishes!)

FOURTEEN

The morning after the interview

J uliet tossed and turned, her mind refusing to let her rest. *Why had she gone on the attack? Why did she always have to be so impulsive, so polarizing? How did she ever think she could be a news reporter when she didn't know how to be objective?*

It was this last thought that hit her hardest. What if it wasn't the men at the *Times* who stood in her way? What if it was her own impulsive, polarizing self?

When it was clear sleep wasn't going to happen, she pushed aside the covers and got out of bed. She showered, dressed, and drank a cup of coffee as if she were going to work and then switched on the radio and parked herself at the kitchen table she'd found at a flea market. It had one wobbly leg and a yellow Formica top and it was her favorite place to write.

The familiar plinking notes of a piano filled the apartment, and then the voice, so unmistakable. Perpetually husky and disheveled, as if he'd just woken up.

Juliet, sleeping in my bed
In my head
She's Juliet, sleeping
She's the one you cannot catch unless you know the words
And the words are always changing

She'll tell you what she wants to hear
And then she'll disappear
My Juliet, sleeping

The thing she hated most about the fucking song was that it was so bloody accurate. She, Juliet Dunne, was a person who too often disappeared. Even when she didn't mean to. Even when the person she was disappearing from was herself.

She flicked off the radio and began to sort through the stack of notes and pages on her desk. Her typewriter was a 1960 Hermes 3000 in mint green that she'd purchased during her first year at the *Los Angeles Times*. Right now, she was working on a piece all her own. This wasn't an assignment. It was, most likely, nothing Boyd Hartley would ever be interested in.

The piece was about sexual freedom. Specifically, the Pill and a woman's right to take it without requiring permission from anyone but herself. Other journalists—she knew of several on the *Times* staff—condemned the Pill as a thing that would promote promiscuity and, if they were believed, the end of the civilized world. Two years earlier, Gloria Steinem had written an article for *Esquire* entitled "The Moral Disarmament of Betty Coed," in which she discussed the changing views on sex among young women. Since then, demand for the Pill had skyrocketed, yet contraception remained illegal in some states.

To Juliet, who considered herself sexually free, the Pill meant a world in which women could enjoy sex while delaying motherhood, enabling them to finish college or pursue careers. She'd been trying without success to interview Margaret Sanger, who had spent her life fighting to make birth control legal. But Sanger, now in her nineties, was reportedly in the throes of dementia. Sanger's son referred her instead to Katharine McCormick—nearly ninety herself—the philanthropist who'd famously funded the research to develop the Pill. And Estelle Griswold, a sixty-four-year-old civil rights activist and feminist who had overseen Connecticut's Planned Parenthood League since 1954 and spent her days shuttling women across the border into New York or Rhode Island so they could procure contraceptives.

These were the kinds of interviews—deep and hard-hitting—that Juliet relished most. But she was on a deadline, which meant the Pill and Sanger and Griswold would have to wait while she wrote up her interview with Dinah Newman.

As she played back the recording, her own voice—too loud, too combative—filled the apartment. She fiddled with the volume, as if that alone would take care of it. And then suddenly, Dinah was speaking.

Juliet's hand fell still. Her crossed leg stopped swinging. She thought she'd imagined the warmth in Dinah's voice and the music of her words. But now they engulfed her, casting light across the desk and the floor and Juliet herself, making her feel small and mean and unfit to work on a Pulitzer Prize–winning newspaper.

Renee picked up the phone on the first ring. It was barely 6:00 a.m., and she'd stayed up past 2:00 because sometimes that was when inspiration struck. Being an ambitious young clothing designer without financial backers or a degree in fashion, she had no choice but to follow the muse, and if the muse didn't present itself—especially during respectable waking hours—you had to shake it loose. Her mom liked to say *You have a duty to honor your gifts.*

But Renee was tired. She hadn't had her coffee. Her hands hurt from the tedium of stitching and sewing. From the constant labor and no promise of success. And her brother the aeronautical engineer, whose house she was living in, had worked the night shift at Hughes Aircraft. One of his many rules was: *Do not wake me unless it's an emergency.*

"What?" she barked into the receiver.

"It's Juliet," said the voice, sounding out of breath, as if she were being chased.

"What's happened? Are you okay?"

"Who is it?" Calvin stood outside her door, rubbing his eyes.

"Go back to bed," Renee told him. "It's a friend."

"Is it an emergency?"

"Yes," she lied. "Is it?" she asked Juliet.

"I don't know."

Renee gave her brother the look she'd given him since they were kids, him just ten months older. All their lives, the two of them against the world. When he'd gotten into UCLA and, after graduation, was handpicked by Howard Hughes, no one—not even their mother—was prouder of him than she was.

"I'll make coffee," Calvin said and padded off, yawning.

Forty minutes later, Renee and Juliet roamed a garment shop at the corner of Third and Los Angeles Streets, not far from the *Times*. Under the neon lights, Juliet looked pale and rattled, as if she'd narrowly survived a natural disaster.

Renee, on the other hand, was caffeinated and feeling energized by the late-night work she had done. She knew already, this early in the day, that she would pick it up again tonight as soon as she was home. The electric-green jumpsuit she was wearing was one of her favorite creations. Its long and flowing silhouette gave it the illusion of being a dress, which meant she could sneak it past the office dress code. Today, she'd paired it with a trio of long chain necklaces and enormous earrings, shiny Bakelite butterflies the size of wind chimes.

Juliet trailed through the shop as Renee handled the fabrics, feeling the texture, which was just as important as the color. The shopkeeper, Elyora Turgunbaeva, had once been an actress. But when RKO and then Universal and then Columbia Pictures insisted on changing her name, she'd walked away. Her career had ended before it began, and now she ran Elyora's Textiles and spent her days sketching and drawing. She was the closest thing Renee had to a mentor.

"Dinah Newman is a dinosaur," Juliet said. "Women like her, they hold us back. They keep us rooted because they don't get it. They're so mired in the past and unhappy, and most of them don't even realize it."

Renee picked up a swath of Day-Glo aqua-blue corduroy and held it up to Juliet. "What do you think of this one?"

"It's blinding."

Renee smiled. "Yes." She tucked it under her arm and, bypassing the pastels, began to sort through a pile of vivid pinks and purples.

"Women like her," Juliet continued. "They're standing in their own way. And by doing so, they're blocking us, but it's like they can't—they won't move aside."

Renee strolled to the front of the store, where Elyora was waiting, making magic on her sketch pad. Renee dropped the bolts of fabric onto the counter and, as Elyora rang up the cost, pulled out her wallet.

Juliet said, "I'm sorry. I know it's early. I know how I sound. It's just . . . why do women buy into what she's selling?"

Renee didn't answer, because there was too much to say, and she didn't want to say it in here. Elyora's Textiles was, to her, as holy as a church.

Back outside, the street smelled of fresh flowers and urine, which, to Renee, completely summed up this city. Her arms full of brown-wrapped packages, she looked at Juliet. "Just because the door isn't open as wide as you want it doesn't mean she didn't have to kick it in before you got there."

"I don't like her." Juliet's tone was petulant. She held out her hands so Renee could place a few of the packages in them. Together, they began to walk in the direction of the *LA Times*, the air growing sweeter, less pungent.

"You don't have to. There's no rule that says we all have to like each other just because we're women. Take some of that anger and pour it into your work. Check the teletype every single day. Steal a story right out from under one of those bozo male reporters. Let all this"—Renee waved her hand at Juliet—"fuel you."

"What about you?"

"What about me? I don't want to be a reporter. I'm only in the Pen till the Chiffons get wise and beg me to join them."

As if to prove this, Renee started to croon "He's So Fine" in a honking, off-key voice. Singing was not one of her many talents. Perhaps to save her ears, Juliet joined in.

They began to bumble the words, first one, then the other, and eventually dissolved into laughter. Renee linked an arm through her friend's.

"Do you know why I started designing in the first place?"

"No. But that seems like something I should know." The song had softened Juliet. She briefly rested her head on Renee's shoulder as they walked.

"Because there was nothing out there that matched the vision in my brain. Not just that nothing fit me as I grew and grew and grew. But because all the clothes on the racks and in the stores and in the magazines didn't measure up to what I wanted them to be. What I knew they could be. So I decided to create them."

Juliet lifted her head, and Renee could see her words had landed. "You're a wise woman, Renee Otero."

"I know."

As they turned a corner, the *Times* building suddenly in sight, Juliet looked up at her. "I'll check the teletype if you submit your designs to, say, five department stores."

"One store."

"Three."

"Deal."

As they closed the distance between them and the building, a breeze caught their hair and sent Renee's earrings fluttering, as if the butterflies were taking flight.

FIFTEEN

The day after the accident

There was not a part of Dinah that didn't ache. She sank onto one of the living room chairs and closed her eyes, as if by closing them she could erase the past twelve hours. She felt a hand on her shoulder and looked up to see Guy offering her a cup of something. Tea, maybe. Or coffee. She took it gratefully and then set it aside because she wasn't hungry or thirsty and anything she tried to swallow refused to stay down.

The hospital had made her leave early this morning. She'd wanted to stay with Del, but they told her to go home. She could come back later. He was in good hands.

So Sydney had driven her the 17.7 miles from Santa Monica to Toluca Lake—17.7 miles that felt like a continental divide. And now here she was, here but not here. Her oldest son perched on the edge of the sofa, arms resting on knees, looking ready to spring into action as soon as she gave the word. While Sydney paced in front of the fireplace, wearing a path into the carpet.

The two men were arguing. The room was heavy with emotion. The weight of it settled into Dinah's bones and pushed her downward toward the floor and the earth below. Del's favorite chair, the oversize green one, sat empty.

"We can't tell Aubrey."

"We have to tell Aubrey."

"What good is that going to do?"

"What if he finds out from someone else?"

"Most execs don't know their ass from a hole in the ground."

"We have to let the crew know."

"I'll handle the crew."

"Why should you handle it?"

"Because I'm the manager. And your elder. And you're required to respect me."

"Yeah, but I'm his son."

From the kitchen, there was the sound of dishes clattering. Sydney had sent Flora home. As long as she'd worked for them, he didn't want to risk the news of Del's accident getting out. So it was Kelly in there making breakfast. Or maybe lunch. Dinah glanced at her watch. She'd forgotten to wind it. Her eyes moved to the window behind the sofa, but the curtains were drawn. It was all noise.

This morning when she arrived home, she had gone directly upstairs and stood by the window smoking cigarette after cigarette, watching the neighbor clean the gutters. She imagined scaling the ladder after him, letting him pull her up onto the roof, kissing him hard and long until they were both dizzy and holding on to each other so that they didn't fall off. Then she imagined climbing back down the ladder to the earth below and returning here, to her house, as if nothing had happened.

The idea of Ted/Tad, of the whole scenario, made her feel somehow normal, as if everything was the same today as it had been the day before and the day before that. As if nothing at all had changed. Except that everything had changed.

Suddenly, there was commotion at the front door, and Shep walked in with Eileen Weld. He looked awake but disheveled, as if he'd been up all night. When had Dinah last seen him? She tried to remember. Had he been home since the accident? And why was he with Eileen?

"Wow," Shep said, taking in their faces and the general mood of the room. "Who died?"

Dinah sprang to her feet. "Where have you been?"

"At the studio. Recording the album." He automatically looked at Guy to interpret for him, the way he'd done when they were kids.

"He doesn't know, Mom," Guy said.

"Doesn't know what?" Shep looked from his brother to Sydney to his mother, then back to Guy.

"It's Dad. He's been in an accident."

"What do you mean 'an accident'?" As much as he'd traveled the world, Shep, as the youngest, was used to being shielded from things that were too hard or traumatic. And, Dinah supposed, she was too. It was what happened when you had a Del, a Sydney, even an asshole of a studio head like James T. Aubrey. You were protected so that you could be you and do the work you were contracted to do.

She stared at Eileen, this interloper, this girl who was now engaged to her older son so that the show could, literally, go on. After all these years and all the money the Newmans had made CBS, it'd come down to this—their fate resting in the hands of a nineteen-year-old actress.

But she wasn't married to Guy *yet*, and as if reading Dinah's mind, Eileen excused herself and disappeared into another room.

"Why didn't you call me?" Shep was saying. "You know I'm practically living at the studio. You couldn't have at least *tried* to get a hold of me?" He was saying all of this to his brother. "What the fuck, Guy?"

Dinah started to cry. In a moment, she felt arms around her and looked up to see Shep. It was the first time he'd hugged her on his own, without prompting, since he was ten years old.

The hug was brief—only a few seconds—and afterward, she reached up and patted his cheek, his beautiful heartbreak of a face. He helped ease her into a chair, and she felt for the armrests, which she clutched with hands that were now numb. She watched as Shep sank onto the sofa beside Guy, so close their arms were touching.

Through tear-filled eyes, Dinah gazed at her boys. The whole scenario—Dinah, Guy, Shep, Sydney, here, in this living room that looked exactly like their TV living room—felt surreal, as if she had wandered through the looking glass into an alternate universe, one in which she and the boys were their TV selves but Del had been replaced by this small, neat man in his small, neat suit. In her head, she heard the announcer's voice—*On tonight's episode, the part of Del Newman will be portrayed by Sydney Weiss.*

It had been Del's idea for them to play themselves, first on radio and later on television. What he was selling was the thing he had missed in his own childhood—a real-life family who loved each other and was there for one another through thick and thin. A family with two nice-looking parents and two nice-looking sons who were wholesome and clean-cut and never wanted for anything. Who navigated problems and issues that were never too tough or too big to solve—and they were *always* solved—in under thirty minutes.

Loud voices brought her back to the living room. Her sons went catapulting off the sofa onto the coffee table and from there to the floor, ricocheting off the furniture, throwing punches—never at the face, which would show on camera, always at the ribs or stomach or groin. They had always done this—shifted in an instant from allies to adversaries, or as Del liked to say, allies to assholes. Sydney tried and failed to pull them apart. Kelly and Eileen came running. Everyone yelling so loudly the walls quaked.

Dinah shouted over all of them, "Enough!"

She was on her feet, fists clenched at her sides, the numbness spreading up her arms until she worried it would fill her lungs. Guy, Shep, Kelly, Eileen, Sydney—they all stared at her.

"Please shut up, just shut. Up. And let me think."

She rubbed her forehead, trying to clear her mind so that she could figure out what needed to be done. What Del would do if he were here. Which he wasn't. Which was why she guessed it was up to her now.

God, she wanted her mother. She wondered if it was something we ever outgrew—that need for our mothers. Hers had died so suddenly, had woken up feeling dizzy and driven herself to the hospital in Charlotte without a word to anyone. By the time Dinah had gotten to North Carolina and her bedside, she was still breathing, still kept alive by a series of tubes and machines—like Del. *Like Del.* But she could tell on sight that her mother was no longer there.

Penelope Shepherd was seventy-five, so beloved in that short hospital stay that the doctors and nurses wept when the machines were turned off and her heart stopped beating. Dinah had always felt like a pale, frazzled shadow by comparison. And she missed her. Oh, she missed her. And while she missed her, she also missed herself at six, twelve, eighteen, twenty-four, forty. Every stage of their relationship.

Now here was Dinah, orphaned at forty-three and everyone's mom. Not just her own sons'—and occasionally her husband's—but the entire damn country's. She wasn't sure how it had happened.

"We need," she said, "to explain your father's absence this week. We have to downplay as much as possible and come up with a perfectly good reason why he isn't here. If Aubrey senses anything out of the ordinary, he might just shut us down for good before the finale. All we need to do is buy ourselves and your father some time."

"We'll tell the crew he's had an accident." Sydney stopped pacing, hands on hips. "Something that's going to keep him from appearing before the camera for a little while, but nothing serious enough to disrupt the running of the show. We could say he has a broken leg."

"And what if Aubrey catches wind and wants us to write it into the episode?" Guy was on the sofa again, leaning forward, hands clasped, as if he hadn't just been beating the shit out of his little brother on the living room floor.

"Tell them he has two broken legs," Shep volunteered from the rug.

"No," Guy said, shaking his head. "What if they say he can *still* appear on camera?"

Shep propped himself on one elbow and shrugged. "Tell them he had a facelift."

Guy gave him an exasperated look. "He'd rather we go down to Cedars and film him in a coma."

"Tell them he had a mental breakdown, then. He's always saying it's only a matter of time before you—okay, and me—cause him to have one."

Shep delivered the line like he was on camera. Lately, whenever he found himself in tough emotional situations, he retreated into his television alter ego. On the surface, happy and carefree, but beneath the surface, moving in a quiet, private world that no one, not even Dinah, had learned to penetrate. Until the age of fifteen, he'd been a live wire, a chatterbox, a ham. This quiet, private world was more recent, as if the more well known he became, the less known he allowed himself to be.

"We need to carry on, business as usual," Sydney was saying. "Don't let on about the accident or the coma. Make them think he's gone away for a while and he's still writing the scripts, giving notes, making the decisions."

"*If* it goes that far," Shep said, plucking at the carpet. "He'll probably be up and back at it tomorrow."

"Yeah, but if he's not . . ." Guy didn't finish the thought. "Who *is* going to write the script? For the finale? And direct the last two episodes?"

"I don't know," Sydney said. "I will, maybe. You." He waved at Guy. "One of the wardrobe gals. Hell, maybe your mom."

The three men laughed at this, grasping at it like a light source. They laughed as if it was the funniest, most preposterous idea they'd ever heard.

"The point is," Syd continued, catching his breath, "I don't really care. All I care about is covering our asses and Del's ass and the ass of the show."

"Guy's the ass of this show."

Guy ignored his brother. "I'd like to direct," he said to the room, his voice firm. "I've already directed an episode." This wasn't technically true, but no one called him on it. No one, Dinah observed, *laughed*.

"It's fine with me," said Sydney. "As for what we tell the crew, our official story is that Del had to fly east to take care of his mother, who's fallen ill. He's always been protective of his past. No one knows that she died years ago. This way, if he doesn't recover . . ." He glanced at Dinah. "If we need to extend his absence, we can."

"And the sponsors?" Guy said. "In case you've forgotten, we're down one. Without someone to fund the show, none of this is relevant."

"I'll handle the sponsors," Sydney told him. "Kodak may be gone, but as Del says, there are plenty of other options out there."

"What do you mean 'maybe your mom'?"

The men looked at Dinah as if they'd forgotten she was there.

"When you said who should write the script and, Syd, you said one of the wardrobe gals and 'Hell, maybe your mom.' And then you laughed. The three of you." Her eyes went from one to the other of them. "Is it—why? Because I'm a woman? Is that it? Because my job on the show is to bake the pies and vacuum the living room?"

"Just that you're an actress, Di," Syd said. "A brilliant actress. You're a singer and performer, not a writer."

"You and I both know that isn't what you meant." She rubbed at her forehead again, at the headache there, and then, before they could protest that they really hadn't meant anything by it, that they were all just overwrought and not in their right minds, she said, "And *I'll* handle the sponsors."

They were silent as she walked out of the room. Instead of heading upstairs, she crossed the length of the house to the garage, putting as much distance between herself and them as possible. There, she climbed the stairs to Del's home office.

Inside, it smelled like him—a mix of aftershave and fresh, clean soap. She breathed it in. The walls were lined with framed photos. Movie stills and gold records—Del's, Shep's, her own—and black-and-white images from *Meet the Newmans*. Magazine covers and promotional posters and family pictures, the boys young, the boys grown. Del and Dinah. Dinah and Del.

Dinah gazed up at them, a lifetime captured on four walls. Memory after memory. There was their first film together, their first project as a family, Shep's first haircut, Guy's first car, the Emmy Awards they had won for best comedy series. Among all the photos, her favorite one—the four of them in the only unposed picture up there, climbing out of the pool in bathing suits, laughing. A second after the shutter clicked, Shep had pushed Guy into the water, and Guy had pulled Shep in with him. Del had cannonballed in and Dinah had followed, everyone splashing each other. The person who had taken the photo was a friend of Guy's, the name lost to her now. But she could remember the way the sun felt on her back, the way her husband's arms felt around her as he carried her through the shallow end, droplets raining down from his dark hair, the smiles on her sons' faces that made them—in that exact moment—look suddenly alike for the first and only time in their lives.

Dinah sank into the chair behind the desk, which sat in front of an enormous bay window. The desktop messy with bills, stamps, scribbled notes. The central feature was the Olympia typewriter Del had bought in 1952 after selling the TV series to CBS. He had written every one of their scripts on it despite owning newer models, electric ones that practically typed for you and that now languished on shelves, gathering dust. A stack of books anchored one corner, napkins, ticket stubs, and other odds and ends marking the pages. The last newspaper he'd read was folded on top. Discarded balls of paper filled the trash can. His sweater hung across the back of the chair. A pillow and blankets sat neatly on a corner of the fold-out couch. He was everywhere and nowhere at all.

There was a blank piece of paper waiting in the typewriter. Waiting for Del's return the way Dinah was. She rested her fingers on the keys, last touched by him. Then, without thinking, she began to type the same three words over and over:

I miss you. I miss you. I miss you.

With a sigh, she stood and started to click off the desk lamp, and this was when she spotted a folder beneath the mess. *Contract 1957.* Five years into the show, bolstered by its success, Del had renegotiated the original contract with CBS. He must have been going over it as he prepared to argue for new terms with Aubrey.

Suddenly, Dinah heard Juliet Dunne asking if she made the same money as her husband and sons. She could open the file right now and know the answer once and for all. But a little voice in the back of her mind—aggravatingly similar to Juliet's—said, *Are you prepared to find out?*

Of course we're all paid the same, she told herself. The contract was for the four of them, the Newman family. You couldn't have one without the others.

Still, it was Del people wanted. Del, who had—over the years—fielded interest from publishers offering him huge sums of money in exchange for the real-life stories behind the stories of the Newman family. He couldn't understand why anyone would be interested. *Because we all have a behind-the-scenes*, Dinah told him. *And maybe it's good for people to see who we really are.*

They ate an early dinner at the kitchen table. At Guy's insistence, Dinah sat while the others served themselves and then her. As they talked around her, she felt remote, as if a window separated them, Dinah on one side and her family—along with Sydney, Kelly, and Eileen—on the other.

The thing she liked best about *Meet the Newmans* was that during every episode, the four of them ate a meal together. And maybe it wasn't a real meal, but it was at least a semblance of one. So much like the meals they had together when the boys were younger.

She missed Del and she missed her sons. She missed the way they all used to need her. Del, after all, was the sun around which they revolved. Everything they had, everything they were was because of him. His tenacity and shrewdness and ambition and discipline and talent and love. It hadn't always been easy. But she could not imagine a world without him.

SIXTEEN

The evening after the accident

Eileen stood up to leave around 7:00 p.m. Shep walked her out, the two of them making their way down the front path side by side. She didn't tell him everything would be fine, that she had this on some higher authority, or that these things happened for a reason. Instead, she was silent along with him, which somehow felt like a gift.

He reached out and opened the door of her red-and-white Nash Metropolitan, but she paused before getting in. He could see her trying to gather herself as she turned back to him, head cocked, hair falling to one side. *Like a waterfall*, he thought.

"Are you going to be okay?" she asked.

"I don't know yet." He gave her a half smile, the best he could muster.

"I'm not planning to tell anyone about the accident. Please make sure your mom knows that." She had a slight Southern drawl that surfaced now and again. Being a musician, he had an ear for accents, which were just another form of music. "For added assurance, though, here's something no one knows about me." She scrunched up her nose, let out a breath. "I was once a card-carrying member of the *Captain Kangaroo* fan club."

"The kids' show?"

She nodded. "I was in love with Mr. Green Jeans. He used to sing this song about a horse in striped pajamas. It's like he knew me. My love for horses. My love for pajamas. I would run to the mailbox every day to see if he'd sent me a letter. I was convinced that by joining the fan club, he'd be able to find me and realize we were meant to be."

"And did he? Find you?"

"No. He's the same age as my grandfather. It would never have worked. But I'm okay. I've learned to accept it."

"Thanks, Lee," he said simply, the name only he called her. She was the single most incomprehensible, bewildering woman he'd ever met, and he felt a rush of gratitude. "And thank you for coming. Sorry if it was weird, but it meant something. To me. And to them."

"You're welcome. That's what friends do."

Friends. Instead of feeling like a consolation prize, the word warmed him.

Something moved overhead. They both looked up at the same time. At first, he thought it was a shooting star, but it was just a plane. They stared at it anyway, watching until it vanished.

His eyes met hers. "I'm glad you came with me to the studio." *Because sometimes I feel alone, even in my family, and I didn't want to feel that way right now. Because my dad is in a coma and I'm going to be a father and I'm not even good at being a son. Because you are the only person in my life who really gets me.*

She nodded and slid into the car. He watched as she turned the key in the ignition, as she dropped her purse onto the passenger seat, as she settled herself behind the wheel. "If you need me," she said, "just call. Don't worry about Mrs. Dennis, the house chaperone. I'll tell her you're my brother and we've had a family emergency."

He glanced up at the sky again, where the plane had been. *Who needs actual shooting stars?* he thought. Eileen made him feel as if the sky was filled with them.

"Where are you from, Eileen Weld?"

"Tupelo," she said, arching an eyebrow. "I believe we've already covered this."

But he had meant *Where on earth did you come from, and how did I get lucky enough to know you?*

He did his best Elvis Presley twitch of the hips and said, "Home of the King." The way he had the first time she'd told him.

She smiled, one that went straight to her eyes. "He's got nothing on you, Shep Newman."

And then she closed the door and pulled away, leaving him standing in the street thinking of a quote from *On the Road*: *A pain stabbed my heart, as it did every time I saw a girl I loved who was going the opposite direction in this too-big world.*

Inside the guesthouse, Guy lay on his bed marveling at how, when the world was upside down, gravity continued to work. Here he was, still rooted to this spinning globe.

Of the two Newman boys, he was the one who had raced motorcycles and cars and flown through the air on the flying trapeze. But he realized here, in the dark, that he was only a daredevil because his parents had always been there to make sure he landed safely.

He tried to imagine being his own net and wondered if one way to do that was to marry Eileen. He pictured the public and private celebration. The gratitude of James T. Aubrey and the studio. The relief of Del and Dinah. The ratings. The magazines. The fans. Each image like a snapshot in an album he was paging through.

But then the snapshots began to fray, their edges curling, going up in smoke. He watched as they burned to ash. To marry Eileen—or any woman—would be lying. Worse, it would be hurting the person most important to him. It was criminal that the world could tell you who to love and who not to love—as if the world had a right to something so private. What was even more criminal was the fact that his father might die before Guy ever got the chance to tell him how he felt about Kelly.

The hall light clicked off. As if he'd conjured him, Kelly's figure appeared. The bed sank with the weight of him, and Guy moved over to give him space. Kelly always slept hot, naked and on top of the covers, one foot on the cool wood floor. But tonight, he slid across the sheets and reached for Guy. He wrapped his arms around him and held him close.

"Your dad isn't done yet," he whispered into Guy's back. "He isn't done yet."

SEVENTEEN

Three days after the accident

D inah spent Sunday in a blur. Sleeping. Not sleeping. Driving to the hospital and sitting by her husband's bedside, wafting into his room smelling of Fleurissimo, the same perfume worn by Grace Kelly and Jacqueline Kennedy. She had imagined rousing him from his coma with the scent of it. Instead, he lay motionless just as he had the day before.

But if there was one thing Dinah Newman understood, it was that the show must go on. Her grandfather had been a postmaster, and she'd grown up hearing the postman's creed applied to every kind of situation—*Neither snow nor rain nor heat nor gloom of night stays these couriers from the swift completion of their appointed rounds.* She was just a different kind of courier—one who delivered entertainment instead of letters.

And so, on Monday morning, she donned a bright dress and matching heels and stood in front of her bedroom mirror rehearsing for a full day of appointments with advertisers, men Del knew and, for the most part, respected. Men they had worked with before.

"I'm so pleased to meet you," she said to her reflection. Hands on hips. Hands at her side. One hand in her skirt pocket. Searching for the most confident pose. "I've personally been using your brand (mention specific product of specific brand) for years." A bat of the eyelashes, the hint of a smile. "As America's Favorite Housewife . . . No.

Because I am America's Favorite Housewife, the homemakers of this country are heavily influenced by the items I use in my own home." She might not know an electric griddle from a Crock-Pot, but she knew how to sell something. "And I glean true pleasure out of recommending yours. Not only do the products speak for themselves, your name and reputation do as well."

She leaned in to the mirror and applied her brightest lipstick, Revlon's Love That Red, the one that emboldened her and made her feel unmissable. As she stepped back to look at herself, she felt a surge of confidence that stemmed not from Revlon but from a deep-seated belief in her own goodness and her own clever mind. She not only *could* do this, she *would*.

Frigidaire's West Coast headquarters were housed in a palatial building near MGM Studios in Culver City. Dinah arrived five minutes early and was offered a seat in the lobby outside the office of Mr. Frigidaire. She flipped absently through a copy of *Good Housekeeping*, tingling with nerves and anticipation, the way she did before she went onstage.

The elevator dinged, and she looked up to see two men in gray suits who sat down opposite her. Another ding, another man. Dinah moved over so that he had room to sit.

Five minutes later, at exactly 9:00 a.m., the door to Mr. Frigidaire's office opened and the receptionist summoned one of the gray-suited men. Dinah set the magazine down. More men arrived and joined her in the waiting area. Mr. Frigidaire's door swung open as the man in gray exited. Another man was called. Over and over. Men went in, men came out.

Only after the waiting room was empty—some ninety minutes later—was Dinah ushered in. She bumbled through her speech, and in less than sixty seconds, Mr. Frigidaire cut her off. "Sorry, sweetheart. We simply aren't interested." He had barely even listened to what she had to say.

Appointment after appointment, the same thing happened. She

waited. She watched as the men were called in before she was. When she was eventually granted an audience with the executive she was there to see, he barely listened, more interested in staring openly at her legs or her breasts, as if she had been whittled down to a single body part.

By afternoon, Dinah felt demoralized and degraded and really fucking fed up. It was the unfairness of it all. The dehumanization of it. As a girl, then as a woman, she'd been made to believe that being sexualized was a compliment. That above all else, sexual value was what she offered, more than her potential, her dreams, her ideas. When she was seventeen, she'd modeled for Hot Point appliances and danced in their commercials wearing nothing but a leotard. The men she worked for and with—even men on the street who had merely *seen* the commercial—thought nothing of inviting her to sit on their laps or chasing her around a couch or, worse, outright grabbing her as if she were one of the vacuums they advertised. Auditioning for movie roles had been just as much of a minefield, but like every other woman she knew in show business, she'd been made to understand that she should make the most of the attention because her value would diminish as she got older.

Just once, she wanted one of these men behind these enormous office doors to know what it was like to go into the world expecting to be valued for your good ideas and instead being treated like a piece of meat.

And so, by the time she arrived at the West Coast headquarters for Sunbeam—the nation's leading manufacturer of home appliances—she'd had enough.

The building itself was beautiful. Gleaming green marble, deco ironwork, travertine floors. But it might as well have been a mud hut for all Dinah cared. She stalked through the lobby and pushed the button for the elevator. As she waited, she hummed under her breath, the way her mother used to, in an effort to calm her rapidly beating heart.

There was a loud *ding* as the elevator doors opened, and suddenly, out of nowhere, a herd of men stampeded past her, upending her handbag and nearly knocking Dinah off her feet. She scrambled to retrieve the contents of her purse, managing to just slide between the doors as they were closing.

Safely on the elevator, she smoothed her rumpled hair and her rumpled skirt, her anger filling the air. Her fellow passengers, with their Brylcreem and their pressed suits, didn't pay her any attention. For some reason, one of Guy's facts popped into her head, something he had told her years ago. There was a creature called the death's-head hawkmoth, which was able to mimic the smell of a honeybee. This allowed it to enter a hive and steal the honey without the bees noticing.

Another *ding* as the elevator arrived at the fifth floor. Still thinking of the death's-head hawkmoth, Dinah elbowed her way out, through and past the men, who had already started their mad rush. She practically sprinted to the reception desk, determined to reach it first.

"Dinah Newman, here for Mr. Sunbeam," she said, winded but triumphant.

"He'll be right with you," the receptionist intoned with practiced efficiency.

Dinah eyed the men who were grumbling behind her and the men who were seated and waiting. "My appointment is at four p.m."

"Yes, ma'am."

"When are their appointment times?" She waved at the others.

"They're not all here for Mr. Sunbeam," the receptionist said.

"I know you're doing your job, but—may I ask your name?"

"Allison."

"Allison. I've just had a day of meetings where man after man was called in ahead of me. Someone I love is very sick. I am very tired. And more than a little ticked off, not at you, not at Mr. Sunbeam—at least, not yet—but at every single one of the men who caused me to wait today, as if my time didn't matter. So if there's any way you can make sure that I get in before them, I would greatly appreciate it."

Allison blinked at her with wide eyes. "Yes, ma'am," she said again. "You have my word."

Heart beating wildly, Dinah walked to the windows and oriented herself, as she always did—the ocean there, the mountains there, the Hollywood sign there. It was easy to find your way in Los Angeles, as enormous as it was. The ocean was always west, the mountains always north. It was the rest of it, the life lived between, that shifted and lost direction.

"Mrs. Newman?" A young woman with a neat plait of hair held out her hand. "I'm Connie Norris, his secretary."

With a conspiratorial wink at Allison, Dinah followed the secretary down a long hallway, turning onto another hallway, until they reached a bright corner office larger than the others. Just outside, a woman of middle age, perhaps older, perched on what must have been the secretary's desk, telephone to her ear.

Mr. Sunbeam rose from his own desk—the size of a Buick—and extended his hand. He was the head of West Coast operations, reporting directly to the CEO of the corporation back in Illinois. He offered her a glass of something—water, whiskey, whatever she desired.

"Nothing for me," she said to Connie, who left without shutting the door.

Mr. Sunbeam told Dinah what a fan he was of the show, how nowadays he didn't get the chance to watch it as often as he would like because the company took up too much of his time, but he appreciated the family values, so rare in this day and age.

Dinah thanked him for these words she had heard thousands of times. And then—without staring at either her breasts or her legs—Mr. Sunbeam offered her a seat and waited expectantly for her to state her business.

She framed it in what she hoped was the best and most appealing way possible, telling him they were planning something exciting and modern—a whole new take on the show, one that would still be in keeping with the family values they were known for while also speaking to today's audience. She cited Aubrey's statistic—twenty-two million babies born between 1946 and 1951 now representing the largest portion of the general population. She mentioned Shep, dangling her hugely famous and popular teen idol son like a carrot in front of this man's nose. She then spoke of her genuine fondness for the Sunbeam products and her loyal use of them.

To his credit, he listened to what she had to say, gray eyes fixed on hers. But when she was winding to a close, he leaned forward in his chair and said, "I'm sorry, Mrs. Newman. Our roster is full right now. I'm afraid our budget for television is already exceeded."

Outside his office, a telephone rang. She heard voices in the hallway.

She said, "But Sunbeam would only be responsible for financing half the show. Listerine is financing the other half. I'm not asking for a full season. I'm asking for a single episode. Our season finale."

The clock above his desk chimed the half hour, an elaborate, endless production. When it was finished, she said simply, "Please." She sat still, barely breathing.

After a long moment, he said, "I admire you and your show. I admire what you're trying to do. But the answer is still no."

He stood then and thanked her for coming in. He was sorry, again, that they could not be of help. He wished her luck and hoped they might work together in the future. And then he extended an arm, as if to herd her out the door, like she was cattle or a lost sheep. After this day—this horrible, humiliating day—it was the last straw.

"I find it disturbing," she said to him in the open doorway, "that corporations which create, market, and sell products for and to women treat a woman so poorly. I'm not just talking about you. You, at least, have been a gentleman. But I am not something to be gawked at or talked down to or dismissed or ignored. Or"—she lifted her chin—"herded."

Dinah Newman turned then, as she had done in 1949 at the end of *Strasbourg* costarring Rock Hudson, wishing she had a mink stole to fling over her shoulder as she made her exit.

She glided past the lobby and all the men lounging on couches and chairs. At the elevator, she punched the button repeatedly, as if this would make the doors open faster, and as she did, she heard her name.

The middle-aged woman who had sat outside Mr. Sunbeam's office stood at her elbow. A pair of cat-eye glasses perched atop her graying curls like a tiara.

"I want to apologize for my husband's shortsightedness and for the shortsightedness of all the Neanderthalic, uninspired bastards in this town."

"Your husband," Dinah repeated.

The woman waved her hand toward the long hallway and, Dinah imagined, the massive corner office beyond. "I've been a fan of yours from your earliest films," the woman said.

At that moment, the elevator doors slid open. A sea of dark suits, wristwatches, and briefcases. A choking smell of pomade and aftershave.

"Come on, sweetheart," one of them said. "We can't stand here all day."

The woman leaned past Dinah. "Hello, Jeffrey. We were just finishing up. Why don't you hold that door a moment longer?"

If Dinah lived to be a hundred, she doubted she'd ever forget the look on Jeffrey's face as he recognized the wife of the president of Sunbeam's West Coast operations.

"I'm sure you're a busy woman," she said to Dinah. "But I didn't want to miss this opportunity to thank you. Maybe it's because you have two boys. I have three. You need to be able to hold your own, and I think for the most part Dinah does. It's more than that, though. The world right now . . ." Mrs. Sunbeam shook her head. "It's not so wholesome. But for thirty minutes every Friday night, I know it will be. And no matter what happens, no matter what you all get into, I know it's going to work out fine by the end."

"But do you think we let people down?" *Specifically me*, Dinah wanted to say. *Do you think I let women down?*

"You make people laugh, and you make people feel good," said Mrs. Sunbeam. "It doesn't need to be more than that. It doesn't have to be profound. It just has to take people out of their own lives for a little while and make them feel better."

She bid Dinah goodbye, and Dinah—Mrs. Sunbeam's words filling her head—stepped into the elevator and said, "Lobby, please."

The man named Jeffrey didn't meet her eye, merely pressed the button. He murmured something to one of his colleagues, but Dinah stood with her back to all of them and pretended she didn't hear.

When she walked into her house, she heard a noise coming from the kitchen. "Shep?" she called, even though she knew it wasn't him. She glanced around for a weapon of some sort—anything that might deliver a blow to the head if needed—and settled for her own shoe.

But as she entered the kitchen, one elegant heel still on her foot, the other in her hand, she found Flora. She watched as the housekeeper puttered and cleaned, tidying the already tidy counters, hypnotized by the precision of her movements.

"I thought," Dinah said, "Sydney told you not to come?"

Flora turned, eyebrows knitting together as she took Dinah in. "He did. But then Arving—Mr. Guy—he called me. He told me about Mr. Del. He thought you might be able to use my help."

Then, as Dinah continued to stand there, Flora dropped the dishcloth and opened her arms wide. It was only after Dinah had gone to her and wrapped her own arms around her that she realized she was crying.

In the wee hours, a sleepless Dinah roamed the dark house, missing her husband and trying to shake the realization that for most of her life she'd been tricked. Led to believe that a little hard work and a lot of imagination were all she needed, that those things mattered—along with kindness and good intentions—to people other than herself. When, in truth, nothing mattered except being a man. What's more, it was Del, not Dinah, they respected.

Juliet Dunne was right—she was a fraud. And the worst thing of all was that the show still didn't have a sponsor.

As she crossed the sunporch, feeling as if—now that her eyes were wide open—she might never sleep again, she spied a flash of red. On the table was the book Juliet had left behind. *The Feminine Mystique.* For some reason, Dinah glanced up and around, even though she was very much alone.

It was too early to go to the hospital, so she picked up the book and carried it back to her room, where she closed the door and lit a cigarette and leaned out the window. She cracked open the spine and began to read.

Each suburban wife struggled with it alone. As she made the beds, shopped for groceries, matched slipcover material, ate peanut butter sandwiches with her children, chauffeured Cub Scouts and Brownies, lay beside her husband at night—she was afraid to ask even of herself the silent question—"Is this all?"

Dinah thought about her body going numb. She wondered what would happen if the numbness was allowed to continue—if it might spread throughout every molecule and particle until she was erased.

Sometimes a woman would say, "I feel empty somehow . . . incomplete." Or she would say, "I feel as if I don't exist."

Somewhere, a clock struck three. And then four. And then five. Still Dinah read, thumbing through the pages as if she didn't dare stop.

Why should women accept this picture of a half-life, instead of a share in the whole of human destiny?

She told herself she didn't feel this way. She wasn't Friedan's target audience. Regardless of what had happened with the advertisers, she lived a very full life.

Sometimes a woman would tell me that the feeling gets so strong she runs out of the house and walks through the streets. Or she stays inside her house and cries. Or her children tell her a joke, and she doesn't laugh because she doesn't hear it.

Or she imagines having an affair with her neighbor.

She read the next page. And the next. She read the entire book as the sky grew lighter and the sun began to rise, having the distinct, unsettling feeling that the words had been lifted from her own private thoughts, ones she herself was—until recently—barely privy to.

EIGHTEEN

Four days after the accident

On Tuesday morning, in the newsroom of the *LA Times*, a half dozen men hunched over their typewriters or scribbled furiously while Juliet brewed a pot of coffee. Over the din of the teletype machine, the coffee maker, chairs rolling across the floor, voices braying all at once—into telephones, to each other—she somehow heard a snapping of fingers. She looked up to see Charlie pointing to his empty mug. She sighed as she poured him a cup and delivered it to him. He didn't say thank you, just reached for it as he continued typing with the other hand.

Back at her desk, she sorted through the pile of things she had been given to do, task after task for Nick, Charlie, Phil, and the others. And then she glanced over the Dinah Newman article she had written, which was just one more unremarkable celebrity puff piece to end up as lining for the cat box.

She got up again and headed this time to the teletype machines. The thing Renee had said about finding a story of her own dug into the gray matter of her brain and took root. It was a slow news day, except for Dr. Lewis F. Ellmore, a Beverly Hills doctor who was apparently treating the Vietcong's victims in Saigon and had revealed that many of them were children—primarily little girls—as young as forty-five days old.

An hour later, she had tracked down Ellmore's family and booked an exclusive interview with him. When Boyd Hartley strode back into the office around 10:00 a.m., Juliet took the story directly to him. He listened, as he always did, looking solemn, as he always did. And then he said, "Good work, Dunne. I want you to give it to Phil."

Before she could protest or tell him why she, and not Phil, should write this, Hartley said, "You're not ready. But your ambition has been noted."

For the rest of the morning, she sat in on the editorial meeting and took the notes because Marcia was still gone. She made another pot of coffee. She edited copy, correcting Nick's punctuation, Charlie's spelling, Ed's sentence structure. She reread the quote Renee had left on her desk: *To realize our dreams, we must decide to wake up. —Josephine Baker, dancer.*

Juliet gazed across the room at Renee and the other women behind the barricade. She might have moved out of the typing pool, but she was essentially still a secretary. As if to confirm this, the telephone on Nick's desk rang.

She rose to answer it, retrieving his message pad from the outgoing letter tray, where she knew it would be buried beneath newspaper clippings, stamped envelopes, and packs of Clove gum. In many ways, she knew him as well as she knew the Musician. The tenor of his voice when he was tired or overworked. The way his eyes darkened whenever he heard about a violent crime. The way he rolled up his sleeves when he was working hard, but the right sleeve—no matter the shirt— always fell down. The way he nodded when he was concentrating or hummed to himself—"Jim Dandy" by LaVern Baker—when he thought no one was listening.

Back at her own desk, Juliet picked up a red pen and a page of Nick's copy—his work always came first—and began to read. Half an hour later, the usual din of the newsroom grew to an insistent, excited buzz that spread like a wave across the expanse of room. Over it, there was the unmistakable click of high heels against the marble floor.

Juliet looked up to see Dinah Newman striding through the labyrinth of desks and reporters, every head turning in her wake. She was windblown and flushed as if she'd run all the way from the valley.

Juliet, like everyone else, stared. And then Dinah came to a stop in front of her. She reached inside her bag and pulled out the book Juliet had left at her house, thumping it down onto the pile of messages and marked-up articles.

"Do you feel like you're living a half-life?" she asked. "As if you don't exist?"

"So you read it."

"You didn't answer my question."

"Yes," Juliet told her. "In some ways, I feel like I'm living a half-life."

Dinah nodded as if Juliet had passed some sort of test. "I don't know that I relate to all of it. But clearly, there are women out there who do." She rummaged in her bag again and this time handed Juliet a stack of envelopes, letters addressed to Dinah Newman. "There are thousands more just like them, from women all over this country asking for help."

One of the men strolled by humming "Juliet, Sleeping." Juliet's face went pink.

Dinah frowned after him. "Do they do that a lot? Hum that song at you?"

"No." Juliet smiled dryly. "Usually, they sing it."

"Come work with me."

"I'm sorry?"

"My husband is away right now. He does everything, as you know, of course." Dinah arched a well-manicured eyebrow. "He writes the episodes, and I've decided to give myself the job of filling in while he's gone. But I need help."

"Help doing what?"

"I need a writing partner. Someone to write a script with."

"I've never written a script before."

"Neither have I."

"How many shows are we talking about?"

"Just one. But it's the most important one because it might be the last. We haven't been renewed. I don't think we will be. This show isn't only the season finale, it could be our grand finale. *Meet the Newmans* meets the end. Also. We don't have a sponsor. Technically, Listerine is still paying for half of the last episode. If we can't find someone to take on the other half, I'm prepared for us to pay for it ourselves."

"Why me?"

"Because you're smart and obstinate and challenging and opinionated. And because you *clearly* have a lot to say. But I don't think you're being given the chance to say it."

"Will I be paid?"

"Of course."

Juliet gazed down at her desk, then glanced around at the high ceilings, the marble floor, the enormous clock on the wall, the dark wood, all the details she loved. "I'm not going to quit the paper. If I leave, I'll have to start over."

"I'm not asking you to quit. But I will need you to be available for the next few weeks. We can work around your hours and meet at my house, which will give us space and privacy."

"You've certainly got it all figured out. How do I know . . ." Juliet trailed off. She was trying to think of how to ask what she wanted to ask, which was *How do I know I won't be overlooked and relegated to some dark corner and treated like a servant?* "How do I know that it won't be more of the same?"

For a second, she worried that Dinah wouldn't understand. But then Dinah said, "The world of television is even more of a boys' club than this place. I can't guarantee you ease or longevity or that you will have a big career. But I can tell you that my husband has complete creative control over our show. It's written into our contract. Which means whatever you write, whatever we write, will make it on the air. As long as the sponsors agree."

Juliet glanced around again at the wood, the ceilings, the floor, the clock. At Nick's desk, the bullpen, the typing pool. At her own desk and the stacks upon stacks of secretarial work.

Then she looked back up at Dinah. The two women regarded each other, recognizing that they were standing on a precipice here, together, in spite of their differences. The air was filled with understanding. It felt to Juliet like the most profound moment of her life.

"I plan to change history," Dinah said. "And I'd like you to help me. I'm not sure yet what that looks like, but I want it to be big. I want us to make a lasting imprint, one they'll talk about for years to come. I want it"—she paused, searching—"to be a revolution."

Us. The backs of Juliet's eyelids stung the way they always did when she got emotional. "Why now?"

"Because they laughed and said I couldn't. Because they made me sit in the lobby while one man after another was called first. Because I want to be a fucking death's-head hawkmoth and steal the honey right out from under them."

It was honest, and it was enough. "When would we start?"

"Tomorrow."

Dinah offered Juliet her hand to shake. It sat there, suspended in the air between them, for several seconds.

Juliet wanted to be more than the girl who took messages for other reporters for stories that weren't hers. She wanted to do more than fix punctuation.

"Okay," she said. She reached out her own hand in return. "I'm in."

NINETEEN

Five days after the accident

On Wednesday morning, Dinah awoke with a prickling excitement that reminded her of Christmas Days in North Carolina. For the first time in nearly a week, she felt up to doing her morning stretches, and these she followed by a hot shower. Afterward, her skin pink and glowing, she wafted into her closet where she took in the multitude of dresses that hung, neatly pressed—silk and cotton and wool and chiffon, slim skirts, full skirts, belted, pleated, sleeveless, collared, cuffed, plain, and patterned.

When had she acquired so many dresses? All this energy she'd invested into being the kind of woman men expected her to be, only to discover that it didn't matter. It would never be enough, because whatever she wore, however she did her hair, no one would take her seriously.

She slipped into the capri pants she preferred, making a mental note to buy more pairs. Ran a comb through her hair, swept powder across her nose, brushed her eyelashes with mascara—otherwise they disappeared—and painted her lips a neutral shade of pink. She had read somewhere that nude lipstick was in and red lipstick was out, because makeup was all about the eyes right now, the windows to the soul.

In the hallway, the carpet—the same pale blue as her sweater—muffled the *slap-slap* made by her ballet flats. Del hated the sound, hated the way she flattened down the backs of the shoes with her heels like they were house slippers. It hadn't occurred to her till now that she did it as a small act of rebellion, a way of saying *I'm still here.*

The *slap-slap* came to a stop outside Shep's door, where she paused, listening. Her younger son lived in chaos, which meant he was almost always surrounded by noise. Right now, there was silence, and she tried to remember if she'd heard him come in last night. Inside his room, the bed was unmade, and with relief, she thought, *No Shep.*

Juliet would be there at 7:00 a.m. Dinah had sent Flora to the hospital to sit with Del, both to keep her out of the house and to be there in case he woke up. It wasn't that Dinah couldn't explain away Juliet's presence to her housekeeper or her sons, but, like an egg not yet hatched, she wanted to guard it for as long as she could. Give her a chance to see what came of it without involving anyone else's expectations.

As she picked up Shep's jacket and draped it over a chair, something dropped onto the floor. A cigarette. She knew she was a fine one to talk, but she didn't like the thought of him smoking. She slipped the cigarette into the pocket of her pants.

On the other side of the house, in Del's office, she managed to push the sofa, that traitor, into the hall, where it sat like an abandoned car. Her grandfather had collected Buicks and Chevys until they sprouted up across his lawn, weeds growing around and through them, twining through wheel wells and engines. She gathered the blankets and pillow, storing them in a hall closet, and then strode back into the office and moved the desk to the center of the room.

An hour later, the two women sat across from each other. Dinah watched as Juliet took in the floor-to-ceiling bookshelves overflowing with books and scripts, the piano and television tucked into their recesses, and the walls of framed photos documenting a career—four careers, actually—that spanned decades.

"I've been looking forward to this," Dinah said, which was both true and not true. The ghost of their first meeting and all that had happened since hung over them. And so did her own expectations, try as she might to contain them.

"Does your husband know you've hired me?" Juliet's eyes lingered on the photographs.

"No."

Juliet's eyes moved to Dinah. "Why not?"

"Does it matter?"

"I'm not sure. It depends on the reason. Maybe he's walked out."

"Would that make a difference?" Dinah asked.

"No."

Dinah felt suddenly shy, as if this weren't her house, as if she hadn't hired Juliet to write with her on *her* show. Juliet, not Dinah, was the one who knew about feminism. Juliet, not Dinah, was the evolved, liberated woman. A wave of frustration—at herself, at Juliet, at 1964, at Del for being in a coma and leaving her all alone to deal with everything and now of all times with Aubrey breathing down their necks, at Del's doctors for not knowing how to make him better so that he could wake up and come home to her, at Kennedy for dying, at the advertising executives in their overstuffed offices, at Betty Friedan for insisting on shaking things up when they had been doing just fine, when Dinah had been doing just fine. Hadn't she? Whatever happened with Del, whatever happened with the television show, whatever happened with her and Juliet, nothing would be like it was before, and she wasn't sure if that was bad or good.

"I know we only have a limited time this morning, so I'd like to get right into it," Dinah said.

"Of course." Juliet scrounged in her bag—the oversize velvet satchel she seemed to carry everywhere—trying to balance her notebook and coffee, hair cascading across her face. "I'd love to hear what you're thinking."

"I don't really have any ideas." Dinah recrossed her legs. "Other than that I'd like to do something new. Original. Important."

In interviews, she claimed to love the sense of collaboration on *Meet the Newmans*, when the truth of the matter was that it was Del writing the lines and telling them where to stand and what to do. Unless a situation came directly from their lives, the only contribution she and the boys made was appearing on-screen.

She thought of Rob, Buddy, and Sally from *The Dick Van Dyke Show*, their casual banter, their quick jokes, their ease with one another as they worked in the fictitious writers' room of *The Alan Brady Show*. She had expected—she didn't know what she expected. That Juliet would roll in, ideas bursting out of her, setting it all in motion.

"I've never written before. Or written with anyone else." Dinah hated to admit—always—that she couldn't do something. It was one reason the kitchen was her least favorite room in the house.

Juliet was upright again, pen in her hand. "I haven't either. Written with anyone else, I mean. The newspaper can be collaborative, but for me, that consists of researching other people's stories and editing copy. Or, let's be honest, fetching them coffee and running their errands."

It felt somehow momentous, their confessions. Outside the window, the sun was already bright, the sky already blue. Dinah thought of Guy and Kelly in the guesthouse, and suddenly, they seemed very far away. The only thing that existed was right now—Dinah, Juliet, the script to be written.

"Okay, then," Dinah said after a few seconds. "Things to remember about writing for television. There's a three-act structure. First, a cold open, which is the scene before the opening credits. This is where you grab the audience and hook them in. *Our* cold open is where we advertise products by our sponsors. After that, act one introduces the situation. Act two is where we try to address the situation and, of course, run into obstacles. Act three is the resolution."

As Dinah spoke, Juliet jotted down notes.

"The tag is the final scene, basically one last laugh. And then we usually end with a number or two from Shep. The network wants more music, so we need to work in enough time for two, maybe even three songs."

Juliet raised a hand. "What about weaving songs into the episode instead of just tacking them onto the end?"

"Why are you raising your hand?"

"Because it feels like I'm in school."

Dinah decided to ignore this. "Now, the setup is important. So is the punch line. With a TV script, there's a certain formula. Basically, setup, setup, joke. Setup, setup, joke. Over and over. Del likes a minimum of three jokes per page. At the end of a scene, you need what's called a *button*. That's either a punch line or a cliffhanger that will propel you into the next one—"

Juliet raised her hand again. "I get that structure matters, but the way I approach a story is to find the idea, the thing I'm burning to say." She flipped through her notebook until she landed on a page covered in chaotic scrawl. "These are just to get the ball rolling. Dinah gets a job. Dinah has an affair. Dinah leaves home to strike out on her own." Juliet glanced up, pen on the page, holding her place. "Since 1962, the divorce rate has skyrocketed. It's higher in the US than in any other country. And the younger people are when they get hitched, the more likely they are to get unhitched."

Twenty. Dinah had been twenty when she married Del.

Dinah said, "Del and Dinah aren't getting divorced. They have a good marriage." *We*, Dinah thought. *We have a good marriage.*

"Of course," Juliet said, but she didn't sound as if she believed her. "Birth control. It's one of the most important issues we face as women. The Pill is changing lives, but you can't get a prescription unless you're married, which means millions of women aren't able to protect themselves from getting pregnant—"

"Dinah doesn't need contraception," Dinah broke in, brimming with frustration. "She and Del never have sex. On the show. They're lucky they're allowed to sleep in the same bed. Can she still have kids? Yes, medically. But Guy is twenty-two and Shep is almost eighteen.

No one expects her to have a baby. Even though she absolutely could if she wanted to." She thought of Dr. Berke talking to her about *the change of life*.

"But think how modern it would be. To show this woman who's such an icon to other women struggling with some of the same issues they're struggling with."

"And then what's next? Dinah has a midlife crisis and sleeps with one of Guy's fraternity brothers? Dinah gets an abortion?"

Juliet sat back, looking defeated, as if someone had pointed a TV remote at her and pressed the Mute button. "I thought you wanted to say something."

"Not *that*."

"Okay, fine. Dinah goes on strike. I don't know. Dinah hires a male housekeeper. Dinah runs for president of the United States. Dinah befriends a talking horse. . . . Who the fuck cares?"

There was something Dinah had once heard Shep say—how he couldn't bring himself to sing words that he would never say in real life. Dinah—the television version—might have been America's homemaker, wearing pearls as she vacuumed and cooked delicious, well-balanced meals for her family, but she was still an extension of her own flesh-and-blood self. She thought of the way she'd strode into that newspaper office, of the speech she'd given this girl, of the promises she'd made.

"She wouldn't do that. Dinah. She wouldn't do any of that."

Juliet closed her notebook. "Then tell me what she would do."

"I don't know. It's been a really long time since someone's asked me. . . . And because I don't know, she doesn't know. Dinah. The on-screen Dinah." She thought, *Maybe the off-screen Dinah too.*

"What happened to changing history?" Juliet said. "To making it big? What about"—she repeated Dinah's words—"'making a lasting imprint, one they'll talk about for years to come'? This is the problem with your generation. You say you want change so that you can—I don't know—appear enlightened and in touch with what's going on in the world, but you don't do anything about it. Have you seen the commercials for Folgers Coffee? The misogyny running wild through their fucking ads? Poor Susan can't make a good cup of joe. But poor Richard has to drink Susan's terrible coffee. Thank god the girls at the office know how to make coffee. Susan can fuck right off. She's out of luck. Until she discovers Folgers, the secret to a happy marriage. At least for one of them."

"You're so . . . angry."

"Yeah, and you should be too. Why aren't you angry?"

"I am angry. You should have seen me on Monday."

"Then why aren't you angrier?" When Dinah didn't answer, Juliet said, "Why am I here? You could have hired anyone."

"You have something to say." *A lot of it.* With a mix of envy and exasperation, Dinah couldn't help thinking how assured this young woman was, how unwavering and uncompromising, as if she knew herself and always had.

"Then let me say it. Betty Friedan writes, 'No woman gets an orgasm from shining the kitchen floor.' I don't think Dinah Newman has ever had one."

"Had one . . . ?"

"An orgasm."

Flesh-and-blood Dinah opened her mouth to say, *Of course I've had an orgasm; I have two children, for god's sake*, even though she knew this would sound insane. One did not mean the other.

"Helen Gurley Brown said women can be equal partners to men. Not just through sex, but that's one place to start."

As Juliet lectured on, Dinah wished for a time machine helmet, like the one she'd seen in an episode of *The Twilight Zone*. She would turn the clock back to the day before, and instead of driving to the *LA Times* office, she would take herself to a movie or stay home and watch the neighbor clean his gutters.

"It's so easy for you to judge me," she interrupted. "To think what you would do in my shoes. It's easy for your entire generation to say, 'You should be braver. You should have done more. Why didn't you fix every-thing so that we don't have to?' But you're looking at me—at us—from the eyes of 1964, not the eyes of 1944 when we were your age. For start-ers, there was a war. Women went to work outside the house, and for the majority of them? It was the first time. You can never understand how enormous that was because you grew up in a completely different era."

"With plenty of the same bullshit, which we've inherited from you."

Dinah needed a cigarette. Remembering the one she'd found in Shep's room, she pulled it out of her pocket and saw that it wasn't a cigarette at all. It was a joint.

Juliet was still talking as Dinah stepped out of her flats and hoisted the window open. She leaned out into the morning.

"What are you doing?" Juliet asked.

"I'm breaking the fucking ice," Dinah said. She climbed into the windowsill, straddling the ledge. And then she lit the joint and in-haled, feeling the sweet, bitter taste of it fill her lungs. She had never smoked marijuana, but how hard could it be? She knew it was some-thing beatniks did, and she was no beatnik. At least not that she knew. Maybe, after all of this was over, she would become one. She tried to picture herself rejecting conventional society, shedding consumer-ism and conformity, beating the bongos, spouting slang, dressing all in black—a beret, dark glasses, her capri pants. She stifled a giggle. Everything she knew about beatniks she'd learned from Audrey Hep-burn in *Funny Face*. She took another hit and then began to cough.

"Are you smoking dope?"

Dinah looked up. "I am," she choked out. It burned. God, how it burned. "If we were my sons, we would be down there on the lawn pummeling each other until we settled this. But since we're women . . . Off the record? Let's just say I found it in my house."

She held out the joint. The truth was, she knew nothing about beat-niks. Truth was, at forty-three, she was discovering there was a lot she knew nothing about.

Juliet handled the joint with ease, an afterthought, as if she'd smoked hundreds of them before. She arranged herself like Dinah, one bare leg slung over the sill, back against the window frame, so that the two women were mirror images of each other.

"What you're describing"—Dinah waved at the notebook in Juliet's other hand—"is burning the proverbial house down. A house that my husband built. That we've all built over the past two decades." She shook her head and kept shaking it until it felt as if her eyes might rattle loose. "We can change history without blowing up the entire world."

Juliet breathed out a plume of smoke and tugged at the hem of her miniskirt. "Sometimes I want to blow up the world."

"Oh, sure," said Dinah. "I do too. You just have to be thoughtful about the way you do it. Especially when you're America's Favorite Mom and Homemaker." She nodded at Juliet's legs. "I used to never wear hose. Somewhere along the way, I became all girdled up." She was wearing knee-highs now, for fuck's sake, under the capri pants.

"So don't wear them," Juliet said simply.

Dinah handed her the joint and threw the other leg over the sill. She shimmied out of the nude-colored stockings, first one, then the other, and dropped them into the flower bed below. And laughed.

Juliet began to laugh too. The laughter was a surprise to both of them. They passed the joint back and forth, and for the first time that morning, Dinah felt at ease.

There was a rattling sound from across the street. The neighbor strode through his yard, tool belt slung around the slight paunch of his waist.

"What is he doing?" Juliet said. "It's barely eight a.m."

"He's always working on a project—mowing the lawn, cleaning the gutters, sweeping the driveway. He's out there every morning and every night. I honestly don't know when he finds time to go to the office. Assuming he goes to an office. I'm not really sure what he does." Dinah sighed. "Off the record, I've been imagining an affair."

"With *him*?" Juliet gripped the window and leaned out a little farther, trying to get a better look.

"There's something so . . . masculine about all that yard work."

"So would you ever actually do it? Have an affair?"

"No. I love my husband." A wistful note in her voice made her sound years younger. "I don't really have women friends, not anymore. But I have two sisters-in-law, and back when I used to go home for holidays, before the boys, before the show, they would complain to me about my brothers. I've noticed women on the set doing this too. Almost trying to one-up each other, like whoever has the worst husband wins. And then they look at me like, *Okay, Dinah, your turn, tell us what you hate about Del*. But I don't hate anything about Del. I love Del." She blew out smoke. "Even when he's being an ass."

Juliet looked out at the trees, at the hills, at the sky. "That's the thing about love. Sometimes you feel weightless, and sometimes you feel tethered to the ground."

"More than the yard work," Dinah said, her voice froggy from the smoke, "it's this indescribable something. That lack of something. That need to feel more."

"The same thing that makes me want to stand up in the middle of the newsroom and tell them all to fuck off. Who knows? Maybe men feel it too, to some degree." Juliet shrugged. "But for me, at least, I feel itchy and angry and I know I'm not alone."

They fell quiet for a minute. Right now, they were two colleagues, two pairs of bare legs, passing a joint between them.

Then Juliet said, "You know I've been angry at you for a long time."

"Really?" Dinah said dryly. "You hid it so well."

Juliet smiled a fleeting smile. "I blamed you for my mom's life. She loves you. She idolizes you. She wrote you a letter years ago, asking for a recipe, and you wrote her back. She has it framed in our house." Juliet shook her head. "She cleans and cooks the meals and wears her pearls so that when my dad gets home from work, she looks like a field of daisies, as if she's spent the day napping and getting her hair done. Meanwhile, her back aches and her head aches and he barely notices her."

"What's her name? Your mom."

"Roberta."

"Roberta," Dinah repeated. She searched her memory banks for a Roberta, but the truth was that the studio answered most of her fan mail. "What is it Roberta loves so much about Dinah Newman?"

"The way you—Dinah—seem to have it all. Handsome husband who loves her. Handsome sons who never give her any trouble. A beautiful house. A beautiful wardrobe. A sparkling kitchen. Friends and time and love to spare."

"But no one has all of that. Not really." In spite of Dinah's best efforts, a note of sadness crept into her voice.

And then she climbed off the windowsill and crossed the room to the desk. She dropped into one of the two chairs, pulled the cover off Del's typewriter, and fed a piece of paper into the machine.

Juliet lowered herself into the chair across from her, opened her notebook, and took out a pen. "Where should we start?"

Dinah placed her fingers on the typewriter keys. "I think it's time Dinah Newman had an orgasm."

TWENTY

Five days after the accident

The entire cast sat around the table in the rehearsal hall above the soundstage, a vast, windowless space that resembled an office building without walls. Aside from Del, only Sydney—who always attended table reads—was missing, having taken a last-minute trip to New York.

Even though the temperature in the room was kept at a perpetual sixty-eight degrees, Guy's neck was damp. A single bead of sweat made its way down his spine. That morning in the editing room, he had watched back the film they'd shot on the day of the accident right through the moment Del hit the ground. If Guy was going to quarterback this family, he had to stop shying away from the hard things, and he knew what Del would say: *It's all a part of the job. We put ourselves out there because other people can't or won't. You've got to be willing to take risks. And maybe you break your leg. Or maybe you break your heart. But let it heal and move on.*

"My dad," he began, "has gone east to take care of his mother, who's very ill. We ask for your discretion during this difficult time. In his absence, I'll be directing the episode. Our last one before the season finale!"

To his own ears, he sounded too formal, even prim. This was why—one of the reasons, at least—Shep called him *Grandpa*. He glanced at his brother, tipping back in his chair. A chair would never slip out from under Shep because he was someone who could balance on two legs instead of four, even when the world was upside down.

"We hope you know how much we appreciate you and what you do," Guy went on, trying to loosen his voice and his pulse, which thrummed beneath his skin. "It's not just thanks to Pop that *Meet the Newmans* runs like clockwork. It's because of you."

He and Sydney had agreed that his words should be succinct and direct. And leave no room for questions. What he did not say was *For you, this is just another episode in a long line of episodes. For us, this is one of our last remaining chances to prove to James T. Aubrey that we are indispensable. And for me, I need to prove that too.*

But as he looked around the table at the faces of his other family, Guy felt the need to say something more. Something rallying. Which was why he borrowed from his favorite speech, one delivered by President Kennedy two years ago at Houston's Rice University.

"'We *choose* to go to the moon. We choose to go to the moon in this decade and do the other things, not because they are easy, but because they are hard.'"

His brother pretended to nod off. Shep treating the table read like recess was nothing new, but if he had been within reach, Guy would have kicked the chair out from under him. Instead, he brought the speech to an abrupt, stuttering end, even though there was so much more of it, every word an inspiration. *Because that challenge is one that we are willing to accept, one we are unwilling to postpone, and one which we intend to win.*

The script for this episode was, in the kindest terms, a hack job. Guy had divvied up Del's dialogue between himself and Shep, and much of the storyline centered around his brother's eighteenth birthday. But the biggest change was to the very last scene, Guy's proposal. Guy the real-life person proposing to the real-life Eileen. The episode would end before Eileen gave her answer so that viewers would be forced to watch the finale to see if she said yes or no.

His dad hated using ploys like this to trick an audience. But Aubrey loved them. He had leaked hints that there *might be something big coming*, bigger than viewers could even imagine, and that audiences could watch as this *big surprise* unfolded *live* on April 24. No one—not the other actors, not the crew, not even Shep—was in on the secret, except for those in the meeting with Aubrey.

That morning, Guy had taken Eileen aside and shown her the last scene of the script so she'd be prepared for the changes.

And do I say yes? she'd asked.

I guess we'll have to wait to find out.

He still had no idea how Eileen felt about their impending marriage. With all that had happened, there hadn't been a moment to ask. Guy himself was conflicted, of course, but strangely, during this wild, uncharted time, he also found it a kind of life preserver, a distraction to complain about, to rationalize, to pour all his emotional energy into.

Here on *Meet the Newmans*, it was tradition that the director read the scene descriptions and action, and so Guy began: "Interior. Front yard. Day. Dinah, Guy, and Shep stand on the lawn waving at Del's car as it rolls away." This was another small change. Sending Del on a business trip to explain his absence.

In spite of that absence, the table read felt like any other table read. Until page four, when Dinah—who smelled faintly and impossibly of marijuana—held up a finger.

"Instead of me cooking a pot roast, why don't I throw on some slacks and go outside and garden?"

On page ten, she once again held up a finger. "I don't understand why I'm cooking a full meal for myself if Del is on a business trip and you boys are at the fraternity house. Why can't I eat in front of the TV? Dinah's off duty. Let's give her a moment of rest."

Shep, still tilted back in his chair, sang, "'Someone's in the kitchen with Dinah.'"

"No one's in the kitchen *but* Dinah," his mother said. "Here on pages six, eleven, fourteen, fifteen, twenty-one. I'm cooking and cleaning, cooking and cleaning."

"Sorry, Mom," Guy told her. "It was already in the script. I mean, that's just what—" He had started to say *that's just what on-screen Dinah does* but stopped himself.

"I don't understand," she said in a clipped, simmering voice, "why I've been relegated to a hausfrau. At what point did your father decide—did I let him decide—that I'm the family maid? Your father is a grown man. You boys are grown men. Why am I washing and ironing your shirts? You live at the fraternity house." She waved at Guy. "Yet you're always walking in the door, bringing me your laundry—"

"Seriously, Guy," said Shep.

"And you." She turned on him. "You can't even make a sandwich. I could be playing bridge with the Women's Club or—I don't know—dancing at Ciro's instead of hanging up your clothes and making your bed."

"Except that Ciro's closed four years ago," Shep quipped.

Dinah turned to Peggy. "Did you know that women aren't allowed to serve on juries?"

Peggy did know this, and so did Eileen, along with a slew of other things women weren't legally permitted to do.

Delicately, Guy steered them back to the script, promising his mother he would make some changes, and the table read continued, Dinah suggesting alterations, Guy taking notes.

As he delivered his last line—*"Eileen, will you marry me? Here and* (a nod to the camera, breaking the fourth wall) *out there?"*—there was a sharp bang of chair legs hitting the floor. Everyone looked up. Shep was now firmly on the ground.

TWENTY-ONE

Five days after the accident

The Golden Sun Saloon was the oldest bar in Los Angeles. It had sat on Eighth Street between Olive and Hill since 1905. It was a five-minute walk from the *Times* building, which was one reason Juliet's colleagues—if they could be called that—went there after work. Juliet had never been invited to join them. But this evening—Wednesday—Charlie Murdock had paused as they were leaving and hollered back to her. "Hey, Dunne. We're off to the Golden Sun if you want to join us."

Her eyes went to Paula Goodman, pecking away at her typewriter. Paula had never, to Juliet's knowledge, been invited to grab drinks with the men. Juliet studied the stacks of work spread out in front of her. She was almost caught up. She could stay in the office a little longer, see if Renee was interested in getting a bite. She could head home. Take a relaxing bath. Order Chinese from the place on the corner, the one that always gave her extra egg rolls. Or she could go to the Golden Sun.

It was nearing sunset, and the air was chilly. Juliet turned her collar up against the breeze, tucked her left hand in her pocket, held on to her bag with her right. Downtown after hours was a different downtown than during the day. Most everyone who worked there fled at five o'clock, returning to the west side or Los Feliz or the valley. Shops closed. Businesses closed. Only bars and restaurants stayed open.

Her eyes searched the street ahead, moving upward to the buildings—shabby hotels, movie palaces, department stores, office towers—ever watchful, anticipating threats. She turned onto Eighth Street and saw the glowing lights of the bar halfway down the block. Without thinking, she quickened her pace. Then she was there, opening the door and walking inside, into the light and warmth, the smell of cigarettes and beer, the sounds of laughter, of music.

It was a long, narrow space lit by flickering lamps. The vibe was cozy and welcoming, and she felt herself relax. The bartender had long hair and a trim beard, and he wore a white T-shirt like Marlon Brando in *A Streetcar Named Desire*. A photo of the Golden Sun's first owner, President Teddy Roosevelt, hung on the wall behind him. She waited for the bartender to ask what she was having so that she could say she was meeting colleagues, thanks. But he merely nodded and went back to mixing drinks.

She walked deeper into the belly of the saloon, no going back now. She scanned the unfamiliar faces and felt a flush of irritation and humiliation. It was a joke, it had to be. Early on, when she'd first started working on the Lifestyle page, she'd asked Nick about the news reporters. She knew they hung out in a pack, like dogs, drinking after work together. "They're a boys' club," he told her. "You'll never be one of them. And you should be grateful for that."

She was turning to go when an arm encircled her waist. She yanked away to see Charlie, laughing, eyes dancing behind his glasses. He smelled like whiskey.

"We're back here," he said, and led her to the darkest corner of the room. She hadn't noticed the table or the men, but now she saw them—Lance and Gregory and Phil and a couple of others she knew by sight but hadn't officially met. The table was already littered with empty glasses and bottles. Lance jumped to his feet and procured an extra chair from nearby.

"Settle this argument for us, Dunne," Charlie said, seated again.

Juliet sat, slinging her purse over the back of the chair but keeping her jacket on. *Not yet*, she thought. She'd see how it went first.

"Do you think Oswald acted alone?"

In the wake of Kennedy's death, and—two days later—Lee Harvey Oswald's, there had been speculation, talks of conspiracy theories and a government cover-up.

Juliet, who had no opinion on this one way or the other, said, "I don't think we have enough information."

When she thought about the president's death, she thought about the president himself, not the man or men who'd shot him. She thought of Jackie in her pink suit, of the Secret Service agent climbing over the back of the car to her. She thought of the news anchors who removed their glasses and wept as they reported that Kennedy was dead. She thought of her own heartbreak and the nation's heartbreak and the heaviness of this new America.

The men seemed satisfied enough with her answer. They continued to debate Oswald and the CIA and Jack Ruby, who just last week had been found guilty of killing Oswald, as they ordered another round of scotch.

Fifteen minutes later, she draped her coat across her lap—a life jacket just in case she needed it—and nursed her scotch in spite of the good-natured teasing to keep up. The only time she had ever let her guard down completely had been with the Musician. The man she knew could be lovely and genuine, sweet and sincere. And funny. That was something you didn't see in his interviews, how funny he was. She rarely recognized the version of him she saw in the press and on television. The preening, smug rooster of a man who wrote songs about ex-lovers, turning them into material, something to make money from.

"Penny for your thoughts," Charlie said in her ear. A prickle of something on her neck—a tiny warning. She brought the scotch to her lips and drank.

"Did you always want to be a reporter?" she asked him. Setting the glass down, running her finger around the rim, round and round until she saw him watching, saw him wet his lips. She folded her hands in her lap, sat back.

"Yes and no," he said. "I actually planned to write books. Overly dense, overly important nonfiction books. I was going to expose government secrets, take down the chemical plants. I wanted to win a Pulitzer."

One of the other men laughed. They went around the table listing their original dreams—chef, politician, entrepreneur, bum. The thing they all seemed to have in common was that none of them had set out to work at a newspaper.

"And what about you, fair Juliet?" asked Charlie. "What brings you to the *LA Times*?"

"I want to report the news," she said out loud. *Not be the news*, she thought. She'd been a headline far too much for one lifetime. "To feel like I'm bringing valuable information to the public, telling them what they need to know."

Until this moment, Nick and Renee had been the only two people who knew her plans. As the words left her mouth, she wanted to chase them and stuff them back in. She held her chin a little higher, hoping to distract from the violent beating of her heart. And because it was out there, she decided she didn't have anything left to lose.

Which was why she added that the reason she wanted to become a news reporter came from a personal need to know, that as a kid she'd sensed things weren't always what they seemed with her parents. Too many conversations behind closed doors, too many hushed discussions when they thought she wasn't around. She'd grown up waiting for whatever lay just beneath the surface of them to break through and devour them all.

For a minute, the men just sat there. When they exchanged looks around the table—with each other, not with her—she realized what she'd done.

"But the news," Lance said, one corner of his mouth hitched up in a smirk. "Come on. You're telling us you're not happy on the Lifestyle page? Don't you want to get married? Pop out a few babies?"

"Settle down and *read* the Lifestyle page instead of writing for it?" This from Gregory, who tilted his beer bottle back and kept his eyes on her while he drank.

"No," she said, her voice sounding like a croak. "And before you ask, I'm not working at the *Times* to find a husband."

They laughed. Gregory muttered, "Who said anything about a husband?"

Her neck prickled again. "Why did you invite me here tonight?" she asked, her eyes scanning the table. She wrapped her hands around her glass, willed her expression to remain cool and placid even though Phil was openly staring at her breasts.

Charlie said, "We thought it was time we get to know you better."

There was nothing provocative about his words, but it was there in their expressions. And then, just so she understood, Phil said, "Tell us about the Musician."

"Excuse me?" She felt the features of her face freeze, locking in place as if she were made of stone.

"You know," and then he sang a few lines of "Juliet, Sleeping," the others joining in until they dissolved into laughter.

Their questions came quickly, overlapping one another. Raucous, infantile boys.

What was it like being a muse?

What's the difference between a muse and a groupie?

I wouldn't mind having a muse. How about being mine?

That's what the newsroom needs. More groupies.

It's chilly out—is that the only coat you brought? Where's your fur skin rug?

It was worse than being hit on. More demeaning. They thought *she* was the joke. Not the punch line but the joke itself. She sat in silence, unable to move. Unable to feel her face. She couldn't even blink. She shouldn't have been surprised. Nick had warned her. So had Renee. So had, in her own roundabout way, Paula Goodman, who from Juliet's first day made it clear they would never be friends. *You are not to stop by my desk to chat, and we do not confer unless we are told to. They already lump us together because of our sex. Let's not reinforce in their minds that we're the only two female reporters here.*

Juliet sat there, unspeaking, unmoving, as they shifted merrily to other topics. And then, at some point, just to make it perfectly clear what they thought of her, Gregory said, "You know they'll never put you on the news desk."

"Paula's on the news desk," she said, her voice a shadow. She should have gotten up when they started hurling their insults. She should have picked up their drinks and emptied them on their heads and then kicked them each, one by one, in the groin.

Someone snorted. "*Local* news."

Someone else added, "What else is she good for? You, though. You've got other things going for you."

An arm on the back of her chair. Charlie staking his claim. He leaned in, whispering in her ear, "Maybe I can help you out, put in a good word with Hartley." Then he reached a hand up under her hair and stroked her bare neck.

She pulled away. She wanted to slap the smile off his face, but she would not give them the satisfaction of seeing her upset. Instead, she calmly finished her drink, neatly set the glass upside down on the table, the way she had watched the Musician do once in a pub on a blustery London street. Picked up her jacket, her purse, slid back her chair, and walked away. It didn't matter how famous your on-again, off-again boyfriend was or how tough you thought you were. A single stroke of the neck was all it took to reduce you to nothing, to remind you where they thought you belonged.

On her way out, she stopped at the bar and ordered another round of their most expensive scotch for the table. "Actually," she said, "send a round to every table in here."

"Your treat?" the bartender asked.

"No." She smiled. "Charge it to my friends. And while you're at it, throw in a bottle of your priciest booze."

He gave her a flicker of a smile that told her he understood.

She watched as he poured the shots, one by one. Shot upon shot upon shot until the bar was covered in them. When he set down a bottle of Macallan Fine & Rare 1926, she picked it up and tucked it under her arm. "That one's for me."

And then she asked him to call her a cab to take her home. She didn't want to brave the night again on her own.

Half an hour later, she stood under the hot spray of her shower, wishing she could cleanse her mind of the last few hours as easily as the water cleansed her skin.

Half an hour after that, she sat in front of the television eating cold Chinese food. When she was done, she hunched over her kitchen table and started writing.

TWENTY-TWO

Five days after the accident

To become a resident of the Hollywood Studio Club, women had to be between eighteen and thirty-five and work in show business. The dormitory itself had been designed by the architect of Hearst Castle. It was an elegant Italianate building with arched windows, porticos, and balconies, which sat on a quiet street in the heart of Hollywood shaded by palm trees. Marilyn Monroe had once lived there, as had Donna Reed and Kim Novak and a slew of other actresses who went on to be famous. Eileen had been living at the Studio Club for nearly a year. It made her feel part of something in a town where you could often feel alone.

It was after ten o'clock. Music drifted out of open windows. Someone was playing guitar. Someone else was singing. Voices and laughter, warm and busy, the sounds of the night beginning to wind down. The air smelled sweet. Eileen sprawled on her bed and ran lines with her roommate, Chloe Danielle, a studio secretary from Nebraska who wanted to be the next Debbie Reynolds.

A knock on the door interrupted them, and the club chaperone appeared. Mrs. Dennis was matronly and tall and wore round glasses that always caught the light. She was a kind woman, deep down, but her presence at your door was rarely a good thing.

"Oh no," Chloe breathed. One of the things Eileen liked best about her roommate was her boundless enthusiasm and her unwavering optimism, but Chloe was—like so many of the girls—scared of Mrs. Dennis.

"Your brother is here," the chaperone said to Eileen.

Eileen's three brothers were, she was almost certain, fast asleep back in Mississippi.

"He looks suspiciously like Shep Newman," Mrs. Dennis added. "And it's after curfew."

"I'm sorry."

"He said it was urgent."

"I'm sorry," Eileen repeated.

Mrs. Dennis stood aside, waiting, and Eileen made her way down the hall and down the main stairs. As rigid as Mrs. Dennis could be, Eileen knew the rules were there for their safety, and she felt a sudden swell of gratitude. She often wondered what life must be like for her, living here, seeing girls come and go—their excitement and youth and flurry, lives just beginning. There was a part of her that would miss it once she moved out and into the Newmans' guesthouse with Guy.

Outside the front door, Shep paced the yard, hands in the pockets of his jeans. Eileen walked out onto the stoop. From inside, a song ended and another one began.

"Is your dad . . ." she began.

"He's okay. I mean, nothing's changed."

"What are you doing here?" She could feel Mrs. Dennis over her shoulder.

"I don't like the script edits. The ones Guy made. You and him. The two of you." He was talking faster than she'd ever heard him, like he was hopped up on something. "What did he mean—'marry me in here and out there'?"

She asked the chaperone if she could have a few minutes. Waited as Mrs. Dennis went inside and shut the door with a sharp *click*. Turned back to Shep.

"It was Aubrey's idea," she told him.

"What was?"

He was going to make her say it.

"He wants me to marry Guy. Actually marry him. On the live finale."

"And you told him to fuck off because you don't believe in marriage."

"Technically, I haven't said I'll do it."

"But you haven't said you won't."

She took a beat too long to answer, which was an answer in itself.

"So you and my brother?" A vein pulsed in his temple.

"He's a great person."

"So it's real, then. Between you. The two of you. You. And Guy."

"I'm not discussing this with you, Shep."

"Why not? I mean, I'm going to be your brother-in-law. We're practically family. Is that why—you and him—is that why we never . . ." He gestured back and forth between them. "Or is this about your career?"

She wanted to snap, *It's about your career as much as mine.* But instead she went right for the sarcasm. "The fact that 'we never' has nothing to do with your brother. And what do you want me to say? It's television? It's a job? It's me not having to worry about tabloid gossip? 'Why is she still single? What kind of woman doesn't want marriage and children?' Do you *want* me to tell you there's no other feeling behind it?"

"So you're selling your soul."

She crossed her arms. "You came here, after curfew, to—what? Lecture me? Or is this your valiant way of trying to protect me?"

"I came here to tell you that if you're marrying him for any reason other than love, you're an idiot."

"I don't need to explain myself to you, and we don't need to talk about it. Any of it. I don't want to get in the middle of your stuff any more than I want you in the middle of mine."

"You could never be in the middle."

And there it was again—this unspoken thing between them that wouldn't go away no matter how much she wanted it to. She waited for him to continue, thinking, *All right, you've got me here. Now would be a good time for you to start speaking the hell up.* She knew him well enough to know he felt a great deal all the time, that he ran far deeper than anyone gave him credit for. But she wasn't a mind reader, nor did she have any interest in pretending to be.

Instead, he looked up at the dormitory. "This place is pretty amazing. Did you know that, back in the twenties and thirties, girls had to have references and a letter from their parents to move in?"

"It's still that way."

"Marilyn Monroe posed nude to earn money to pay her rent."

He waggled an eyebrow at her, and she realized he was trying to *charm* her the way he did other girls. This, more than him showing up here, more than him thinking he had a right to who she dated or married, pissed her off.

"And," she said flatly, "one of the women here was murdered by her boyfriend. Right in there." She pointed behind her. "And then he killed himself."

"Jesus." Shep dropped his smile.

Eileen waited for him to say something else about how sorry he was for butting in or about how the girl at the recording studio meant nothing to him. Instead, he just stood there looking at her. Communicating with Shep was a little like learning a new language. All relationships were like that to some degree, but she got the feeling it would be even more so with him. Which was yet another reason to never sleep with him.

She sighed. "Well," she said briskly. "If that's it, then."

The words sounded final, an ending. He moved closer, leaning against the doorframe. The two of them stood inches apart. She felt the slow, burning heat of him and wondered—not for the first time—if touching him would make her catch fire.

"I'm writing a song for you," he said.

Then he reached out and fingered a strand of her hair. As corny as it was, she caught her breath. In that moment, it felt like everything changed between them.

And then the strand of hair fell back against her shoulder and he shook his head.

"So what was that about?" she asked, her voice husky from the night air, from the proximity of him. "At the studio." Even though she didn't really want to know.

"With Lorrie?"

"Yes." *Lorrie.*

"Complications."

"Complications," she repeated.

"Yes." He said it to their feet, to the ground below them.

Then he looked up at her.

"Oh," she breathed, because in that moment, he didn't need to say anything. It was all there, on his face. She felt her heart crack in two. He was tied to this girl. This Lorrie. And so there really was nothing standing in her way of marrying Guy.

From above, a girl leaned out of her window and cried, "Holy shit! It's Shep Newman!" Then she turned inward, and Eileen could hear her shouting, "Shep Newman's outside! Shep goddamn Newman!"

She was still caught up in *complications*, in the vision of herself marrying the wrong brother, and it took her a second to find her voice. "You'd better go before the mob arrives."

Behind and above, there was the sound of running and shrieking.

He didn't move. Eileen placed her hand on his chest, in the space over his heart, and gave him a little push.

"Go," she said.

And then she closed the door in his face.

TWENTY-THREE

Six days after the accident

This time, they began on the window ledge of Del's office. Dinah lit a cigarette and offered one to Juliet, who leaned forward, lighting hers from the one in Dinah's hand. For a moment, they sat there, like bookends, enjoying the silence, the warmth of the morning on their skin, the sight of the smoke as it curled lazily upward. And then Juliet began to tell Dinah about the Golden Sun Saloon. She nodded toward the desk, where her notebook lay, indicating that she'd written it all down.

In turn, Dinah told Juliet about the table read and the way she'd spoken up for that little brown wren version of herself who cooked and vacuumed and dusted and wore aprons and baked pies and acted as a sounding board for her husband and sons, who rarely exhibited interests of her own outside of her household and family.

"Everything," Juliet said aloud, "is material."

"But do we dare use it?"

"Why not? These things that have happened—they're ours. They belong to us." She studied the burning tip of the cigarette. And then she studied Dinah's profile as she gazed out across the lawn and rooftops toward the lake beyond. "Where is he really? Off the record."

"Where is who?" asked Dinah.

"Del." It felt wrong calling him this, as if he were the father of a childhood friend.

"He's away." Dinah's tone was careful, her expression suddenly wary. She brushed invisible ash off her pants and didn't meet Juliet's eyes.

Juliet sighed. For the most part, she considered herself an open book. Just because she and Dinah had smoked a joint together didn't mean they were friends. And sometimes when working on a story, you had to barter. It was all about reciprocation—I'll give you something and you give me something in return. So she began to tell Dinah about the messy, complicated nature of her relationship with the Musician, not just the public relationship but the private one, and her fear of losing herself again.

"It wasn't just that stupid fur skin rug or being in the public eye. I saw the other wives and girlfriends—they call them WAGs. They'd be at home alone with the kids while the guys—these men they love, the fathers of those kids—went out on the road. I've interviewed bands before. I know what happens when they're on tour. They live one life out there and a totally different life at home. I didn't want to be just another woman sitting around waiting for her man to come back and her life to begin again. And I couldn't figure out if I was the wife in that scenario or the girl on the road."

It was as if the windowsill were magic. A portal for baring one's soul. And then, because she was already talking and why stop now, she told Dinah about the pregnancy scare, the one she'd had last year. This was after she'd been outed as the girl in the fur skin rug, after she'd broken up with the Musician and moved out of their house on Wonderland because she couldn't live his lifestyle and her own at the *LA Times*. She found herself with no partner, no home, no support system. She couldn't imagine bringing a child into the world, and the memory of her own childhood in a cold, unhappy house haunted her. What if she, like her own mother, wasn't cut out for it?

So she went to her doctor. *I can't help you*, he'd told her. But later that evening, she received a phone call from a voice she didn't recognize giving her a name and a telephone number for someone in

Reno, Nevada. She borrowed money from her landlord and flew there alone. A woman met her at the airport. She handed Juliet a blindfold and told her she needed to put it on, that anonymity was crucial. They drove for what felt like hours, and then the woman led Juliet inside a building where—still blindfolded—she was helped onto a bed that felt more like a table, hard and cold beneath her back. Only to discover that somewhere between her apartment and Reno, she'd miscarried.

At this, Dinah said, "I'm so sorry."

"It's okay. I'd been preparing myself to not have the baby, and in many ways, I was grateful I didn't have to make that call myself."

"Do you trust him? The Musician?"

Juliet blinked at her, at the photos covering the walls, at the sun pouring in the window, at the shine of the sill beneath her, gradually coming back to this office, this moment. When people asked about trust, they usually meant do you trust him not to cheat on you, do you trust him to be honest, do you trust him to be good to you. Even when they were exclusive, she knew *exclusive* was just a word.

"Yes," she said. "It's me I don't trust."

A small part of her—the part that would always yearn for an understanding mother—wished for an acknowledgment. A *thank you for sharing* or a simple *you're okay*.

Dinah said, "I think I know what you mean."

And Juliet felt a wave of something—not love. Camaraderie, maybe. A kinship with this woman, nearly twenty years her senior. Emboldened, she swung off the sill and pulled a stack of papers from her bag.

"I have something to show you. It's the interview. The one I did with you. After the saloon, I rewrote it. I just—I'd muted myself and you, and I don't want to do that."

She handed Dinah the pages, neatly typed and stapled.

"Del always says, 'There are enough people in this world who will tell you no. Don't be one of them.'" Dinah smiled at the thought of him, then looked at the pages in her hand. "Should I read this now?"

"Now or later. It's up to you. I'd like to hear what you think, though."

Instead of returning to the windowsill, Juliet stood by the desk, face aglow with youth and the early-morning sunlight. In that moment, she felt fearless.

Dinah began to read. Juliet dropped into the desk chair. Then stood and began to pace. When Dinah reached the end of the second page, she looked up. "What is this?"

"Our interview."

"I realize it's our interview. Why did you write it this way?"

"Because it's honest."

Dinah flipped through the remaining pages. And then she pulled them apart, freeing them from the staple, and sent them flying.

"Why did . . ." Juliet rushed to the window and watched as her hard work came to rest in the dirt, the grass, a bush, the pool.

"Know your audience," Dinah said. "It's one of the first rules of television. Anyone interested in reading an interview with me isn't going to want to read that." She nodded toward the ground. "Maybe they think they do, but they don't."

"People love seeing behind the scenes, and this is a dialogue. A very real conversation between two women from two generations who see the world differently, who live vastly different lives, yet are bonded by the same laws and some of the same experiences."

As Juliet spoke the words, she felt the idea catch fire. *Yes,* she thought. *You are onto something here.*

"No," Dinah said simply. She stubbed her cigarette out and stood. In a cool voice as crisp as autumn leaves, she told Juliet, "I think we should take the rest of the day and work separately. You go home. I'll be here. And we'll spend some time thinking about what it is we're trying to do and why."

The two women stared at each other. Without a word, Juliet gathered her jacket and all the shit that had somehow fallen out of her bag and onto the floor, and only in the doorway to the office did she stop and look at Dinah.

"You know what? Why don't you give me a call when you're ready to do this. Whether you like it or not, this is a relationship, even if it's just a fleeting one, and I'm only interested in being here if I can be honest. Oh, and as far as your audience? We've already seen how out of touch you are with them."

With that, Juliet banged through the hallway and down the stairs and outside. She stood in the driveway, trying to catch her breath, half expecting Dinah to come after her. But there was only the distant cry of a coyote, splitting the morning in two.

TWENTY-FOUR

Six days after the accident

D el lay in his hospital bed, with the strange, vacant look of a shell that had been discarded. Dinah dropped into the chair beside him and began recounting her heated exchange with Juliet, which—an hour later—still had her bristling. Del loved it when she got fired up about something, and she ranted to him about this new generation. They were impatient, too eager for change. They were so critical of her and her contemporaries, as if the world and all its ills were their fault.

She tried to imagine what her husband would have said if he were conscious. Reassuring words to let her know she wasn't alone, that he felt this way too. Then something to make her smile, maybe even to make her laugh. Somewhere along the way, that man she'd first fallen in love with had gotten lost. She supposed the girl she'd been when he first fell in love with her had gotten lost too, although she couldn't pinpoint the exact moment it happened.

"Mrs. Newman?"

She turned to see Dr. Carson, standing just inside the doorway. It occurred to her that he had dropped the pretense of *Thornhill*. Nurse Benny stood behind him.

The doctor moved into the room, positioning himself at the end of Del's bed. "I'm afraid there's no change." He still didn't quite meet her eyes, and she wondered if it had more to do with her being a woman or with some terrible news he was about to deliver.

"The swelling in his brain?"

He shook his head, consulted the chart he carried under his arm. She wondered if he was actually reading or only pretending to. She doubted he had to consult his notes to tell her that her husband, at this moment, was trapped somewhere between this world and the next. She accepted the chart reading as a kindness, and suddenly she was in tears, because these days, the tears, like the numbness in her limbs, were never far away.

"And what are the dangers of keeping him like this?" she asked.

"In a comatose state?"

She nodded.

"The longer the brain goes without oxygen, the greater the chance he could experience permanent damage."

"Brain damage?"

"Yes. But in your husband's case, I'm optimistic."

She waited for more—why he was optimistic, what it was about Del's particular circumstances that made him say something like this to her, knowing she would grab on to it with both hands.

She glanced at Nurse Benny, at the doctor. She forced herself to say, "And if he's like this next week? Or three weeks from now?"

"Then we reevaluate. We discuss our options."

She knew that doctors, like reporters, were supposed to maintain objectivity, but she flinched at the flat turn of his voice. Her brother Tripp was a doctor back in North Carolina, and she had phoned him to ask what he knew about medically induced comas. *Is everyone okay?* he'd asked. *Yes,* she lied. *It's research for an episode.* Then he told her about a woman in Chicago who had been comatose since 1941. And another man who had awakened from a coma suddenly able to speak three new languages.

Dr. Carson said, "We'll let you have some time alone with him."

Dinah stared down at the man in the bed, so still and placid and un-Del-like. He was a person who lived in constant motion. He would hate for anyone to see him like this, especially strangers.

"Mrs. Newman?"

Dinah looked up. Nurse Benny lingered in the doorway.

"It's important that you don't lose hope. Important for you, but mostly important for him. He needs you to not count him out."

The same goes for all of us, Dinah thought.

She was heading out of the hospital parking lot when a familiar sports car turned in. She honked the horn, and the car slowed, pulling up next to her Impala. Dinah and the other driver rolled their windows down, engines idling.

"When did you get back from New York?" she asked, shielding her eyes from the sun.

"Last night." Sydney looked grim. "I met with sponsors while I was there."

On the steering wheel, her hands were numb. It always surprised her how quickly it came on. Of course he hadn't trusted her to find a sponsor herself. What smarted even more was that she'd been completely unsuccessful, just as he'd expected her to be.

"No one wants to take us on," he said, "not even by half. Not even with television's wedding of the year as bait. However." His tone lightened, a sliver of blue sky peeking out from behind a cloud. "I swung by Cincinnati on my way home. To meet with Procter & Gamble."

Procter & Gamble financed *The Dick Van Dyke Show*.

"And?"

"They said they'd think about it."

She wished he hadn't told her. Even though, as Nurse Benny had said, it was important to not lose hope, *thinking about it* felt every bit as hopeless as *no*.

Later, before going home, Dinah stood at the corner of Ocean and Colorado Avenues and stared at the entrance to the Santa Monica Pier and the ocean just beyond. A palm tree near the curb still bore a deep gouge, which she assumed was from the accident. She reached out for it, then jerked away as if she'd been burned. A pinhole of blood pooled on the tip of her index finger. She pulled a handkerchief from her pocket and wrapped it to stop the bleeding.

Across the street was a gas station. On the other corner, a vacant lot. If this was Del's destination—any farther west and he would have been in the Pacific Ocean—then it had to be the pier.

She stepped beneath the blue archway—*Santa Monica Yacht Harbor, Sport Fishing, Boating, Cafés*—and onto the rough wooden planks of the boardwalk, the lights and sounds drawing her toward them. She passed the merry-go-round, the carousel horses sitting frozen and silent. The place had the lonely, run-down look of a ghost town. People still turned out for the Hippodrome, and there were usually fishermen at the railings with buckets and poles. But she couldn't remember ever coming here with Del. Maybe once as a family, back when the boys were little. Maybe not even then.

Why had he driven here last week?

By now, twenty-three years in, she and Del knew everything about one another. She could predict him just like he could her. She knew his daily routine down to the minute. They never went anywhere without telling the other. She pushed aside the memory of her visit to Dr. Berke. For some reason, she told herself, that didn't count.

Dinah strode into the wind, the collar of her coat turned up, her hands deep in her pockets. The results from her blood work were normal, which meant she was healthy. Dr. Berke had delivered the news the day before, and she'd barely had time to digest it. *Everything is good.* She should have been relieved, but it would have been easier to have a medical diagnosis, something she could treat with a pill or an injection. Instead, Dr. Berke had given her the name of a psychotherapist.

She heard her father's words again, about the hysteria that ran through her mother's family tree, and it made her feel ashamed, like there was something wrong with her. Like the numbness was her fault, a choice, and she was somehow inflicting it upon herself.

Dinah passed a man and woman, their heads bent toward one another, attempting to shield their faces from the breeze. It gave them a clandestine look that unsettled her. Her husband was a handsome man who'd had a few girlfriends before she came into his life. She wasn't blind to the fact that women found him attractive. But she was not a jealous person. It had never occurred to her—until right now—that Del might be involved with someone else and that he could have come here to meet her.

The two of them were happy, though, weren't they? In spite of sleeping separately. In spite of the distance that had grown between them. They were, after all, Del and Dinah Newman.

Yes, there were bumps. Everyone had bumps. But they always managed to work things out. Yes, Del was busy. They both were. But that was the nature of this career they had chosen. One day, they would have time again to do the things they used to do. Dance in the living room, eat by candlelight, read passages from their favorite books aloud to one another, lie in the backyard and stare up at the stars, go for walks on the beach, park on Mulholland—the city spread out beneath them—and neck like they were teenagers.

Before she knew it, she was crying. *When had they stopped making time for each other?*

The man and woman looked up, both of them, their eyes narrowing at her. She had been staring at them, and now she was crying at them.

"Sorry," she whispered, too low for anyone to hear. She kept walking, the wooden slats of the boardwalk uneven so that she wobbled a little, unable to find her footing.

She walked until she came to the very end. The waves pounded below, surging against the pillars that held the pier aloft. *What if one enormous, deadly wave rose up and it all collapsed beneath me?*

Her eyes stung from tears or the wind, or both. She hated the possibility that she didn't know her husband as well as she thought she did, that he had come here—what? To meet another woman? To engage in something nefarious? To throw himself off the end of the pier? She couldn't imagine what would have brought him to this place, on a Friday night, when he was expected at home. The thought that she couldn't ask him, that he couldn't explain himself, made her feel helpless and small and alone.

Dinah gripped the wooden railing. The handkerchief she'd tied around her finger tore loose and fluttered away. She watched it, white against the black of the water, until it dropped into the sea and disappeared.

She caught her breath. Lost it. Caught it again. And then she opened her mouth and screamed.

TWENTY-FIVE

One week after the accident

J uliet perched on a corner of Nick's desk and watched as he read. When she was younger, she had chewed her nails to the quick in nervous moments like this one. But now she sat on her hands the way she did whenever she felt the urge and waited, her eyes going back and forth from Nick to the pages of her article.

She had come in that morning to find Boyd Hartley waiting at her desk. "You interviewed Dinah Newman recently. How about doing a follow-up piece on her spring wardrobe or favorite Easter recipes?"

When he stood, she saw the day's Post-it note from Renee: *I've always believed that I could do whatever I set my mind to do. —Alice Coachman, first Black woman to win an Olympic gold medal.* Below it was a hand-scrawled bill for the Golden Sun Saloon. It sat atop a mountain of work as high as her chin, even though the research department—with its dozens of employees—was only one floor down. *Charlie needs by noon. Lance needs ASAP. Gregory needs by 3 pm.*

She crumpled the bar bill and then—so that Charlie, Lance, Gregory, and the others would be sure to see—walked it to one of the communal trash cans and dropped it in. As far as she was concerned, *they* owed *her.* A debt that couldn't be repaid, the naïve part of herself that had momentarily believed they had finally accepted her as one of their own. She hadn't told Nick about that night. Hadn't mentioned it to anyone—not Renee, not the Musician, whom she hadn't seen or talked to in a week. The only person she'd told was Dinah.

Nick set her pages on his desk and tapped them once with his index finger. "And here I thought this was just another celebrity interview."

His eyes met hers. Impossible to read. She had the feeling of holding her breath, as if his verdict on her story would be the deciding factor for her career, for her. If he loved it or even liked it, she would know she was right and Dinah was wrong, that she was saying something meaningful and true. If he didn't like it, if he hated it, what then?

Nick sat back, crossed his arms, stared at the pages. She knew him well enough to know he was trying to choose his words. This wasn't necessarily a bad sign, but it wasn't a good one either.

After a moment, he said, "It seems personal."

"It *is* personal," she said, hearing the defensiveness in her voice. "It's an interview."

"Not like that." He met her eyes and leaned forward again the way he did when he was about to level with someone. "It feels like you were looking for a fight, and she gave you one. This here is not what the assignment was. There's nothing objective about it."

"It's more interesting this way. It's more honest. It's a conversation between two women of different generations—"

"No," he said. "It's not. It's too one-sided to be a dialogue. Your opinion is all over it, Jules. Why write it this way when you know damn well what we're looking for?"

If she knew why, she could tell him. He was, she believed, someone she could trust. He knew what it was like to be discriminated against and overlooked, underappreciated, disregarded, judged before people took the chance to get to know you. The two of them understood each other without talking about how or why they understood each other.

"If I don't write the truth," she said, "then what's the fucking point?" She wanted to say, *Take my side. Tell me I'm right and Dinah is wrong.*

He handed Juliet the pages, and only now could she sense his frustration with her. "Hartley's never going to approve it. And I can't either. You know this. It's first-year reporting. You're better than this. You, of all people, understand what it's like to be unfairly gone after by the press."

"But it's an important dialogue about women. The issues we face—our differences, our similarities. Friedan's book—that was one point of view, one type of background. Too often, as women, we tear each other down. Just because we're women doesn't mean we always speak the same language." She knew she was all over the place, but in her mind, it was all connected. "I'm trying to show we can talk about what's happening to us. Our experiences. Not only that we can, we should."

"Then write it that way. If you're going to be a news reporter, you *have* to be impartial and objective." To his credit, he didn't placate or soften his voice or change his tone in any way. "I wonder if you're capable of doing that."

He studied her, waiting. Nick Mitchell was the fairest person she knew. But she still felt like she needed to win him over. It was what happened when you were a woman in a man's world.

She had torn up the puff-piece version, but she could rewrite the interview, maybe find some happy medium between brutal honesty and frivolous fabrication. She could explain to Dinah that she'd simply been having a bad day. She could invent some excuse as to why she'd felt the need to pick a fight with everyone's favorite mom.

Or she could forget the interview entirely and just move on. Write something on the new Beverly Hills Women's Club cookbook or the proper ways to wear tights this season.

When she didn't vocalize any of this, only sat there, Nick said, "I look forward to reading it when it's done."

She wasn't hungry for dinner, so she sat in the video room and watched *Meet the Newmans*. It was the episode where Shep is punched by a girl while trying to protect her from a bully. Dinah hands Shep a towel for his bloody nose and then examines his face for additional signs of trauma. It was the way she hovered over him that made the lump rise in Juliet's throat. It was the words Dinah uttered to him afterward—"Here's the thing about girls—sometimes we're stronger than you think"—that made her start to cry.

With impeccable timing, Renee appeared. She frowned at the monitor and the happy black-and-white images of the Newman family, and then she frowned at Juliet's wet cheeks. Before she could ask what was wrong, Juliet wiped her eyes and snapped off the television. She was a news reporter. She was objective and capable and she didn't cry at work.

"What's going on?" she said.

"You tell me."

"Hormones."

Renee gave her a look that said she didn't believe her but would get it out of her sooner or later. And then she told her, "There's been an earthquake in Alaska. It's big. They're calling it the second largest on record."

"Shit." She and Renee rushed back into the newsroom, where all hands were on deck. The teletype machines stood in a frantic line, humming with news from the world. A cluster of men hovered over them, reading the latest reports as they came in.

"I'll never get in there," Juliet said.

"You don't need to. Look on your desk." Renee winked and walked quickly away, a blur of orange and pink fabric, her hair sprinkled with little flecks of gold—like stars—that caught the light and held it.

Sitting on Juliet's typewriter was a piece of paper. *What we have so far*, Renee had typed at the top. The earthquake had lasted for nearly three minutes. Experts were already calling it the second largest on record. The epicenter was somewhere in Prince William Sound, the impact felt as far away as Kodiak, where some areas of the coastline had been raised thirty or more feet. There was an underwater landslide in the Port of Valdez. A thirty-foot tsunami had destroyed a village. At the bottom of the page was a list of phone numbers, including a survivor of that village and the mayor of Anchorage.

Juliet blinked up at the men, huddled around the teletype. One million words arrived every hour, history being recorded as it was made. She had always marveled at the fact that they were able to witness the world almost as it happened. It made her feel at once small and larger than herself, a part of something greater.

She picked up the phone and dialed. It was moments like this, even in the face of tragedy, that she remembered why she wanted to be a reporter.

Several hours later, Juliet walked out of the *Times* building to the parking lot across the street. It was getting toward 11:00 p.m. on a Friday night. Downtown, so busy in the daytime, was now vacant.

She both heard the footsteps and felt them. Without glancing over her shoulder, she quickened her pace, reaching her car just as a body thrust itself against it. She opened her mouth to scream—someone had told her this was what she needed to do. A TV show. A magazine. Her mother, maybe. But then she saw it was Charlie Murdock.

Annoyance quickly replaced fear as she unlocked her door and pulled it open. He reached past her and slammed it close.

"What do you want, Charlie?"

"You think you're pretty clever, and I'll hand it to you. You're not stupid."

"If this is your idea of foreplay, I'll pass."

"See? That's what I mean. Clever." Only he wasn't laughing. "We're out a grand total of thirty-five hundred dollars thanks to you."

"Seems awfully expensive. Maybe you should find another place to drink." She kept her voice steady, even though the rest of her was not.

"Here's what I don't get. You acting like some schoolgirl, like a fucking nun when everyone knows—literally everyone knows—you're all about a good time."

She faded from color to black and white, from black and white to gray. She hated men like this because they reminded her that the world could be a cruel, ugly place, that she was, at best, a second-class citizen. And perversely, infuriatingly, they made her long for the arms of the Musician.

Juliet shoved past Charlie, managing to fling the car door open again. Before she could dive inside, he trapped her between the door and himself. In the dark parking lot, alone, the lights of the *Times* building behind her, his body seemed to expand.

Into her ear, he breathed, "Don't screw with me, Juliet Dunne." His breath was hot on her neck, her hair, her cheek. He didn't touch her, didn't need to, but as he pulled away, she could feel it—he had left a mark.

TWENTY-SIX

Eight days after the accident

K elly rose with the sun to rustle up breakfast—bacon, eggs, and his famous cheese grits—so that Guy would be fortified for his first day of filming. This was him trying to be there for Guy, but truth be told, Kelly was ticked off at James T. Aubrey and the machine that was CBS, at Del and Dinah Newman for always presuming their son's patience and good nature and his sense of duty to the family. And he was ticked off at Guy for not standing up for himself and telling Aubrey and the lot of them where they could stick their sham marriage.

But. *But.* His mind kept circling back to a teacher of his named Walter Wurley. This was in Missouri, when Kelly was in eighth grade, before his entire family moved to California so that he could become a movie star. Walter Wurley taught math, one of those educators who truly cared about educating and his students. By the time Kelly arrived in his classroom, he had been teaching for twenty-five years.

Until someone started a rumor that Mr. Wurley lived with a man. The rumors escalated, and one day, Kelly showed up at school to find Mrs. Mason, the home economics teacher, sitting behind Mr. Wurley's desk. She was there the next day and the next and all the ones after that. According to Kelly's dad, Mr. Wurley had been fired because, as a federal employee, the government believed he posed a threat to national security. Kelly imagined him creating diabolical mathematical equations and bombs in his basement, but of course, he'd done neither.

Two years later, a cousin in his former hometown told him that Mr. Wurley had closed his garage door one night and turned on the engine. Kelly went out that day and joined the Mattachine Society, which stood up for the rights of gay men and women.

Which was all to say that—as he stirred the grits and poured the coffee—Kelly was conflicted. Torn between wanting to support the man he loved and the privacy that protected them from hatred and prejudice, and wanting to tell him he was making the biggest mistake of his life. This wasn't taking Natalie Wood to Dan Tana's for a steak dinner. This was marriage.

When the food was ready and Guy still hadn't emerged from the bedroom, Kelly walked in to find him lying on the bed, clothes on, shoes on, staring at the ceiling.

"I can't do it," he said without moving. "Whatever I do, it's going to be wrong. It's not going to be the way Del would do it or the way the show's always done it or the way Aubrey wants it or CBS or our one remaining sponsor . . ."

"Or Wanda in Texas or Jim Bob and his kinfolk over in West Virginia or the Swansons up in Minnesota." Kelly settled against the doorframe. "There's no pleasing any of them."

"You're not helping." Guy's eyes remained on the ceiling.

"How about if I give you permission not to go? Let your mom and brother sort it out. You can stay right here and feel bad for yourself and never try anything again."

"Great pep talk."

"I'm not done. Or you can get your ass out of bed and go eat the food I made you so lovingly and drive to CBS and show them the way *you* do things. There's a reason this house is crammed full of books on directing. You are the most prepared person I know. And even if you don't believe you can do this, well—*I* believe you can."

He ambled over to the bed and stretched out beside Guy.

"But if all that's too much, I'll just lie here with you. Call Jack Warner, tell him to fuck right off, they can shoot around me."

Guy turned his head to look at Kelly. "I don't want to screw this up."

"I know. And you might. But you gotta start somewhere."

They lay there listening to the sound of the coffee percolating in the kitchen and the morning weather report playing on the living room radio.

"I was thinking," Guy said at last, "that we should have Eileen over for dinner. So you can get to know each other."

"Because you know her so well?" Kelly couldn't resist saying.

"I can't do this without you."

Oh, but you are.

Without another word, Guy stood up. As Kelly watched from the bed, Guy tidied his hair and tucked in his shirt and got himself ready for the day.

Shep emerged from an all-night session at the recording studio to find Lorrie sitting in her car. His instinct was to pretend not to see her, but the combination of Jack Daniel's and no sleep meant that he was moving slower than usual. He split off from the members of his band and planted himself in front of her Volkswagen, thinking, *Please just run me over.*

She got out, slamming the door, the sound of a coffin lid closing, burying Shep alive. "You didn't call me back. We need to figure it out, Shep. Babies cost money. Doctor appointments and diapers and formula and cribs. We need to figure out what we're going to do. Where we're going to live. What it means for this baby and me if you're not going to be part of it."

He wanted to ask if that was actually an option, to not be part of it, but instead, he let her talk until she'd said all she wanted to say. She wasn't, he realized, wanting answers—not really, not yet. She just wanted to yell at him because she was upset. And he got that. Boy, did he get it.

"You just need to grow up," she said once she was done. He wished everyone would make up their minds. *Grow up*, they all told him, yet they mostly treated him like a kid.

He and Lorrie made a date to talk about it further—really talk, no more of his "usual hemming and hawing"—and he watched her drive away. Then he began to walk down Sunset. To the north, the Hollywood sign glowed white against the hills. He wasn't sure where he was walking, just that he needed to move. He lit a joint he didn't want and then was stuck holding it. It would serve him right if it burned his fingers off and he wasn't able to play guitar ever again. But what did it fucking matter? Eileen would marry Guy, and Shep would be alone because one day he would be washed up and no one would remember him and by then his heart would have calcified so that he was incapable of loving anyone.

Someone caught up with him, huffing and puffing. Tommy Hutchins, better known as Hutch, his guitarist and friend. It warmed what was left of Shep's calcified heart to know he'd stuck around.

"I thought you guys broke up," Hutch said.

"I wanted to quit her," Shep told him. "But I can't. I'm in too deep."

The two of them walked along Sunset Boulevard for another few blocks, Shep's pulse starting to slow. And then he looked at his watch and saw the time and, without a word, turned around and started back the way he came. Shep thinking that with any luck Guy was going to kill him. Hutch thinking that he sure was glad he didn't have a sister.

Guy sat stewing, his neck broken out in a bright red stress rash that even Linda couldn't make disappear. Shep was two hours late. This meant that Guy had been forced to shoot out of order. He'd marked the script up so much it was indecipherable. "Shep Turns Eighteen." That was the new name of the episode. An enormous birthday cake sat melting beneath the lights waiting for the party scene, waiting for Shep to show up.

There were television shows that were rumored to be cursed—*The*

Little Rascals and *Superman* came to mind. Cast members dying tragically and young. Guy wondered if, after all these years, their time had come, if one day people would say the same about *Meet the Newmans*.

He could feel his mother's eyes on him, and he looked up. "Here," she said and placed a cool washcloth around his neck, the way she'd done when he was little and had a fever. "Go easy on Shep. He's upset about your dad, even if he doesn't fully realize it."

"He always does this. He only thinks about himself." Little drops of water fell from the washcloth onto the script. He didn't bother wiping them away.

Before Dinah could respond, the prodigal son himself strolled onto the set, eyes bloodshot and looking high as a kite. Guy could smell the booze from where he sat, and he was pretty sure Shep was wearing the same clothes he had on yesterday.

"You've got to be fucking kidding me." As Guy flew out of his chair, the washcloth fell to the floor. "You were supposed to be here two hours ago," he hissed at his brother.

In response, Shep opened his arms and hugged him tight. And then lifted him off the ground. Guy tried to pry himself loose, aware that the set had gone quiet.

"Put me down," he huffed, feet dangling.

Cast and crew stood watching the two of them with varying expressions of surprise and amusement. Shep hung on the way he had as a kid, not wanting to let go until his brother forgave him.

"And get your shit together. Show up when you're supposed to and be ready to go. We can't wait around for you to decide we're worth your time."

Shep's only reply was to carry him away from the lights and the cameras. After a few seconds of struggle, Guy managed to free himself and, as his little brother started to laugh, swept his legs out from under him—a move he'd learned on the football field. Shep landed flat on his back but then made a lunge for Guy, tackling his ankles and sending him sprawling.

As everyone looked on, they wrestled across the floor, one crawling off only to have the other pull him back. Over and over until Shep managed to break away. He wobbled to his feet and took off, eyes still on Guy—and ran smack into the birthday cake. Without faltering, he scooped a chunk off the top and hurled it at his brother. Guy was up now, frosting dripping from his hair, and grabbing his own fistful, which he launched at Shep. Back and forth they went until the four-layer cake was a three-layer cake and their mother shouted, "Enough!"

The brothers froze, blinking through icing-laced lashes at Dinah and the crowd—open-mouthed—just beyond.

"Both of you," Dinah thundered. "Clean yourselves up so we can get back to work."

With tails tucked between legs, Guy and Shep slunk away single file down the hallway that led to the dressing rooms, their mother's voice—apologizing to the cast and crew—fading as they went.

"Asshole," Guy muttered.

"Grandpa," Shep said behind him.

In the makeup room, Linda took one look at them and tutted. She handed them each a towel and told them she was going to fetch Roz, who was in charge of hair.

The boys sat side by side, doing their best to scrub themselves clean.

"You know," Guy said, eyeing his brother in the mirror, "someone's gotta be the grandpa so someone else can be the star. If it weren't for me, you wouldn't get to be Shep Newman. I make it possible for you to be you. But every now and then, it'd be great if instead of acting like a selfish prick, you paid attention to what's going on with everyone else."

Shep tossed the used towel into the laundry bin, a perfect free throw. "You mean like you and Eileen getting married? Like that kind of paying attention?"

In the mirror, Guy met his eyes and then looked away.

"Marriage," Shep said. "That's a pretty big step. I didn't know you felt that way about her. I thought she was just your on-screen girlfriend, and she hasn't been that for long. How well do you even know each other?"

"Well enough to marry her, apparently."

"So you're telling me the two of you—you and Eileen—you've been going out. Together."

"It's not going to affect the show. If that's what you're worried about."

"I don't care about the show."

"Of course you don't. You don't care about anything. You don't even care about Dad. You haven't been to see him once."

"Fuck you."

It was said softly, but Guy felt the sting. For the thousandth time in his life, he had the urge to get up and walk away from his brother, his family, the show. To drive home to Kelly and then to the desert, maybe, where the two of them could fall asleep on the ground, the stars shining above them—countless and limitless.

We get to do this, his dad always said. *It's a lifeline, not a deadline.* But how long had it been since he felt that way? If he really did marry Eileen, he would have to live with her, and Kelly would have to move out, and that would be that.

"Yeah, fuck you too," he said to Shep.

But the air had gone out of him, and the words were uttered softly, with familiarity. Not fighting words at all.

After a beat, Shep said, "Sorry I was late."

"You can't pick me up in front of the crew. It undermines what little authority I have."

"Unlike, say, engaging in a food fight."

Touché, Guy thought. "Also you need a shower."

"And you've got a . . ." Shep waved at the rash on Guy's neck. "You should really get that looked at."

Linda returned with Rozhin, better known as Roz, the child of immigrants, who, through her own hard work, had become one of the most sought-after hairdressers in the industry. Roz's eyes darted from one Newman to the other.

"Sometimes," she sighed, "I wish I'd become a librarian instead."

After Guy and Shep were put back together again, they were sent to Nathan in wardrobe. Once he'd replaced the soiled shirts with identical ones, they walked side by side down the long hallway toward the lights and voices.

"Listen," Guy said, "I'm going to see Dad tonight if you want to come with me."

"No thanks."

"Look, I know you're worried. I know it's hard. But you need to see him."

"Even when he's in a coma, you still kiss his ass. The perfect, dutiful son."

The only reason Guy swallowed down the words that came boiling up was that he and Shep had reached the set. Everyone was as they left them, the scene lit for the next shot, the cake restored, except for a small dent in the top layer. Dinah's expression said, *Keep the peace, you blockheads.*

"Hey." Shep was looking at Guy, his face gone serious. "Don't try to be Del Newman. Out there." He nodded at the set, the lights, the cake, the people waiting for them. "Be Guy Newman. Whatever that looks like."

"Thanks," Guy said, meaning it, and for the first time since they were kids he had the urge to hug him. When you had a younger brother who outshone you, you became grateful for any ounce of praise he directed your way, even if you couldn't stand him most of the time.

They saved the party for the final shot of the day. As the camera rolled, surrounded by his mother and brother and by the actors who played his friends, Shep made a wish and blew out the candles. The dented side of the cake was turned away from the camera. It took several takes, doing it again and again—lighting the candles, blowing them out—until Guy was satisfied.

Off camera, after they wrapped, cast and crew congratulated Shep and slapped him on the back, forgetting that he wouldn't actually be eighteen till the following week. When Tommy Hutchins asked what he'd wished for all those many, many takes, Shep's eyes went to Eileen. She looked up and then quickly looked away because that's how it was now. Her over there, keeping him at arm's length. Him over here, an entire world away.

"Just once," Shep told Hutch, "I'd like to celebrate my birthday on the actual day." It wasn't *the* wish but a wish.

Only Hutch understood what he meant. And while everyone else was raising a glass to Shep and throwing gifts at him, Hutch thought he wouldn't trade places with his friend for anything.

TWENTY-SEVEN

Nine days after the accident

Dinah and Juliet hadn't spoken since Thursday. When the telephone rang early Sunday morning, Dinah—in Del's office—laid a hand on the receiver, resisting the urge to answer right away. She'd imagined the scenario countless times over the past four days: Juliet calling to apologize as Dinah listened, forgave, and established new ground rules for moving forward on the script. *Rule one—we put the interview behind us and never discuss it again.*

On the fourth ring, she picked it up. "Hello?"

"We did it," Sydney said. "Well. Technically, *I* did it."

She sank a little at his voice. "Did what, Syd?" *Rule two—no more sharing of personal stories. The work comes first.*

"Procter & Gamble has agreed to help sponsor the finale!"

He crowed as he told her all about the deal he'd brokered, and how P&G, as he called them, might even consider sponsoring *Meet the Newmans* if they were renewed for a thirteenth season.

"Now what we need," he said, "is a script. A bang-up, blow-your-mind motherfucker of a script. The sooner, the better."

"Which is exactly what you'll get," she sang with forced confidence. Her relief over Procter & Gamble was being completely eclipsed by a feeling of *Oh shit.* "I've found a talented scriptwriter who's already hard at work."

They talked for a minute more, and before they hung up, Sydney said, "By the way, in case you haven't seen it, there's a piece about you in the *LA Times*."

Dinah found the newspaper at the end of the front walk, where it had been impaled on a bush. She approached it like a crime scene, ignoring the neighbor as he boomed hello from his yard.

There were her name and face splashed across the front of the Lifestyle section. There was the byline: *Juliet Dunne*. There was the headline: *An Interview with Dinah Newman*.

She stood on the lawn reading. It wasn't the version Juliet had shown her. It was a tamed-down, heavily edited piece, as sweet and fluffy as a meringue. Dinah felt both victorious and disappointed. She read it and then reread it before carrying it inside.

"Flora?" She followed the sound of running water until she found the housekeeper in one of the downstairs bathrooms, on hands and knees as she mopped the floor.

"Yes, Mrs. Newman?"

"Are you fulfilled?"

"What kind of question is that?" Flora sat back on her heels.

"Lately, I just . . . I realize I've never asked if you're happy in your work."

Flora returned to the mopping, shaking her head, clucking to herself. "I am always pleased with a job well done." Then she flicked her rag at Dinah's feet. "Shoo."

In that moment, Dinah missed her mother. The grief came and went, sometimes so sharp, like a knife twist, that she lost her breath. If it had been Penelope Shepherd here and not Flora, Dinah would have told her that lately she'd been feeling as if she'd woken up after a long sleep and realized that, for the past decade, she'd been coasting through her life. In an almost catatonic state. Going about everything like she had all the time in the world. Forgetting about any dreams she might've had once, and essentially telling other women to do the same.

What have I done? she thought.

"What's that?" Flora asked, and Dinah realized she was still standing there, in her way.

"Nothing, Flora. Thank you. And please, for god's sake, use a mop. It will be so much easier on your knees."

Dinah dropped the newspaper into the bathroom wastebasket and walked away, into the living room, where she stared down at the telephone.

It's important to give of yourself, her mother used to tell her. *But you have to keep something for you. Don't let them have it all.*

Part of her had hoped the *Times* would publish the version of the interview Juliet showed her. The real version. In some ways, it would have been a relief. So much of what Dinah hated about being a Newman was the pretense. It would be so nice not to pretend anymore.

On the other side of the hill, Juliet was in her apartment *not* thinking about Dinah Newman. Although Juliet's name appeared in the byline of the interview, it wasn't her piece. It was just an arrangement of words that meant nothing. It was Juliet doing what she'd *had* to do to keep her job. All the quotes Renee left on her desk from courageous women—how disappointed they would be in her. Almost as disappointed as she was in herself.

She flipped to the front page of the *LA Times* and reread her Alaska earthquake story, which *was* her piece but had been attributed to Nick. Then she tossed the paper aside.

She ate leftover Chinese food, straight out of the fridge. She tried to digest a few pages of the latest Marilyn French novel. She worked on the article about the Pill, most of it a blur except for one line, which wasn't even hers. It belonged to Simone de Beauvoir.

Her wings are cut and then she is blamed for not knowing how to fly.

When the telephone rang, she almost didn't answer it, but something made her pick it up.

"You didn't print it," Dinah said, by way of greeting. "The version you made me read. The one you were so high and mighty about. Why didn't you print it?"

"This was the only version they would publish."

There was silence from the other end of the line.

"Hello?" said Juliet. "*You* called *me*." She nearly slammed the receiver into its cradle.

But then Dinah let out a breath. "I've been going numb. For the past six months. I haven't lost all sensation, but it's more like a deadening. I went to the doctor and he did blood work, but everything is normal. Which means it's most likely psychological. I think there's some part of me—some part of me that needs more."

"Why are you telling me this?"

"Because I wasn't completely honest with you about Betty Friedan's book. I related to it more than I said. Too much of it, actually. There are whole sections of it that won't let go. And because you're right. If this is going to work, we need to be open with each other."

Now Juliet went quiet.

"Hello?" Dinah said, mimicking her.

"I get in my own way sometimes. I lose my cool, and I overreact. So. I'm sorry."

"I'm sorry too," said Dinah. "I'm a little touchy about being out of touch. And you're just so—young. And so relevant. And so ready to take on the fight."

"Well," Juliet said. She was learning that you couldn't always stand up for the things you believed in, no matter how vital they were.

"By the way, we just found out—the finale is fully sponsored."

"Well," Juliet said again, a little brighter. "Then I guess we have an obligation to write it."

After they hung up, Juliet stood in front of her living room window gazing out into the early evening, past the lights of Hollywood Boulevard and the hills, until she could see all the way to Indiana and her younger self. Then she sat down at her desk and opened her notebook—the one she'd bought just for *Meet the Newmans*.

While over in Toluca Lake, Dinah searched the kitchen cabinets for jars of Folgers, thinking of the sexist commercials Juliet had ranted about during their first script meeting. Flora always bought in bulk, as if feeding a family of twelve, and sure enough, there were six unopened jars arranged in a neat line. With a sinking feeling, as if knowing what she would find, Dinah pulled one out and examined the label. There on the back it read: *The Folger Coffee Company. A subsidiary of Procter & Gamble.*

She tossed the jars, one by one, into a trash bag and then carried the bag outside and dropped it in the metal garbage bin with a satisfying bang. Without their sponsorship, there would be no *Meet the Newmans*, and without *Meet the Newmans*, there would be no season finale, and without the season finale, there would be no chance to create something that would be remembered. But that didn't mean Dinah had to personally support a brand that didn't support women.

Confidential

MARCH 31, 1964

Where Is Del Newman?

The rumor around town is that **Del Newman**, America's Favorite Father, is missing. We have a source that says his family—wife **Dinah** and sons **Guy** and **Shep**—are being cagily silent about his whereabouts, and Guy has taken over the directing of the show. Our queries to the Newmans, executive producer **Sydney Weiss**, and CBS have gone unanswered, which leaves us drawing our own conclusions.

Wherever Del is, they don't want us to know.

While it's whispered that he's flown east to take care of his ailing mother, it appears that she died in 1951. So if it's true he's gone east, who was he really going to see? But if he didn't go east—as *we* believe—then where is he now?

In the meantime, the other Newmans appear to be doing just fine in his absence. **Oldest son Guy** and roommate **Kelly Faber** (Guy's Best Man . . . ?) took part in a civil rights protest down at Woolworth's on South Broadway and afterward were spotted at the Playboy Club on Sunset Boulevard. Noticeably absent were their usual dates, or any dates for that matter. Maybe these fellas prefer to go stag?

Teen idol Shep isn't about to settle down anytime soon, even though rumor has it he's spending a lot of time lately with someone named Mary Jane.

While **mom Dinah** has been spotted around town on the arm of **Sydney Weiss** (whom she dated before marrying Del).

Which leads us to ask—could there be trouble in paradise? Is America's Favorite Couple on the skids? And if so, what does this mean for America's Favorite Home?

TWENTY-EIGHT

Twelve days after the accident

On Wednesday, April 1, his actual eighteenth birthday, Shep Newman awoke in a strange bedroom with a strange girl. He was naked and the girl was naked, and she was snoring beside him. The night before, he'd talked to her about Carl Perkins, his idol, and then *On the Road* and Kerouac and the Beat Generation, who believed, as he did, in the truth of the heart. He'd tried in vain to spar with her the way he did with Eileen, but instead, she had listened with wide, shining eyes and claimed to have read not just Kerouac but Allen Ginsberg, William S. Burroughs, *and* Lawrence Ferlinghetti. Afterward, she'd invited him back to her place—he remembered, vaguely, something about UCLA and a sorority house.

He looked up at the walls of her room now—and instead of bookshelves lined with volumes by the Beat writers, there was his face plastered everywhere, across three walls, the fourth wall being taken up by windows. Shep smiling. Shep playing the guitar. Shep staring moodily into the camera. Shep in color. Shep in black and white. *Shep. Shep. Shep.*

It was an experience he'd had before, but that didn't mean it wasn't seriously weird.

He managed to pull on his jeans and find his shirt and his keys before she began to stir. He left the shoes—he guessed she wouldn't mind—and fled the room for the hallway, the stairs, down two flights, past closed doors with girls' names, Greek letters, his face, the faces of Paul McCartney and Elvis, his face again.

He managed to get to the front door before someone screamed *Shep Newman* and there was a pounding of feet and then he ran like hell, all the way to the street—where had he parked?—and then began to run faster, the girls behind him. He raced past a motorcycle, his motorcycle, and for a single heartbeat, he considered letting them have him.

What did it matter? His dad was comatose. His brother was marrying the girl he loved. There wasn't even a birthday cake to look forward to. In the eyes of the fans and the viewers, he had already turned eighteen. He couldn't remember ever celebrating his birthday off camera.

There'd only been one time on the show that it had fallen on his actual day. He was thirteen. He'd gotten the Harley-Davidson XLCH Sportster he'd been begging for and a cake five layers high. But only the bottom layer was real, and he'd had to send the motorcycle back because the studio wanted him to have a bicycle instead to please their sponsor—Schwinn.

He stood motionless on the street thinking about the disappointment of his thirteenth birthday and listening to the girls bearing down on him. Let them rip him to shreds. *What would it matter?* he told himself again. *Who would care?*

But then he thought of the album not yet finished and his unborn baby and *Eileen, Eileen, Eileen*, and he backed up, threw himself on the bike, and took off just as the throng of young women arrived, claws out, teeth bared, his name on their lips a long, high-pitched shriek.

He broke out in a cold sweat, the way he always did when this happened. He woke up sometimes, his own name ringing in his ears, the sheets tangled from fighting them off in nightmares. Who could he have taken this to? His dad, in a coma? His mom, in a world of her own? Guy, who wasn't nearly as famous? Hutch, who always looked on the bright side? Anyone would tell him to stop complaining about problems any red-blooded man would love to have.

And so he swallowed it down like he swallowed most everything and tried to think of a way to put the whole fucked-up situation that was his whole fucked-up life to music.

In Toluca Lake, Shep bypassed the guesthouse, not wanting to see Guy, if he was even home and not out somewhere making the moves on Eileen. A car he didn't recognize, a VW Beetle, was parked in the drive, but he went right on by. He opened the door to his parents' house and called for his mom, and when she didn't answer, he walked into the kitchen. Every year on April 1, Flora baked a chocolate cake with vanilla icing, his favorite. It sat on the counter now, as it always did, this time with eighteen candles. Next to the candles and the cake was a stack of messages. On slips of pink paper, in Flora's tidy handwriting, they read: *Lorrie called 10:15 a.m. Lorrie phoned 11:45 a.m. Lorrie 1:03 p.m.* On and on.

Shep dug through his pockets for his lighter and lit the pieces of paper. He tossed them in the garbage pail and watched them burn. And then he lit the candles one by one. The flames flickered like stars and he held his hand over them, feeling their heat. Closer and closer until they practically licked his skin.

Back when he was sixteen and performing at a sold-out Atlantic City Convention Hall, the venue had caught fire. He had felt the heat in his lungs. It had seared into him as if from the inside out, and the smoke had made his head go light and heavy at the same time. He'd thought, *This is it.* And then there was the sound of banging followed by splintering wood and a fireman had appeared, only Shep in his delirium saw a monster moving toward him in slow motion.

He had let himself be led through the tunnel of flames to the outside, where the monster had removed his helmet and asked for an autograph even as people screamed from inside.

They need you, Shep had said.

But the fireman just cradled his helmet under his arm and told Shep about his girlfriend's daughter who loved Shep Newman. That's all he heard the livelong day—Shep this, Shep that. The fireman told him boy, it sure would go a long way to get him in good with the girlfriend if Shep could help a buddy out and get him in good with the kid. The whole while, his fellow firefighters were racing back into the building and coming out with people in their arms and shouting at the guy to do his fucking job.

Shep jerked his hand away now and examined the blistered tip of his index finger. No one had died that night, but if they had, it would have been on him. Just like Del's accident was on him. If he hadn't goaded his dad, Del wouldn't have joined the football game. If he hadn't joined the game, he wouldn't have hit his head.

As the candles flickered, Shep thought of all the things he wished for and then settled on the most pressing—*Please don't let her get married.* Just like he had on set, he blew them out in one enormous breath, and then he cut himself a slice of cake and carried it to the backyard.

He circled the pool until he reached the deep end and climbed the steps to the diving board. He walked out until he stood at the very end.

There he ate the cake in three big bites as he stared at the mountains in the distance, dotted with light. He wiped his hands on his jeans. And then he shucked them off, down to his boxers, stepped off the edge, and dropped into the water.

When he came up, there was a figure standing on the side. Kelly, in swim trunks, looking like he'd lost his best friend. "I thought you might be Guy," he said.

"Not in a million years," Shep replied, flipping onto his back, letting the water carry him. Although there had been a time, not too long ago, when he'd looked up to his brother. Not to the point of wanting to trade places with him—it was more of an admiration, a recognition that they were destined to be two very separate people who happened to share parents and a single unique experience. Until Shep became the brother who sang and played music and the divide doubled in size. And then Guy became the one who got the girl.

All of this he was thinking as he floated across the pool. As he drifted past Kelly, he heard, "Hey, happy birthday, by the way."

Then there was a splash as Kelly dove into the pool and began to swim laps, each one more furious than the next, as if he were trying to outdistance something swift and deadly.

In the office over the garage, Dinah and Juliet watched Shep and Kelly from the windowsill. And then Dinah glanced up at the photo on the wall of the four of them by that same swimming pool, at the broad shoulders and laughing face of her husband.

"He had an accident. Del. He's in a coma in the hospital." Twelve little words. She had spent so much time worrying about saying them aloud, and now that they were out Dinah felt something inside her burst like a dam. She began to tell Juliet about the separate beds and the wall that had grown up between them without her noticing. Even as a part of her whispered, *She is a reporter. She will expose you and your family.*

Afterward, Juliet said, "I'm so sorry that happened. Not just the accident. But all of it." Her voice cracked with sincerity, as if she felt the ache as well.

Dinah sighed. "It never occurred to me to worry about losing myself. For so long, Del and I have been like one person, at least that's what I've always thought. Maybe that's not such a good thing. In that way, I did lose myself." She shook her head. "My husband is corny. It's one of the things that made me fall in love with him. The corniness you see on the show? That's real. As tough as he can be, he has a way of looking at the world. He has all these sayings. 'The only limits are those we put on ourselves.' 'They aren't deadlines—they're lifelines.' See? Corny." A broader smile this time. "That's why when Walter Kerr wrote that awful piece for *The New York Times*, it didn't bother me, because honestly, most of what he said is true. But that kind of thing devastates Del. Shep has that same thin skin. The two of them, they're the true artists in the family." She smiled, sad and wistful. "I could have killed Walter Kerr for hurting Del."

"'Writing well is the best revenge,'" said Juliet. "Dorothy Parker."

One week in, and the script still didn't exist. With just under three weeks to go, they had no story, no pages, no order—only a random, stream-of-consciousness collection of scene ideas, wild and rambling. Dinah waved a hand in the direction of the pile.

"Where do we start?" She felt a little hopeless. More than a little overwhelmed.

"The power of television," Juliet mused, "is that it pulls you into another world and makes you part of it, as if you know the people in there and they belong to you. I watched the episode that aired the week after Kennedy was shot, and the four of you—you went about your regular, everyday lives. It was like what happened to the president happened somewhere else. You might as well have been living on the moon."

Dinah waited for the point—for *here's where we start*. When Juliet simply sat there, Dinah said, "I think we felt—Del felt—that what viewers needed more than anything was normality."

"There's normality, and then there's out of touch."

Juliet slid off the windowsill and took a seat at the desk. She threaded a fresh sheet of paper through Del's typewriter and began to type.

"Interior. Newman house. Morning." She looked up.

With a dancer's grace, Dinah moved to the chair across from her. "Dinah takes off her apron." It was the first thing that came to her mind. "She drops it in the trash can and says, 'If I never see another ham loaf or veal cutlet again, it'll be too soon.'"

"Bigger," Juliet said, fingers flying across the keys. "She hands the apron to Guy as he and Shep enter the kitchen. 'Here,' she tells them—"

" 'I am not your hausfrau anymore.' "

Juliet frowned. " 'Hausfrau'? No one talks like that."

"I talk like that. Dinah talks like that. On the show."

Juliet looked at her.

"Fine." She sighed. " 'Here,' Dinah tells them. 'Your turn.' "

"And just like that," said Juliet, "we've begun."

Life

Shep Newman Comes of Age

America's favorite little brother is all grown up. This week Shep Newman turns eighteen. To commemorate the occasion, we asked him to tell us where he is now and where he hopes to be down the road. Here, unfiltered, is what he had to say. . . .

I love life, but it'll break you. All I ever wanted was to make music. Not the kind CBS wants me to make. I'm talking Carl-Perkins-on-a-bender kind of music. Son House, Robert Johnson kind of music. The kind that's like a needle in the vein. A magic carpet trip. A fucking mystical experience on a whole other plane.

There'll be a time when it ends. No more concerts. No more all-night recording sessions followed by early mornings on the set. No more autographs. No more screaming crowds. I can't wait. I think I'll feel good when it's over. I can't feel much worse. I'll still play music because that's what I love, only I'll play the music I want to play and not what everyone else tells me to play.

There's a big deal being made about me turning eighteen. It's like all of a sudden you're supposed to be twenty-five or thirty or whatever and someone says to you, *Okay. Now you're a grown-up.* Take my parents, though. They're in their forties and they still don't know what the fuck they're doing. Everybody thinks they have their shit together, but they don't. Trust me. They're just as fucked up as the rest of us.

Even when I was a kid, I wasn't a kid. I worked long hours. I promoted the show. I snuck cigarettes and drank coffee. I got into my dad's LSD, and for a while I liked it. I lost my virginity when I was fourteen to this girl with long hair and a tattoo of a dolphin on her ankle. She was dreamy. A real flower child before that was even a thing. She gave me some dope and we smoked it together to take the edge off, but there was no edge, because when you feel everything, you get real good at feeling nothing.

Have there been other girls? Plenty. Have there been other drugs? Sure. After a while, they blur together. Not the girls, not the drugs, but the experience, until you start thinking it's more about you than it is about them. What I mean is that it's about you running, always running away from yourself because you're not wild about who you are. Of course, it's hard to be wild about who you are when you don't even know who that is.

Think of all the roles we play every day depending on who we're with. All our different selves. Doing television is strange. It's strange to play yourself, especially when you don't recognize the person you're pretending to be. Making music is the only thing I'm really good at. It's where I'm most myself. But sometimes, even when I'm singing or playing guitar, I'm not so sure there is a real me. Maybe he doesn't exist. Maybe he's just someone created by his father and CBS for television and radio and records. A pretty face to sell pictures. Maybe that's all there is to Shep Newman.

I guess only time will tell. If I got the chance to do my own thing, I'd be grateful. Play my own tunes. Live my own fucking life. No rules. No expectation. Just me deciding me. There's this quote by Jack Kerouac. He says, "What is that feeling when you're driving away from people and they recede on the plain till you see their specks dispersing?—It's the too-huge world vaulting us, and it's good-bye. But we lean forward to the next crazy venture beneath the skies."

That's what I want. To see myself in the rearview mirror. To drive away from Shep Newman, teen idol. To lean forward to the next crazy venture.

TWENTY-NINE

Two weeks after the accident

The newest issue of *Life* magazine hit newsstands across the world on Friday, April 3, on a sunny, crisp morning that felt like fall. Readers were treated to a cover featuring a good-looking young man who sat on the edge of a dock staring out toward the horizon. His shirt was off. The top button of his jeans was undone. There was a tattoo on one bicep—the words *mad to live*. A cigarette dangled from his lips.

For Shep Newman, the image itself was an act of rebellion—a way to banish the boy-next-door persona his father had created for him. But as the magazine landed on doorsteps and newsstand shelves, that act of rebellion—depending on who you talked to—felt like a betrayal, a *fuck you* to the generation that had come before, not to mention Del, Dinah, Guy, and the studio that had birthed him.

Shep knew from experience that when you caused trouble, you had two choices—you could run away from it or you could own up to it. In his eighteen years, he'd done more running than owning, but with the arrival of *Life*, he decided he was going to head trouble off at the pass. As much as the piece had been about him, the fallout affected all of them, which was why he made his way to the executive wing of CBS and told James T. Aubrey's secretary he wanted to see him.

Before she could buzz the intercom on her desk, the man himself appeared, a copy of the magazine in one hand—rolled tight like a weapon—his face red with fury. "You," he said.

Inside the office, behind the slammed door, Shep took a seat on the arm of the couch. He thought back to times in the Hollywood High principal's office when he had denied everything. And other times when his father or Sydney had been forced to intervene on his behalf. *This ain't my first rodeo, bub.* The catchphrase he himself had coined when he was a rascally, precocious ten-year-old.

"What the fuck were you thinking?" Aubrey wanted to know. He was smoking ferociously now, as if the cigar were the only thing on earth keeping him alive.

"I was thinking I'd give an interview. Weren't you the one who said all publicity is good publicity? Oh, wait. That was Phineas T. Barnum."

"That," Aubrey said, "is debatable."

"I'm pretty sure it was Barnum."

Aubrey cast him a withering look. "It's debatable that this"—he threw the magazine across the room—"can be considered anything but a grenade hurled on a stockpile of ammunition hurled on a fire and doused in gasoline."

And then he started to rant. Shep pretended to listen. Yes, the show was in trouble. Yes, they would most likely be canceled soon. If not this year, it was coming. They all knew it was coming. But Shep was also very aware that his fan mail flooded the CBS mail room each week like a tsunami—tens of thousands of letters. And his current record sat at number six on the Billboard charts, right behind the Beatles, who were hogging up the top five spots. In addition, he was the only rock 'n' roll star at CBS Records, unless you counted Dion, which Shep did not.

More than all of that, he didn't regret the cover photograph or the things he said in the article. Not for a second. He would have given that same interview again if he could.

He didn't say any of this aloud. He just let Aubrey scream. And once he was done, Aubrey told him to get the hell out, but not before holding up a threatening finger, the smoke from the cigar rising over him like a storm cloud, and delivering one last warning.

"I am watching."

On the set, still happily oblivious, Guy Newman finally appeared to be in his element. Shep had to admit that the environment his brother was cultivating was more relaxed than their father's, the actors encouraged to offer suggestions on line readings and actions, the crew working with a kind of renewed vigor. Even Eugene Balboa, the pompous old goat of a cameraman, had stopped fighting Guy on every single take.

Today, the air felt momentous, partly because they were filming the party scene that would end in Guy's proposal, which meant both the regular cast and the background actors—except for Dinah, who wasn't needed—wore suits or dresses. And partly because in the twelve-year history of the show, the only kissing that had been done on camera was between Dinah and Del. Until now.

When Guy announced to the cast and crew that he'd added a kiss between Eileen and himself, Howie let out a wolf whistle. Shep shot him a look that shut him up quick. He and Eileen hadn't talked since the night he'd gone to see her at the Hollywood Studio Club, and the distance between them left him feeling strange and unmoored, like an abandoned boat drifting in the water.

As the cast members took their places, Shep stood a little to the side, which was where he always felt most comfortable unless he was holding a guitar. He tried to imagine a world in which Guy would understand why he'd said everything he said to that reporter at *Life* and why he told them to photograph him without a shirt and with a cigarette. It was about trying to carve out something for himself, but it was more than that. It was about finally staking a claim, saying, *This is who I am*.

He felt a tap on his shoulder. Eileen, wearing a dress that took his breath away. The top was sleeveless, black and fitted with a high collar, the skirt a cream color with a kind of netting over it, flowers stitched throughout. Her hair was pulled back in a ponytail. Her lips were painted red. Maybe it wasn't the dress that took his breath away. Maybe it was the girl.

She said, "Are you okay?"

She was asking about his dad without mentioning his dad since no one was supposed to know. Because Eileen Weld was considerate and thoughtful and a better person than he could ever be. *Don't do that*, he wanted to say. *Don't ask me how I am. It only makes things worse.* He didn't want her to show anything like care or interest, because it was easier if he could put her out of his mind the way he was trying to put Del out of his mind. If he didn't talk to Eileen, it was because she was just a work colleague, not someone he wanted but couldn't have. If he didn't see his father, it was because he was off somewhere on business, not laid up in a hospital.

"Earth to Shep," she said, a little smile on her face. It was a smile he'd only ever seen her give him.

He said, "Sure. I'm good." And looked away.

"I meant the *Life* article." She tilted her head and studied him. Then raised an eyebrow, waggled it. Fanned herself in a pretend swoon. "Pretty sexy stuff there, Shep Newman. Guy hasn't seen it yet."

"Are you telling me or asking me?" He hated the idea that she, as Guy's fiancée, would know something about his brother that he didn't.

"Neither," she said. "I'm guessing by how chipper he is."

The two of them watched as Guy moved—quicker and more sure of himself—around the set. Then, as if he knew he was being discussed, he yelled, "Places!"

Eileen looked up at Shep. "For what it's worth? I think there's a lot more to you than anyone knows." It was, in that moment, the loveliest thing anyone had ever said to him.

Distantly, he heard his brother call, "Action!" and watched as the fraternity party jumped to life, everyone dancing to an instrumental version of one of Shep's songs, which filtered through the stage speakers. The only records they ever played on the show were his, the only music that existed in their black-and-white world.

Guy strode up to Shep and, in character, said, "How about doing a favor for your big brother?"

"Depends."

"On what?"

"On who she is."

"She is her." He pointed to Eileen. "I promised I'd walk her home, but I can't leave before the party's over."

On cue, Shep gazed at Eileen for a beat too long. He blinked away, back to his brother, suddenly all smiles, eager to help. "Well, why didn't you say so?"

As he walked off, Guy called out, "A little less enthusiasm, please."

The next scene had Shep and Eileen strolling up the walk to her house, their pace slowing the closer they came to her front door. She wore his suit jacket over her shoulders so that he was in his rolled-up shirtsleeves. She was to turn away from him to put her key in the lock, and when she turned back, Guy would be there, down on one knee.

Eileen's arm brushed Shep's, just barely, and the feel of her skin was enough to send him through the roof.

"Gosh, it's a lovely night," she said.

"The loveliest," he agreed, sneaking a glance at her.

They slowed their pace even more until it looked as if they were walking in slow motion. This made them laugh, which was unscripted, but felt right and real, so Guy kept rolling.

When they finally climbed the steps onto the porch, Shep and Eileen looked up simultaneously at where the sky would have been. Standing with her like this, it was easy to forget that the rafters above them weren't the moon and stars.

As scripted, Eileen said, "Shep?"

Thanks for walking me home. That was what she was supposed to say before turning away from him to unlock the door. *Of course* was the next line, spoken by Guy. Followed by Eileen wheeling around to find him on one knee.

Instead, Shep said, "There's something I need to tell you." Which wasn't in the script.

And then he placed his hands on either side of her face, like she was made of glass, something to be protected, and kissed her.

Her lips were soft and sweet. Immediately, she was kissing him back, and for a few glorious seconds, Shep lost himself in her. He felt her arms reach for him, one hand resting on his shoulder. Distantly, he heard his brother yell, "Cut!" Heard Howie, Clint, and the rest of them start to cheer and whistle. Heard Hutch pick out a guitar lick to a song of his called "You Are the Only You for Me."

Finally, they broke apart and stood looking at each other. Everything but the two of them had faded away.

"Eileen," he said. It was hard to read her face.

And then she was shaking her head, as if she was attempting to shake herself awake from a spell, and suddenly Linda was there, powdering her nose and cheeks, reapplying her lipstick, and all the while Eileen kept her eyes on his.

In front of everyone, Guy yanked his brother aside. "What the hell were you thinking?"

Shep still felt the burn of Eileen's skin against his own. "I was thinking," he said, "that it's time Pop stops being the only one calling the shots. And that it's time you and I get out from under his shadow. Something I thought you, of all people, would understand."

She found him after in the parking lot, and the two of them sat in silence watching the traffic. Shep thought he could be content to sit here like this with her for the rest of his life.

But then Eileen said, "We shouldn't have done that."

We. Not *you.*

"It complicates things that are already complicated," she said.

He stared down at her hand, which was right there. He wanted to take it in his own, but then she pulled away, moving it out of reach.

I think I love you, he wanted to say. *But I have no idea what that means.*

They sat like that a moment more, and then she stood and looked at him, her eyes dark and sad as she delivered her line. "Thanks for walking me home, Shep Newman."

And as he watched, she climbed into her car and drove away.

Woman's Own

APRIL 6, 1964

Dear Young Brides

by Dinah Newman

As I prepare for my son's on-screen wedding, here is some advice on how to have the perfect engagement and ceremony. Marriage is a giddy, exciting time, and it is only too easy for young people in love to overlook these little details. But I am here to help!

• Don't put every penny you have into your special day. It's not too early to start a nest egg! Talk to your groom about realistic expectations. Compromise your own grandiose visions if necessary. The important thing is that the two of you love each other!

• Before, during, and after the wedding itself, do not give into the temptation to display your love for each other in public. Too many affectionate embraces will only embarrass those around you!

• When socializing with others prior to the wedding, make sure to do so *only* with other females unless your groom-to-be is there too! It does not look good for you to go dancing or to a party with men who aren't your fiancé even if they are just part of your crowd!

• At your wedding reception, serve plentiful refreshments to your guests, but nothing too heavy or indulgent. The last thing you want is an empty dance floor because the guests are feeling bloated! I recommend a nonalcoholic sherbet punch, ambrosia salad, a pecan cheese log, coffee, and cream cheese mints. I served this at my own wedding and there wasn't a single wallflower in sight!

• After you cut the wedding cake, wrap a piece in tinfoil and sleep with it under your pillow for good luck!

• On the honeymoon, lingerie is not only expected, it's encouraged. Once you're home, invest in pretty slips and girdles, and—if you must dress comfortably—a fetching housecoat.

• Don't forget to douche. Every husband, old or new, wants his wife to be feminine, which means you have a responsibility to keep yourself clean and fresh. Yes, a dab of perfume behind the ear is important, but don't neglect your delicate insides.

• Invest in an elegant, quality stationery set and send thank-you notes promptly upon your return. No one likes a tardy Tessy!

THIRTY

Sixteen days after the accident

Dinah knew nothing about comas other than what she'd learned over the past two weeks. When Dr. Carson said, "The swelling in his brain has gone down—I'd like to bring him out of it," she pictured taking Del home with her that very night. Until the doctor told her it would be a process and that it could take days for the sedatives to wear off, that even when they did, Del's first signs of consciousness might be a simple instinctive reaction to light or sound. Blinking. Moving a finger. Twitching his mouth.

"His responses will be slow," Dr. Carson said. "But we will bring him back."

That evening, alone in Toluca Lake, Dinah poured herself a drink. She took two aspirin, kicked off her shoes, and helped herself to the leftover cake in the fridge. Suddenly ravenous, she laid down her fork and ate with her hands. The taste of icing on her tongue, the jolt as the sugar hit her bloodstream, the simple pleasure of it.

Her emotions were a mix of elation and worry. The ache in her heart, which had been there since the accident, was lighter and weightier at the same time. Del had survived. *We will bring him back.* She imagined him here, where he belonged, at the studio, where he belonged. Del, recovered. Del, in charge.

She carried the glass of gin into the den and put on a record, one of her old ones. An album called *He's the (Golly Gee) Guy for Me.* She cranked up the music—at once a celebration and an attempt to silence her busy, whirling mind. Del coming back was a good thing. The best thing. The thing she most wanted. She was happy. So happy. She wasn't worried about what it meant for the script. For the time she'd spent with Juliet. For all they were hoping to do.

She started to hum and then to sing along with her recorded voice, which sounded so painfully, enthusiastically, stupidly young.

The louder her thoughts, the louder she sang, throwing out one long leg. Then the other. Choreography from a movie she'd made at— *god*—eighteen or nineteen. She involved her arms, her hips, her legs again until she ran out of moves she remembered.

Then there, on the soft carpet, she started to twist. When the gin sloshed onto her arm and onto the rug, she set the glass down and shook her hips, twisting all over the room. *Did they still do the twist?* She wasn't sure. She morphed into the swim and then the jerk, and then combined them into one spectacular dance, the choreography all her own.

She felt like the Tin Man, rusted and in need of oil, but with every move, she grew a little less creaky. Her body was remembering, and soon, she was moving with maybe not the old gusto but something close to it.

As another song played and then another, Dinah shook off all she was carrying—shook it right onto the rug—until it wasn't a part of her any longer.

At some point, distantly, there was the ringing of the telephone. She turned up the music and ignored it.

Ever since the *Life* article, they'd been barraged by interview requests. As far as Shep was concerned, he'd already talked about himself and done what he'd set out to do. Dinah had so far managed to avoid the wrath of Sydney, but it wasn't as easy to dodge Aubrey. He had booked her on *Art Linkletter's House Party*, another CBS show, to do damage control. She agreed to it only to appease him and his growing questions—*When is Del coming back? Isn't there anyone else who can take care of his mother? Doesn't he know he has a goddamn show to run?*

Eventually, the ringing stopped and then started again. She wanted to turn the music up louder or yank the line from the wall, but a voice inside said, *It could be the hospital. It could be about your husband.*

"Hello?" she breathed, the receiver in one hand, the other reaching to turn off the record. For a few seconds, her voice sang on until she was able to flick the switch. "Sorry. Hello?"

"It's Syd." And then he launched into an earsplitting rant about *Life* magazine and what in the name of hell had Shep been thinking and had she seen the latest ratings, which were their lowest to date. *Sixty-eighth.*

After about five minutes of this, he finally told her the thing he'd actually called to say. "Procter & Gamble has dropped us. And so has Listerine."

She was surprised by Listerine, but the Procter & Gamble thing stung. It was like being broken up with by someone she hadn't even wanted to date in the first place.

"They only just took us on," she said. And then, in the next breath, "Well. We'll just find someone else." She would not be sorry over this. Folgers should be sorry. Procter & Gamble should be sorry.

"Who?" Sydney roared. "Tell me who. Because as far as I can see, there's no one left. We've exhausted our options. And now we need *two* sponsors, not just one. I don't know what the fuckity fuck fuck we're going to do."

As he fumed on, Dinah felt herself go surprisingly calm. Yes, *Meet the Newmans* was back where they had started. Further back, actually, given that now they had *no* sponsors and they would have to pay for the finale themselves. Yet somehow they were light-years ahead of where they had been.

In Del's office, Dinah rummaged through the drawers of the file cabinets and the desk. She had always thought of her husband as organized, but when she couldn't find their financial records, she wondered how well she knew him after all. *This is your fault too,* she told herself. *You should have been more involved. Instead you just handed everything over to him.*

The office closet was stuffed with old props and keepsakes and other memorabilia from their years on the show. The collection continued downstairs in the garage, spreading like a virus into bins and boxes and old wooden crates that read *CAL-CREST, Finest California Oranges.* She recognized some of the keepsakes from their early days together, just the two of them, and the boys' childhoods. Love letters written during their first year of marriage, when they were apart on separate film sets. Guy's baseball glove and baseball cards. Shep's lasso. Guy's football cleats. Shep's first guitar. Family photographs and albums. Old children's books—*Curious George*, *Pippi Longstocking*, *Stuart Little*, *Adventures of Huckleberry Finn*. The covers were worn, the pages yellowed. She thought of Shep insisting on reading, even when he didn't know all the words, and Guy pretending to pay attention because his little brother demanded an audience.

She stood on tiptoes as she returned the books to the shelf, and then she saw the shoeboxes lined up against the wall in neat stacks. They were labeled by year, going back to 1956.

She sat on the floor of the office, covered in bank statements and credit card statements and receipts, as if the ceiling above her had rained down paper. There was no question, she had thought there would be more money. The amounts in the accounts were much, much lower than she'd expected. As in worryingly low. So low that she wondered if they'd been robbed. She thought immediately of a bank teller in North Carolina who had impersonated another man and stolen his life savings.

For the past two decades, there'd been no shortage of money. At some point, she'd stopped thinking about how much she spent or what she spent it on. Sitting here, at forty-two—*forty-three*—she was no longer that sixteen-year-old girl who, once upon a time, saved up all her earnings from babysitting and working at the local hardware store so that she could come to California to live in a tiny studio apartment with two roommates and wait tables while she studied and auditioned.

She reached for another box. This one wasn't a shoebox like the others. It was a cardboard candy box with a cartoon image of the Newman family. *The Newmans love Peter Paul Almond Joy.* There was Shep with a guitar next to a grinning Del and Guy, and there she was in her apron and pearls. Those fucking pearls. It was amazing they hadn't choked her by now.

Inside the box was a deed to a house. In Del's name. And copies of checks, dated monthly, addressed to *M. Leslie.* The checks went back twelve years, the exact amount of time they'd been on television.

Mary Leslie. Marie Leslie. Miriam Leslie . . .

Could this M. Leslie be someone Del was having an affair with? Was she the person he'd been going to see the night of the accident?

Her stomach heaved, and for one awful minute, she thought she was going to be sick. She stared into the Almond Joy box and waited for it.

She pictured another wife, another life. Possibly other children. She saw him giving piggyback rides and bandaging scraped knees, bringing his other wife flowers on Mother's Day, perfume and lingerie on her birthday. He would tuck her hair behind her ears, the way he did Dinah's. He would make up outrageous bedtime stories, and they would go on car trips to Big Bear Mountain or the desert.

He would tell this other wife that he loved her best. No, that he loved her and only her, that he'd never loved another woman. When she asked about Dinah, he would laugh. *That old hag,* he'd say. *Her best years are behind her.* The other wife, who Dinah imagined was much, much younger, would beg him not to go back to Dinah and the boys. *Stay with me,* she'd whisper as she lay in his arms. *You don't need them anymore.* He would kiss her and agree, and Dinah would never see him again. They would find her here in his office, her body buried beneath a mound of paper.

Don't borrow trouble, her mother used to say. But that is exactly what Dinah did. She sat. She stewed. And, after a while of this, she gathered the files until they were stacked in a neat, angry pile, and then she stood up, smoothed her dress and her hair, and phoned Sydney.

"Sydney Weiss."

"Syd, it's Dinah again. What do you know about a person named M. Leslie?"

"Emma Leslie?" He was somewhere loud, the sound of music and people in the background.

"*M* as in the initial. Last name Leslie."

"If it's a person, I have no idea who that is."

He sounded like his usual impatient self.

"There are all these canceled checks dating back to 1952. There's also a house." She reached for the deed. "I don't recognize the address. But I need to get my hands on any additional statements, anything you can—"

"It could be an investment property, a place he rents out."

"There's no record of rental payments coming in."

"Why don't I come over there tomorrow and take a look."

"No offense, Syd, but I've looked. You're his business partner. You should have been on top of Del, on top of the money—"

"No offense, Di, but that's not my job. I'm a producer, not an accountant."

"Clearly." She slammed down the phone. She was angry. Not so much at Sydney or the sponsors for not having balls enough to honor a business deal. Not even at James T. Aubrey. She was angry with her husband, who had left her alone with all this mess.

She had a strange urge to call Juliet. Instead, she left the office and went down the stairs into the main house. When she reached the kitchen, she opened the freezer door, stuck her head in, and stood there until she cooled down.

The truth was she might never find out who M. Leslie was or why Del owned a house at 156 Fraser Avenue in Santa Monica, because Del might never wake up. He would be gone and would take M. Leslie with him.

THIRTY-ONE

Seventeen days after the accident

T he city was just beginning to stir, lights blinking on, the sky over downtown glowing pink and blue. Juliet tried to focus on the beauty of the sunrise, but the pink made her think of Jackie Kennedy's suit, covered in her husband's blood.

Before she realized where she was going, she had driven up into the hills. And then she was turning onto Wonderland. Behind the faint mist that had settled over trees and houses, the canyon looked heavy-eyed and quiet.

In the car, she sat for a few minutes outside the Musician's bungalow, which twinkled with the fairy lights they'd strung up when they first moved in. It had been a hot July night, sticky and star-filled. No breeze. No relief from the heat. The two of them had lingered outside naked, drinking cold beer and making up nonsense lyrics, because the heat had affected their brains. The sound of a piano floated toward them. Mama Cass lived up there, the earth mother of Laurel Canyon, the canyon itself an oasis where you were welcome anytime, and were at home with people who loved and accepted you, no matter what.

The Musician had said, "I like this place. It gets me."

And Juliet knew exactly what he meant.

He had wrapped her in strands of lights, and then she had wrapped him in lights, the two of them twinkling and shining and twirling about until they were breathless from laughing. It was in those moments that she felt her breath catch and her heart catch, and she knew she would never truly leave him, not even when she left him—finally, definitively—one day. She had never in all her life felt so happy.

Since the breakup, there had been other men here and there. An actor from London—charming and pomaded—who turned out to be married with kids. A bearded screenwriter who loved to hear himself talk. A carpenter who built sets for Warner Bros.—not her usual type, but the *aw shucks* smile swayed her. He'd seemed sincere until, without warning, he stopped returning her calls. Disappointment after disappointment, until she stopped dating altogether.

Now she found herself walking up the drive, across the grass and the gravel. She didn't knock, just let herself in and followed the sound of a guitar. It led her onto the back porch, which looked out over the canyon. The Musician was alone and barefoot, shirt loose and unbuttoned, long curling hair like a cloud around his face. The beads that pressed against her flesh in the shower, that dangled over her as they moved together in the dark, were hanging from his neck.

Juliet stood for a moment listening to him. Even though she'd given up all rights to him last spring when she broke it off, she was more relieved at finding him alone in their house than she liked to admit.

When he looked up, she said, "What do you think of Shep Newman?" It was the first thing that came out. She waited for him to be dismissive, the way he was about almost everyone who wasn't one of the blues greats—Lead Belly, Son House, Muddy Waters. His heroes.

He gazed at her, lips parted, joint dangling from his fingers. Even though he was looking at her, she knew he was looking beyond her at the question.

"He's more talented than people give him credit for. His songs are pretty layered, guitar work is decent." He shrugged, indifferent, then took a drag on the joint. "But his voice, man." A flicker behind his dark eyes. "It's older than he is. He's what, just a kid, right? Seventeen, eighteen?" The Musician was all of twenty-seven. "His voice contains worlds."

She could hear a whiff of envy. The Musician's own singing voice was raspy and distinctive, infused with electricity just like he was, something that made him a great front man for a rock band. But Shep's voice contained something extra she couldn't quite put her finger on. As if he had lived many lives.

"Don't tell me you're leaving me for him."

"I've already left you."

"Yes and no," he said and grinned.

Juliet opened her mouth to argue, but she couldn't, because here she was. Also, the grin was disarming. The grin was what had first drawn her in. It was equal parts warm and wicked, like he knew a secret about her, something dirty but harmless.

She had come here tonight to tell him she was working on a project that would keep her from losing herself, the way she had lost herself in him. But he began to pick a tune on the guitar, slow and seductive. It was different from anything she'd heard him play before, and she was momentarily captivated.

"What is that?" she asked.

"It's new."

He held out a hand then, beckoning her over. Juliet thought of a million things she should do instead—leave, go to work, go home, go anywhere else but here. But instead, she joined her hand with his and let him pull her over so that she was next to him, their legs pressed against each other's, close enough to breathe him in.

"I miss you," he said. He laid the guitar aside, balancing the joint precariously on top of it. "I miss us."

They were impossible, she thought. There was no way it could work. Only in private, if it could be strictly the two of them—no bandmates, no public, no press. But he didn't belong just to her, and they were in different orbits with different trajectories. She imagined telling him now about Dinah Newman and what they were trying to do, but it was easier to let it be.

"Me too," she said and left it at that.

She is every color as she shines,
As she shines,
She is lit up by the sun
And she is mine,
She is mine

After he'd played her the entire new tune, he looked at her in a way that let her know she was still here with him, his present. While he was her past. *This will be the last time you come up here*, she told herself. She was a feminist, for fuck's sake. What had the press called her? *A witchy wood nymph, a seductress, a slut, a murderess muse.*

"Don't put my name in this one," she said.

"Hey now." When he wasn't singing, that famous voice was soft and rumbling. It was, she thought with a pang, one of her favorite sounds. It was a birdcall in the morning on a bright, blue day. It was the hypnotic rhythm of ocean waves outside a window. It was sweet music from somewhere close by, the kind that made you think of childhood and summer days and freedom.

He took her hand in his, and she watched as their fingers intertwined. She had known him in another life. Anything she felt in this life was merely a lingering. That's what she told herself. Yes, she still loved him. Which made everything so much easier and so much harder at the same time.

THIRTY-TWO

Eighteen days after the accident

On April 7, Juliet and Renee stood over the teletype reading the stories as they arrived across the wire. In Ohio, a minister had been killed by a tractor during a civil rights protest. In Chester, Pennsylvania, so many demonstrators were marching against segregation in public schools that the city had deputized trash collectors and firefighters to assist the police force. Alan Gartner, the chairman of the Congress of Racial Equality, predicted that the summer would be one "of great and anguished violence."

There were still things to celebrate. The *Los Angeles Times* reported that public support for Kennedy's—now LBJ's—Civil Rights Bill had risen. The Beatles announced their first world tour. (Today, Renee wore black and white, her nod to their tailored black suits, though hers was a wild checkerboard pattern paired with green tights and silver boots.) And the World's Fair was coming to New York, the theme *Peace Through Understanding*. Yet the world felt anything but peaceful. It felt, for good or bad, awake.

For much of the morning, Juliet and Nick worked on a story about the thirteen women murdered by the Boston Strangler between June 1962 and January of this year. They wanted to remind the public that these women were more than "victims"—that they had been living, breathing human beings with loved ones and lives. Women as young as nineteen and as old as eighty-five. Anna Slesers was a seamstress and a mother, Nina Nichols a physiotherapist, Helen Blake a nurse, Patricia Bissette a receptionist who was one month pregnant.

Investigative journalists Loretta McLaughlin and Jean Cole Harris were the first to connect the murders for the *Boston Record American*, and it was McLaughlin who had coined the name "the Boston Strangler." Even though Juliet didn't know them personally, she felt a sense of pride at the work they had done. They inhabited a small, elite sphere of female reporters that she herself aspired to join.

"Look at this." Nick sprang from his chair and set something in front of her. As Juliet studied the newspaper clipping, he leaned over her, and they read together. *The stocking was the instrument of death.* Each of the women had been strangled with articles of their own clothing, and this seemed to Juliet the most chilling detail of all.

Hours passed. These were the days she loved—the two of them chasing leads and sharing information, discussing angles and inroads, how to find the heart of the story, humanizing the victims. Days like this made her forget about the News page and focus on becoming an investigative reporter. She left the desk only to get a cup of coffee. When she returned, Nick was answering her phone.

"*LA Times*, Juliet Dunne's desk."

He flashed her a cheeky smile, and she wondered, as she had before, what might have happened if she and Nick had met somewhere else, if they weren't work colleagues. He was handsome and smart and kind and insightful. His punctuation was shit, but he was a good writer, and most vital of all, he cared.

"Yes, she's right here." He was still looking at her, but his expression had shifted to one of surprise. "Of course, no worries. . . . She'll be right down."

He hung up, folded his hands, and said, "Dinah Newman is downstairs. Care to tell me now or later?"

"Later."

Juliet took the elevator, trying to imagine what on earth Dinah was doing here when they were supposed to meet later that evening. The only thing she could think was that something had happened with Del.

The elevator was crowded and stopped on every floor, people taking their sweet time getting on and off. When at last the doors opened onto the lobby, she spied Dinah immediately in dark glasses and a trench coat, standing by the door.

"You look like you're in a Hitchcock film," Juliet said to her.

"Not here."

Juliet followed her outside into the day, and when they were two blocks from the *Times* building, Dinah began to talk. "We lost the sponsors. Procter & Gamble and Listerine—they've dropped us. And apparently, my husband has been paying money to someone named M. Leslie every month—a salary, child support, I don't know—and he also owns a house in Santa Monica that I never knew about. And now, on top of everything else, there are the hospital bills. So who knows if we can even afford a finale, much less groceries and gas for the car? I'm sorry, I had no right to involve you in any of our mess, and it is a mess, a much bigger mess than I ever knew. I don't know if I can keep paying you, much less afford to fund the show, which means—which means—"

"The money doesn't matter, at least not for me. It was never about the money. It's about what we're doing." Juliet found herself talking as fast and feverishly as Dinah. "We've come this far. We can still—"

"I'm not sure we can. Even if we find a sponsor, I don't know that I have it in me."

"You'll survive this," Juliet told her. "*Life* magazine. If that's really why . . . It hasn't even been a week. Take it from me. I've survived way worse."

"This isn't about *Life*." Dinah emitted a short bark of a laugh. "Well, maybe it is about life, but not *Life*. I'm not sure the Fates want me to be a revolutionary."

Juliet told her about Estelle Griswold, who had opened her clinic in direct defiance of the law and smuggled people across state lines so they could get abortions or birth control. And Dr. Mary Calderone, Planned Parenthood's first female medical director, who, at thirty, enrolled in medical school despite being a divorced mother of two. And Lucille Ball—just think of all the important strides she'd made for women.

She strained to think of other people, heroes of hers, who might change Dinah's mind—Margaret Sanger, Zora Neale Hurston, her friend Renee, even Paula Goodman. She told her about Anna Slesers, Patricia Bissette, and the other Boston Strangler victims. She told her about Loretta McLaughlin and Jean Cole Harris.

But Dinah simply stood there, unmoved and unmoving. And then Juliet had an idea.

"We can talk to women—regular, everyday women—so we get a better idea of the impact we might make. We could interview them. We could interview them *together*. I have a friend in New York; she's part of this consciousness-raising group where they discuss and debate women's issues."

Juliet had never felt part of a group. Not at the newspaper. And not with the girlfriends and wives of the Musician's bandmates. In this moment, on this street, she suddenly yearned for the deep and meaningful companionship that something like this could give her. It was, she thought, what she'd been missing. Women as allies. Women as champions of one another. Juliet's mind caught hold of this and started to run.

"We create our own version of that. We ask them what they're up against, the things they'd change if they could. We create the dialogue I wanted our interview to be. . . ." Juliet could see it so clearly, but Dinah just stared at her. And so Juliet said, "'She stood there until something fell off the shelf inside her.'"

Dinah blinked, expression blank.

"From *Their Eyes Were Watching God*. My friend Renee, she writes down these quotes by inspiring Black women and leaves them on my desk. That's how I feel, like something has fallen off the shelf inside me and I can't put it back. I don't want to put it back."

"No," Dinah said. "I'm sorry."

"You're doing it again. You're shutting me out. Like a goddamn yo-yo. We're on, we're off, we're on, we're off." *Like the Musician*, she thought. "But I'm your partner here. You may be paying me or not paying me—at this point, I don't really care—but I'm one half of this team, and I should have a say."

"I'm sorry," Dinah said again. "I'll get you the money I owe you." Then, as if she were being chased, she hurried away.

As Dinah rounded the corner from First Street onto Spring, her pulse quieted as if she had just dodged something fatal. She brushed at a stray piece of hair, and as she passed a newsstand, there was her face and Guy's face and Shep's face and Del's face. All their faces staring back at her.

She didn't wait to go home. She marched to the nearest pay phone, where she called Sydney and told him that all future articles purporting to be written by her must be run past her first. And then she slammed down the receiver and watched as the sky opened and the rain began to pour. She listened to it drumming against the roof of the phone booth like a thousand hammers banging a thousand nails. And then she opened the door and stepped out into it.

As she returned to the newsroom, Juliet was greeted by the sound of laughter. Charlie Murdock, with feet up, lounged at his desk with a couple of other reporters, talking out of one side of his jaw the way he always did, perfectly secure in his place in the world.

Something inside her snapped. She was fed up with fucking everything. She loved the Musician, but she didn't want to love him. Dinah had ended their partnership, just like that. Being a woman in 1964 was legally like being a child.

For all these reasons, she marched over to the men—no more than a gossipy, middle-aged coffee klatch, like the one her mother belonged to back in Indiana.

Charlie smirked. "Is there something you need, Dunne?"

"No," she said. "Actually, just this, and you should probably hear this too." She nodded at Phil and Gregory and the others. "Do not follow me or any other woman as she's walking in the dark by herself. We're already conditioned to be afraid. Don't intentionally threaten us. Do not try to cop a feel without our permission. Do not make sexist, degrading comments about our bodies or us in general to try to make us feel smaller than you, because we aren't smaller than you and you'll only make it clear to everyone else that you are the small one."

She couldn't resist glancing at his crotch.

"And by the way? You can sing that song all you want." She directed this at all of them, not just Charlie. "It was written by a man you could never understand, because you and he are different species. The song only reminds me all over again of the kind of person I deserve. And the kind of person who isn't worth my time."

As she walked away, Juliet caught Renee's eye. Behind her typewriter, Renee raised both arms like a boxer, like Muhammad Ali winning the World Heavyweight Championship, and Juliet couldn't help it—she swaggered all the way to her chair.

THIRTY-THREE

Eighteen days after the accident

When Kelly first moved to Los Angeles, he'd bought a tourist map of the city that divided it into areas—here was where the Japanese lived, there was where the Koreans lived. This was the Jewish sector. These were the Mexican neighborhoods. The Blacks were here and here. So that, apparently, you could identify which parts were "safe and civilized." When he asked someone, sarcasm dripping from his big-sky Missouri voice, "What about the homosexuals? Where are they?"

"Brother," he was told. "They're everywhere."

He had thrown the map away and sought out the places people warned him about. The jazz clubs of South Central Avenue, the Chicano dance halls of Boyle Heights. He joined the Non-Violent Action Committee, which picketed businesses like Woolworth's, Thriftimart, Ralphs grocery, and Bank of America for employment discrimination based on race.

They staged sit-ins and shop-ins and what they called *sip-ins*. Protestors were often arrested, and sometimes there was violence against them. Kelly longed for something more—other men like him advocating for the right to love freely—but the Mattachine Society, at least as it existed in Los Angeles, wasn't confrontational. And so he fought for the rights of other repressed groups. Which was why, on the evening of Wednesday, April 8, he stood with a dozen other N-VAC members outside Van de Kamp's, a wholesome family establishment that refused to pay Black and Hispanic employees—when they hired Black and Hispanic employees—as much as their white coworkers.

Kelly and the others carried signs—*Freedom Now!* And *No one is free till everyone is free*—and marched up and down outside the front doors. It was peaceful and organized. Like a hundred other protests he'd taken part in, each one similar yet different. It was the energy that separated them and linked them—that feeling that you were risking everything for something that mattered more than you did.

The night was a cool one, and underneath his jacket, Kelly wore the GAY IS GOOD shirt he'd hand stenciled earlier that afternoon. Of all Kelly's many selves, this was the one he didn't show most people. There was the Kelly that got a lot of satisfaction from the work he did and understood that the only way to continue doing that work was to pretend he was something he wasn't. There was the Kelly who loved Guy Newman, who had built an entire world with him inside the Newmans' guesthouse. There was the Kelly who had been raised in Missouri by two conservative parents who, in spite of their beliefs, were loving and kind. There was the Kelly who was, at heart, just a self-proclaimed country hayseed who thought he could be happy roping cattle and living on a ranch somewhere in Montana.

It was important to all of these Kellys that he wear the shirt, even if it stayed zipped beneath his jacket. Just like it was important to him that Guy be there to join the picket line. It was, he felt, the least he could do, given the engagement to Eileen and his recent absences from home.

Guy was trying to fill his dad's shoes and satisfy the CBS publicity machine, all while keeping the show afloat and, most of all, protect Kelly and himself. Kelly understood all that. But Guy not being on the picket line right now was, in his book, just another excuse. The things that were taking up Guy's time weren't real. Sure, his career. But the engagement to Eileen was a whole other animal. It was a deception that went beyond a dinner date with a movie starlet. This was inventing a story and putting it out there, bold, purposeful trickery. While Guy and Kelly being forced to disguise their relationship—that was guarding something real and true, and keeping your mouth shut to protect your livelihood and your life.

When Daniel Alexander, a young writer who loved his daughter and Spider-Man and fighting for human rights, asked where Guy was tonight, Kelly didn't feel like going along with the lie. He said, "I don't know."

When, an hour later, the cops showed up and shouted at everyone to go home, Kelly and Daniel Alexander and the rest of the N-VAC stood their ground. Only when the batons were flashed and threats of tear gas were made did Kelly and the others start to run.

The Whisky a Go Go was crowded for a Wednesday, especially for midnight. The air was smoky, a haze of alcohol and electricity. The dance floor vibrated with bodies—tight pants, miniskirts, long hair—quaking and jerking, limbs free. In a glass booth suspended overhead, a beautiful blond spun records. On another elevated platform made to look like a cage, three girls in white boots glittered in fringed miniskirts and halters.

No one noticed Shep Newman as he made his way through the sea of people. Hutch bumped along behind in his usual role as friend and bodyguard. They ordered drinks and watched the crowd: the impeccable Cary Grant, as suave in real life as he was on the screen, and every inch a movie star; Jayne Mansfield, hair shining under the spotlights; Steve McQueen, who'd done most of his own stunts in *The Great Escape*, now gyrating on the dance floor.

When they were on the road, it was impossible for Shep to blend in. Wherever he went, he was mobbed the minute he walked into a place. But LA could be a great equalizer, and in this moment, he was grateful for the Whisky, grateful for Steve McQueen and Cary Grant and Jayne Mansfield, grateful to have his star eclipsed.

Shep downed his drink, handed the empty bottle to Hutch, and made his way onto the floor. The DJ was named Joanie. He knew her name because he knew the names of all the attractive girls. She was the one who'd designed the glittery fringe costumes worn by the dancers. Shep had met her on the Whisky's opening night but ended up leaving with Lorrie.

He looked up now at the three girls on the cage platform and spied her short white-yellow hair. Another thing he was grateful for—the distance between them tonight.

Someone pressed something into his hand. A girl with raccoon eyes opened her mouth to show him the pills on her tongue and then danced away, a mirage. Shep stared down at his palm at the three red bennies and then popped them into his mouth and swallowed them whole.

Over the music, Hutch shouted, "What're we doing?" It was a loaded question. Hutch wasn't anyone's conscience, but Shep could hear what he wasn't saying: *Shouldn't we be working on the album right now?*

"We're joining the party." Shep flashed him a smile and let himself be consumed by the sea. He was a good dancer. He'd been king of the prom, had taken girls in his arms and led them. He'd danced on the show with his "dates," and when he did, America swooned. Now, he grooved as everyone else did, vibrating alone, disconnected, solitary, yet part of something. *Life* magazine was the first step out of the box his father had built for him, and he felt both lonely and free.

The music was fast—Johnny Rivers, Little Eva, the Ronettes, Elvis. This was what Shep missed most about fame—being one of the crowd, just another body. His shirt was wet through and stuck to his back, a second skin. Hutch had disappeared, but it was hard to tell how long ago, because time didn't seem like a real thing in here. Someone passed him a joint, which he took, feeling anonymous, unworried about reporters or cameras. He took a deep, languid inhale and passed it to a girl in tight pants, who leaned in and blew smoke into his mouth, biting his lower lip as she pulled away.

"I've always wanted to do that," she said dreamily.

Before he could react—pull her back into him, kiss her again, try to lose himself in the feel of her—Joanie the DJ blasted a new song from up in her booth. The club shook with the tight, frenzied sound of the Beatles. "I Want to Hold Your Hand" morphed into "Can't Buy Me Love" and then "A Hard Day's Night."

This last one nearly undid him. It was partly the Beatles, who were taking over the whole fucking world right now, leaving no space for him or the kind of harmless rock 'n' roll he was known for. But the main reason was that it felt like the words were reaching into him, gutting him and leaving pieces of him all over the dance floor.

He stopped moving, and the world continued gyrating and shaking around him on all sides. He looked up at the go-go cage, where Lorrie stood, looking down at him. *Why can't you be Eileen?* he thought unfairly. And at the idea of her—Eileen—he started to cry.

Through the crowd, Hutch caught sight of his friend and thought, *Oh, shit.* He tried to untangle himself from the girl he was dancing with, breaking free just in time to see a body slam into Shep.

Shep barely registered the jolt, lost in the moment and Eileen and the cloud of smoke and a feeling of weightlessness, of no one knowing where he was, of the song filling his brain and his bones until there was nothing left of him. He gave in to all of it, letting himself be carried by the current.

At midnight, Guy met Kelly at Pink's hot dog stand in the heart of Hollywood. There was a bruise over Kelly's left eye that looked angry, but not as angry as Kelly. Overwhelmed with guilt and tenderness, Guy reached out to brush away the hair that fell across his boyfriend's forehead, but Kelly ducked away.

"Where were you?" was all he said.

"Sorry. I was late at the studio, and then Eileen and I had this press event, but whatever, it's not important. What happened? Who did this?"

"Cops came and chased us off, and my face collided with a streetlight."

Normally, Kelly would have turned it into a long story, unbothered about making himself the punch line, but he clearly wasn't in any mood right now.

They walked in silence the 350 feet to 7013 Melrose Avenue, where a man named Bob Damron ran a place called Red Raven. Guy and Kelly had never been there, but Clint had heard about it from a mutual friend of theirs. Clint said that in addition to running the bar, Damron was in the midst of compiling a guidebook of all the gay-friendly places in Los Angeles.

Inside Red Raven were throngs of men and only a handful of women. The place was dark and cozy, with a bar that curved in a half-moon along one side of the room. Guy and Kelly stood, taking it in, temporarily forgetting their anger. The bartenders, the pomaded men in suits or shirtsleeves. Young men. Old men. Men of all ages. The music, the cigarette smoke. The easiness of the mood. The freedom. To Guy, it felt like a world that had only—until this moment—existed in his head. A place where it was okay for them to hold hands and kiss each other without anyone batting an eye.

Outside, the Sunset Strip was flooded with bodies. They were young bodies with long hair and beards, tight pants and short dresses, dark glasses and hippie beads, who stopped traffic as they clamored from club to club.

Not so long ago, Shep had been one of them. They'd started letting him in when he turned fifteen because he was famous, but he never forgot what it was like to bum around out there, dreaming of what lay on the other side of those doors. It had been a little like the Emerald City.

Right now, he found it hard to breathe, as if those bodies were consuming all the air, none left over for him. He walked, hands shoved in pockets, head bowed, unsure of where he was going, while

Hutch did his best to keep pace. It was only when Shep heard voices from above that he looked up. There were some kids around his age who'd climbed up one of the billboards. They sat, legs swinging, in front of the ad for Fremont Hotel & Casino Las Vegas, smoking and passing bottles around. A guy with a mustache and tattoos chugged his and then threw it onto the ground, where it shattered.

"Where're you going, pretty boy?" said a voice behind him.

There were three of them, and immediately, he recognized them—not in the sense that he *knew* them, but he knew guys like them. Hulking, hotheaded, itching for a fight. He'd gone to school with boys like this. Most were bullies out of boredom, looking to kill time, but lately, it was like everything in the world was heightened. Like they'd been living all cinched up for so long and now the threads were coming loose. There was an ugliness in the air, like all you had to do was light a match and the whole place and all its people would go up in flames.

In the best of times, he found this kind of confrontation hard to resist, even though he liked to think he was—as blues musician Lazy Lester sang—a lover, not a fighter. But this was not the best of times. As much as he longed to feel *something*, Shep knew fighting was more trouble than it was worth. Suddenly, he wanted his bed and sleep and the deadening quiet of the Newman home.

And then, from above, like a spark, a beer bottle cracked one of the meathead guys on the skull. Someone threw a punch. Someone went down. And suddenly, it was a wildfire, consuming the Strip. A flurry of motion on his left, and Shep locked eyes with Hutch, who was there beside him, the two of them against the world. Shep felt a surge of love for his best friend, and when Hutch went down swinging, Shep dove into the fray.

Twelve miles away in Santa Monica, Dinah left the hospital, where Dr. Carson had informed her of Del's progress. Two days earlier, they'd stopped the sedatives. Del had blinked. He had twitched. He had moved his big left toe. But other than that, he showed no signs of waking up. Carson was worried. She could see it on his face before he told her *I'm concerned that he's slower to respond than expected.*

She had sat at Del's side, convinced he only needed to hear her voice. But when she asked him to blink, to twitch, to move his toe, he merely lay there sleeping.

Instead of driving home, she drove southwest to a neighborhood near the ocean. She parked her car outside 156 Fraser Avenue. The house was a simple beach cottage, similar to the other beach cottages that lined the street. From what she could tell in the dark, moonless night, it was painted green.

The windows were closed and curtained except for the largest one to the right of the door, but she couldn't see any movement. She imagined knocking on that door and introducing herself and asking her—M. Leslie, this mythical, hypothetical woman—what the hell she thought she was doing in her husband's house. She wondered if this woman was worrying about him. If that was the reason she was still awake this late at night. Had she known him before Dinah? Had she given up her dreams to be with him? Did she even remember what those dreams were?

This thought, more than the sight of the house itself, was sobering. When she had saved up her money and come to Los Angeles, sixteen-year-old Dinah Garfinkle had never imagined a husband who kept secrets, sons she loved but barely knew, a failing television career, middle age. Did Del's mistress have any of these thoughts and fears?

Before she realized what she was doing, she was out of the Impala and crossing the street. She was careful to stop at the narrow, grassy curb, aware enough to know that the sidewalk in front of the house was a dividing line—on one side, her marriage, her life as she knew it, her sanity. On the other, the person who lived at 156 Fraser Avenue. Who was important enough to her husband to have been kept secret for over a decade.

Dinah stepped onto the lawn. She was numb again, not just her skin this time. She wondered vaguely how long a person could live after their heart had stopped beating, because hers seemed to have gone silent. While she could still move, she crept closer to the house itself. One of the darkened windows sat open, a sliver, enough to let in the ocean breeze. There was the muffled noise of a television or maybe the radio, but she couldn't tell if it was coming from inside or farther down the street.

She needed to see in the other window, the larger one. Her skin prickled—a warning, which she ignored. She hunched over so that she wouldn't be seen, picking her way through the bushes that stood watch, blocking her path. A scratch on her bare ankle. The scent of blood. But she was there now, just below. She rested her fingers on the windowsill, feeling the solid realness of the house, which was a thing that existed on this earth, not a figment of her imagination.

She caught her breath, and her heart began to beat again with a kind of ferocious, desperate intent. And then she lifted her head enough so that her eyes were level with the sill and she could see inside.

In the distance, a siren. The sounds of a city.

Without thinking, Dinah straightened to her full height and stared at the room—its pale gray walls, its matching armchairs and sofa tastefully arranged around a coffee table. Bookshelves. A fireplace. Framed photos on the wall. But the focal point, a television set, newer and nicer than the one they owned in Toluca Lake.

The living room, where its occupant lived, was empty, but the set was on, tuned to *The Tonight Show Starring Johnny Carson*, which played in blazing color. Dinah wondered what, if any, right she had to this house and its furnishings. She'd earned the money alongside Del, which meant this lawn was part hers and that television set was part hers and the books were—

"You there," a voice called. "What do you think you're doing?"

Dinah turned in the bushes to see a woman standing in the street, a leash in her hand, a dog at the end of it.

It was as if the Sunset Strip had overflowed into the West Hollywood Sheriff's Station. Teens in tight pants and hip-huggers were crammed into what they called the Show-Up Room, where they usually conducted lineups. On nights like this, it was a containment cell for anyone under the age of twenty. Angry parents filed in, demanding to know where their children were. The air was hot and stifling and loud.

Hutch kept one eye on Shep and the other on the door. In the end, he'd been the one to make the phone call. He didn't think he'd ever understand the dynamics between Shep and his family, and was grateful all over again to have two regular parents who weren't in showbiz and two brothers who were at least a dozen years older than he was, essentially making him an only child.

"How did he sound?" Shep asked. His lip was split and he had a bloody nose.

"He wasn't there," said Hutch, pressing his handkerchief to his ear, which wouldn't stop bleeding. "So I called Sydney."

Great, Shep thought. Guy was the only person he remotely wanted to see. Sydney ranked up there as the last, just above his mom.

They sat for over an hour, the room gradually emptying out, before a uniformed deputy came looking for "Moe" and "Larry."

"Is that us?" Hutch asked.

"You know Syd." Shep sighed. "What a comedian."

They followed the deputy out of the room, past vagrants and hookers and law enforcement officers. Elbowing their way to the front desk, where Sydney Weiss gesticulated wildly under the fluorescent lights, face livid. Hutch pushed toward him, but Shep's eyes went past Syd to Lorrie, who sat on a bench, coat thrown over her Whisky costume, the little vinyl purse she always carried balanced on her knees.

Shep rubbed his mouth with the back of his hand, remembering too late the split lip. "This night just keeps getting better and better," he said to no one.

When she saw him, she jumped to her feet and pushed her way through the throng.

Before she could open her mouth, Shep said, "What are you doing here?"

"I came to bail you out. After you got taken away, someone came running in crying her eyes out because 'Shep Newman got arrested, Shep Newman's gone to jail.'" She flapped her hands in clear imitation before zeroing in on the split lip. "Hey, are you okay?" Her face and voice softened a little.

"All good. Thanks for coming."

"Here." She handed him a pair of dark glasses and a hat. "Don't make it worse. This place is lousy with reporters." She cast a narrow glance at the men who loitered near the desk and the exits, cigarettes burning, an antsy, shifty look to them.

Feeling ridiculous, Shep donned the disguise, but in the crowd, no one seemed to notice.

Lorrie said, "You know you're going to need to stop doing stuff like this. Getting into fights. Hanging out on the Strip like a bum." But she didn't sound preachy, she sounded tired, like she needed to get off her feet.

"You work on the Strip."

"That's different. And I'm not working there much longer, because I won't be able to." She shook her hips, and the miniskirt made a swishing sound. She smiled then and so did he, and it was a nice moment. Not romantic but almost friendly.

Something caught Shep's eye, and he watched as a familiar head of dark blond hair cut across the room, like a football player barreling past the opposing team. Shep waved, then hollered, which caused heads to turn, including Guy's. His brother changed direction, making for Shep and Lorrie, and that's when Shep saw Eileen bumping along behind him.

"You came," Shep said to both of them. His eyes were on Eileen.

She took in the split lip, the bruised eye, and whistled.

"What are you doing here?" Guy stared at Shep, at Lorrie, who was frowning at Eileen.

"Hutch tried calling, but you didn't answer." Shep's voice was flat.

"I wasn't home," Guy said. "I was here. We were here."

"They got arrested," Eileen offered. "I was their one phone call."

"Of course you were," said Shep, avoiding her eyes. He said to his brother. "We didn't see you in the Show-Up."

"What's the . . . who's 'we'?" Guy looked at Lorrie again.

"Hutch." Shep nodded over at Sydney and Hutch, still over at the desk.

"Syd's here? Jesus." Guy rubbed his hair so violently Shep thought he'd pull it out at the roots. "Is there anything else I should know? Did you kill anyone?" It was his self-righteous big brother voice, the one Shep hated. "Got any murders I should be covering up while I'm at it?"

"Well, well, you're one to talk. What did they cart you in for? Doing twenty-five in a fifty zone? Or did they finally get you for being the world's biggest bore?"

"Are you high right now?"

"Marginally."

Lorrie glanced over her shoulder at the reporters. "You should maybe keep it down. . . ."

But suddenly, Guy Newman couldn't keep it down any longer. "We were at a bar. Kelly and me. Having a beer at the end of a long day. A fucking beer. There was a raid. Because here, in this town, in this country, in this world, it matters where you drink and who you drink with."

He continued, unleashing years of frustration in the lobby of the West Hollywood Sheriff's Station. Frustration at having to forever play the supporting role so that his younger brother could be the star. Never given a choice as to the role itself because his only concern when he was ten years old was to make his dad proud. He'd studied fencing, he'd studied *the fucking trapeze, for fuck's sake*, just to carve out something for himself, but did it work? No. And now here they were and here he was, still with the goddamn rash on his neck, this rash that wouldn't go away, that might never go away, and he was sick of it. Absolutely sick of it.

As Guy threw the tantrum he had never thrown as a child, the one he'd been building toward all his life, Shep stared unblinkingly at Eileen, as if expecting her to interpret for him. In the noise of the station, his brother's speech was an impassioned jumble, and to Shep, it sounded like *fencing trapeze the fucking trapeze the thanks I get and this fucking rash out of my misery*. But Eileen was focused on something just over his shoulder.

"Um, guys?" she said.

Shep and then Lorrie and then Guy turned to follow her gaze. And watched as a woman was escorted from the direction of the cells. She was tall and blond and slender—a little rumpled, a little breathless— and wore a pair of sunglasses Shep recognized because they belonged to him.

They stared, unspeaking, as an officer marched Dinah Newman by the arm through the masses and deposited her at the front desk.

Guy's mouth dropped open.

Eileen whistled again.

Shep turned back to Lorrie. "You should sit down," he said. "We could be here awhile."

THIRTY-FOUR

Nineteen days after the accident

T hey traveled in a caravan from West Hollywood to Toluca Lake, Sydney leading the way with Dinah beside him, the window rolled down so she could feel the air on her face. Her Impala was still parked on Fraser Avenue in Santa Monica, and she had no idea how she was going to retrieve it. In the side mirror, she could see Guy's car, and, behind it, she could just make out Eileen's Nash. Hutch had ordered a cab back to the Strip and promised to get Lorrie home.

When at last Syd turned onto their street, Dinah stared as two cars of girls drove past, slowing down, searching no doubt for their house. She wondered how much longer Shep's fans would do this. And if there would be a day in the not-so-distant future when he—when all of them—wouldn't have fans at all.

Syd parked in the driveway and followed Dinah inside, where she pulled off her earrings and dropped them into her purse, which she shut with a loud snap. She was furious with Shep, furious with Kelly, furious with Guy and Eileen and that strange girl in the go-go costume for witnessing her humiliation, furious with the West Hollywood Sheriff's Station. Furious, most of all, with herself for getting arrested. The woman with the dog had gone back to her house two streets over and called the police. The insanity of it—she, Dinah Newman, accused of being a *Peeping Tom*.

"Would you like a drink?" she asked Syd, who stared at her before erupting into laughter.

"You have," he chortled, "a twig in your hair."

At first, she had an overwhelming urge to hurl something at him—her shoe, her purse, the copy of *Life* magazine. She reached up and felt for the twig, tangled behind her ear. As she plucked it from its blond nest, she felt her mouth twitch, and suddenly, she was laughing too. It was more tree limb than twig. How on earth hadn't she known it was there?

She laughed until the tears ran down her face. She tried to imagine describing to her husband everything he'd missed since the accident, right down to the stick in her hair, and the more she imagined it, the harder she laughed.

When she'd recovered enough, she poured herself and Sydney a glass of whiskey, the liquid shaking with her shaking hands that had not been numb for days, and the two of them—old friends—continued to laugh as they clinked glasses.

"To Del," said Syd. "Thank god he can't see us right now."

"To Del," she agreed and drank.

Outside, Guy and Eileen watched as Kelly climbed out of Guy's Buick and strode off to the guesthouse. He had taken the back seat, giving Shep the front, and hadn't said more than two words during the ride home. While Shep had slept most of the way, was still sleeping, something he'd been able to do his whole life, even when the world was caving in.

"You didn't have to follow us back here," Guy said to Eileen.

"I wanted to make sure you're okay." She glanced at his car, at the boy with closed eyes, head resting against the window.

"I'm okay."

Guy tilted his own head back now and took in the stars. When he was younger, he'd wanted to be an astronaut until his father talked him out of it. As a consolation prize, Del had gifted him an Omega Speedmaster Moonwatch, the same make and model that had orbited the earth six times on the wrist of Wally Schirra as part of the October 1962 Mercury mission.

Guy might have accepted the fact that he would never be part of NASA, but Del couldn't stop him from learning about space. Facts like the number of stars in the Milky Way is higher than the number of humans that have ever existed. And one million earths can fit inside the sun.

He thought about one million earths, imagining one million Guys in one million different lives. He wondered if they were looking up right now wondering about him.

Eileen said, "Give him time. He's got a lot to process. Us, most of all."

Guy's eyes searched for Kelly in the dark and then turned back to the sky.

"Do you think we're making a mistake?" he asked her.

"If we get married? Yes. You don't love me. And I don't love you. Not like that."

"So why go through with it?"

He meant what reasons did she have. He was well aware of his own, which only felt clearer and more crucial after his run-in at Red Raven. There could be fallout he wasn't yet aware of—LA cops were known to talk to the tabloids—and this went beyond the TV show, beyond TV itself. Fallout would follow him wherever he went. It was only a few years ago that respected scientist Frank Kameny was, after two decades, fired from his post with the army for being a homosexual and afterward struggled to find anyone who would hire him.

"I mean, there are worse things a girl can do than marry Guy Newman." She smiled.

"But you're not going to."

She shook her head. "I don't think I can. I keep telling myself marriage is just a legal agreement. It's not that different from the contract I signed when your dad hired me to be on the show. And if I marry you, it's one less thing to worry about. One less pressure."

He understood this—marriage as a place to hide, to keep safe from the outside world—more than she knew.

"But." The softest sigh escaped her. "There are too many hearts at stake."

Guy pictured one of those alternate earths where he and Kelly were free to marry each other, or at least free to love each other honestly and openly.

"When I was little," Eileen said, "I wanted to be a firefighter and, later, a prosecutor. When my dad told me that women weren't allowed to do either of those things, I couldn't understand why not. Like, why was a body part, or lack thereof, the thing keeping me from living a totally different life?" She looked up at him. "You and Kelly. I want you to know that whatever you are to one another, there's nothing wrong with it."

There was a stirring from inside the car, and Eileen straightened.

"I'd better go," she said. "I'm already in enough trouble with Mrs. Dennis." She rolled her eyes and, on tiptoe, kissed Guy on the cheek. Then she climbed into the Nash and sped away down the drive.

"I guess that's all she wrote," a voice said. Shep emerged, stretching his limbs, rubbing his eyes. "Where's she going in such a hurry?"

"Studio Club."

"Did you know one of the girls there was murdered by her boyfriend?"

"Jesus."

"It was a long time ago."

Shep leaned back against the Buick. There was an overall quiet to him that made Guy feel unsettled. He sensed a storm was brewing. He joined his brother against the car so that they were shoulder to shoulder.

"What really happened tonight?" Guy asked. "Not with Mom. With you."

"I can't remember. Everything. And nothing."

"And the *Life* article?"

"A long time coming."

They exchanged a look, Guy nodding because he knew exactly what he meant. *Life* magazine was Shep's version of his tantrum in the sheriff's station. Because that was the thing about trying to shoulder the world—you couldn't carry it around forever.

"And the girl at the station? Lorrie?"

"She dances at the Whisky."

"But you're not together."

"No." Shep's gaze returned to the driveway as if he could still see the red-and-white Nash Metropolitan.

Guy followed his eyes, and what he saw there was something he should have seen all along. "Because you like Eileen."

Shep wouldn't look at him.

"Does Lorrie know?"

"I broke up with her a while ago. Before Pop's accident. Not that it matters. Eileen's engaged, you know." He shot his brother a look.

"So why was Lorrie there tonight?"

The expression on Shep's face meant he was coming up with a hundred different stories, things that would make him seem less guilty. For some reason, this reminded Guy of how they would sneak out of the house when they were kids and go swimming in the lake. They would swing from vines like Tarzan, hitting the dark water with a splash, going under, then coming up again beneath the starry sky.

"She's pregnant," Shep said.

"Shit."

"Yeah."

Guy's first thought was that his little brother's luck had finally run out. All their lives, things had come easily to him. Shep, the charmed one, exerting half the effort of anyone else but reaping twice the rewards. Guy having to work harder at everything, including their dad's approval.

But Guy understood that none of that mattered right now, and so he took his time reacting. His father would have flown off the handle. His mother would have gone quiet but livid, a controlled burn. Guy didn't want to do either of these things, because he knew his brother well enough to know that whatever anyone said couldn't be worse than what he was already saying to himself.

His mind went—as it did now and then—to the Dionne quintuplets, the first quintuplets known to survive infancy. The girls were identical, created from a single egg cell, and in 1934, when they were months old, their parents relinquished them to the Canadian government. They grew up as a kind of zoo exhibit—a nursery was built especially for them with an outdoor playground where thousands of tourists flocked daily to observe them behind one-way screens. The girls could hear but not see them, and the crowd was warned not to speak to them. They were treated as test subjects, and their contact with the outside world was limited to Quintland, as the tourist attraction was called, even as their likenesses were used to advertise products and their father set up a souvenir shop next door.

Guy felt he and Shep had been created from a single cell as well, one that no one else shared. The whole nature of them, of growing up Newman behind a one-way screen, was something only they could understand.

"Are you okay?" he asked.

Shep had always been a strange creature—solitary and quiet, yet full of bravado. Guy knew he took the world in and held on to it, unable to let it go.

"No," his brother said. He sighed. And then looked at Guy. "What was that about back there? At the station? Your little monologue?"

"Nothing. Just letting off steam." Guy considered telling him the truth—*I'm gay and I'm in love with Kelly*. But after the night they'd had, it felt good to be the older brother right now. And so, before Shep could ask anything else, he said, "She's not engaged, by the way. Not anymore."

Shep stared at him.

"You know. For what it's worth."

In the den, Dinah and Sydney tipped back tumblers of whiskey as Carl Perkins crooned loudly on the stereo. Dinah looked up from the enormous plaid chair, the one Del had insisted on even though it was the size of a pickup truck, to see Guy and Shep standing in the doorway.

She held up her glass to them. "I've decided to think about tonight tomorrow," she told them. "For tonight, we . . ." She squinted at Sydney. "How did you say it?"

"'For tonight, we'll merry, merry be.' It's from an old English drinking song." He knocked his back and poured himself another, dancing the twist as he went, Guy and Shep looking on in dismay.

Dinah sang out, "'May we never go to hell but always be on our way.'" She took a long sip, waving for the boys to come join them. As Sydney poured them each a drink, she got to her feet and held out a hand to Guy.

"What?" he said.

"You know I started as a dancer, but did you know your dad and I once won a dance contest? Our specialty was the Carolina shag."

She spun him out, pulled him in. In a family of musicians, Guy, bless him, had no rhythm. He clomped on his mother's foot, cracked his ankle against the ottoman, and then banged into the stereo, causing the record to skip to the next song. Mercifully, Shep cut in, spinning Dinah, the two of them twirling expertly as if they'd been practicing for this moment all their lives.

When it was over, she dabbed at the perspiration on her forehead and said, "I need to talk to you." She pointed at each of them one by one. "You. You. And you."

"What happened to thinking about tonight tomorrow?" Shep asked. He helped himself to more whiskey.

"This isn't about tonight. This is about us." And then, instead of explaining why she, Dinah Newman, had been slinking around in someone's bushes, and instead of yelling at Shep for the *Life* magazine debacle and at Guy for getting arrested in a known homosexual bar, Dinah told them about the sponsors dropping them.

"We need to get renewed," she said, "but I don't think we're going to be. It's time to start thinking about what life looks like beyond the show."

"But first—" Syd held up his glass. "First, we give them one hell of a final episode. Which reminds me—where the hell is the script?"

"That's a funny story," Dinah began. "So I had a writing partner, but now I don't."

"But you wrote the episode," Sydney said.

"No."

"Must be the music. It sounded like you said 'no.'"

"No. But 'with a little luck and a whole lotta pluck, we'll turn this ship around.'" It was a line from one of her early films.

"Yeah," Guy said. "About that."

Dinah listened as Guy told them the engagement was off. *Bang* went Sydney's glass onto the coffee table, and he immediately started in on how now was not the time to be selfish, now was the time to pull together and deliver. He invoked Del and the Virgin Mary and James T. Aubrey and his own mother, and still he was only just getting started when Dinah said, "Syd," and shook her head.

"I'm sorry," said Guy.

"It's okay." Even though she wasn't convinced it was. "We'll just— we'll figure something else out. It's just one more thing to add to the list. To do: Find a way to pay for finale. To do: Cancel the wedding."

"To do," Syd said, "write the fucking script."

Dinah lifted her glass again, a toast to the universe. "But for tonight, we'll merry, merry be."

"Also," Guy said.

Sydney groaned.

"I dropped out of law school."

"Okay," Dinah said. This was less of a surprise than the wedding news. Their oldest son becoming a lawyer was Del's dream, not Guy's. "Have you told Kelly yet?"

"He knows."

"Not about law school. About calling off the engagement."

"What? No."

"You should."

A look passed between them—surprise on his part, something like perceptive all-knowingness on hers. *Maybe*, she thought, *I understand you a little better than either of us knew. Maybe my eyes are finally open and I'm seeing the world and everything in it and everyone in it a little more clearly.*

Syd cleared his throat. "That's all well and good, but who's going to tell Aubrey?"

The palms of Dinah's hands tingled. "I will," she said. "Let me worry about him."

She stared at her sons' faces—so different, yet so similar. She had loved these faces since the instant she first laid eyes on them. In her sons, she saw traces of her mom. She saw her dad and her grandparents. But mostly she saw herself and Del, the good moments and the bad. Drives along Mulholland when they forgot what time it was, the ache she'd felt whenever they were separated, the feel of her hand in his. She wanted to think of the good right now, with him lying across town, still as a turnip. If she thought of him as a helpless turnip, it made the fact that he'd squandered their money easier to swallow.

"Mom?" Shep looked at her, then at his brother, and Dinah wondered how long she'd been lost in thought.

"Sorry." She shook her head, wishing it was that simple—a single shake of the head to clear the mind. She was thinking of Del, who in reality was neither helpless nor a turnip. Who, for better or worse, had put them here. She arranged her mouth in a tight little smile. *That self-righteous SOB.* Boy, did she have some things to say to him when he woke up.

For now, though—she explained the plan. Sydney was going to handle the selling of Del's cars. After that would come the collections and the art. The gruesome surrealist charcoal drawings by Odilon Redon and Victor Brauner.

"We don't need them," she said, "and your father—if he recovers—will be lucky if I ever let him drive again."

"Are you saying we're broke?" Guy's drink was still untouched. He swirled it round and round in the glass.

"Yes," Dinah told him. "We are. Turns out, your father is terrible with money. Ever since they put him in a coma, I am learning so much about him."

"Did the *Life* piece—" Shep said, rubbing a knuckle over his split lip. "Did that have anything to do with losing the sponsors?"

"Yes," Dinah said again. "It absolutely did. But I don't care about the magazine. Actually, I do care about it because clearly you had something to say, and while a heads-up might have been nice, I get why you did it. Syd is pissed, but it's his job to be pissed at things we do. He'll get over it." She looked at her old friend and manager, and then at her sons. "Because that's what we do. We get over it. We move on. It's the only way we know to be."

Inside the guesthouse, Guy found Kelly sitting in the dark at the kitchen table. He was barefoot in jeans, still wearing the GAY IS GOOD shirt, and the bruise on his forehead was the deep blue purple of a stormy sky.

"Will you let me help you with that now?" Guy flipped on the overhead light and started rummaging through the cabinets.

"We moved it, remember?" Kelly's voice was tired. "The first aid kit. It's in the pantry."

Guy unearthed the metal box that had been there for as long as he'd been alive and started digging through, coming up with alcohol, cotton, antibacterial ointment. He knelt on the cold tile floor and brushed the hair off Kelly's face.

"Ice will be the best thing for it, but we want to make sure it's clean."

Guy had a distant memory of a childhood fight with his brother, his mother uttering similar words as she tended to their injuries while their dad lectured them. *If you have to fight each other, never aim for the face.*

Then he said, "This is going to hurt." But Kelly didn't flinch, not even as Guy poured the alcohol onto the cotton and pressed it against the wound.

The silence between them was heavy. After ice had been applied, Guy sat back on his heels, his hands resting lightly on Kelly's thighs.

"I'm sorry," he said.

"You can't marry her. I want you to marry me."

"You were the one who told me to. You said sometimes this is just what we have to do."

"I was wrong."

"Kel . . ."

"No. I need you to listen. I know we live in a world where that can never happen. But that doesn't mean I love you any less. And it doesn't mean I want to see you marry someone else just because you can. I understand the stakes here. I know all the stories—this person lost his career, this person was shunned, this person was, I don't know, stoned in a public forum. I get that we risk losing everything." He chuckled at the way it sounded, like dialogue from one of his movies. "But I'd rather lose everything than lose you."

He reached out and touched Guy's cheek with a single finger.

"We called it off," Guy said.

"You . . ."

"Called it off."

"What about CBS?"

"Fuck CBS. It would be a lie. I can't live like that. Can you?"

Their eyes met and held. It was something they'd always been able to do—hold each other without holding each other. And then Guy reached out to this man he loved in a way he'd never loved anyone else, and took his face in his hands and kissed him.

At 2:00 a.m., Dinah was still awake, the house too quiet. She threw back the covers and stole down the hall to Shep's room, where a light shone beneath the door.

Every night of her childhood and every morning, Dinah's mother had told her daughter she loved her. *I want it to be the first and the last thing you hear each day*, she'd said. Dinah had vowed to do the same with her children, and for a few years, she had. But at some point along the way, *I love you, happy dreams* gave way to *Good night* or nothing at all. The boys, gangly and independent, growing rapidly, had been anxious to guard what time they had away from the studio and the show. She hadn't wanted to bother them or annoy them or, god forbid, have them accuse her of being sappy. Del, always so good at solving problems, became the person they went to—when they went to somebody other than one another—and Dinah had stepped aside.

She knocked twice on Shep's door and waited for his "Come in."

He was lying on the bed, headphones on, guitar beside him. His hair fell across his forehead in messy waves, making him look younger, her little boy.

"Shepherd," she said with a softness she reserved only for him, her mystery child, the one who carried her mother's maiden name as his own.

"Mom?" He pulled off the headphones, a woman's voice continuing to belt out whatever song he was listening to. "Have you ever had the dream where you're flying?"

She didn't answer right away. When he wasn't on camera, Shep spoke so unpredictably these days—sometimes in great bursts, other times not at all—that his questions deserved some thought.

"Yes," she said finally. "Not often enough, though. It's one of the better ones, as far as dreams go." She nodded at the headphones and the music filtering out of them. "Who is that?" Because it had been a long time since she'd ventured behind the walls and engaged him like this, trying to figure out the things that made up his daily life, that made up *him*.

"Lesley Gore."

He held the headphones out to her and she slipped them over her ears. The woman's voice was a cry, an anthem. The music stirring. Declarative. Rousing. It made her feel like weeping. It made her feel like climbing onto the roof and shouting to the world that there was so much more to her than they knew.

You don't own me

Two minutes and thirty seconds later, as Lesley Gore's voice faded into the middle distance, Dinah handed Shep back his headphones and said, "I wanted to talk to you about the finale. I'd like you to write a new song. Make it your own. Whatever that means. I trust you."

"Are you sure?" He reached out a hand, laying it on the guitar the way Del had once reached for her in their bed, in the night, making sure she was still there.

She wanted to ask her son how he was, deep down inside himself where he lived. But instead she said, "I'm sure." And then she added, "I love you."

"I love you too, Mom."

She closed his door before he could see her blinking, which she did all the way down the hall to her room. As she climbed back into her bed, she heard the sound of a drawer being pulled, a familiar creaking of floorboards. She had a memory of Del loosening one, back when Shep was fourteen and sneaking out, in an effort to catch their slippery younger son when he came home. The memory made her laugh, and instinctively, she stared down at the empty space beside her. Then there was another sound—the gentle strumming of guitar strings.

She rested a hand on her husband's pillow, leaving it there for a few seconds. And then she clicked off the light and closed her eyes because there was work to be done and she needed her sleep.

THIRTY-FIVE

Twenty days after the accident

T he idea came to Dinah in the middle of the night, the way the best ideas often do. It woke her up and kept her up—she blamed the alcohol, Lesley Gore, and her own busy, feverish brain. But it wasn't until nine o'clock on Thursday morning that she could set it in motion.

She picked up the telephone and dialed information. "Hello, operator?" she said. "Please put me through to Mrs. Sunbeam, wife of the president of Sunbeam's West Coast operations."

At home in her apartment, Juliet felt adrift. The *Times* had once filled her waking hours, any remaining hours belonging to the Musician or to her alone. But then she'd started working with Dinah, and her days had expanded and she had expanded, as if she'd been granted extra time. Now she felt herself shrinking to fit into twenty-four hours once again.

Which was why, on Thursday morning, she decided to telephone her mother. Five minutes into the call, she regretted it. Her mother told her about the neighbor, whose begonias had died due to the frost; her cousin, who was getting a *d-i-v-o-r-c-e*; her father's work at the dairy; his boss's wife, who was in the hospital with a burst appendix.

Then, to Juliet's surprise, Roberta said, "I read the interview. With Dinah Newman. What was her home like? Was it beautiful? I bet it was beautiful. What was she wearing? She looks so lovely in blue. Did she serve you food? I use her recipe for lamb stew every Christmas. You would know that if you ever came home."

"It was fine. She was fine. . . ."

"You know, years ago, I wrote to her, and she wrote me back. . . ."

"I know, Mom. I remember. You have the letter hanging in the kitchen."

"Of course." Roberta laughed, a thin, nervous sound. "I hope if you see her again you'll tell her how much it means to me. Are you still watching the show? I can't believe how big those boys have gotten, and so handsome—"

"You should come out here and see it," Juliet said impulsively. "The finale is filming live on April twenty-fourth."

"Oh, I couldn't leave your father."

"You could bring him. It would be great to see you."

But she knew her dad well enough to know it would never happen. He didn't believe in travel—he was content to remain in his own back-yard and felt others should be too. And her mother would never go anywhere without him.

Roberta said, "What on earth would I do in California?" Like Juliet had invited her to the moon.

"You told me once that you wanted to write," her daughter said, happy to change the subject. "Was that true? Did you ever plan to be a writer?"

"Oh, I don't know. Maybe when I was younger. In my teenage years. That was a long time ago now. . . ."

"You went to college for a year. Did you take writing classes?"

"I think so. One or two. Again, that was so long ago."

"Because I read about this woman who wrote her first book at sixty. You're only forty-four."

"I'm not a writer," Roberta said. Her voice had tightened. "But how wonderful for her, this woman. You'll have to let me know the name of her book so that I can read it."

"And Betty Friedan wrote *The Feminine Mystique* when she was forty-one."

"Oh, your father told me about that book. It sounds outrageous."

Juliet huffed out a breath. She had called her mother in a misguided attempt to seek even a smidgen of maternal comfort. It wasn't as if she was asking for a lot. Just a reminder that she was loved by someone who had birthed her. She was also, maybe, making an effort to try to understand Roberta—to try to better understand Dinah. But here they were, going round and round as usual and getting nowhere.

"Are you happy, Mom?" she blurted.

A brief pause.

"Of course I'm happy, Juliet. What a question."

The conversation moved on to the church bake sale—Roberta was planning to make Dinah Newman's famed chocolate pound cake—until finally Juliet told her mother she had to get back to work. Her hand shook as she hung up the receiver, and she sat there staring at the phone.

It rang almost as soon as she hung up. She answered without thinking. In case it was her mother calling back to tell her she loved her and that she'd changed her mind, she was coming to California after all. Or, more conceivably, in case it was Nick or—even more pressing, but impossible—Boyd Hartley with a news story he needed her to cover.

"Ms. Dunne?"

"Yes?"

"Delivery for you. I can bring it up in a bit, but I'm helping Mrs. Wallis with her dogs."

"That's okay, George. I'll come down."

Juliet took the stairs to the lobby of her building, which was far more elegant than the apartments themselves. She crossed the tile floor that shone beneath heavy chandeliers and carved wood ceilings. George, the doorman, was kneeling in front of an older lady with silver hair, attempting to untangle the leashes of her three dachshunds.

An enormous flower arrangement sat on the desk, and as Juliet started toward it, George called, "That's not the delivery. Yours is there beside it."

She picked up a slender package wrapped in newspaper. She carried it upstairs unopened and then tore the paper off. Inside were two television scripts.

I Love Lucy—"Lucy Is Enceinte." Season 2, Episode 50. Written by Jess Oppenheimer, Madelyn Davis, and Bob Carroll Jr. 1952.

And *The Dick Van Dyke Show—"That's My Boy?" Season 3, Episode 64. Written by Bill Persky and Sam Denoff. 1963.*

Attached was a note on pale blue paper written in lilting cursive.

They made history. So can we.

—Dinah

THIRTY-SIX

Twenty-two days after the accident

T he women were scheduled to arrive at noon on Saturday. With Dinah and Juliet's help, Flora arranged the Newmans' living room seating into an informal circle. There would be six of them in all, possibly seven, if Juliet's colleague Paula Goodwin decided to show. Although Flora said nothing to this, she couldn't help tsking under her breath. Really. How was she supposed to plan refreshments if she didn't know how many people were coming?

"No," Juliet said, pulling her hair back from her face and holding it atop her head. "This looks too formal. We don't want them to feel like they're in a lecture hall."

Flora had never personally seen a lecture hall, but she couldn't imagine anyone would mistake the Newman living room for one, with its floor-to-ceiling French drapes and pale green sofa.

As Juliet stood frowning from beneath a fringe that needed a decent trim from a good pair of scissors, Flora and Dinah pushed and pulled the furniture until it was less of a circle and more of a casual square. Finally, Juliet nodded as if satisfied, letting go of her hair so that it tumbled free, and Dinah bustled around in capri pants, shoes *slap-slapping*, placing ashtrays and lighters on tables, tidying throw pillows. Flora busied herself double-checking surfaces for dust— even though she knew she wouldn't find any.

"I thought we'd serve refreshments when they get here," Dinah said to her. Then, to Juliet, "Give them a chance to break the ice before we start in with the conversation."

But Juliet was busy with her tape recorder, pushing buttons, shaking it vigorously.

Flora walked out and then returned, quietly setting a notebook and pen on Juliet's chair. Her brother worked for the Danish government, and she knew enough not to trust technology.

As to what the purpose of today was, she hadn't figured that out. Dinah had told her it was research for a project and later mentioned "the show."

Flora wished that Mr. Del were here. First, because she liked him best of all the Newmans for the way he electrified every room he walked into and always complimented her food. But second, because she preferred order and routine. There was a fairy tale by Hans Christian Andersen that she'd been raised on—"The Red Shoes." So horrified was she by the image of the peasant girl Karen literally dancing herself to death that she had taken the moral of the story to heart: Obey your elders, avoid sin, and only wear black shoes to church.

By 12:15, the Newman house was filled with laughter and chatter. Actresses Eileen Weld and Peggy Livingston from CBS. A young, very tall Black woman dressed head to toe in vivid purple—from her feathered marabou party hat to her vinyl kitten heels. A nurse named Benny from St. John's Hospital. And the unreliable Paula Goodman, who at least had the decency to ask before entering the living room if she should remove her loafers.

They passed around the hors d'oeuvres and finger sandwiches Flora had spent the morning making, a few of the women smoking, and most everyone drinking the wine or coffee that had been offered. They made chitchat—about the traffic, about the unprecedented heat wave of the past two days, about the Beatles, about General MacArthur's death. The entire time circling one another warily, taking each other in. Flora, who had no idea why these women were here, wondered if the women themselves knew.

She surveyed the room, ascertaining that everyone had a drink and a seat, and then she moved to leave. After years as a domestic servant, she had perfected the art of making herself invisible when necessary. She was nearly through the door when Dinah said—much to Flora's horror—"Please stay. We'd like you to join us."

It was then Flora noticed the eighth chair, which told her that Dinah had been planning this all along. With a deep, impatient sigh, she lowered herself onto it, careful to arrange the skirt of her uniform over her knees, shaking her head at Dinah's offer of coffee and—heaven forbid—wine, and folding her hands in her lap.

Dinah said, "Now we are eight," and there were a few titters around the square. "As my grandmother used to say, what I'm about to tell you should be kept in the strictest of confidence. Juliet here has been helping us with the last script of our season." She held up a finger, a mock warning. "But that doesn't leave this room. In fact, none of this does."

Flora stared at Dinah, but Juliet was talking now, her kohl-rimmed eyes moving from one guest to another. "It's no coincidence that we're all women," she said. "We're especially interested in what it means to be a woman right now in 1964. That's what we want to talk about. Whether you work outside the home or not, whether you're married or have a partner, whether or not you have kids."

"Does this mean my on-screen cookie-baking days are over?" asked Peggy. "Because, Lord, I hope so." More titters. Flora frowned. "I've read that book, you know. I'm familiar with the problem that has no name." Peggy twirled around in her chair in an effort to see the door. "Betty Friedan's not going to walk in here, is she?"

Flora wanted to ask *what* book, but Juliet held up the tape recorder and asked their permission to turn it on, and now the girl in vivid purple—Renee—said, "I wish she would walk in here."

She wriggled out of her jacket and tossed it over the back of her seat, where it missed and slid onto the floor. Flora started to rise—she would hang it properly in the hall closet—but Dinah shook her head.

"I've got a few things to say to her," Renee continued. "For starters, what she claims to be the 'woman's experience'? She means the *white* woman's experience."

The nurse, who was also Black, was nodding. "She completely leaves out the women who aren't married, who don't have kids, who can't afford a house. . . ."

"Exactly," said Renee. "She only focuses on white middle-class women, as if no other type of woman exists."

"It's a start, though," Juliet said, scribbling something in the notebook Flora had set out for her.

"Not good enough." Renee slipped off one kitten heel and scratched the back of her other calf with a stockinged toe. "I mean, if you're going through all the trouble to write the book, don't leave out half the female population."

"Listen," said Peggy through a cloud of smoke, "I'm a middle-aged white woman with a lot of money, but Friedan doesn't speak for me either. I'm too old to be liberated."

"You're only a year older than I am," Dinah said.

"And don't you feel settled?" Peggy waved her cigarette hand. "Kind of just stuck in? It's like whenever I think about divorcing Eddie. It took me twenty years to break him in. Why would I want to start over with someone else?" She nodded at the younger women. "It's too late for us, ladies. Save yourselves."

"Tell us more about what you're looking for here." Paula frowned at Dinah, with a secondary glance at Juliet. "What exactly do you plan to do with this information?"

"And what is it you're doing with the script?" Eileen Weld looked back and forth between Dinah and Juliet. "Can we ask that?"

"We want to . . ." Juliet closed the notebook. "We'd like to modernize the Newmans a little. And that includes giving Dinah something more to do than just cook and clean."

Dinah glanced at Flora. "Not that there's anything wrong with that."

"Not if you get paid for it," Flora said dryly.

Peggy hooted, and the others laughed. Flora's eyebrows shot up, but the room felt suddenly lighter, the tension cut in half. Everyone but Flora seemed to relax a little.

Over her cigarette, Peggy eyed Dinah. "And Del's okay with this?"

"He's got so much going on right now." Dinah tried to sound casual—*You know Del*. "He's barely aware of anything at the moment."

Sadly, this was true. Flora had been to see Mr. Del twice. Both times, she'd read to him from *Catch-22*, a book she didn't much like but that he loved. The doctor had brought him out of his coma almost a week ago, but since then, he hadn't done anything more than blinking and twitching. Flora had a secret fear that he would remain that way, and then what would become of her? She was too old to start over in another household with another family.

"The women Friedan leaves out of her book," Juliet was saying. "Is the problem that has no name relatable to all of us?"

Renee leaned forward. Her kitten heels, Flora noticed, had been discarded, and the young woman was in her stocking feet, legs crossed, one leg swinging wildly. "Are we all in this together, one big happy family regardless of skin color? Yes and also no. Hell no. Just because you're a white woman and men discriminate against you doesn't mean you don't discriminate against Black women."

Nurse Benny said, "The rights the rest of you fight for are going to look different from the rights we fight for. And our fight—Renee's and mine—is more of an uphill battle. It's the big steps and the small steps. The size of the step, that's not what matters. It's *taking* the step."

She sipped her wine. All the women, Flora observed, were now drinking wine by the glassful as if it wasn't early afternoon. And then, as she watched, the nurse spilled a little on the chair and dabbed at it with her napkin. Flora stood immediately, but Dinah placed a hand on her arm. Flora sat back down, eyes locked on the stain that was slowly darkening the chair cushion, no doubt settling in forever.

"We need to be able to acknowledge our differences," Benny said, holding out her glass as Juliet refilled it. "And the difference in the way we're treated. But do we have some things in common? Ways we're held down or held back? Yes. Because we're women." She smiled at Flora, a warm, genuine smile that seemed to say, *We're in this together.*

In spite of herself, Flora felt her cheeks ripen. And then, the smile causing her to momentarily forget the spilled drink, she asked, "What book are you talking about?"

"*The Feminine Mystique,*" Dinah said, "by a woman named Betty Friedan."

Flora had not heard of this woman or this book, but she nodded as if she had because all their guests—Mrs. Newman's guests—seemed to be very excited about it, and they were guests after all.

"Whatever our skin color," Renee said, as if Flora hadn't interrupted, "men think they have the right to what's inside it."

"Whether they're married to us or not," quipped Peggy. She lit another cigarette and wandered to the window, glass in hand, staring out across the backyard. This time, Flora was on her feet before Dinah could stop her, handing Peggy an ashtray, attempting a smile so as not to make her feel bad for ruining the rug.

"Thank you, Flora," Peggy said, then turned back to the room. "I'll tell you what I can't stand—the way some men like to pit us against each other. The stories I could tell you, and not just about Hollywood."

"It's the same at the hospital," said Benny.

"At the paper too." Paula snorted. "They like it better when we don't agree. Boyd Hartley's fairer than most, but," she said to Juliet, "don't let his Gary Cooper *High Noon* act fool you." She spread her arms wide. "'Two households, both alike in dignity, in fair Verona, where we lay our scene, from ancient grudge break to new mutiny, where civil blood makes civil hands unclean.'"

Flora slipped out of the room silently. In another life, with another upbringing, she might have made a good cat burglar like the one Cary Grant played in *To Catch a Thief*.

Now there, Flora thought, *was a man.*

Minutes later, she returned, carrying a tray with two new bottles of wine and a fresh pot of coffee. As Flora set down the refreshments and refilled empty glasses, Dinah was talking about her mother. "She used to call it the patchwork quilt method. Little pieces of time you take for yourself to write or paint or dance or study or whatever it is you like doing. Whatever you need to do for you. You take these pieces of time when and where you can, and before you know it, you've cobbled something together."

"I feel like a lot of women give up too quickly," Paula said.

"Like they forget all about their dreams," added Renee. "Or they come up with some excuse to justify the fact that they're not even trying anymore."

"If," Juliet said, "they were even allowed to dream."

Eileen took her glass from Flora with a soft "Thank you." This girl who was marrying Arving seemed polite and decent, but she was an actress, so you never could tell. To the wider group, she said, "I think feminism is meant to give women the chance to choose the life they want. So if they choose to be a stay-at-home mom, that's feminism. Just like if they choose to work."

"The problem is we don't have systems in place to help women thrive." Paula was picking the cucumber out of the finger sandwiches and discarding the cream cheese, fresh dill, and white bread—soft as a pillow—that Flora had so carefully assembled. "As employees," Paula said as she was chewing. "As mothers. So we always feel as if we're failing somewhere. You find yourself thinking, *I'm not a good reporter. Not as good as the men I work with.*"

"*Not a good wife, not a good mother*," Peggy added. "Anytime you move outside the bounds of preset social roles, you get slapped back." She ambled about the room, making sweeping gestures with her hands, ash scattering in her wake. Flora would have to hire someone to deep clean the carpets.

They discussed the women they knew, both famous and not famous, who had existed beyond those roles, and the Pill, abortion, their non-existent rights to their bodies. A glass was pressed into Flora's hand, and Dinah was waving her back to her seat, even though most of the guests were on their feet now, heated and tipsy.

Benny said, "Do you realize it isn't until after menopause that our bodies actually belong to us?" She sighed. "And by then, no one cares what we do with them."

Flora had been married once, twenty years ago, to an Italian man named Ricardo. The marriage itself had been short-lived. She had loved him. He had died. She had no desire to go through it—any of it—again.

"Back when I was your age"—Peggy nodded at Juliet, Renee, Eileen—"I used to be whistled at on the street. And then I turned forty and it stopped. I thought, *That's it. I'm over the hill. I'm no longer de-sirable. I've gone invisible.* But why did I need that attention to *not* feel invisible? Why did how men see me or not see me become a factor in how I feel about myself?"

"We should start whistling at them," Dinah said to laughter.

"They'd like it too much," said Renee.

Flora thought about a time long ago when she was less stout and less gray and men called out things to her on the street. Dirty things. Un-seemly things. The comments and catcalls had made her feel guilty, as if she were somehow responsible. She took a sip from the glass in her hand and was suddenly transported to a terrace in Italy, where she sat across from her husband, the sleeves of his shirt rolled to his elbows, his dark head thrown back in laughter. He had loved wine, the dryer the better, and she had learned to love it too. For them, it was reserved for celebrations and milestones. She wondered if this forum of women, gathered here in an informal square in the Newman living room, counted as such.

"I don't know," Eileen said thoughtfully, almost dreamily. "Not all men. Some of them don't like the attention."

Peggy laughed at this, but Renee said, "That's the thing, right?" She was looking at Juliet. "They're not all bad. And we can't help loving some of them. And that's okay. As long as we don't lose ourselves."

Juliet stared at the floor, as if she saw something or someone in the rug. "Friedan believes"—she looked up again—"that women have to experience sexual fulfillment before they can truly know their full strength as human beings. And if we're sexually realized, we have higher self-esteem. If we have higher self-esteem, we're freer to be ourselves."

"Orgasms," said Peggy. "It always comes down to orgasms."

"Yet they don't even belong to us," said Juliet. "Some doctors believe the whole reason we have them is so that men can express tenderness. And so that we'll be knocked out, basically horizontal, giving the sperm a better chance of getting to the egg."

"Most men," added Renee, "couldn't find a clitoris if it were attached to them."

The women erupted into laughter, which dissolved into a discussion of where a clitoris might be attached to a man for him to find it.

"His penis," Eileen said finally, decisively. "That's the only place he'd look for it."

Peggy cackled. "And even then, he wouldn't know what to do with it."

As Flora sat in her employer's living room, listening to these women talk about orgasms and penises and sex, she tried not to appear as shocked as she was. But she couldn't help feeling that it wasn't just *The Feminine Mystique* she'd been in the dark about. It was as if all this time there'd been a rule book she'd never heard of—one that women hated, one that, as a woman, *she* should hate too.

Paula Goodman said, "This theory of Friedan's about being sexually realized—she's saying our sexual fulfillment is dependent on someone else."

"Not just someone else," said Benny. "A *male* someone else."

"Exactly," said Paula. "But what about fulfilling ourselves? What about those of us who aren't sexual beings? Does that mean we'll never be fulfilled?"

"If I was my 'true self'"—Dinah made air quotes—"I don't know if I would have gone along with Del taking charge of every element of our lives. I mean, where was I the past twenty years?"

It was a haunting question, one that made Flora almost as uncomfortable as sex. Dinah Newman was an institution. She was everything Flora believed in. But then, Flora knew, Dinah couldn't actually cook, couldn't clean, couldn't sew. And she also knew that before the accident, whenever she had changed the sheets and made the beds, Mr. Del's side wasn't being slept in.

"What I want to know is," Juliet said, "do you think we can have it all?"

Flora's husband had talked like this. *One day*, he would say to her as they climbed into bed each night, *we're going to have everything we ever dreamed of.* She had laughed at him, told him to stop being so Italian, but inwardly, she had thought, *I already have more than I need.*

"God, do we *want* it all?" Peggy pulled out another cigarette and tapped it thoughtfully against the package.

Benny sat back in her chair. "Give me my work, my home, my friends. An occasional date here and there. That's what 'all' means to me."

"I think women are capable of having it all," Paula said. "I just don't know that society's built in a way that makes it possible."

"I can tell you right now it's not," said Renee.

"I think," said Flora, frowning deeply, "that if I wanted to, I could have it all. I just don't know that I'd want it."

The sound of her own voice surprised her as much as it surprised the others. Everyone stopped and stared at her.

"All is too much," she continued. "If a woman is told when she's a child, *You can have it all*, how will she feel when she grows up and goes into the world and learns that she can't?"

Juliet turned those dark-rimmed eyes on her. "Are you saying it's better we don't let girls grow up thinking they can do anything they put their minds to?"

Flora opened her mouth to say no, but instead, she said, "Believing you can do anything, that's different from having everything."

"So maybe that's not the goal," Eileen said to Flora, to Juliet, to all of them, her young voice filled with passion. "Maybe the goal is to have enough for you. Whatever that looks like."

They fell silent at this, everyone lost in private reverie.

"I feel too big for this room," Peggy said. "We should go kick some doors in."

"We should run naked through the streets!" said Renee, hoisting her glass heavenward, liquid sloshing over the side and onto the rug.

Juliet laughed. They were all laughing now except Flora. But the energy in the room was hopeful and electric and so charged that she felt herself vibrate.

"The lake," said Dinah, eyes gleaming. One by one, they turned their heads to stare out the window in the direction of the six-acre body of water around which the neighborhood had formed. "We should go swimming."

Eight women—fueled by wine and solidarity—descended upon Toluca Lake in the middle of the sunlit afternoon, laughing and shrieking as they stripped to their underwear and went splashing into the water. It was a Saturday, which meant there were sailboats floating by and families dotting the banks here and there for picnics or fishing.

Dinah was the first one in, shivering beneath the sun because the air was warm but the water was cold. Then Juliet, then Peggy, then Renee, and so on, until it was just Flora standing resolutely on the shore. She watched as they dove and swam and shrieked some more. They reminded her of seals, mouths open, limbs splashing. They turned cartwheels in the shallows and chased each other into the depths, looking ridiculous. As if the great Amelia Earhart had never lived here. As if distinguished movie stars like Frank Sinatra and Bette Davis, or that delightful singing cowboy Tex Ritter, had never walked the short distance from their homes onto these banks and waded into this very lake.

Still. When they drifted farther and farther toward the horizon, Flora felt a strange pang in the center of her chest. She didn't want to be left behind. She glanced around her. Quickly, before she could change her mind, she slipped out of her sensible shoes, set them neatly aside, and walked into the water.

"Flora!" Dinah shouted.

The rest of the women turned to watch her, joining in.

She took a breath. Let it out. Then, still wearing her neatly pressed uniform, pushed toward them, until the water—as chilly as Julsø, the lake of her youth—reached her knees, her thighs, her waist, her chest, all the while they were screaming her name.

Afterward, as they lay on the grassy bank, Dinah said to the sky, "I feel like I'm still learning how." Her voice was dreamy. She didn't say what it was she was still learning to do. "And most of the time, I feel like I'm failing at everything."

"I want the chance," said Juliet, sitting cross-legged and shaking the drops from her hair, "to be a full person in this world." She opened her arms wide, encompassing the other women, the lake, the city, and beyond. "To go anywhere a man can go."

"I'll tell you what I want." Renee stood and stretched. Her underwear was the same brilliant purple as her outfit. "The freedom to be an asshole. The freedom to be selfish. The freedom to be unlikable if I want to be."

"The freedom to stand up for yourself," said Paula, face tilted upward, eyes closed.

"The freedom to *like* ourselves," Dinah added. "Because we're not really supposed to."

"I want the ability to be great without having to apologize or make it okay for others," Benny said, propping herself on her elbows. "To lift my own self up."

"And the freedom not to have to feel afraid all the time," said Juliet. "To not be harassed wherever we go."

She held up a hand, and Renee helped her to her feet. The two of them stood side by side, one a head taller than the other, and Renee threw an arm around Juliet's shoulders, an instinctive, easy gesture. In that instant, Flora envied their friendship.

"If all of these things changed—the things that need changing—would you think of yourselves as equal?" Dinah asked them, shading her eyes against the sun.

"Oh, better than equal," Peggy said, which inspired laughter.

Sitting next to her, Flora was listening to the sound of her own heartbeat. She gazed down at her shoes, sturdy and black, and imagined them—just for a moment—a bright, dazzling red.

The women raced each other back to the Newman house, everyone but Flora in their underwear. The damp fabric of her dress was a second skin as she pushed to keep pace with Dinah, Juliet, and the rest. It had been so long since she had run, she was surprised her body remembered how. But instead of the heavy ache of her joints, she felt as light as the breeze.

As they reached the front gate, Flora heard a crash. She turned like the others to see the next-door neighbor on his riding lawn mower, which—upon seeing half a dozen women of multiple ages running nearly naked down the street—he'd driven headfirst into a palm tree.

THIRTY-SEVEN

Twenty-three days after the accident

On Sunday, April 12, Los Angeles woke to light showers and a sky clouded with gray. The high was expected to be sixty-two, the low thirty-four, the heat finally breaking. It was an unusually wet day, but rain was more common in spring than Angelenos liked to admit.

Dinah normally hated weather like this, but today it made her feel cozy and cocooned. She sat in the office, listening to the recording of the focus group, now and then pausing the tape to write something down so that she would remember. In another part of the house, the telephone rang—she had banished the office extension to the closet so as not to be disturbed—far enough away that she didn't have to worry about it.

She pressed Play. Then Stop. Then Play again. Over and over, enjoying the feel of her pen against paper and the sight of the words beginning to fill the blank space. After a whole lot of trial and error, she and Juliet had written a bare-bones script. It was thin and needed padding in places, trimming in others, and there were entire pages that were marked up and slashed through, Juliet's wild scribble and Dinah's neat cursive in the margins. But it was a thing that existed, that they had made.

Thunder cracked overhead, so rare in LA that she squinted out the window as if trying to place the sound.

There was a knock, and Dinah swiveled in her chair to see Flora in the doorway.

"A Mrs. Sunbeam is on the telephone for you," Flora said. Her eyes moved across the office, taking in every change Dinah had made to it in the days Del had been gone.

"Mrs. Sunbeam," Dinah repeated. She jumped to her feet and followed Flora down the stairs and into the main house, where she picked up the receiver in the den. "This is Dinah," she said.

"Dinah, it's Mrs. Sunbeam. Great news. I've spoken with my husband, and we—the Sunbeam Corporation—would like to sponsor *Meet the Newmans*. This is just for the finale, with a possibility of renewing sponsorship should the network pick you up for next season. . . ."

Dinah didn't hear the rest. Suddenly, in this moment, she felt brand new, the way she had at sixteen when she first arrived in Hollywood, like she had when she and Del fell in love. The two women spoke for a few minutes about official paperwork and next steps, and when the call ended, she immediately picked up the receiver again to phone Juliet.

"Hello?" a male voice said.

"Hello?"

"Is this Mrs. Newman?"

"Yes, it is. . . . Sorry, the line didn't even ring. I was about to make a call. . . . Who is this?"

"This is Dr. Carson from St. John's Hospital."

He sounded grave. In words clipped and precise, he told her his news.

"I'm sorry," she said. "Could you say that again?" She was trying to make sense of what he was telling her. She wanted to be certain she understood.

"It's your husband," he said again. "We lost him earlier today. His heart stopped. We got him back, but I suggest you come now."

THIRTY-EIGHT

Twenty-three days after the accident

G uy rode the gas pedal like he was at Le Mans, knuckles white on the steering wheel. His mother beside him in the front seat, Shep and Kelly in the back. It was now raining hard, which meant the city's drivers were driving too fast, driving too slow, or sitting at a standstill blocking traffic.

Dinah stared out the window, even though she couldn't focus on anything other than Del. How were you supposed to say goodbye to someone you'd spent half your life with? Her mother had died so suddenly and out of the blue that Dinah hadn't had the chance to prepare. Her mother was just gone. But now that Dinah did have warning, she wondered how on earth you ever prepared for something like this.

What had she been doing at the exact time he coded? As Del died and was brought back to life, where was Dinah? She should have sensed it, felt him leaving her. She didn't expect the world itself to stop, but she should have known.

In the seat behind her, Shep closed his eyes, unable to look at the rain or his family—his brother's profile, jaw clenched and serious. The back of his mother's neck, which had gone rigid. Kelly's hand resting on his brother's head, a gesture so tender that Shep looked away even though he wasn't sure why.

For once, Guy wasn't trying to spin the situation to try to make it better, and as much as this particular characteristic had always bugged the shit out of Shep, the lack of it made him feel worse. He felt sick. He felt numb. He mostly felt sorry. It had been three weeks, and he'd never gone to see his dad, not once.

Something nudged him, and he looked up to see Kelly. He was asking without asking if he needed anything—a comforting hug, a brotherly shoulder to cry on—because this was how distant Shep was. He could go to bed with strangers, girls he barely knew or didn't know at all, but his family—and by now, Kelly was like family—understood not to touch him without permission.

He opened his hand, and Kelly wrapped his around it. Shep closed his eyes again and, in the five minutes left to the hospital, sent up approximately eight thousand appeals, entreaties, prayers—whatever you wanted to call them—to the universe that this wasn't the end.

The Newmans burst into the emergency room, forgetting to disguise themselves. They heard the recognition as it happened, sparking and spreading. Sydney was nowhere to be seen, and so Dinah, Guy, Kelly, and Shep hurried to the check-in desk, ignoring the stares and the whispers and the general sound of buzzing, a thousand cicadas on a hot summer evening.

"Yes," said the nurse, who wasn't Benny, before any of them said a word. "Come with me."

It struck Dinah how unfair this was, with an emergency room full of people waiting to be seen or waiting for their loved ones. But she didn't complain or tell the nurse to take these others first, because she and her family might already be too late. Del might already be gone.

They followed the nurse through the double doors into the emergency room, where no one noticed or cared that they were America's Favorite Family. There was the smell, Dinah thought, of antiseptic and blood and death. She faltered, her legs not working. She almost told the boys to go on without her, as if she were an anchor tying them to the ocean floor. But then she saw Sydney, in his dark blue suit, as if he were dressed for a funeral, speaking with Dr. Carson.

An arm around her shoulders, and Guy was beside her, helping her walk. They moved together, the four of them, in a clump, braced and ready for what lay ahead. She watched as first Sydney and then Dr. Carson turned to them.

"It's Del," said Dr. Carson. "He's awake."

For a few seconds, no one spoke. It was as if they hadn't heard him.

"What's that?" Guy asked. "Did you say—"

"He's awake," Sydney blurted before Dr. Carson could repeat himself. He met Dinah's eyes, his own eyes brimming over. "Del is awake."

A few more seconds as they stood there, Dinah, Guy, Shep, and Kelly, trying to take this in. Then Shep voiced the thing that each of them was thinking:

"Oh, fuck."

The Return

One week before the finale

THIRTY-NINE

Seven days before the final episode

Del Newman stood in the back garden of his house and breathed in the lake air. You had your ocean air and then you had your lake air, and to him, both smelled like California, this state he loved in spite of its own self-importance and everyone back east who called it vapid and cultureless. Give him palm trees and mountains and ocean and sunshine anytime. Frankly, he'd always found LA—unlike the Big Apple—to have a sense of humor. If the city was a joke, it was in on it.

Birds were singing high up on the branches above him. Their music was a concert at the Hollywood Bowl on a clear summer night. It was the sound of an audience cheering, a standing ovation during an Emmy Award acceptance speech. Each time he tested one of his senses and found it worked, he was filled all over again with a gratitude so enormous he almost broke down. *Was it his imagination, or were those senses even more heightened?*

Beyond the birds was the white streak of an airplane, soaring to places unknown. He could feel it as well as hear it—that rumble of the jet engine. It was swallowed by all that blue. And there was the moon, faint but visible, and the burning gold orb of sun. There was an entire world in the sky. Yet another thing—there were so many—he'd taken for granted. What was it Will Rogers had said? *If you want to be successful, it's just this simple. Know what you are doing. Love what you are doing. And believe in what you are doing.* In his head, Del added one more line—*And always take time to look up.*

The doctors had kept him for a couple of days to make sure he was strong enough and clear enough to leave the hospital. But now it was Friday, April 17, and he had been awake for five and a half days. He figured if unconsciousness were going to reclaim him and drag him back into the Great Darkness, it would have done so by now. He was home and, for the first time, out of bed. What's more, he had walked out here on his own, using the wall as a prop as he eased himself down the stairs from the bedroom. It felt as momentous as the time he'd been grand marshal of the Rose Bowl parade.

And so, filled with all this gratitude and life, he did the thing he most felt like doing. He began to sing. The song that came to him was "Back in the Saddle Again," that old Gene Autry classic. A song Del had always liked but never thought much of until now. His voice, he was happy to hear, sounded clearer and stronger than ever. There was a timbre to it he hadn't noticed before. He envisioned dueting with Shep on *Meet the Newmans*. Perhaps even reigniting his long-dormant singing career.

When he had sung every verse and every round of chorus, he launched into a rousing version of "Don't Fence Me In."

Oh, give me land, lots of land under starry skies above,
Don't fence me in

The song captured how he felt in this moment, standing in this spot, free of the hospital, restored to his family. He had spent twenty-two days somewhere else. In darkness. In dreams. But now the world was bright and possible and real, and he was part of it once again.

Upstairs, Dinah stood at the open window of the office, out of view of the backyard, listening to her husband sing a medley of Gene Autry's greatest. Her husband, who was—miracle of miracles—back from the dead, the very thing she had yearned for and prayed for every day for the past three weeks.

On Wednesday, when she brought him home, Dinah had wanted to crawl into the bed and tell him everything that had happened since he'd been gone. But the car ride from Santa Monica to Toluca Lake had worn him out. So instead, she had kissed his forehead and come to this office, where she wrote and then collapsed on the foldout couch, which still sat in the hall outside the door.

She lit a cigarette, sinking into the cushions. Inhaled deeply, pursed her lips, expelled the smoke in a delicate stream, the meandering, lazy uncurling of a hypnotized snake. He was home and he would be fine. She waited for it to sink in, for the weight she had been carrying since March 20 to detach itself like some sort of gigantic bloodsucking tick, from her shoulders, her head, her heart. Del's doctors had warned her that he should pace himself. What he needed was the routine of home. Nothing unusual. No excitement. Also, it was normal for coma patients to awaken feeling depressed. Sometimes their memories were hazy. If he appeared forgetful or confused, that was to be expected.

But Del seemed mostly like Del. In the past three weeks, he was the only one who hadn't changed.

What are we going to do? Guy asked as the four of them—Dinah, Kelly, Shep, himself—left the hospital on Sunday, the day of Del's miraculous reawakening.

Let's get him home first, Dinah had said. *And then we'll figure it out.*

What Guy had meant, of course, was what did Del's being back mean for the rest of them? Would they be out of a job? Dr. Carson had been vague about when exactly Del might be up for working again. But they all knew Del Newman well enough to know he wasn't one to listen to medical experts or advice. Sunday night, Dinah had thanked god, her mother, the universe—any powers that be that might have had a hand in saving her husband's life. And then she delivered up an urgent prayer: "Please keep him out of the way until we finish writing the script. Or until we begin rehearsals. Or, actually, until we shoot the finale."

When he came home, days later, he was too weary to talk, and so she was able to dodge the subject of the show. But she wasn't sure how much longer she would be able to do so.

It was one reason she sat here on this sofa when she could, should, be down there with him. More than that, she was up here because she was angry. And hurt. Whatever explanation for M. Leslie and the fact that they were broke, he had betrayed her. Not only her but *them*. The them they'd been when they first fell in love, the them they had promised to be. And these were things she wasn't sure how to tell him.

Juliet had visited movie and television sets before. As a reporter living in Los Angeles, writing for the Lifestyle section of a major newspaper, it came with the job. She liked to think she wasn't a person who was easily starstruck. But as she walked onto the CBS set of the Newman family home, she was overcome with a sense of something like déjà vu. More a cousin of it than the actual feeling of having been there before. It was, she decided, a sense of coming full circle. She had grown up watching *Meet the Newmans*, and now here she stood, the guest of Dinah Newman, with whom she was writing the very last script of season twelve. Possibly the very last script of the series.

She pushed her sunglasses onto her head and took in everything, her reporter's eye memorizing details—the lights of various sizes and shapes that hung from the rafters, the heat they seemed to give off even though they were dark, the camera, cumbersome and attached to a rolling base, the colors of the living room furniture, vivid greens and blues and oranges. It was strange to see their world in color when she was so used to seeing it in black and white.

The soundstage was strangely, almost eerily quiet. While she waited for Dinah, she crossed from sofa to fireplace. She examined the framed photographs that hung on the set walls, the magazines spread on the coffee table, the books lining the shelves, the sweets in the candy dish. It was like being in a museum she'd heard about for years—the Louvre, the Met, the Smithsonian. Everything perfectly preserved. She was afraid of touching the exhibits, terrified of disturbing anything.

"They're real. You can have one."

Juliet jumped, then turned to see Dinah striding toward her, dressed again in capri pants and very little makeup. The way she moved, long legs graceful, a swing to her hips, the way her freckles shone across her nose and cheeks, she looked almost like a teenager.

"The candy," Dinah said. "But I wouldn't recommend it. God knows how long it's been there. Shep used to swap out pieces and replace them with fireballs and this awful black taffy that stained your teeth and stuck them together like glue."

Juliet set the candy back in its dish, unaware of having picked it up. "It looks just like your house."

Dinah surveyed the living room. "It should," she said. "We spent enough time and money making sure of that. Right down to . . ." She crossed to the set beside it, the Newman kitchen. Juliet followed, watching as Dinah opened the refrigerator door. "Right down to the loose handle on the fridge, courtesy of my sons, who were wrestling one day—this was years ago. Crashed right into it. Added a dent." She moved the door back and forth so that Juliet could see the slight dip in the shine of it. "And forever broke the handle."

"That's . . ." Juliet wanted to say, *That's so weird and lovely.*

"Too much detail. Maybe you've heard, but my husband's a stickler." At the word *husband*, Dinah frowned. And then she was waving Juliet onward through the shadowy spaces of backstage to her dressing room, which looked like something from the golden age of Hollywood. The room itself was done up in varying shades of sky blue, the enormous makeup mirror and gleaming white vanity its focal point.

"Where is everyone?" Juliet asked.

"Regrouping."

Dinah closed the door and sank onto the curved sofa. She immediately began to rub at her temples, as if the weight of her head was too much.

It was a gesture that seemed private and personal, not a thing Juliet was meant to see. Instinct told her to stand very still. It was something she'd learned in the early days of reporting. When a person had something to say, a single movement could disrupt their train of thought and make them go silent.

Dinah's hands dropped into her lap. "Del's back."

"When?"

"Yesterday."

From the door, Juliet said, "And he's okay?"

"He's great." Dinah brushed at her eyes as if she were brushing away a cobweb. "Tired but good. Surprisingly good. I mean, this is what we've been hoping for. Del waking up . . . Del recovering . . . that's the only thing I've wanted since the accident." She sounded as if she were trying to convince herself. "At first, he took a turn . . . I mean, he was literally dead. We went to the hospital, and when we got there, he was awake. Just sitting there. Smiling . . ." Her voice trailed off. She picked over and over at a thread on the couch. "Just smiling and smiling and so happy to be back and to see us, and the only thing I could think was, 'Why couldn't you have woken up after the final show?'"

Juliet moved then, taking a seat beside her. "Is he coming back to work?"

"He's not supposed to, not anytime soon, but he's well aware of the fact that we're due to shoot the season finale next week . . . and the doctors don't know my husband."

"Oh."

"Yes. Oh. Yes." Dinah hopped to her feet. "It's just that . . ." She checked her wristwatch. "I don't have long. Right now, I mean. I had to make up a reason to leave the house. And yes, it's not as if the show just stops or the world just stops, but if we let on that we're here, he'll want to know what exactly we're doing for the finale, and I don't want him to ask me anything, not yet, but I don't know how long I can . . ."

She shook her head. "How am I supposed to work on the script with him underfoot?"

Juliet said, "You have to tell him."

"I can't go back to how things were. I don't want to. It's almost like I've been in my own coma for the past few years." Dinah began to pace. "But here I am, and he has no idea . . . It's not like I've told him what we're doing . . . but I can only imagine . . . At the same time, I don't care! I'm not the only one keeping secrets." She was growing more and more animated. "I can't very well climb back into the goddamn box when I'm telling women that they don't have to live in one. Can I?"

"No," Juliet said simply. "You can't. And *that* is our show. Del. The coma. Freeing Dinah from the box. And then he wakes up."

Time seemed to slow. *Of course*, Dinah thought. *It's so simple.*

Juliet set her bag on the floor. She pulled out her notebook and flipped through until she found a blank page. She wrote as they talked over each other, words spilling around them, filling the room—an accident, a coma, a wife and mother navigating the aftermath. It was wartime all over again, women leaving the house to work in factories, finding their freedom in the workplace. Only this was 1964. This was Dinah Newman.

Someone—maybe Eileen—can give Dinah a copy of The Feminine Mystique. *And that sets it all in motion. And then Guy can take his mom to a civil rights protest, help her see what's really going on out there. Dinah can smoke grass with Mama Cass. Or go dancing at the Whisky while Shep plays a new song.*

They were up and down—on their feet acting out their ideas, on the couch writing, writing.

Or she can take over for Del at his work, even though no one—probably not even Del—knows what he does for a living. She lives all these lives while he's incapacitated. We liberate her and then he wakes up, but she no longer fits in the box.

The air around them pulsed. Dinah felt flammable, one match strike and she would go up in flames. Juliet—so accustomed to taking dictation—couldn't write fast enough. She reached into her bag and found the recorder. What Dinah had said about feeling invisible around men, that needed to go in. Also what Juliet had said about losing herself when she was with the Musician. Eileen could take those lines, and Dinah—no, *Peggy* could daydream about an affair with the milkman. . . .

The ring of the telephone was too loud, too shrill, as if it had to scream to be heard. Without thinking, as if it were part of a scene, Dinah picked up the receiver.

"What are you doing there?" Del said.

She felt herself crash back to earth. "I left my sunglasses. No one else is here. Just me. . . ."

"Weren't you wearing them this morning?"

"Not those. The brown ones." Some ingrained human part of her remembered to ask, "How are you feeling?"

They talked for a minute, and then she promised him she'd be right home. When she hung up, Juliet was still writing.

Dinah didn't want to leave. She said, a little wistfully, "I wonder if this is what a real writers' room is like."

"No." Juliet shook her head. "In a real writers' room, the men would do all the talking."

FORTY

Seven days before the final episode

As she watched Dinah drive out of the CBS lot toward Toluca Lake and home, Juliet felt a sudden stab of longing. She didn't want the day to be over. She wasn't sure when it had happened, but she'd started looking forward to these sessions with Dinah. She was left—at the end of each of them—feeling restless and wanting more. There had always been so much to say, and now, finally, she had a chance to say it and to a much larger audience than the *LA Times* could give her.

She should have gone back to her place and caught up on the sleep she needed, but every part of her was awake. And so she drove until she found herself heading north on Crescent Heights—which would morph into Laurel Canyon once she crossed Sunset Boulevard. It didn't help that her car seemed able to navigate to the Musician's house all on its own.

Juliet managed to wrest control over the steering wheel and went screeching eastward instead, pulling over outside Schwab's Pharmacy. She had planned to come here—or some other drugstore—as research for her article on the Pill, but between the newspaper and her work with Dinah, there hadn't been time.

The bell jingled as she pushed through the double doors. Inside, Schwab's was teeming with wall-to-wall people and smelled of the malts and sundaes the soda fountain was known for. Juliet bypassed the long, crowded counter, where, decades ago, Lana Turner had—according to legend—been discovered and Harold Arlen had reportedly composed "Over the Rainbow" on a napkin, and made her way to the druggist at the back of the store. He was not much older than she was. A harried smile. A tight-knit brow. He looked as if he was nursing a headache.

"I'd like to buy a package of condoms," she told him, shouting over the noise.

"Is your husband with you?"

"I'm not married."

"Sorry," he said. And, just to be clear, he shook his head.

"What do you recommend I do?"

"Talk to your doctor."

"But he won't even prescribe the Pill. Because, as I mentioned . . ." She held up her left hand to show him the lack of wedding ring.

"Sorry," he said again.

"Access to contraception *should* be a fundamental right. No one should be allowed to decide whether I'm free to have sex or not, whether I protect myself or not. It's not as if I invented the Pill or condoms or birth control. These things exist for a reason."

She could feel the bubbling of her blood, the acceleration of her heart. It was a challenge, and she loved a challenge. But it was also the thought of the Musician in their house, free to sleep with whomever he wanted without worrying about the fallout. It was men like Charlie Murdock and her father and her mother's long-forsaken dreams. It was Del Newman back from his long winter's nap.

"I'm twenty-six years old and I'm not allowed access to any kind of contraception. It should be my decision if I want kids now or later or not at all. It shouldn't matter who I am or how much money I have or where I come from or if I'm married or not married. What am I supposed to do?"

"Abstain," the pharmacist said dryly and then glanced over her head at the enormous clock. And sighed.

There was a lot she wanted to say to this man, but her words would be lost on him. He wasn't the one who had created these laws. He was only doing his job, counting down the time until he could punch out and go home.

The air was so close that she was beginning to suffocate, and so she moved toward the exit. As she did, Juliet felt someone tug at her sleeve. "It's bullshit," said a young woman, nodding toward the pharmacist. "This is 1964. No one cares who a man sleeps with."

The woman—Hannah—told Juliet how much she loved Betty Friedan for what she'd tried to do with her book. How she'd devoured Helen Gurley Brown's *Sex and the Single Girl*, which she related to even more. Juliet thought of the letters women wrote Dinah from across the country, and as she squeezed Hannah's hand and walked out of Schwab's, she felt even more restless, even more awake.

Her apartment, only minutes away, was too far, and so she sat in her car outside the drugstore and—by the glow of the streetlights and the passing headlights—wrote the scene.

What Dinah needed was a buffer. Before she'd left the studio, she telephoned her sons and Sydney to invite them to dinner, and then she called Flora to ask her to set four extra places.

Del, his color improved, his eyes brighter, sat at the head of the table in the chair Dinah had begun to think of as hers. He was dressed in his dark blue pajamas, the ones that matched his eyes, jet-black hair combed and styled, a red handkerchief—his nod to dressing for dinner—folded neatly in his breast pocket.

Dinah sat at the opposite end, Guy and Sydney on one side, Shep and Kelly on the other. As they passed the food Flora had left for them, they filled Del in on all the things he had missed. The death of General Douglas MacArthur. The earthquake in Alaska. The first driverless train running on the London Underground. The heat wave they'd been having recently.

On and on, the conversation focused strictly on the news of the greater world. Del unable to get a word in edgewise, head turning, eyes following the volleys they were serving up across the steak and potatoes and green beans and braised carrots, all his favorite foods, which Flora had so lovingly cooked in his honor.

Kelly talked about the film he was shooting, a political thriller that starred Kirk Douglas and Burt Lancaster. Sydney told them about the plays he'd seen while he was in New York, and Guy said he was thinking of getting a dog, which he wasn't—he and Kelly were far too busy for a pet—but he was running out of things to say.

"Let's put on some music," Dinah said, sensing a lull was coming. "Shep, do you want to choose something? How about the Beatles? Del, they're really quite good."

"I know who the Beatles are," he said, watching as his younger son left the room. Opening guitar riffs followed by drums—so much banging—the whole thing sounding like it had been sped up, as if playing on the wrong speed.

Shep sat back down. "Groovy, right?"

"The Beatles arrived in February," Del said. "How long do you think I've been gone?"

No one answered this. Instead, they passed the food around again, and Sydney said if he ever got a dog, he'd get a basset hound or another breed that was good with scent. That way, it would warn him when any of his ex-wives came around. Kelly told them about the pet goat he'd had as a kid that was always running away to the neighbors'. Shep remembered a childhood buddy whose dog used to eat socks and pantyhose and glass Christmas ornaments. And then Dinah and Guy reminded everyone about the time when Shep was six and had insisted on eating out of a bowl on the floor and being taken for walks.

Del stared at all of them as if they'd lost their minds.

Then Dinah brought out the Baked Alaska, and the topic returned to the earthquake. Guy talked about earthquakes on the moon, how they were called *moonquakes*, how Mars had marsquakes, how there were even suspected spacequakes, which were temblors in the earth's magnetic field. The others came up with many, many questions for him about space, all of which he answered at great length. None of them—Dinah, Guy, Shep, Kelly, or Sydney—had ever worked so hard in their lives.

At some point, Del sat back, arms folded, staring at his family with the look he usually reserved for James T. Aubrey. It was a look of skepticism and suspicion. They chose to ignore it and babble on until Del stood, lifted the edge of the table, and moved it several inches toward him. He dropped it down with a bang and said, "What the fuck is going on with the show?"

They all stared at him. Only Shep continued to eat, plucking the food off Kelly's plate, which was now in front of him.

Dinah waved her hand. "Oh, we shot your last script, the one you wrote before . . . We divided your lines between Guy and Shep."

"I meant the finale. The live season finale, which, if memory serves—and I don't seem to have amnesia—is next week."

"Del," Dinah began, "you're only just home, and Dr. Carson said the last thing you should do is think about work. Your only job is to get better."

Del said nothing. Dinah looked at Guy, who looked at Shep, who looked at Kelly's plate. Then, all at once, the two of them stood, these children she had birthed and raised, gathered their plates, and ran. Guy and Shep, who had only ever cleared their places after much nagging or, on a few occasions, much yelling. She watched them leave the room through narrowed eyes.

"What about Aubrey? Where does he think I am?" Del said, once again taking a seat.

Aubrey. At the mention of his name, Dinah thought, *Shit.* In all the commotion—between hiring Juliet and the focus group and Del rising from the dead—she had forgotten to tell Aubrey that the wedding was off.

"Shit," she said.

The others stared at her.

"Sorry. I just . . . remembered that . . . I have something . . . on the stove . . . that I forgot to turn off. And I should have taken it off the burner a long time ago. Back when we first talked about it. Back when I told you all that I would take care of it."

She stared at Syd, willing him to understand.

"I'll check on it for you." Kelly leaped from his chair and went jogging off to the kitchen, which, presumably, had swallowed her sons like one of those black holes Guy loved so much.

Sydney said, "Who wants a cigarette?" And, carrying his whiskey glass, disappeared.

Dinah heard the back door slam and knew she had been abandoned. *Cowards*, she thought.

She looked at Del.

"Hi," he said.

"Hi."

"Aubrey?"

"Right." She shook her head, attempting to gather herself. "We told him you were visiting your sick mother."

"My mother who died?"

"Yes."

Del's eyes were still on hers. She opened her mouth to tell him how Aubrey had seemed—believe it or not—to buy it, and to launch after that into some long excuse about how lost they'd been while he was in the coma and how they'd done their best to find their way in his absence, when Del erupted into laughter. His laugh, always infectious, reached into her and grabbed hold of her heart and squeezed it for all it was worth.

Dinah began to laugh too, unsure what exactly they were laughing about, but not caring in the least because, just like in the old days, they were doing it together.

Del, the night owl, had gone to bed early, his energy still a shadow of its former boundless self. As Dinah sat before the typewriter, the office window open a crack so that she could feel the cool night air, she thought that their relationship felt tentative, precarious. The muscle memory was there, but they had all this new terrain to navigate. He was, after three weeks, a stranger.

She looked down at the paper, at the single word she'd typed. *Grateful.* She was grateful that Del was recovering, that he was here. Even if his being here wasn't the best timing.

She picked up the script she and Juliet had been working so hard on and dropped it into a desk drawer. Then she threaded a new page into the typewriter and started at the beginning—Dinah waiting for Del to come home from work and burning the dinner. Dinah pouring herself a drink. Dinah getting the call that Del had been in an accident. The coma. The hospital. She spent less than a page on these because she didn't want to bring the mood down. Moved on quickly to the family trying to figure out what to do without their leader.

As she wrote, she didn't stop to worry about setups and punch lines and scene buttons and laughs. She simply put it all down as it had happened.

Hours later, she fell onto the couch without even bothering to open it. She lay not sleeping, because not sleeping was what she did now. While across the house, in their bed, Del lay not sleeping too. Both yearning for the other and missing them—not necessarily the way they were right before the accident but the way they once were. The way they wished they could be again.

FORTY-ONE

Six days before the final episode

Everywhere Dinah turned, Del was there. She deflected and distracted and handled him with kid gloves, trying to appease him, soothe him, and—when he told her he was anxious to return to the studio—discourage him. *Not yet. You're not ready. You need rest.*

All I've been doing is goddamn resting since they put me in the goddamn coma.

He was able to bathe himself, and he was maneuvering the stairs twice a day. But his body—always so strong and infallible—was weak, which meant he had to depend on Dinah more than he liked. Overnight, his spirits had turned. So far, he had only wandered as far as the backyard, but it was only a matter of time before he ventured to the other side of the house and his rearranged office or—and this was what she really dreaded—down into the now-empty garage. Then she would have to explain to him, in a way that wouldn't upset him and put him back in the hospital, that because he had spent all their money, they would need to live on what they'd gotten for the cars and the art and the other collections.

In the living room, Del settled into his favorite chair. Dinah fetched him coffee and toast and the newspaper, but looking at it only reminded him—as if he needed a reminder—that time was passing and the season finale was six days away. And so she took away the newspaper and handed him a carefully curated stack of books, none of which dealt with comas or frustrated artists or car accidents or wives keeping secrets from husbands, and most of which—in an effort to keep him occupied—were over four hundred pages long.

"I know what you're doing," he said to her. "You're trying to keep me out of the way."

"I'm trying to keep you calm. Dr. Carson doesn't want you getting overexcited."

"Well, this is a great way to see to that." He tossed the copy of *Moby Dick* onto the floor. "I need to know what's happening with the finale. Is there a script? Of course there isn't a script. I still need to write it." He started to push himself up and out of the chair, but Dinah flew to him and gently eased him back down.

"All you need to know is that your family has stepped up. We're taking care of the show until you're able to come back."

Something made her lean down and kiss him. She meant to give him a quick peck on the forehead but instead found herself touching her lips to his. She waited for the awkwardness between them to disappear, as if this were a fairy tale and she was kissing him awake from a spell. But he only stared unhappily at the book on the floor, and so she left the room.

She enlisted Flora to watch him, which meant no strenuous activity. Especially not working or driving. No office. No garage. She must do whatever she had to in order to keep him calm and preoccupied in this portion of the house. And then Dinah drove to Juliet's apartment, which was small and cozy and reminded her of the first place she had ever rented all on her own, at the base of the Hollywood Hills. A funny little place that smelled like mole poblano from the Mexican restaurant down below.

They had four days until the first rehearsal, which meant three days to finish the script and edit it into shape so they could share it with the cast and crew. *Three days*, which didn't count the fact that Juliet would be spending most of each day at the *Times* and Dinah would need to work around her husband.

"Okay," Dinah said in an effort to center herself. "Okay, okay, okay." She flipped through the existing pages, the ones she had typed the night before. She had decided not to tell Aubrey about the canceled wedding. She didn't want to risk his ire or give him an excuse to yank the season finale. What was the old saying? *Better to ask for forgiveness.*

Still, it weighed on her. The way everything right now weighed on her. She could feel the world starting to crowd in, flattening her where she sat until the only thing left of her would be her clothing in a pile on the floor. She covered her face with her hands.

Juliet set her notebook aside, gently took the pages from Dinah's lap, and began to read. The little apartment was quiet except for the rustling of paper. Eventually, Dinah uncovered her face and waited.

Several interminable minutes later, Juliet looked up. "It's good." Her voice was scratchy from emotion.

"It's not finished. I should have waited for you. . . ."

"No," said Juliet. "We just need to punch it up. Maybe trim a little. Add the ending." She got up, sat down at the typewriter, and began to write. "'Interior. Newman house. Night.'" She talked as she typed. "'The grandfather clock strikes midnight. . . .'"

Dinah rose, starting to pace. "'Dinah stands at the window, worried, angry. Beyond her, we can see a table set for two.'"

Guy and Sydney met Mr. and Mrs. Sunbeam in the lobby of CBS and escorted them to Studio 33 to give them a tour of the sound booth, the wardrobe room, the rehearsal hall, the set itself. They waited until the sponsor and his wife were seated comfortably in the TV living room— marveling at the vivid hues of the curtains, the furniture, the rug!—to break the news that *Meet the Newmans* needed two additional cameras and two additional camera operators for the season finale.

Mr. Sunbeam couldn't resist interjecting, "Why don't you ask for two more years on-air while you're at it?" He frowned at his wife. The only reason he was doing this was for her.

Guy said, "That would be fantastic." He couldn't help the sarcasm in his voice. This was business, and he wasn't asking for anything un-reasonable. "But that's not why we're here. All we're asking for is a chance to shoot this show before a live studio audience, and we can't tape the show in front of an audience unless we have more cameras."

Sydney jumped in, "Just wait'll you see it. Everyone's going to be talking about it. We're bringing the Newmans into the 1960s. Picture this—a new song by Shep Newman. Del, Dinah, and Guy as you've never seen them before." He hadn't been included in script discussions, didn't even know what the episode was about, but he knew what words to use with sponsors. "They're still the Newmans we love, but more modern, more with it. . . ."

"Why don't you just shoot the blasted thing in color?" Mr. Sunbeam let out a laugh, as if he couldn't imagine anything more preposterous.

"That's exactly what we plan to do," said Guy, his voice steady, his gaze steadier. Mr. Sunbeam's smile faded. Guy said, "Sir, I've done my research, and I predict that next year, over half of all network programming, at least in prime time, will be broadcast in color."

The Lucy Show had been filmed in color for the past year but was still shown in black and white. Last year, CBS had only broadcast in color when advertisers agreed to share the financial burden. But color was the future. It was as clear to Guy as Mr. Sunbeam's gray mustache or the peacock feather in Mrs. Sunbeam's hat.

He continued, "Imagine you're one of the millions of Americans watching the show. Not only do you get to see this living room in all its vivid hues, but you get to see the Sunbeam logo *in color*, blazing across your TV screen. And then there come your appliances—every product as dazzling as it looks in real life. It's the next-best thing to walking into a store and seeing it for yourself. It's even better than photos in a magazine, because these are moving, breathing images—look at how this vacuum gets rid of dirt! Look at this toaster, this Mixmaster, this coffee maker—they not only work like a charm, they'll look great in your home."

Mr. Sunbeam regarded Guy, already—at twenty-two—a seasoned veteran in the business, brimming over with boyish confidence and a curious blend of experience and hope. But there were concerns other than money. There were the rumors that had come to light in the past few weeks—rumors that may not have been new but that were new to him as someone investing a major stake in *Meet the Newmans*. Del and Dinah, a marriage on the skids. America's not-so-innocent kid brother, Shep Newman, with a taste for drugs and wild women. Straightlaced older son Guy, who maybe wasn't so straight after all. Things that were none of Sunbeam's business but that, as a business-man, he bore the responsibility of looking into.

"I've heard rumors," he said. "About your parents. About your brother. About you."

Guy didn't flinch or look away.

"Are they true?" asked Mr. Sunbeam.

"Does it matter?"

Mr. Sunbeam sighed. He didn't personally care what the Newmans did on their days off. Mrs. Sunbeam was his second marriage. The first had been unhappy and short-lived, a youthful error in judgment. His own adolescence had been indecorous, to say the least.

Guy said, "And what if they're all true?"

The sponsor turned to his wife again. He trusted her more than anyone on this planet. "What do you say, Ellie?"

"I say we're in the business of selling products. So are the New-mans. The TV show is a product. The characters are products. The way of life they sell—a product. Our alarm clocks aren't going to run any slower or faster because Victor in the Chicago office leaves his wife for his secretary."

Mr. Sunbeam sighed deeply, eyes still on his wife. She nodded. He nodded. Then he got to his feet.

"All right, then," he said, extending his hand. "If Ellie says we've got a deal, we've got a deal. Work up the cost estimates, the list of equipment you need to buy. Send everything over to my office, and I'll cut you a check."

Once the Sunbeams and then Sydney were gone, Guy shut off the stage lights and stood alone in the darkened living room. When it was like this, it looked like what it was—a television set built by television carpenters—and not an actual house that people lived in.

But Guy could see it—the lights, the actors, the crew, the cameras, the live audience. He could hear the laughter and the applause. Now all he needed was a script.

He drove straight home, hoping Kelly was there so he could tell him about the meeting. But when he turned onto their street, he found his foot easing off the gas until he stopped altogether in the middle of the road, half a block away.

Guy stared out at the gate and beyond it the driveway and beyond it the main house, where his father was no doubt waiting for one of them to walk in so that he could demand to know what was going on with the show that he had created and produced and written and directed and starred in up until three weeks ago.

Cars drove around him, but Guy didn't move. Not until he heard a tap on the window and saw Kelly, eyebrows raised, mouth hitched into a smile.

"You do know we live right there," Kelly said, sliding into the passenger seat. He was still wearing his stage makeup from Warner Bros., which meant that he was only getting home himself.

"Can you . . ." Guy motioned for him to close the car door. A truck veered past, horn blaring.

"Maybe we could just mosey on over to the curb," suggested Kelly.

In excruciatingly slow motion, Guy did so. He put the car in park, left the engine running, and continued to sit there. "Sunbeam said yes."

"To shooting in color?"

"To everything."

Kelly whistled and threw his arms around Guy.

When they broke apart again, Guy said, "I'm not sure what I'm doing out here." He meant out here on the street, but he also meant out here in the world of television, which, after all these years, suddenly felt like new and uncharted territory.

"I'm pretty sure you're avoiding your dad."

"Do you blame me?"

"No. But you're going to have to go in there eventually, if nothing else to get a change of clothes."

"I just need some time," Guy said. "Just a little more time to keep going before he can take the reins away. Or tell me all the ways I'm going to blow it and let this family down."

"Why don't you just tell him how much this means to you?"

Guy snorted. "Okay. 'Hey, Pop, I know this may be our last show ever, but I'm going to direct it.' How's that sound? Or how about 'I actually liked it when you were in the coma because you couldn't take my dreams and crush them until all that was left was a deep, black void in my soul.'"

"Yeah, not that one."

"Oh, but wait, there's more. 'I dropped out of USC because I will never be a lawyer. Because I would rather gouge out my own eyes than read one more tort.' And, get this, I've saved the best for last. 'Guess what, Pop, the wedding's off. I can't marry Eileen or any woman because I like men. Specifically one man.'"

Kelly took Guy's hand. The two of them stared down at the marvel that was their intertwined fingers, the current that ran from one of them into the other and back again.

Kelly said, "We can stay out here as long as you need to."

All Guy needed, he thought, was another five minutes. Just five more minutes to live in the day.

When—much too soon—the five minutes were up, they opened the gate and rolled in to the drive and parked the car by the guesthouse.

Guy turned to Kelly, one hand still on the wheel. "I may never have the opportunity to tell the world how much I love you, Kelly Faber. I hope I will. But for now, this will have to do."

And then he leaned over and kissed him.

Shep met Lorrie at Ben Frank's on Sunset after she finished work at the Whisky. They sat in a booth toward the back of the restaurant, where it was less noisy. Frank's was open twenty-four hours and was always filled with young people like themselves nursing coffee after drinking too much at the clubs, sleeping heads on tables, eight or ten crammed into a booth.

Lorrie said, "I'm tired and I need some sleep. What do you want?" She was still angry, and he didn't blame her.

"I want to say thanks for coming to bail me out."

She shrugged. "Whatever."

"And I thought we should talk about the baby."

She shifted in her seat but said nothing, clearly waiting.

"It's just . . . you started right in before I even had a chance to process . . . talking about Holmby Hills and the Buckley School. I needed a moment to catch up. But I'm sorry I was an asshole. You don't deserve that."

"And now you're caught up?"

"Mostly."

She let out a long sigh, loud enough to be heard blocks away.

"I'm doing my best here," he said, even though he wasn't sure if this was true. He wanted to do his best, and surely that had to count for something. Since his dad had come home, he'd been staying with Guy and Kelly, because he didn't want to risk being alone with him. They'd offered him the second bedroom, which looked as if no one had ever set foot in it, and at night, he heard them talking behind Guy's closed door.

"Shep, look," Lorrie started. "You don't want me, and I'm not sure I want you, not anymore. But I think I want this baby."

"Why?"

She looked genuinely surprised at this. She stared down into her coffee mug as if she could read the answer there. "I don't know. I guess I want the chance to do better."

There was a lot she wasn't saying, but he thought he understood, because in many ways, he felt the same. It was the chance to do something beyond yourself and your family and the greater imperfect world.

"Okay," he said in a minute, and in that one word, under the harsh lights of Ben Frank's, amid all the noise of the after-party crowd, his baby became very, very real.

FORTY-TWO

Five days before the final episode

Every time Del woke up, he thought, *I'm awake*, and then took immediate stock of his appendages for confirmation that this state of awakeness was real and not some sort of hallucination. He had dreamed in the coma. The doctor, whose name he couldn't remember, had said it was possible. Del had dreamed of going to the moon and an indistinguishable European city, somewhere with subways and sidewalk cafés and ancient buildings that lit up at night. He dreamed of music—a strange, ethereal music that he couldn't begin to describe or replicate. He dreamed of President Kennedy, who was very much alive, and a world that was at peace. He dreamed of strange animals—a tiger with a giraffe's head, a zebra that glowed in the dark, a sloth that loped like a cheetah through the Los Angeles hills. And he dreamed of Dinah.

The first time he met her, he knew, *Buddy, your life is about to change.* When he'd told her this, she laughed. It was a sound he'd never heard before. Bright like a bell.

What Del didn't tell Dr. What's-his-name was that he had felt his heart stop the instant he coded, heard the medics announce his time of death, saw them working on him to try to bring him back to life. It was an empty, helpless feeling of standing in a desert with no one or nothing for miles. He had dreamed of Dinah then too.

He wanted to tell her this and also that he missed her in their bed.

Not just because every night he closed his eyes, he worried he would never open them again. Not because he was anxious in a way he'd never felt before. Afraid to place his hand over his chest for fear there wouldn't be a heartbeat. He wanted her here with him, and together they could stay awake the way they used to, back before the boys came. Laughing and making love and eating a box of Cracker Jack in bed, talking until the sun came up because there was so much to say and not enough time to say it in.

"Daisy?" he said now. It was Sunday.

He got out of bed, a little steadier on his feet than he was the day before or the day before that. Once upon a time, he had sprung right up and into calisthenics—one hundred push-ups, jumping jacks, sit-ups—followed by a quick five-mile run around the lake and possibly a swim to cool off, and all this before 7:00 a.m. Now he barely recognized his own body, which gave out after any exertion, no matter how mild.

Del made his way downstairs where the early-morning sun was pouring through the windows, lighting the rooms with a beatific glow. He called for his wife but got Flora instead, striding out of the library with a dusting cloth in one hand and a can of Pledge in the other.

"Did you need something, Mr. Del?"

He adored Flora for her stoic, sensible Danishness and her indbagt svinemørbrad—pork tenderloin in puff pastry. He also adored the fact that she was not a hoverer, or at least she had never been one until now. He was not a stupid man. He knew his family was shielding him from something, which he suspected had to do with the show. And that they had enlisted Flora to help them.

"Just my wife, Flora."

"She's not here."

"Where is she?"

"I'm not sure."

"Flora . . ."

"Mr. Del. You need to eat something." And she disappeared into the kitchen.

Lately, it seemed that every time he walked into a room, everyone else walked out. The doctor had told him to get the old blood circulating, and so he didn't wait for Flora. He made a sweep of the first floor before taking the stairs to his office. He paused halfway up, wheezing like an old man, and then continued to the top, where he was met with the sofa. He tried to remember when and why he had moved it into the hallway. *Don't be alarmed if you experience some short-term memory loss*, the doctor had said.

But Del was different. He was a warhorse, his mind—like his body—a reliable, intricately constructed thing that had never failed him. He told himself he remembered the sofa. He had moved it because he wanted to erase the temptation to simply go to his desk and work all night, as he sometimes did. It had been a matter of his health.

He swung the office door open and stared inside. The desk was no longer by the window. It sat in the middle of the room, a chair on either side. The books on the desk were different from the ones he remembered keeping there. Beneath them lay a copy of *Life* magazine. He shoved the books aside, and there was Shep on the cover. Half-naked. With a cigarette. And a tattoo. *I will kill him*, Del thought.

Momentarily worried that he had woken up in an episode of *The Twilight Zone*, he was relieved to see his typewriter. A single script lay beside it.

He leaned over and flicked it open to the first page.

MEET THE NEWMANS
"The Finale"
Network CBS-TV
Produced and Directed by Guy Newman
Written by Dinah Newman & Juliet Dunne

Who the fuck was Juliet Dunne? And what the fuck was going on? Del flipped through the pages. It was clearly a rough draft. Sections were crossed out, notes scribbled in the margins. There was

Dinah's handwriting mixed with another he didn't recognize. Juliet's, he guessed, whoever that was. *Whomever*, he heard Dinah correcting him.

He skimmed the lines, some of which were good, some not so good. From what he could tell, the story was autobiographical. Del wakes up from a coma to find that the entire world has changed around him. Dinah has gotten some sort of job outside the house. Guy is giving up law school and joining civil rights protests. And Shep is apparently dating Guy's ex-fiancée, Eileen.

"No," he said aloud, his voice sounding—at last—like his pre-coma voice. Strong, firm, clear. "No," he said again. "No, no, no." He repeated the word again and again as he marched out of the office and down the stairs to the garage.

Which was empty. The cars he had collected and paid good money for were missing, except for the cherry-red 1903 Ford Model A—the first car produced by Ford and one of just 1,750 ever made—he'd bought when they sold *Meet the Newmans* to CBS. The one that barely ran and always overheated and had a top speed of twenty-eight miles per hour.

He looked around as if for an answer. He might have forgotten moving the couch out of the office, but he would never have forgotten selling his automobile collection.

Kelly answered the pounding at the door to find Del standing on the front steps of the guesthouse, dressed—for the first time in days—in something other than pajamas.

"He's not here," Kelly said. "If you're looking for Guy." He stared at the pink flush of Del's face, the dampness of his brow. "Do you need to sit down?"

"Is he at the studio?"

"Yessir." Kelly could lie, but frankly, he was sick of lying.

"Great. Do you think you could drive me there?" Del seemed to flicker and wobble like a mirage.

"Here," Kelly said and steered him to the couch. He would have made a great third grade teacher, he thought. Being part of this family—even on the fringes—had more than prepared him for dealing with children.

Once Del was safely seated, Kelly went to the kitchen to get him a glass of water.

"I'm not a tyrant," he said when Kelly came back.

"Good. Tyrants usually meet a bad end."

Del took a long drink and then raised the cool glass to his forehead, to his cheeks. "All I want to know is what's going on around here. You always level with me."

"Thanks," Kelly said, trying to remember a time when he'd ever leveled with Del Newman. "As for what's going on, I'm not the one you should be asking."

"My wife apparently is writing a script. And my son is directing."

"You were in a coma."

"Yes, but I'm back. The script isn't done. All this time they've had . . . The finale is this week." He stared up at Kelly, a lost little boy. "I love my wife, but she doesn't know the first thing about writing. People think if they have an idea and a typewriter, they must be writers. If they can write a letter, they can write a book. If they're witty at a dinner party, then how hard can dialogue be? And Guy? A director? He's not built for that. He doesn't have the right personality. You must see that. As a director? As a *producer*? He's too compliant, too—I don't know—*yes, sir; no, sir; whatever you think, sir*—"

"Stop it," Kelly said. "Listen to yourself. Your son knows plenty about this business because he's grown up watching you. And he's a shit ton tougher than you give him credit for. The fact that you're saying"—he waved his hand as if wiping dirt off a window—"all this? It's because you don't really know him. Guy is unwavering. Does he want people to be happy? Sure, which is why he goes out of his way to go along with things and be courteous. Which is why he almost let James T. Aubrey and CBS marry him off to someone he doesn't love. But he would have done it for this family, for the show, for you. And doing it would have killed something in him because Guy Newman is always who he is. No matter what. You don't know that because you don't take the time. If you did, you'd know that all he wants is your attention. That's it. And to direct."

"He wants to be me . . ."

"No. He wants to be anyone *but* you. But the thing he loves most is directing. Can't you see that for years he's tried to carve out something just for him? I mean, come on. Do you know how hard it is to be part of this family? Guy is who he is because he listens. He sees every-thing. And he would be a fucking great director. If someone would only give him the chance."

Kelly scooped up his keys from the hall table. He was slow to anger, but there were a couple of hot-ticket items that did it every time—the biggest being *Don't insult the people I love*, Guy topping that list.

"I'm on my way to Warner Bros. You're welcome to hang out here, but, Mr. Newman, sir? I'm going to share something a wise man once told me. There are enough people in this world who will tell you no. Don't be one of them."

Kelly delivered this last line with an emphatic, agitated wink. Del stared up at him.

But Kelly wasn't done. "See, all this time, all of us? We've been lis-tening to you and believing you when you give us advice. So your wife? And your sons? They're not telling themselves no anymore."

Dinah, Guy, Shep, Juliet, Sydney, and camera operator Gene Balboa sat around the Newmans' dining room table in Studio 33 at CBS Tele-vision City and listened as Dinah and Juliet talked them through the new concept for the script.

"When can I see it?" Balboa, better known as Boa, wanted to know.

Dinah and Juliet answered in unison, "Soon."

Boa threw his hands in the air. He was a man who loved gestures, who relied on them when words simply weren't enough.

"You'll have it in three days," Dinah told him.

"Three days?" Boa stared at the men—Guy, Shep, Sydney—to see if they were as outraged as he was. "Three days is not enough. When will I have the new cameras? When will I have the new operators? Will I have time to train these people? To choose my angles?" Hands flying, he directed his last few questions to Sydney, the man closest to his age.

Syd said, "You'll have them tomorrow, Gene."

"Boa," Dinah said. "We're all working as fast as we can. If that isn't fast enough for you, I'm sure one of the other camera people will be happy to step in."

He met Dinah's gaze with piercing dark eyes beneath wild brows that curled out like spider legs. He had always unnerved her. But now she wondered why. He was just a little man with an enormous ego who had once, nearly two decades ago, won an Oscar. She opened her mouth to remind him that Del had given him steady work and a pay-check, that most of his contemporaries were either retired and long forgotten or dead, while he at least continued to work, creating a legacy that—whether he liked it or not—would live on long after he was gone.

But then her gaze moved past him to the figure that stood in the opening between living room and dining room. Everyone turned.

He did not look like a person who had been in a coma for the past few weeks. Quite simply, Del looked like Del.

He was casually but immaculately dressed as if he were reporting to work. He had lain motionless in the hospital for twenty-two days, yet he still had the physique of a football player. From where Dinah sat, her husband seemed taller than six foot one, but then he had always seemed larger than life. His hair waved thick and black like Superman's. His jaw still chiseled from stone. He looked, she thought, infallible.

But the expression on his face was one Dinah and Guy and Shep would never forget. It was one of betrayal.

"Del," she said, pushing away from the table. Her chair scraped against the floor. "Honey. Did you drive here?"

For a moment, she thought he would respond. But instead, he walked out.

FORTY-THREE

Five days before the final episode

T he minute Del saw them at the table, he realized what had happened. He was Rip Van Winkle, the man who slept for twenty years, only to awaken and find the world had kept moving. Worse than that, it had changed.

He exited the studio via the large central hallway instead of the Artists Entrance, which was what he'd meant to do. It was like a scene from a film—he was nearly run over by the traffic of people and prop trucks. He was Roger Thornhill outrunning the crop duster in *North by Northwest*. No. He was Don Birnam in *The Lost Weekend* waking after a four-day bender.

Someone called to him, but he kept walking because he needed to be outside. If he didn't get outside, he knew he would run out of air, and if he ran out of air, he would die here in the main artery of CBS Television City.

"Mr. Newman!"

His name again. Del felt his lungs tighten as he bumped into a group of people dressed in feathers, headdresses like peacocks. One of them squawked at him, and all of them started to laugh, only their laughter sounded like crowing and then hooting, like they were peacocks themselves.

There was a loud blast of horn, and someone yanked him out of the way of a truck that was barreling down on him. Del gazed into the face of Larry, the security guard, his old and trusted friend.

"Larry," he said and embraced the man.

"Mr. Newman?" Larry patted him. "You okay? Listen, I sure was sorry to hear about your mom—"

"She died." Del released him.

"Oh, Christ, I had no idea. No wonder you're wandering around out here like you just lost your best friend. I never would've said if . . . I thought 'cause you were back . . . maybe she was better?"

"I'm afraid not. Listen, Larry, I have to go. Because if I don't . . ."

He didn't finish, just walked away as Larry stared after him. Then out into the parking lot, squinting like a mole in the sunshine. And then behind the wheel of his 1903 Ford Model A, which puttered out of the CBS lot at a top speed of twenty-eight miles per hour.

Dinah arrived home just minutes after Del. The Ford was parked haphazardly, half in the driveway, half in the grass. She heard a voice from somewhere behind her and turned to see the neighbor, waving at her through the gate. He seemed out of context there, without a lawn mower.

"I wanted to make sure he was okay. Your husband?"

From where she stood by her car, she called, "Oh, he's fine. Thank you."

The neighbor was looking at her expectantly, like a bellman waiting for a tip. He was dressed as he usually was, in clothes that said, *I'm here to do yard work.* She pictured his closet. Polo shirt after polo shirt arranged by color—beige, tan, orange, brown. There was nothing wrong with him. But Dinah wondered now why she had ever fantasized about rolling across the grass with him. She gave him a quick, impatient smile and strode into her house.

She could hear her husband upstairs, and she was grateful that she had this moment to compose herself, something she hadn't been able to do on the drive over. She set down her things. She removed her shoes. Then slipped them back on because somehow they made her feel more in control. Then took them off again because she didn't want to announce herself, and besides, they were only shoes.

Dinah stood in the living room with its vaulted ceilings and cheery yellow walls, and she breathed. Not because she was afraid of telling Del what they had been doing in his absence. But because if he was capable of showing up at the studio, he was capable of explaining the house deed, the money, and M. Leslie. And once she knew the truth about these things, she couldn't unknow them.

She found him in their room, sitting on the foot of their bed, staring at the wall. He was still dressed in the navy sweater and slacks he had worn to CBS. The *Life* magazine with Shep on the cover lay next to him.

Del said, "I've been trying to remember why we chose this wallpaper."

She followed his gaze. "We'd just been to Monet's house and gardens and I wanted to live in flowers."

"And I surprised you while you were making that picture, the one on the cruise ship . . ."

"*Out of My Dreams*. Frank Sinatra. Bing Crosby."

"That's right."

She removed her earrings, set them on her vanity. She approached cautiously as if he were an animal that might run away. She sat beside him on the bed, *Life* magazine between them. "Del," she said. "Shep's just a kid. We forget that sometimes."

"The press vultures sure were happy to have me gone. I turn my back for three weeks, and suddenly, it's open season on the Newmans."

"Del," she said again.

"I found the script."

"You found the . . ."

"The script." He looked at her.

So not *Life*. Not the tabloid gossip.

She said, "That's why you came to the studio."

"Was that Juliet Dunne? The girl who was there today? The one you're writing it with?"

"Yes. Woman. Not girl."

"And you hired her."

"She's a reporter for the *LA Times*. She interviewed me that day—the same afternoon as your accident. She had a lot to say about women and Betty Friedan and equality. She called me square and old-fashioned. She essentially blamed me for the fact that so many women are feeling lost in their own lives. I kicked her out of the house. But when I wasn't sure . . . when I didn't know . . ." She couldn't bring herself to say *when I wasn't sure whether you would survive*.

"You thought I might die."

"We all did."

"Sorry to disappoint you."

"Stop it." It came out too sharp, like he was a sulky child.

"And Guy is directing. . . ."

"He filled in while you were gone."

"And there are going to be three cameras, apparently. Which need to be paid for. And cameramen. And we're shooting in color? Is that what I overheard?" There was heat in his words. He was beginning to catch fire.

"The show had to go on. You taught me that."

He didn't seem to hear her. "And you've decided to write about us. About me. The accident, the coma, this life I've trapped you in against your will—"

"I'm writing about the Newmans. Those people we play on TV. You always say don't think of them as us, except when we aren't in front of the camera, and then you say remember who we are, this family that everyone admires and wants to be."

"And do you?" He finally looked at her. "Still want to be a family?"

"What kind of question is that?"

"So let me ask you—what am I supposed to do while you're at work? Put on an apron? Go to the Women's Club?"

"Why not?"

"So now you're the man of the house, is that it?"

"Are you asking if Dinah is the man of the house or if I am? Because there's a difference."

Instead of answering her, he said, "I knew the show wouldn't just stop, but today . . . seeing you gathered like the White House cabinet, discussing state secrets . . ."

"Trying to keep the show afloat and ourselves afloat. Not knowing if you were coming back." Her voice caught, but she cleared her throat, tossed her head. Suddenly, she was on her feet, hands on hips, and then Del was on his, which meant that she had to look up. Dinah was so sick of looking up.

"And where are my cars?" he said.

"We sold them. Along with the artwork and some of the other collections gathering dust."

"You sold my—why the hell would—you're kidding."

"No."

"Without consulting me?" He was getting louder. "You thought, what, he'll probably die, he won't need this stuff, not where he's going? We'll just get rid of it like it was never there, like he never even existed? You're trying to retire me just like Aubrey wanted. . . ."

As he ranted, Dinah crossed to her bedside table, sparks shooting off her. She opened a drawer and pulled out three pieces of paper. She slammed the drawer and then, one by one, threw the papers onto the bed. Bank statement. House deed. Canceled check to M. Leslie.

She straightened, hands back on hips. "We had to sell them, Del. Because apparently, we barely have enough to live on otherwise. Not for long, at least. Because you spent it. All that money we earned and worked so hard for."

Come on, she thought. *Lay it on me, big fella.* And then she decided she didn't give a damn about the doctor's warnings not to upset him or overexcite him. *She'd* been really damn upset, thank you very much. *She'd* been overexcited for the past four weeks, and no one was warning *him* not to upset *her* again. Besides, she'd waited long enough in her life.

Out it came, within the four flowered walls, which formed just one more fucking box. The overdue bills, the empty accounts, the pilfered trusts, the overspending, the cars, the art, the gifts to employees and their families, the house deed, the monthly payments to M. Leslie, her own numbness—all the things that had led them here.

Now, she was glad to see, her husband was on the defensive. He tried to tell her he had it handled. There was that time last year when Aubrey and the sponsors had made layoffs. He'd paid the salaries of the people they couldn't afford to lose. The cars, they were just something he admired, something he'd always wanted when he was a kid and lived in a cramped house where they took the bus or walked everywhere. They were, like the art and the other collections, an investment. He didn't say anything about the house deed. Or M. Leslie.

Dinah interrupted him. "Why were you in Santa Monica the night of the accident?"

"I needed to clear my head—"

"No. Why were you there? Were you going to the house? The one you own? Is that where she lives? M. Leslie?" She picked up the house deed and waved it at him. "Did you buy the house for her? For the two of you? A place to escape from the boys and me or just from me?"

"Dinah, no . . . I mean, yes, I bought it. . . ."

"I've been with you for *twenty-three years*. That girl I was when we got married, she's someone I don't know. I can barely remember being her. And this person, the one I am right now, I don't know her either. But at least I want to. But if you don't . . . if we have secrets like this? Like the fact that you've spent all this money—money we earned together—on all these things, on a house, and a mistress? And you have a love nest—"

"It's not a love nest." He dropped like a stone, back onto the bed. "It's for my father. I bought it for him."

"Your father?"

"Matthew Leslie."

"Your parents are dead."

"My mom is dead."

"The theater that they ran, the one you grew up in—"

"Dinah, stop. Please. Give me a chance here."

His voice was loud but not angry. And so she crossed her arms and shut her mouth and waited. She could see him trying to find the words, the right ones, the ones that would explain what he needed to explain.

In a moment, he said, "Your mom was exceptional. As a mother and a human. Mine . . ." He shook his head. "I invented a story about my past because I didn't like the past I came from. Mom ran off when I was a kid. My dad raised me. We had a falling-out when I was maybe sixteen. I haven't seen him since."

"But the house . . ."

"The reason I went to Santa Monica was to visit him. At the gas station where he's worked for the past forty years."

"The one across from the pier."

"The day before the accident, he sent me a telegram—it came to the studio. He said he needed to see me. He's been diagnosed with cancer. I wanted to go not just for him but to say I was sorry for my part. And to help pay his medical bills and find him a specialist."

"And the monthly checks . . ."

"Those were for him and also for me. Same with the house. To make me feel better about cutting him out of my life. I loved my mom. But I was never close to my dad. He was too strict. Too unreachable. When she left, it's like all the love that had existed left with her. I had to go too if I ever wanted the chance to do something, to get out from under him and be someone I wanted to be."

She strained to absorb everything he was saying. When had they last talked like this, no-holds-barred, the two of them out in the open? "What else have you lied about?"

"Nothing," he said. "Daisy. I swear."

"You have a father. Does he . . ." She almost asked, *Does he know about the boys and me?* but of course he did. She had seen his television set with her own eyes. "I don't know anything about him. What's he like?"

"Stubborn. Stoic. Dry sense of humor. But"—he shook his head—"the man I remember may not be the man he is now."

"None of us are." She gave him a faint smile.

"Anyway," Del said. "You'll meet him. We both will."

The weight of it all was too much. She sat down beside him. This was the thing they didn't tell you about love. It was being able to talk about the hard things and forgive the disappointments and try not to break each other's hearts again and again in big and small ways. And if you did, it was saying you were sorry and meaning it and letting them say sorry too.

"You talk about living in a box," he said in a moment. "I don't think that's only true of women. My little prison might look different. Maybe it has larger parameters. Maybe it's a prison of my own making. But it's still a prison."

"That's a good line," Dinah said.

He didn't exactly laugh, but he made a chuffing sound, which was in the vicinity. He looked at her sideways, arching one dark eyebrow. "Should I wait till you can get a notebook?"

"I'll remember it." She bumped his shoulder with her own, and he bumped her back. Something they used to do when they were just getting to know each other before anyone had proclaimed his or her love.

"Do you really feel that way?" He looked at her. "Lost in your own life?"

"Yes. I think I do. I think I did."

"Me too."

She reached for his hand, and it was right there.

One to Watch: Fashion Designer Renee Otero

By Clarise Joy

For Henri Bendel's Department Store

"Fashion should be controversial. It should evoke a reaction—people love it, people hate it. There's no such thing as pleasing everyone. But that's not why I do this. I do this because the world needs more color."

Renee Otero, 25, has been enamored of color since she was a child growing up in San Diego, California. She found inspiration in the orange trees outside her house, the green of the hills in spring, the vibrant hues of the Cuban food her father cooked, and the blue of the ocean.

She began designing early, mixing and matching and creating outfits from items found in her mother's closet. At ten, she taught herself to sew on her grandmother's sewing machine, and at thirteen, she earned her first commission—a dress for her neighbor's school dance. "It was loud and the execution was pretty clumsy, but she wore it, and afterward, everyone was talking about it." She laughs. "Although no one else commissioned me for a while."

Like the iconic **Mary Quant**, maker of the miniskirt, Renee spurned fashion school for art school, believing it gave her more creative license and freedom. "I have a wild imagination," says Otero. "I dream in Technicolor, and the last thing I want is for someone to stifle that."

She credits her mother and grandmother for encouraging her

imagination, and Elyora Turgunbaeva, owner of Elyora's Textiles (garment district, Los Angeles), for mentoring her.

Says Otero, "As a woman—as a Black woman—I'm either targeted or discounted, overlooked, passed by. Color is my way of saying, *Here I am. You can't ignore me. You cannot silence me no matter how much you may want to.*"

A selection of Otero's Originals will be included in Bendel's fall catalog.

FORTY-FOUR

Four days before the final episode

When Juliet walked into the newsroom Monday morning, Nick was sitting at her desk, elbows on the armrests of her chair, fingers steepled. He wasn't scribbling notes on something for her to go over, the way he often did. He was simply waiting.

"Nick," she said.

"You're late."

"By two minutes. Since when do you care?"

"Is there anything you need to tell me? Are you quitting?"

"What? No. I love my job. I mean, I don't love my job. But I love this newsroom in spite of . . ." She glanced around at her male colleagues, who weren't actually colleagues, at least not to their thinking. "And I plan to become a news reporter as soon as they'll let me. That's still what I want to do."

He nodded but didn't look convinced, and she noticed the tense line of his mouth. "More," he said.

"Okay." She lowered her voice. "Confidentially? I'm working on something with Dinah Newman. Actually, she asked me to write the season finale of *Meet the Newmans* with her." And then it all came spilling out—Del's accident, the day Dinah had shown up at the paper, their disastrous first attempt, their disastrous second attempt, the focus group, the Sunbeams.

By the time she was finished, Nick was grinning at her. For one lovely moment, they were the only two people in the room.

"But," he said, the grin fading, "it sure is a white world they live in."

"It is."

"And a man's world."

"It is," she repeated.

"I'd like to see one of them join Reverend King in a march for civil rights."

Juliet tried to imagine it. In August, she and Nick had traveled to DC with Boyd Hartley and a handful of other reporters from the *LA Times* for the March on Washington. Under a cloudless sky, in front of a crowd of 250,000-some people, Dr. Martin Luther King Jr. stood on the steps of the Lincoln Memorial and delivered a speech unlike any other she had ever heard before. *No, no, we are not satisfied and we will not be satisfied until justice rolls down like waters and righteousness like a mighty stream.* . . .

"It's only one episode," Juliet said. "But we're liberating her. Dinah Newman." A little beam of pride escaped her and floated into the room.

"And you were going to hate her forever."

This made Juliet laugh, a great, barking sound that caused heads to turn and her to clamp a hand over her mouth, as if she was afraid of what else might escape. "And you were going to miss me." It was the closest she'd ever come to outright flirting with him.

"But now I don't have to." Nick's voice and eyes were warm and direct. Something new rippled in the air between them.

Then he stood and Juliet sat, the seat warm from him. She tried not to think about his body heat, about his smile, which was easy but genuine. About the way he furrowed his brow when he was concentrating. The way he looked her in the eye and listened whenever she talked, as if whatever she was saying was important. The way he remembered things and noticed things about her, about others. The way he alone, out of her colleagues, believed she had what it took to become a news reporter.

As she dropped her bag into one of the file drawers and draped her jacket on the back of her chair, she asked if there was anything he needed. He told her no, he was good, and started away. Then he backed up until he was standing there again, tapping on the edge of her desk.

"Actually, I do have a request." She assumed he wanted a cup of coffee or maybe a sandwich from the café downstairs. But he said, "There's a lead in my mother's case. I'd like you to help me with the story—after the season finale, of course. It means working outside of the office. I'm not sure it's something Boyd would publish. I'd probably try to sell it to *The Atlanta Constitution* since the murder was committed in Georgia. But I need to pursue this. And the two of us would share the byline."

"Why me?" she asked before she could help herself. She remembered posing the same question to Dinah not too long ago.

"Because we work well together. And I trust you. This story. I don't have to tell you what it means to me."

She nodded once, confirmation that she could only imagine what it meant, which wasn't the same as knowing, but was as close as she could give him.

"Anyway." He tapped her desk again. "Think about it and get back to me when you can. And actually? I have one more request. This one's for the Newmans."

"What is it?"

"You could start by making the world they live in a little less white."

The script was finished that evening as the sun dipped below the horizon and the lights came on across the city. In the parking lot of CBS, Dinah and Juliet sat on the hood of Dinah's gold Impala and stared up at the hills. They shared a cigarette, passing it between them as Dinah told Juliet that, after two decades of marriage, she apparently had a father-in-law.

"Life," said Juliet. As in you never knew what might happen.

"Life," Dinah agreed.

Juliet tipped her head back and counted the stars, which were infinite. It wasn't just the blue sky she had come for. It was this one too.

Dinah said, "When I first moved to LA, I used to drive up to Mulholland around this time of day and park my car—I had this beaten-up old Buick that barely ran, and the stuffing was coming out of the seats." Her voice was hushed. "So I never knew if the car was going to make it back to my apartment, but it was worth it, going up there. I would sit, windows down, and just watch everything light up. It was like the world's loveliest magic trick. The whole city like a carpet rolled out before me. A carpet of stars."

Juliet sighed, a little dreamy. "Makes me want to drive up there right now."

They looked at one another and began to laugh. The night air and the cigarette and the sense of camaraderie—it was nothing compared to the feeling of what they had done.

On a dusty turnout on Mulholland Drive, Dinah and Juliet sat once again on the hood of Dinah's car, the engine warm beneath them, and gazed down at the miles and miles of bright little stars.

Juliet asked Dinah to drop her in Laurel Canyon, high up the hill on Wonderland. She didn't want to sleep. She wanted to stay awake all night. She could call Renee, convince her to meet her out somewhere, but she wanted to see the Musician and tell him about the script she had written. She wanted to lie in his arms and feel him around her and inside her, like music. It wasn't that she needed him, it was that she wanted him, and wanting him wasn't anything to be embarrassed by.

"I'm happy to wait," Dinah said over the idling engine.

Juliet leaned in the open window. "It's okay. You get home."

She wanted to let Dinah in on all her justifications for going to see this man right now, on the heels of such an important moment. But instead, she reached out and squeezed her hand, a form of thanks—for the evening, for the project, for not judging her.

As she started across the grass, Dinah called, "Hey, Juliet?"

Juliet turned back.

"We did it." Dinah's face was half in shadow, but her smile was brilliant.

"We did." Juliet blew her a kiss and watched as Dinah backed up and rolled away, taillights disappearing around the bend. The night was quiet except for the howl of a coyote, somewhere in the distance.

The house looked still and sleepy. The two front windows were open, the curtains blowing gently in the breeze. The same curtains Juliet and the Musician had found three years ago at a flea market somewhere east of downtown. Juliet tried the door, which was, as usual, unlocked. She remembered to catch the screen with her foot so that it wouldn't slam behind her.

Inside, it smelled of incense and dope and blackberry jam. But it felt lifeless. She knew without checking the closets that they would be empty, that the guitar he loved but rarely played would be gone from its spot beneath the windowsill. A strand of his beads still hung from the hook by the door, forgotten at the last minute. The fairy lights still twinkled on the patio. It was as if he'd just popped out for a few minutes to visit Mama Cass or walk down to the Canyon Country Store.

Juliet felt the way she always did when something ended. Bittersweet. Aching. Hopeful. She needed to sit at her typewriter and write because that was where her emotions made the most sense.

Before leaving, she lifted the beads off their hook and slipped them over her head so that she could feel them against her chest. He had worn them all the time, even in the shower, and she wondered if he'd left them for her to find. She stood still for a minute, touching them like a rosary and snapping a mental photograph of her former home so that she could take it with her.

As she let herself out of the house, the screen door banging behind her, she was flooded by memories. Painting furniture, hanging curtains, making the little house theirs. Staying up all night, lying next to him, sharing a joint, pondering the single light above the bed, having very deep and important conversations. In the early days of their relationship, she would spring up hours later, new and refreshed, and bounce out into the California sunshine. There were always places to go, friends to see and do things with. Activity. Work. Life. And then her feelings grew more complicated, which meant they—the two of them—became more complicated.

She was halfway down the mountain when she saw the headlights. In the dark, it was hard to tell the color of the car. She scrambled into the scrub and brushwood at the side of the road, and watched as the car slowed, as the driver's window rolled down, as Dinah leaned out and said, "I didn't feel right about leaving you."

They drove in silence. Back at CBS, Juliet's car was one of the few left in the parking lot. Dinah pulled up beside it, and they sat there as the engine idled, Juliet thinking about her own mother, whom she loved in spite of the fact that she didn't understand her. Dinah wasn't her mother. She was a friend. But tonight, she had needed both, and Dinah had been there.

"Thank you," she breathed.

𝕷𝖔𝖘 𝕬𝖓𝖌𝖊𝖑𝖊𝖘 𝕿𝖎𝖒𝖊𝖘

APRIL 18, 1964

Mrs. Mock Ends Solo Round-the-World Flight

The Flying Housewife Becomes First Woman to Encircle Globe Alone

by Juliet Dunne

After 30 days and more than 22,000 miles, **Jerrie Mock** set her single-engine plane down in Columbus, Ohio, at 9:36 p.m. Friday night and became the first woman to fly solo around the world. The 38-year-old housewife descended from the red-and-white *Spirit of Columbus* to hugs and kisses from her three children and husband, Russell, and cheers from thousands of spectators.

Mock left Columbus March 19, flying east to Bermuda, Africa, and on around the world. She began her long flight home Friday morning from Tucson. She logged about 200 flight hours and is the first woman to fly solo across the Pacific.

"When I was 10 or 11, I found out that Ohio had something called 'women's protective laws'—that meant that women couldn't do some things," Mock said. "I was never going to abide by man-made laws that told me what I could and couldn't do. I knew one thing: I wanted to see the world. I decided that when I grew up, I would fly my airplane around the globe. Everyone laughed at me, and I laughed right back at them."

"I remember one of the first newspaper interviews I gave before the flight. I took the time to explain all sorts of technical things to the reporter about how I'd navigate my plane. The head-line the next day said: 'She'll Circle the Globe in Her Drip-Dries.'"

Articles mentioned her height, her weight, her figure. She quickly discovered that acceptance in a male-dominated arena wasn't as easy as flying. "Women were often laughed at around the airports," Mock said. "I'd hear them, and I'd ignore it."

She didn't have to hear them when she flew. Jerrie Mock knew what she could do. But upon stopping in Dhahran, Saudi Arabia, she was greeted by a crowd who reminded her of her gender.

"I landed, got out of the plane, and got a big round of applause," Mock said. After soldiers searched the plane and found no one else aboard, she received a second ovation.

"They thought I had a man hidden inside the cockpit. When they saw there was no man at all, they went wild."

When asked what's next for her, Mock said she hasn't yet decided. The only thing she knows is that it will include flying.

"Always I had the feeling that I was supposed to do something special, that I must, really. So now I have. I hope that my doing something that hadn't been done will encourage someone else who wants to do something very much, and hasn't quite had the heart to try."

FORTY-FIVE

Four days before the final episode

S hep drove to the Hollywood Studio Club to see the girl he loved. As he pulled up outside and walked to the front door, he didn't have a plan other than to ask to see her. The windows burned with light, all this life contained within. The sun had set a while ago. He had no idea what time it was. He knocked anyway.

Suddenly, Mrs. Dennis, the chaperone, stood before him, frowning. *You again*, her expression said.

"Good evening, ma'am. I'm here to see Eileen Weld. My creative life depends on it."

He had been trying and failing to figure out the song for the episode. Usually, if he had one bad day of writing, the next day would be good. But he'd had several bad days in a row, coupled with a bad mood. He'd gone around feeling hopeless and blue. He was a terrible son. A terrible Newman. A disappointment to Eileen and to Lorrie and probably, one day, to the child that was coming. And now he wasn't even a good musician.

"I'm sorry," Mrs. Dennis said, not sounding one bit sorry. "It's after visiting hours. You can contact her tomorrow."

"It's urgent, though."

"Then you should have come before curfew."

It was just one more should. He *should* go home to see his dad, who had survived no thanks to Shep. He *should* go to the recording studio, where Hutch would tell him it's okay, we all have off days. But Shep didn't want anyone to try to make him feel better. He knew he could count on Eileen not to do that.

"You see," he told the chaperone, "'the only people for me are the mad ones, the ones who are mad to live, mad to talk, mad to be saved, desirous of everything at the same time.'"

Mrs. Dennis remained unmoved by him and by Kerouac's words. "Good night," she told Shep before swinging the door closed. He could hear her locking it from the inside. Through the open windows came music, laughter, voices rising and falling. And here he was, once again on the outside.

Shep considered his options. He could climb the fire escape or the trellis and let himself in. Bang on the door until Mrs. Dennis reappeared so he could tell her that it wasn't just his creative life that needed saving, it was the rest of him, that his entire life depended on seeing Eileen tonight. It felt like the truth. Like if he didn't see her, he might fade away to nothingness.

She was just out of reach
And the rain came, and the rain came

His own words might be washed up, but that didn't mean he couldn't borrow someone else's. He backed up a few paces, then crossed the grass. He planted himself on the lawn of the Hollywood Studio Club and began to sing.

It was an old Ralph Stanley tune, but he altered the lyrics to fit his own story. Above him, windows were thrown open, girls leaning out, elbows on windowsills, hair pulled back to allow a view of the boy standing below. They couldn't see him well, but the voice was unmistakable.

If I meet my darling girl again
I'll tell her sorry for the trouble

"Eileen!" someone yelled. "Hey, Eileen!"

Another window opened. Another girl leaned out. This one with a long ponytail.

Just tell the girl I love
I'm sure sorry for the trouble

When he finished his serenade, he stood waiting, conscious of his breathing, the dryness of his palms, the murmur of his heart, which should have been pounding but somehow knew to be quiet. All but one of the girls clapped and cheered and shouted, "Encore!"

As he turned to go, she called, "Wait." Eileen vanished from the window.

Now his heart began to pound, and his eyes went to the front door, willing it to open. In a moment, he heard her say, "Hey, Shep Newman." She was above him again, her hair loose. "Watch out below."

Something fell from the sky and landed on the grass at his feet. He bent down and picked it up. An elastic hair tie, the kind she always wore. This one was the dark brown of her hair.

"I'm sorry too," she said.

He felt himself sprout wings, able to fly to her without touching earth or needing the help of stairs or the vine-covered trellis that climbed to the second floor.

When she disappeared again, the window shutting behind her, Shep slipped the band onto his wrist, where he would wear it for the rest of his life.

Thirty minutes later, he walked into his parents' house and told them about the baby. In the living room where they sat, Dinah and Del stared up at him, mouths open. His father, Shep was glad to see, looked like his old self, but also not like his old self. His eyes were brighter and seemed to exist only in this room, only in this moment, not ten steps ahead like usual.

"Is it . . . It's not Eileen?" Dinah asked.

"No."

"But you and she . . ."

"I don't know." He snapped the band on his wrist. *Maybe*, he thought.

Del looked at Dinah. "Eileen Weld?"

His wife merely nodded.

"I need to tell you something else," Shep said. "Remember when I played the Atlantic City Convention Hall last June? There was a fire?" He waited until he saw the recollection on their faces. "The fireman who rescued me, he asked for an autograph while people were still inside. There were other firemen, but he should have been doing his job. It sounds stupid, but it made me feel expendable. People sometimes, they walk up to you and take a photo and walk away like you're a tourist attraction. It really did my head in for a while. Maybe still. I was, like, fifteen when all this started with the music and the touring, and suddenly, everyone was paying attention to me but not always in the best way. So. Yeah. I'm sorry." He directed this to his dad. "For playing rough on the set. For egging you on. For not going to see you in the hospital."

Del coughed, as if trying to expel all the things he wanted to say to his younger son, who inhabited the same charmed world he himself had, until recently, inhabited. *How could you be so reckless? How many times have I told you not to knock someone up?* But he thought about how his own luck had run out, and he forced himself to say, "After all we've weathered . . ." He coughed again. "We can navigate this too. None of this is on you." He paused. "Well. The baby. That's on you. But what happened to me is not."

A moment followed that felt like something to soak in. There was love in this room, in this house, between these people.

Shep said, "Hey, this means you guys are going to be grandparents." And started to laugh. He laughed all the way to the kitchen, where they heard him rattling around in the fridge.

Dinah and Del stared at one another.

"Grandparents." Del was suddenly overcome—as he'd been in James T. Aubrey's office—with an overwhelming urge to drop to the floor and start doing one-armed push-ups.

"No," Dinah said. "We can't be . . . That's not . . . I mean . . ." Her expression said *Look at us.* "You remember my grandmothers," she said to Del. He did. Short, squat women with gray hair who had never been young, not even when they technically were.

The old Del would have killed his son for getting some girl pregnant. And then he would have forced him to marry her, whether he loved her or not. He thought about why Old Del would have done that. Because of how it looked. Because of how it would reflect on the show and their reputation.

He sat there waiting for Old Del to push forward and take charge of the situation. But New Del—he was going to take some getting used to—felt content to sit here with his wife and think of all the years behind them and all the years ahead, ones that now—apparently— included a grandchild.

Later, after Del and Shep were asleep, Dinah sat in the sunroom and reread the script she and Juliet had written. Soon, everyone would have a hand in it, and it would no longer be theirs, not in the way it was now.

She stretched out her hands, which had forgotten to go numb for some time. Instead, they had typed and written and carried the things she had needed to carry.

Whatever else happened, Dinah and Juliet had done this. She wanted to keep it to herself just a little while longer.

FORTY-SIX

Three days before the final episode

D inah opened her eyes to the sky—pink and gold and blue. She had fallen asleep beneath the stars, there on the sunroom couch, the script lying against her chest. It was the way she used to hold Guy and Shep when they were babies and couldn't sleep. Heartbeat to heartbeat until mother and child eventually drifted off.

And soon there would be a new baby. Her grandchild. It was impossible that she could be a grandmother at an age when she was still medically able—no matter what Dr. Berke insinuated—to have a baby. A grandmother, when she was feeling the youngest she had felt in a long time—possibly ever.

Last night, she had stood in front of one of the bathroom mirrors and examined her face for new wrinkles. Then she had moved on to her hair, hunting through the blond until she found the little nest of gray along her part. It had first appeared on her fortieth birthday, and she had been coloring it ever since. For the past couple of years, Del had been graying around the temples, but—as was the way with men—it only made him look handsomer, more distinguished. She wondered why no one ever said that about women. She thought she might look elegant with gray hair. Dinah Newman, writer, actress, wife, mother, silver fox.

The sound of a familiar lawn mower, like an alarm, brought her to her feet. The day was a busy one, and she was due at the studio in an hour for the table read. While their contract gave Del ultimate creative control, the Newmans were required to share the script with their sponsors and with CBS. And when they did, it would be Del's name—not Dinah's and Juliet's, not Guy's—on the title page as writer and director because that was what the network would expect.

When she didn't find her husband in the bedroom, Dinah went on a search throughout the house. When she still hadn't found him, she suddenly got a bad feeling. She took the stairs two at a time to the office, where he sat at the desk typing hard, with what appeared to be great purpose and concentration. There had been a time when she loved watching him, loved just the sound of him typing because it meant his brilliant mind was at work. Now her first thought was that he was trespassing.

"What are you doing?" she asked from the doorway, not trusting herself to be within arm's reach of the typewriter, which—depending on his answer—she might be tempted to throw out the window.

He finished typing whatever he was typing before looking up. "I know you and Juliet are working on a script, but it doesn't hurt to have a backup."

"You're writing a backup script?"

"This isn't me second-guessing you. It's just that we're three days away from shooting the finale. And since it's a live broadcast, there's zero room for error. We put the wedding back in, everybody's happy."

"Everybody except our son and Eileen. Not to mention Kelly." She was in the room now, standing over the desk.

"What does Kelly have to do with anything?" He narrowed his eyes at her. "What do you know?"

"Del, you need to understand a few things. Juliet and I are writing the script. We've written the script. Actually, we've written it more than once now. We'll want your input, but it's our script, hers and mine." She rapped the desk for emphasis, resisting the urge to rap him on the head. "I know you couldn't help it, but you weren't here. And while you were away, this is how we decided to run things."

His eyes left hers, seeking the window.

"You also need to come to terms with the fact that Guy is directing. And Shep is in charge of the music. I've asked him to work on something new."

His gaze returned. "Shep? No." He sat back, shook his head. "He's too unreliable."

"He has more raw talent than either one of us, and the music . . . that's where we can count on him. It's time we let him go." It was, she was trying to say, time to let Shep see what he could do. To let them all see what they could do. "We're not trying to replace you. I know it must feel like that. But the boys have stepped up. Both of them. We all have. Because we had to. And along the way, we figured out we're pretty good at this. But it's not the Newmans without you. So why not let it be a collaboration? A Newman family project."

He stared down at the typewriter, at the words he had written. He said, "Do you remember when we first started—I think it was our third or fourth episode? Ratings weren't good yet, and we lost Quaker Oats as a sponsor, so we were scrambling, trying to find someone who would take us on."

"And you said, no matter what happens, we stop when it's not fun anymore."

"When's the last time you had fun with this?" He nodded at the typewriter, at the photos on the walls all around them.

"Now," Dinah said, with a sudden rush of feeling. "The past few weeks. Working with Juliet. Working with the boys." As much as she didn't want her husband in the way, she wanted him to feel what she was feeling—this sense of standing on the edge of a cliff, arms out, nothing but a long, bottomless drop below and only the sky overhead. Armed with the knowledge that she could jump and be just fine, that somehow she'd acquired the ability to fly.

She took his hand in hers. His face was a conflict of emotion. He looked up at her and said simply, "Okay."

Inside the rehearsal hall, Dinah circled the table, placing the script into the hands of her costars. "I know we're cutting it close on time, which is why we want your feedback on this one," she said. "It's— well." She cleared her throat. "It's possibly the last episode we'll ever film. Which makes it the most important one."

As she took her seat, she looked at Del, and he saw the anxiety that she was trying to hide. They had lost each other over the past few months before his accident, but not completely.

"We're going to go out with a bang," he said to the room, flashing the old smile. "The only way to go." He could see the cast take a collective breath, which felt both like a relief to him and a betrayal to his wife and sons.

There was the sound of rustling, of chatter, of settling in, as a dozen scripts were opened to the first page, and then the cast waited to begin, their eyes on Del.

"In the words of Ann Hodges," Guy said, and all eyes flew to him, "the only person in history to be hit by a meteorite, 'We had a little excitement around here today.'" His smile, not quite as broad and blinding as his father's, had its own charm. It hitched a little higher on the right side, his only rakish feature. "This," he said, "is our meteor."

Then—at the same time—he and Del began reading the stage directions. Everyone froze, glances exchanged, eyes darting back and forth between father and son.

"You go ahead, Pop." Guy's voice was tight.

"No, no," said Del with forced cheer, a muscle in his jaw twitching. "You're the director. The director always reads the directions."

I've read them for the past twelve years, he thought. *Just because this might be the last table read we ever have, why should I read them to-*

day? He sat back, trying to seem gracious and not what he actually was—a displaced person, or maybe *replaced* was a more accurate word.

Afterward, Del excused himself while the others were giving their feedback. He was objective enough to recognize when something was good. And what Dinah and Juliet had written was good. Although it was hard for him to dwell too long on this. He wasn't above professional jealousy, even of something that included him as this did. Even when it was being jealous of his wife.

Dinah, like her mother, shone her light on others wherever she went. At Penelope Shepherd's funeral, so many people—many of them strangers—had said, *She always made me feel like her favorite person, like whatever I had to say was the most important thing in the world.*

Until now, that was how Dinah had always made him feel—like he was the most important thing.

In the quiet of his dressing room, he opened his copy of the script and reread it. When he finished, he thought, *The script isn't just good. It's really fucking good.*

He set it aside. For a long time, he sat, elbows resting on knees, head down, thinking about the accident. How he could have died. How he did die, technically, until the doctors brought him back to life. How grateful he was and how sorry he was that everything had changed. And then for some reason he thought about Walter Kerr at *The New York Times.* Boy did he hope the miserable sonofabitch would watch their season finale.

It was a clear, bright night. From the roof of the guesthouse, you could see the dark sprawl of the lake and—in the distance beyond the city— snowcapped mountains, just like a postcard. Shep Newman lay back against the tiles, cradling his guitar, and strummed the chords he had written over the last few hours.

She was just out of reach, I could see her there
But then the rain came, then the rain came
And washed her away

He wasn't sure about *And washed her away.* He liked the sound of it, but worried it wasn't accurate. This was the kind of girl who didn't leave you.

He sang, " 'But then the rain came, then the rain came and tried to wash her away.' "

Still not it exactly, but better. The song as he heard it started soft but grew into a hard-thumping beat. He stamped against the Spanish tiles, keeping time, until Guy's voice shot up from below. "Get the hell off my roof. Some of us are trying to have a quiet evening."

They had come up here as kids, escaping their parents and the responsibility that came from being on a hit television show. On the rooftop, they were just two brothers who had dreams of their own.

Shep, unbothered, kept playing and stamping until he got to the end, and then sighed deeply and took in the sky, holding the guitar against him and fiddling with the hair tie around his wrist. Guy was edgier than a cat these days, as if his life hinged on this single episode. The thing Shep didn't tell him was that he was feeling it too.

He was loaded down with expectation—his own, more than anyone else's. The new song needed to be good because it was about Eileen. And it needed to be good because it was the first Shep Newman original to appear on the show, which meant it was quite possibly the most important three minutes of his life.

A head appeared, and suddenly, his brother was there, hauling himself up and dropping down beside him.

"I'm writing," Shep said.

"On my roof," said Guy.

Shep didn't respond, because he was thinking about this quote by Carl Perkins that he loved—*If it weren't for the rocks in its bed, the stream would have no song.* He guessed the best thing he could do was play what was in him, rocks and all.

"We used to come up here," Guy said, staring out toward the lake. "It's been a while."

Shep strummed the guitar.

"Listen," he said in a minute, "thanks for letting me stay. Sorry for taking Kelly's room." It was his way of saying, *Hey, I know there's something more going on than you're letting on.*

When Guy didn't respond, Shep played a few more chords.

"Yeah. I sure do hate to uproot Kelly. From his room."

"All right," Guy said. "That's not Kelly's room. My room is Kelly's room. And mine. It's ours, actually. I mean, they're both our rooms because they're in our house, but we only sleep in one of them. . . ."

"You know, it's easier just to tell me he's your boyfriend."

Guy's eyes met Shep's. "How long have you known?"

"Just because I'm young doesn't mean I'm stupid." Shep strummed the guitar and cracked a smile. "This ain't my first rodeo, bub."

"And you're okay with it?"

"What's between you, that's no one's business but yours. 'Life must be rich and full of loving—it's no good otherwise, no good at all, for anyone.'"

"Jack Kerouac."

Shep stopped strumming and stared at him.

Guy shrugged. "It's your favorite book. Of course I read it."

Shep thought that if he lived to be a hundred, people would never stop surprising him. Then Guy lay back, arms crossed beneath his head. After a beat, Shep set the guitar down and did the same. Legs outstretched, arms folded beneath him, mimicking Guy the way he used to. The Newman brothers, side by side again.

FORTY-SEVEN

Two days before the final episode

At 7:00 a.m. on Wednesday, Juliet stood on the front porch of the Newman house. Here, in Toluca Lake, you didn't hear the roar of the freeway or the clatter of a busy restaurant or the shouts of drunken passersby. There was only birdsong, a breeze through the palm trees, and the growl of a car in the distance.

The door was opened by Del Newman. He seemed taller in person, broader through the shoulders, the famous head of wavy black hair, the dark blue eyes. He was, she thought objectively, the handsomest man she'd ever seen.

"Dinah's in the office," he told her. "I'm assuming you know your way."

He was polite but cool. She had watched this man for years on television. He was a skilled physical comedian—especially for a big man—known for his charisma and humor in front of the screen and his dynamism off. But this Del Newman seemed muted, his colors faded.

"I'm so glad," she said without thinking. "That you're okay."

He looked surprised, but then nodded. "Thank you."

Dinah and Juliet worked for over an hour, Juliet at the typewriter while Dinah went over the feedback from the table read. They discarded half of it—Howie's suggested *Rebel Without a Cause* car race between Dinah and Peggy and a dream sequence starring himself and all the sorority girls. Artie's proposed monologue at the end of the second act. Boa's idea to change Del's coma to a drinking problem or intestinal cancer. They implemented the notes they felt would make the script stronger, Juliet retyping the pages where they had changes.

"Does Del have any suggestions?" she asked when they were through.

"If he does—and I can't imagine he doesn't—he hasn't shared them," said Dinah. She didn't mention the backup script he was writing, that he might still be writing. The Del she knew would never have given up control that easily.

"And how are you doing?" Juliet propped her chin in her hand. "The two of you."

"Oh. It's touch-and-go. I think I had this vision of how it would be when he came out of the coma—Deborah Kerr and Burt Lancaster embracing in the waves. But we've been finding our way to each other again. Slowly." Dinah sighed. Then brushed her throat in reference to Juliet's necklace. "How about you?"

Juliet reached for the beads, running her fingers along them. They were her portal to another time, another life, one she had both hated and loved. "Also a bit touch-and-go."

"Have you heard from him?"

"No."

The two women exchanged a smile, comrades who had weathered something—who were still weathering something—not exactly *together* but at the same time.

Juliet glanced down at the script. "There's just one thing missing." She looked up again. "Dinah never got her orgasm."

Dinah laughed because, of course, Juliet was joking. "You know I only meant it metaphorically. God, can you imagine if we actually gave her one?"

"Why not? It's nothing to be ashamed of. Not that we show it happening. But we have her say the word. She can compare something to having one—taking off her pearls, going to work outside the house, hanging up her apron. And not just any old orgasm but a good one."

"The censors would never allow her to say *orgasm*."

"So she doesn't say it outright. She says it without saying it. But it's clear to everyone what she means."

Dinah studied Juliet. The brown eyes, direct and open. Body tilting forward in her chair, as if ready to take off in a sprint. Always so effortlessly her.

"You don't need to worry about losing yourself," Dinah told her.

Juliet held her gaze. She blinked rapidly until the tears retreated. And then, without a word, she turned back to the typewriter. Dinah opened her copy of the finished script, flipped it to the final page, and together, they wrote the last line.

Mr. Sunbeam and three of his colleagues arrived early to CBS Television City to watch the run-through of the show. From the set, Guy spotted them as they strode into Studio 33, heads swiveling at the iconic soundstage where so many TV series had been filmed.

"They knocked down a football stadium to build this place," he heard Mr. Sunbeam say as they approached the first row of audience seating. As a director, Guy was finding that he had a kind of magic ability to zero in on multiple conversations, and over the din of last-minute lighting and prop changes, the running of lines, the general wild flurry of activity, he was now focused on his guests.

"Gilmore Stadium. Before that it was the Salt Lake Oil Field, owned by Arthur F. Gilmore. He was a dairy farmer till they struck oil . . ."

"It's true," Guy said, crouching down at the foot of the stage. "He was digging for water one day, and out came oil instead."

"You're Guy Newman," one of the executives said, and Guy started to laugh. Then he gave a whistle and on cue, Del, Dinah, and Shep broke away from the bustle. One by one, the four of them filed down from the stage to shake hands with their guests.

"We're certainly looking forward to this," Mr. Sunbeam told them. "Are we your only audience today?"

"That's right," Del said. "We always give the sponsors first view."

Mr. Sunbeam introduced his colleagues, two of whom asked Guy and Shep for an autograph for their daughters, the third of whom wanted Shep to sign a record for his wife. He had brought it from home, her favorite album. And then Mr. Sunbeam presented Dinah with an enormous box, wrapped in glittering paper and tied with a bow.

"You may already be familiar with the Mixmaster," he said. "It was the first mechanical mixer to have two detachable beaters. You'll find attachments in the box. Bowls, graters, a slicer-shredder . . ."

"A juice extractor," volunteered one of the other men. "And a drink mixer."

"Meat mincers and dough hooks," said another.

"This here is the 1965 model." Mr. Sunbeam glowed. "It won't hit stores till Christmas."

"Thank you so much," Dinah gushed and immediately handed it to Del.

In their twelve years on television, the Newmans had filmed 420 shows, which meant 420 times advertisers had sat in the audience like this and afterward offered their critiques and concerns. The sole purpose of them being here was to make sure everyone was on the same page and that they had the sponsor's full support.

But today was different. This episode was different. On the set, the Newmans tried to forget all that was riding on its success, and the fact that a big part of that success meant having the sponsors on board from the very first scene to the last.

As the cast was taking their places, Del pulled Guy aside. "No matter what anyone tells you, first-time nerves are no joke. I made a disaster of the *Red Skelton Show* radio episode I directed before I created *Meet the Newmans*. Red himself told me to stick to acting, and I was so disheartened I actually considered it."

Guy had heard the story before, one of his dad's favorite examples of turning your own luck around and showing everyone what you were made of. But now he heard the things Del was saying specifically to him—*You should be nervous.* And *Don't forget who created the show.*

"This is just to say," his father continued, "if at any time you need me to take over for you, I'm right here."

"Thanks," Guy told him. "I'm okay." Usually, he would have said something placating, such as he'd be sure to go to Del if he needed him, and boy was he glad he was there, et cetera. But this time, he resisted the urge, which, for him, was as momentous as John Glenn orbiting Earth two years earlier.

They began the rehearsal. INT. NEWMAN HOUSE—NIGHT. Guy did his best to ignore his father, even though—with every movement and every line—he could feel him there, like an American kestrel, a tiny bird of prey known for its exceptional hovering skills.

Halfway through the first scene, Del interrupted. "Dinah, try reading the line like this. . . ." He quoted her dialogue, acting it out as he did. "More Jane Wyman, less Myrna Loy."

Dinah looked at Guy, who said, "Dad. I've already given my actress direction."

"Of course. But it's good to try multiple line readings."

"Not when you're on a schedule, and not when you have an audience."

Del's eyes slid past Guy to Mr. Sunbeam and the other men who filled the seats. Then, with a forced smile, he held up his hands. "Of course," he repeated. "The last thing I want to do is step on your toes."

In the background, Shep snorted, and his father shot him a look.

They continued with the scene, managing to get through it and move on to the next one before Del stepped in again. Once more, Guy wrestled back control and his father retreated. But it happened over and over, and by the time they finished running through the script—minus Shep's new song—it was almost 7:00 p.m. They looked out into the audience and saw that Mr. Sunbeam and the other men were gone.

"Good work, everyone," Guy told the cast and crew. *Everyone but you, Dad.* "A messy run-through only means a smooth rehearsal and an even smoother live show."

He tried his best to sound cheery, but his heart wasn't in it. There was no way in hell he could go through this again tomorrow.

Back at home, at the end of this interminable day, Guy drove to Toluca Lake and let himself into the main house. He called for his father until he found him standing in the backyard, staring out at the treetops.

Before Guy could launch into the speech he'd rehearsed on the drive over, Del held up a hand. "Listen."

"What?"

"Do you hear the woodpecker?"

"No."

What's gotten into you? Guy wanted to say. Del wasn't one to care about birds or nature. When a northern mockingbird moved into their garden one long-ago spring, he'd chased it away with a broom.

"What were you trying to do today?" Guy began, even though his father was still, apparently, lost in the bird sounds. "At the studio? With the show? The one I'm supposed to be directing. What was that?"

Del listened to the bird a second longer, as if it were the most important thing in the world, before turning to his son and saying simply, "I was trying to help you."

"I don't need your help."

"It's your first show, and it's a big one. It could be our last one."

"And you're afraid I'm going to screw it up. And hey, I might. But I'm going to get at least some of it right. I've got my own way of doing things, which I'm just starting to figure out. And there's no way I'm going to figure it out if you take over. If you want to make suggestions, great. Do it off the set. Not in front of my cast and crew. Don't undermine me. I need them to respect me and take me seriously."

Del sighed. "What happened while I was gone?" He was asking Guy but also the woodpecker and the universe.

"A lot." Guy took a breath, reminding himself of all his dad had been through. "Think of it this way. When I was little and learning to ride a bike, you gave me training wheels, the fastest on the block. And I could go anywhere on those three wheels. But then I got too big for that bike and you got me a bigger one. With two wheels instead of three. And I fell off over and over again."

"And you got back on the tricycle, even though your knees were up to here." Del held his hand up to his forehead. "And you said, 'Why do I have to ride on two wheels when I can ride on three?'"

"And you told me, 'Because you've outgrown that third wheel. And you're ready for two, even though you don't know it.'" Guy cleared his throat, suddenly emotional. "Well, Dad, I'm ready for two. And that's because of you. You got me here. But you need to let me ride."

Del studied him. "You know your mom and I always joke about you being her son and Shep being mine. Not because you're both blond, not because your brother is a musician. But because I understand his temperament. It's why we butt heads. You, though, you're strong like your mother. And you get things done."

"I'm more like you than you know."

"I'm starting to see that."

In the silence, they heard it—the drumming of the woodpecker. Guy watched his dad's profile as he listened to the sound. He looked transfixed, almost serene. Maybe the coma had changed him too.

Del said, "If that little fucker comes for our house, it'll be the last thing he does."

That night, as Dinah was sitting at her bedroom vanity, various pots and bottles before her, Del emerged from the bathroom, hair wet from the shower. She watched him in the mirror, towel around his waist, as he searched through his dresser for the pajama bottoms he'd started wearing to bed after Guy was born, around the time she'd begun wearing a nightgown. Before that, before the boys, they'd slept naked.

Del dropped the towel, and she averted her eyes, out of respect for his privacy, this stranger in her bedroom. It was ridiculous, the looking away. She was his wife. She applied a layer of cold cream to her face and tried to remember the last time they'd had sex.

"Do you remember why you started sleeping in your office?" She met his gaze in the mirror and then began tissuing off the cream, and the day's makeup with it.

"I was an idiot," he said.

"The real answer."

"That is the real answer." He lowered himself onto the bed. "The longer answer is . . . well, I became consumed by the show. I was doing it all. The more I did, the more I needed to do. And somewhere in there, the money became a problem. . . . The lack of money, I should say." He shook his head.

"And we stopped talking." She picked up her brush and ran it through her hair, grateful for this simple task. "After all the years we talked about everything, we just stopped."

"You know, I was gone for three weeks, but it feels like years. I'm trying to catch up, Daisy. I'm not doing a great job of it. I'm an old man who's set in his ways. But I'm trying."

She put down the brush and turned around. "What was it you told me once? You can't film all the scenes at the same time. There's an order for a reason. It's okay if you pace yourself. No one's expecting you to catch up right away."

"That's a good thing," he quipped.

They smiled at one another.

"Move back in here," he said. "Sleep in our bed."

"Where will you sleep?"

"Next to you."

They were two people who had been together for two decades, but Dinah felt a rush of heat in her cheeks and between her legs. She suddenly wanted to go to him and mess up his hair and kiss his mouth and press her bare flesh against his. But she would pace herself too.

"Okay," she said.

They turned the lights out and kept their pajamas on and lay down on top of the covers as if they were strangers. She thought of Claudette Colbert and Clark Gable in *It Happened One Night*, dividing the room in half with a sheet.

"'Have you ever been in love, Peter?'" she said, quoting the movie. Quoting it was a bit they used to do when they were first married. Now it was a test, she realized, to see if they could be in sync again, to see if he even remembered.

Beside her, he said, "'Me?'"

"'Yes. Haven't you ever thought about it at all? It seems to me you could make some girl wonderfully happy.'"

"'Sure, I've thought about it. Who hasn't? If I could ever meet the right sort of girl. Aw, where you gonna find her? Somebody that's real. Somebody that's alive. They don't come that way anymore.'" He skipped ahead. "'She'd have to be the sort of girl who'd . . . well, who'd jump in the surf with me and love it as much as I did. You know, nights when you and the moon and the water all become one. You feel you're part of something big and marvelous. That's the only place to live . . . where the stars are so close over your head you feel you could reach up and stir them around.'"

"'Take me with you, Peter.'" Her voice was soft, a little breathless. "'Take me to your island. I want to do all those things you talked about.'"

In the dark, he found her and pulled her to him. His arms around her, solid and reassuring. Her body pressed to his. Enveloped and cocooned until they fell asleep.

MEET THE NEWMANS

"The Finale"
Network CBS-TV
Directed by Guy Newman
Written by Dinah Newman & Juliet Dunne
Produced by Del Newman & Sydney Weiss
Music by Shep Newman

INT. NEWMAN HOUSE—NIGHT

The grandfather clock strikes midnight. Dinah
stands at the window, worried, angry. Beyond
her, we can see a table set for two.

She sits, picks up a book, continues to stare
out the window. The phone RINGS, loud in the
quiet. She jumps from her chair.

> **DINAH**
>
> Hello?

> **DOCTOR (O.C.)**
>
> Is this Mrs. Newman?

> **DINAH**
>
> Yes. . . .

> **DOCTOR (O.C.)**
>
> I'm afraid there's been an accident.
> We have your husband down here at
> Central Hospital. He's alive but hasn't
> yet regained consciousness. . . .

Dinah drops the phone and starts to race
about the house, one shoe on, searching for
its mate, finally settling for two shoes that
don't match—one heel, one flat. She grabs a
coat—not hers—and the first keys she finds—
also not hers—and exits the house.

EXT. NEWMAN HOUSE—NIGHT

The keys are to Shep's motorcycle. Dinah takes
a beat before climbing aboard and driving
off into the night, coat billowing like a
cape. . . .

FORTY-EIGHT

The morning before the final episode

At 8:00 a.m. on Thursday, Del, Dinah, and Sydney were summoned to the office of James T. Aubrey, where the president of CBS Television, Mr. Sunbeam and one of his partners, and a somber wall of executives, including three CBS censors, were assembled. The two Newmans and Sydney Weiss took their places on the low, cramped sofa like they were awaiting execution by firing squad.

Aubrey, as usual, spoke first. He held up a copy of the final script and waved it over his head. They had waited as long as they could to share it with him, and now, seeing it in his grubby little fists, Dinah wanted to spring from her seat and snatch it from him. "What is this shit?" he roared.

Thump went the script as he slammed it onto his desk. Like the bang of a starter pistol, everyone launched in at once. The episode was offensive and deplorable. They hated the feminist message. Hated the reference, as veiled as it was, to an orgasm, which was *unacceptable* on network TV. *What the fuck did they think they were doing? This wasn't the Newmans. This wasn't what audiences wanted. Had they lost their fucking minds?*

Over the cacophony of voices, James T. Aubrey stalked back and forth across the rug, dropping cigar ash as he went.

"Where is the goddamn wedding? Do you realize how much money I've already sunk into the promotion of the goddamn wedding? Why did no one tell me that the goddamn wedding was canceled? You do realize I can just as easily air a rerun of *Petticoat Junction* or *Candid fucking Camera*."

All the while, Mr. Sunbeam sat on the edge of his chair, his lips pinched so tight beneath his mustache they practically disappeared.

"We're worried about our core audience," his partner said as if his job was to interpret for his boss. "And we just don't feel this script is representative of our values as a company."

"But it's finally representing the world we live in," Dinah said. "Besides, no one here has exactly been a fan of the show as it was. At least not lately."

"All this feminism bullshit," said Aubrey. "I'm assuming that was your idea." He pointed the cigar at Dinah. She started to cough, the smoke causing her eyes to burn.

She wanted to say, *Look here, jackass, not only was it my idea, I wrote the fucking thing.*

"Yes," she said coolly. "I only wish there had been room for more."

"And what do you have to say about this?" Aubrey roared, wheeling on Del. Behind him the executives suddenly looked stricken, as if one of the prop trucks had veered out of the main hall and was coming for them where they sat. "You've been MIA for months. I'm guessing this is as big a surprise for you as it was for us."

"Actually, I've only been gone for three weeks," said Del. "And as for the script, it's about damn time someone talked about what's going on in the world. You're so busy producing garbage about aliens from Mars and sexpots running hotels in the boondocks . . ."

"Don't forget the hillbillies," prompted Dinah.

"Right," said Del. "You can't see the possibilities that exist in real life. The world is changing. I know that better than anyone, and we're all aware this episode might be our last. So let us go out swinging."

Dinah didn't need her husband to stand up for her, but as he joined her in the fight, defending her and her words and her right to say them, she felt herself falling in love with him all over again.

They hadn't done themselves any favors with Aubrey, the executives, or Sunbeam. In something resembling shell shock, Dinah, Del, and Sydney made their way down the busy main corridor to Studio 33, Dinah wondering vaguely how much longer they would make this walk, if maybe this was the last time.

"That went well," said Sydney dryly.

"Thanks for jumping in there, by the way," Del said.

"Don't drag me into this. Even if I could have gotten a word in, the two of you were doing just fine."

"They're going to pull it," said Del. "They're not even going to give us the chance to put it on-air."

"It's not up to them," said Dinah. "It's up to Mr. Sunbeam. If he agrees, if he gives us the okay, we're good."

"That's a mighty big *if*," said Sydney.

"It's too bad his wife wasn't there," said Del. "Didn't you say she was the one who got him to sign on to begin with?"

They stepped out of the way of a rolling wardrobe cart, and then again out of the way of a line of camera equipment. Del and Sydney continued on, but Dinah had stopped walking. *Of course*, she thought.

When the two men realized she wasn't with them, they turned to look at her. People and equipment and props continued to rush past, everyone but Dinah in motion.

"Daisy?" Del called.

She could see it. As if it were right there in front of her. She knew how they would win.

FORTY-NINE

The afternoon before the final episode

I t took Mrs. Sunbeam three short hours to assemble the wives of Sunbeam's most important executives in the first few rows of Studio 33.

Her husband had shared the script with her, the way he shared almost everything relating to the business. She was his sounding board, a job she took seriously. The episode was good. It was funny and heartfelt. And it also had something to say. As talented as Del Newman was, she knew it had not been written by a man.

The wives laughed and clapped and cheered throughout, and during the last scene, Mrs. Sunbeam pulled a handkerchief from her clutch and dabbed at her eyes. Afterward, the women jumped to their feet and applauded, a standing ovation, and she thought, *No, Dinah Newman, you have not let us down.*

FIFTY

The night before the final episode

At the recording studio, Shep and his band experimented with arrangements for his new song. It was the part of the process Shep liked best—the freedom to play with melodies and styles. Rockabilly, blues, soul, country, folk, psychedelic, good old fashioned rock 'n' roll. Or a little of each. What he was looking for was the mood of the song. What it was trying to say. In the past, his father had not only made the producing and marketing decisions but chosen the music too. Shep didn't plan on letting him hear this one until they shot the episode.

As was his custom, Shep closed his eyes while he sang, something he'd been doing since he was a kid. It enabled him to feel the music more, whether here in the studio or onstage. Rarely did he look up, but a mere glance from him, beneath long lashes, was enough to make his fans swoon. He'd never understood how one glance could knock someone off their feet. Not until he met Eileen.

As he sang, he thought of her. He thought so hard about her that he conjured her. Because there she was, standing behind the sound engineer in the control booth.

Shep turned to Hutch. "Do you see her too?"

He half expected Hutch to ask him what the hell he was on about, but instead, he grinned. "Clear as day, brother."

Shep handed the guitar to him and told his bandmates to take five.

He met her in the lobby. She was dressed in a green vinyl raincoat and white half boots, her hair dripping wet from the rain that was now falling over the city. The floor around them was covered in puddles from people tracking it in.

"I love the song," she said. "Even more than that, I love the sound."

"I'm still finding it."

"You'll get there. But it's a great start. It's more you. It's soulful. It's trippy. But also it's got an edge. It reminds me of the Kinks. Of the Zombies a little. But also there's some Carl Perkins in there. And something else I can't describe. Growing pains. Heartache. Fury. Hope. Something that's all you."

For some reason, coming from her, this meant just about everything. Her getting his music and responding to it—understanding it, understanding him—felt more intimate than anything he'd ever done with Lorrie or any other girl.

"I wrote it for you."

"I know."

They stared at one another.

"Are you with her?" Eileen asked.

"Lorrie?"

She nodded.

"No. But she's having the baby."

"Okay." She pulled the hair tie—identical to the one he wore on his wrist—from her ponytail and shook her hair loose. He watched as she combed it with her fingers—something she did when she was thinking—and tied it up again. "I get that you're going to have responsibilities to her and your child. And I also get that sometimes it might not be easy for either of us."

Her eyes, brown with a burst of amber around each pupil, met his.

"But I'm willing to try. As long as you talk to me. I can't try with you if you're not going to talk to me." She smoothed the ends of her ponytail, then put her hands in the pockets of her raincoat. "I'm not a mind reader. I'm not interested in talking only about myself. I know how I feel. I want to know how you feel too. I deserve that, Shep Newman."

"You do," he agreed. "And I'm not great at it. As you know. But for you, Eileen Weld?" He nodded vigorously. "Maybe on my more reclusive days, I can write down how I feel and sing it to you."

She smiled, rolled her eyes a little, shrugged. "I don't like when people promise me things. It's one thing if you hurt each other—that's bad enough—it's another altogether if you made promises first. Just as long as you're doing the best you can. Because that's all any of us can do."

"I will." He'd never meant two words more.

"I will too."

It was all he needed. He took her face in his hands and pulled her into him. In a moment, her arms wrapped around his neck and his arms found her waist underneath her jacket, and their lips met and then met again, over and over until they both forgot where they were.

Hutch walked out long enough to see where Shep had gone off to, then turned around and strolled back into the recording studio. He unplugged his guitar from its amp and said to the drummer and bass player and rhythm guitarist and sound engineer, "I'm pretty sure we're done for the night, fellas."

In the guesthouse, Guy and Kelly were hosting an impromptu party—Howie and Clint and Trent and a few of their other friends, and the new camera operators, a young couple, David and Terrie Walker. The rain thwarted their plans for a cookout, so instead, they crowded into the living room, music on the record player, food spread out in the kitchen, drinks flowing.

At some point, Kelly noticed Guy was missing. When he couldn't find him anywhere—not their bedroom, not the roof—he walked across the lawn to the main house. He found Del in the kitchen making a pot of coffee.

"I can't seem to locate your son," Kelly said. "We're having people over—I thought it would help keep his mind off tomorrow. He seemed like he was having a good time, but then, like the great Houdini, he disappeared."

"I have a pretty good idea where he is," Del said. "Go back to your guests; I'll send him home when he's ready."

Guy's childhood bedroom hadn't changed over the years. The same striped bedspread, the same dark blue walls, the same sports trophies and football gear and books upon books on the shelves and the heavy wooden desk. Unlike Shep's room, it was tidy and clean. Guy had never been one to make a mess, and this realization—like the fact that he was good at pretending—hit Del square in the chest. It was as if his son had been worried about taking up space.

He found him standing in the middle of the room, holding his high school football, the one signed at the end of their last season by his fellow teammates.

"Kelly was looking for you."

Guy turned to see Del in the doorway. "I just needed a little air."

"You know," his father said, "nerves are good. It's part of the adrenaline."

When Guy didn't respond, Del went on. "You captained your team to victory two years in a row. You've actually been directing for years. So I'm not worried about how you're going to do tomorrow. But if you weren't nervous, then maybe I would be." Del pulled something green and shining out of his pocket and held it in the palm of his hand. "Did I ever show you this?"

"Is that an earring?"

"One of your mom's. She gave it to me the night before we debuted the radio show. She said, 'I tried to find a four-leaf clover, but this will have to do.' I've carried it with me ever since."

"A good-luck charm."

"Your mother's my good-luck charm. This is just a token. But it doesn't hurt to have something that reminds you who you are and what you can do." He nodded at the football.

Guy stared down at the ball and then up at his dad as if waiting for more.

"There's a lot you think I don't see," Del went on. "And maybe I haven't always paid enough attention. But that doesn't mean I'm not willing to. The thing I want you to know is that I'm here. If there's ever anything you want to talk to me about or let me in on . . ."

Guy lifted his eyes to meet his dad's. "You mean the fact that I dropped out of USC?"

"What? No. Wait. When did you . . . ?" Del stopped himself. Now was not the time. "You know what. We'll revisit that later."

"So you meant I can talk to you about anything *other* than dropping out of law school."

"Guy."

"Sorry." He smiled, the moment lightened but still warm, still private, just the two of them. "So you're saying you want me to tell you I'm in love with Kelly Faber?"

A single beat, long and loud.

"Yes." And though he might never understand it, Del Newman thought, *It's about damn time you said it.*

The night air was warm and heavy from the rain. In the office windowsill, Dinah and Juliet sat facing each other, listening to the sounds of the party below. They had finished going over the script for the dozenth time. It was as ready as it would ever be.

"Should we join them?" Juliet asked, thinking she could sit here like this forever, on the eve before, cloaked in the satisfaction of what they had done.

"In a minute," Dinah said. "I want to soak it in a little longer."

They sat in companionable silence, Juliet imagining the faces of her father, the Schwab's druggist, Charlie Murdock, and the rest of her male colleagues as they watched the finale. Dinah wishing her mother were here to see it come to life.

Sometime later, the two of them emerged into the backyard and stood watching as the party guests played a loud and raucous game of football on the rain-soaked grass. Bodies leaping and running and falling. Laughter. Shouting. And there, in the midst of it all, was Del.

"Oh, good god," Dinah said.

The ball came sailing toward them, a missile launched from unseen hands. Juliet reached up and caught it and sent it flying back. Then kicked off her shoes and dove into the fray.

Dinah remained on the sidelines, watching as new friends and old friends ran in all directions. Howie, Clint, and Trent, these boys she'd known since they were pimply-faced kids, who had grown up with her sons. Shep and Eileen, looking almost conspiratorial, in a little world of their own. Guy and Kelly, both so golden, so good. She sent up a little prayer to whoever was listening—*Please make it as easy as possible on them.*

The football came soaring once more in her direction, and this time, she plucked it from the air and threw it to Del, who ran far, far, not looking where he was headed. She said another prayer and watched as he executed a perfect leap into the air—he was Balanchine, he was Chaplin at his most poetic—and returned to earth, the ball in his arms.

Afterward, feet firmly planted, his brow was wet, his expression clammy, his breathing labored. But Dinah saw only the young, invincible man she'd married years ago. In that moment, she was consumed by love, and this was another thing they didn't tell you—that you could fall in love with the same person again and again. And then the rain began to pour and the wind began to blow in great, wet gusts, sending them running for cover.

APRIL 23, 1964

Dear Holly Thomson,

Thank you so much for your letter. You began it as so many do, with the words "I know this may never reach you. . . ." Well, Holly, you are right. The television studio doesn't always share the letters that arrive for me. They have created a boilerplate template for replies and a stamp for my signature so that everyone is guaranteed a response. But I want you to know that this is actually me.

It is interesting that the subject of your letter was "Can a woman have it all?" Because lately, this has been very much on my mind. Allow me to answer your question by way of a familial anecdote.

My father used to complain that my mother's people were too emotional and prone to hysteria. His proof was my great-aunt Sally, who was called "eccentric" and even "crazy" by the men who met her. A widow and childless, Aunt Sally never conformed to what her family believed should be her predestined role as a quiet, demure, retiring woman of a certain age. She traveled, she read, she argued, she wrote. When she was in her forties, she even sent herself away to college in a far-distant town. She told me, "I have to spend so much time with myself. I want to be good company."

I tend to agree with Aunt Sally. You don't need to turn heads to know that you are beautiful. You don't need a man telling you what you can and can't do with your body, your mind, or your heart. You don't need to put everyone else's needs before your own. You don't need to solve world peace or cure disease to be important and make a lasting impact. You don't need to do those things and be a mother, a wife, a partner, a housekeeper, a cook, a businesswoman, a sharpshooter, a visionary.

As long as you are in good company when you're on your own. That, I believe, is the secret to having it all.

With love,

Dinah Newman

FIFTY-ONE

The final episode

Dinah sat in front of the mirror in her CBS dressing room, clad in her first costume of the night—dress, apron, pearls, heels. Because they were shooting in color, she had chosen to wear her favorite bright-sky blue, the same shade as her eyes. She knew her lines and her stage directions and, of course, knew everyone else's lines too. The only thing she didn't know was what Shep was planning to sing, but, as she'd told Del, whatever it was would be fine. It would, after all, be the theme that would play them out as the Newmans faded to black.

Juliet was running late. *But it's okay*, Dinah told herself. The two of them had done the work. Now it wasn't just up to them to bring it home, it was up to the entire cast and crew, the audience, and the wives of Sunbeam's executives, the ones who had shown up at the eleventh hour and saved them.

There was a knock on the door. "Fifteen minutes, Mrs. Newman."

She walked the long hall that led from her dressing room to the set. Coming from the opposite direction was her husband in a neatly pressed suit the color of midnight, his hair combed, his shoes polished and spit-shined. Beyond him, she could hear the buzzing of voices and laughter, the sound of a theater filled with 250 enthusiastic, excited people.

"Howie's warming up the crowd," he told her.

"Oh god."

She reached up and, out of habit, straightened his tie. Her eyes met his. They held each other's gaze. It was hard to believe they were here. Twelve years on television. Before that, ten years on radio. The past twenty-three years had led them to tonight. After all this time, they were still in it together.

Dinah pulled Del's face to hers and kissed him softly. Whatever they had gone through, whatever they still had to go through, she had loved this man for each of those years.

She paused to take a breath, to look at him, and then she kissed him again as he gathered her in his arms. The two of them reached for each other, there in the hallway of Studio 33.

They broke apart again. Threw themselves together. Broke apart. Threw together. Over and over, knowing they should stop but unable to stop.

"Oh, screw it," Del muttered.

Without a word, they bumped and jostled and stumbled down the hall, pressing each other into walls. When a doorknob poked at the soft flesh of Dinah's bottom, she gave it a turn and then a push. They fell into a narrow janitor's closet that stored brooms and mops and buckets and cleaning products. Del slammed the door behind them, his lips on her throat, her mouth on his neck, his pants down, her skirt up, and then he was inside her, one hand cupping her ass, the other braced against the wall as if he were holding it up and not the other way around.

She twined her arms around his neck and for several glorious, feverish minutes, forgot about her hair and makeup and wardrobe, the waiting audience, the sponsors' wives, the network, James T. Aubrey, and where the four Newmans would be tomorrow, as she lost herself in the man she loved.

At 8:30 p.m. on Friday, April 24, in front of a live studio audience and a live broadcasting public of forty million viewers who were expecting the wedding of the year, the Newmans filmed—for the very first time in color—the final show of their twelfth season.

The episode opened with Dinah—hair and makeup redone—waiting for Del to get home from work, the dinner burned because—truth be told, she confesses—she's never actually known how to cook. What's more, she can't actually clean either. All these years, she's only been pretending to.

When she gets the call that Del has had an accident and hasn't woken up yet, she drives to the hospital on Shep's motorcycle, where the doctor talks over her head. Del is in a coma. He might never wake up. Dinah reels at the thought of being left on her own without him. A feeling that only grows when she stops by the market afterward and is told she cannot legally obtain a charge account without her husband. She proceeds to learn all the other things she can't do without him. Procure birth control. Apply to an Ivy League school. Serve on a jury. Practice law. Become an astronaut. Run the Boston Marathon. Receive a salary equal to men's.

And all the things she can. Like go to work in her husband's place.

Meanwhile, she inspires Peggy and Eileen and her new friend Renee, played by a young Black actress named Hillary Grey, to stand up for themselves. They are each given a funny, impactful speech about what they will and won't be doing anymore as a modern woman. Eileen picks Shep up for a date instead of the other way around. Peggy starts opening doors for Artie and telling him not to wait up for her when she goes out with girlfriends. Renee invites Dinah to march with her for civil rights. Dinah teaches her sons how to heat up TV dinners in Sunbeam's Automatic Electric Frypan with removable heat control.

Shep asks Eileen to be his steady girl. And there's a new boy in the fraternity house—Kelly, played by popular young movie star Kelly Faber. As he and Guy shake hands, there's a moment—just a moment—where they lock eyes and don't immediately let go.

Then Del wakes up, but guess what? Dinah doesn't want to go back to being a housewife. What's more, she has dreams too. To be a writer.

To be a singer. "Why should I limit myself," she says to him, "just because the world tries to limit me?"

When she announces this to Del, he wonders what her newfound independence means for him. The two of them not only need to navigate his feelings but their marriage.

"Do you still want to be a family?" he asks her.

"Of course. My wanting to do something for me doesn't mean I love the three of you any less."

"And what am I supposed to do while you're at work? Put on an apron? Go to the Women's Club?"

"Why not?"

"So now you're the man of the house, is that it?"

"No. I'm the woman." (Cheers from the audience.)

"You talk about living in a box," he says to her later in the episode. "I don't think that's only true of women. My little prison might look different. Maybe it has larger parameters. Maybe it's a prison of my own making. But it's still a prison."

And then, still later, he tells her, "All these years, you've been there for me and for the boys. How can I be there for you?"

Cut to Del cooking and cleaning, going to the market, sewing buttons, baking pies, and doing the thing he's done all along—listening to his family and offering guidance. Leaving Dinah free to go off to her new job, working at a newspaper. As she gets ready to exit the house, Del hands her a briefcase and gives her a kiss and sends her on her way. He walks her out, watches her climb into her car, but then she gets out and runs back to him.

"I forgot something," she says. "The way I feel right now is beyond myself. It's greater than Dinah Newman. It's true what Betty Friedan says. 'No woman gets an . . .' Well."

And here Dinah broke the fourth wall and spoke directly to the audience, who in this moment were 250 sponsor wives, network executives, members of the press, friends, family, and forty million viewers at home.

"'You don't get one from shining the kitchen floor.' But my god, I feel like I'm having one now."

Then she opens Del's hand and lays her pearls in his palm and sashays down the walk, away from the house, and out into the world.

Then, because *Meet the Newmans* wouldn't be *Meet the Newmans* without a musical finish, they wind up the episode on the set of a nightclub where the entire cast gathers to dance and drink. Dinah takes the stage dressed in an original Renee Otero creation—a thousand glittering shades of red from head to toe, singing Peggy Lee's "I'm a Woman."

Then the finale of the finale—at the same club, Dinah introduces Shep. Del joins them now, twirling his wife around the dance floor as Shep and his band debut "The Girl That Doesn't Leave You."

It is an entirely new sound for him—a melding of rock 'n' roll, country, blues, and psychedelic pop—and it brings down the house. The studio audience jumps to their feet once more, and when the song ends, Shep and his band play it all over again for an encore.

As Guy yells, "That's a wrap!" the audience erupts into applause so loud and long that the show runs three minutes over its allotted time, delaying the beginning of *The Twilight Zone*.

Long after the live show finished, the seats in Studio 33 at CBS Television City remained filled, no one wanting to break the spell of the evening. Dinah took the microphone and gazed out at the sea of faces.

"The world does not believe in women. When a young reporter said these words to me recently, I told her she was wrong. Of course they believe in us. Look at the strides we've made since our mothers were our age. Look at all we can do. We are mothers, wives, and daughters, but we are also doctors, scientists, students, teachers, and writers. We have ferried military planes, won the Nobel Prize, invented the windshield wiper, the chocolate chip cookie, and the peephole, and helped discover the DNA double helix. And yet this young reporter is right. For some reason, the world too often discounts us."

Her eyes met Juliet's.

"I never thought someone so young could give me insight into who I am at this point in my life. Which taught me a very important lesson about judging others without getting to know them first."

Dinah continued in this vein and then offered Juliet the mic. But she merely smiled, Mona Lisa–like, and shook her head. She was done with the spotlight. She had said what she needed to say in the pages of the script.

So Dinah continued. "Someone I love was in an accident recently and had to be placed in a medically induced coma. It's true what doctors will tell you—that coma patients can actually hear what's being said to them. What I learned was that you can't assume someone isn't listening just because they aren't talking. I think we all have to assume that the things we do in this life reach far beyond us and what we know. So if you take away anything from this family of ours—"

She swept her arms wide to include not just her husband and two sons but Juliet and Kelly, Eileen, Hutch, and the rest of the cast, Renee, the crew, Sydney in the wings, Mrs. Sunbeam and the wives of all the Sunbeam executives, and the friends who were gathered, including Flora, Paula, and Benny. And, down in front, on the end of a row, her father-in-law, a wiry man of seventy-five with silver slicked-back hair and glasses.

"If you take away anything," she repeated, the audience suddenly blurring as her eyes grew wet. "Dammit," she said and wiped the tears away. She laughed and the audience echoed her. "If you take away anything," she said for the third time, chin up, shoulders back, regal as a queen. "It's this."

She took a beat, the most dramatic of pauses, and made eye contact with as many people as she could.

"'You don't get an orgasm from shining the kitchen floor.'"

The audience erupted once more as Del, Dinah, Guy, and Shep Newman joined hands and together took one final bow.

FIFTY-TWO

May 8, 1964

Two weeks after *Meet the Newmans* aired its final episode, Dinah and Juliet met downtown at the Original Pantry Café, with its line out the door. Inside, it smelled of bacon and hash browns and burgers from the griddle, and its waiters—in crisp white dress shirts and black bow ties—expertly navigated the overcrowded tables.

"So," Dinah said over the din. "What do we do next?"

Juliet, as usual, had written down ideas. She ran through them quickly, then came to the last one, which she had circled over and over with her pen.

Meet the Newmans had been canceled without fanfare. No final cast party. No goodbyes. The Newmans had simply been left off the fall schedule, and everyone who'd worked on the show went their separate ways. There wasn't even a last showdown with James T. Aubrey who, ten months later, would be let go from CBS under a cloud of suspicion. Headlines would shout: NEVER HAS A TELEVISION EXECUTIVE FALLEN SO FAR, SO FAST!

For the first time in their lives, the Newmans were left not knowing what came next. The cancellation meant Shep would be able to walk away from CBS Records. He had his eye on Capitol, which promised he would be free to make the kind of music *he* wanted to make. The day after the final episode aired, Guy was offered the chance to direct an episode of the number one show in the country, *Bonanza*. And Del was contemplating writing a movie. But there were no more twelve-year guarantees.

"What about," Juliet said, "a TV series about two women from two different generations who have to navigate the political and sexual landscape of a busy big-city newsroom?"

She looked up.

Dinah leaned in. It wasn't enough to hear Juliet say it; she wanted to read the words in the notebook. "Two women," she repeated, "from two different generations who have to navigate the political and sexual landscape. . . ."

"—of a busy big-city newsroom," Juliet finished.

"And the older of the women, she's been at the paper awhile, while the younger one has only recently started working there. And the younger one right away starts judging the older one for not breaking down more barriers."

"And the younger one," Juliet said, "is wondering why on earth the older one, who's really so much older, hasn't ever questioned the sexism at the paper. I mean, it's so rampant."

"And the older one," said Dinah. "I really wish we could stop calling her 'the older one.'" She tapped her chin. "Let's refer to her as Rosalind."

"Like Rosalind Russell? *His Girl Friday*?"

"Yes, so Rosalind tells the younger one—"

"Eve," said Juliet. "After *All About Eve*."

"Cute," Dinah said. "So Eve doesn't begin to understand what Rosalind's been through. And something like, 'I was raised to believe we shouldn't rush to judgment, and we shouldn't judge others based on what we think we know about them.'"

At the familiar words, spoken long ago, Juliet met Dinah's smile with one of her own. Their coffee arrived and with it the menus. They decided to order lunch, and while they waited and then while they ate, they began to argue and throw out ideas, Juliet thinking that Dinah was still so set in her ways and out-of-date, it was a wonder they had ever written anything together. And Dinah thinking it would be a miracle if she didn't kill Juliet before they even decided on the first scene.

Juliet returned to the *LA Times* office feeling the strange sense of relief that always came when she knew what she was writing next. In spite of the way she sometimes lived and the way the public had perceived her, she was not a person who enjoyed floating here and there without some sense of direction. At least not when it came to her work.

"There's a package for you at your desk," Renee sang as she walked past, a cloud of sparkling flowered silk. She opened her eyes wide at Juliet and batted them coquettishly.

Juliet was not in the habit of receiving packages at the *Times*—or anywhere else, for that matter. The only person who might send her something—her mother—didn't even have this address.

The envelope—large and brown—waited on her chair. Juliet picked it up and sat down. *To Juliet Dunne*, it read, *care of the Los Angeles Times.* From: *A planet millions of miles apart.*

She almost held it to her face to breathe it in—the scent of England, that distant land. But instead, she tore it open, and the contents fell out—a compact cassette tape, the type she used to record interviews. There was no note. The only bit of writing was on the cassette itself— *For Juliet.*

Her heart was starting to beat in a quick, frenzied rhythm, a percussive instrument all its own. She dug in a drawer for her tape player and then, without a word to anyone, not even Nick, carried the tape player and cassette outside to the street.

On the nearest corner, she leaned against the cool stone of the building and pressed Play.

She is every color as she shines,
As she shines

That familiar voice, raspy and distinctive, infused with electricity, just like he was—but quieter here, less of a growl. *Almost*, she thought, *a lullaby.*

She is lit up by the sun
And she is mine,
She is mine
She is every color as she shines
As she shines
But she belongs to no one
And she's fine
Yes, she's fine

When it ended, four minutes and twelve seconds later, she started it over, her heart drumming faster and faster, outdistancing the beat of the song.

She began to walk, not paying attention to where she was going. She walked and listened to the words, which didn't mention her name but were clearly about her and for her. About a moment she had shared with the man singing it. A moment in time when they saw each other, really saw each other.

She had loved him. She still loved him. She would maybe always love him. And that was okay. Because she was fine. She was fine.

Five Years Later

April 1969

The year before everything changed for good, the four Newmans set out from points in Los Angeles near and far and converged upon the house in Toluca Lake for the last time.

So much had changed—the house was currently for sale, advertised as *America's most famous home.* Enough time had passed that some of those coming to view it had neither seen nor heard of the TV show it had starred in.

Dinah and Del had bought a lovely bungalow in Laguna Beach that sat on a cliff overlooking the ocean and the horizon beyond. It would be a new chapter, a welcome one.

Guy and Kelly were living in the Hollywood Hills, where, on a clear night, they could see all the way to Catalina Island. Kelly, unwilling anymore to play it straight for the moviegoing public, had moved behind the scenes as a producer, hiring writers, actors, and directors blacklisted during the Lavender Scare. Guy had become one of the most sought-after directors in television. He had a gift for it—the pace, the schedule. He liked how fast it was, how immediate, and he liked the freedom it offered him to spend time with their children, two-year-old Ginny, whom he had adopted earlier that year, and four-year-old Amy, adopted by Kelly. Their fame had made adopting easier—the first "single father" to adopt a child in California had done so just last year—the only caveat being they could not, under any circumstances, mention their sexuality.

Shep and Eileen tied the knot weeks after he turned twenty-one. She had landed in television too, in a sitcom called *The Newly Wed*, but continued to make films when she was on hiatus. Shep still toured with Hutch and the band and made records when it suited him. Sometimes he took months off and stayed home with the kids—Jessica, age three, his daughter with Lorrie, and Daisy, his one-year-old with Eileen. After being lousy with boys for so long, Del observed, the Newman girls had arrived.

Del's memoir was published in 1966—*Meet the Newmans: The Real-Life Story of America's Favorite Family*. He'd written more books since—a series of Hollywood mystery noirs that had seen some success. But more than anything, he loved being a grandfather. His own father, Matthew, had died four years earlier, barely getting the chance to know Del's family. They'd been fortunate to have one year together.

Del could enjoy his grandkids in a way he hadn't been free to enjoy his sons. He discovered that he spoke the language of children, and they followed Grandpa around as if he were Mary Poppins. He wiped tears, bandaged scrapes, and made them laugh.

Flora—called *Mormor* by the kids—was by nature more reserved, but she could produce a sweet out of thin air, her pockets seemingly bottomless, and she had a mind full of fables and fairy tales that the children loved. Now, as Del and Dinah's sons and partners and grandkids took over the house, Flora stood back and watched the happy chaos. It had been a long time since the place had been this full of noise and people.

Three generations of Newmans took their time moving from the yard, the living room, the den, the kitchen, to the dinner table. Once seated, it was Dinah who offered up thanks, not just for loved ones but for the long and happy life they'd lived in the house.

It would be the last time the four of them sat at a table together. Twelve months later, one of those chairs would be empty.

As robust as he was, Del hadn't fully recovered from the accident. Much the way he liked to say he'd left a part of himself back in his football days on the field of the LA Coliseum, he had left a part of himself at St. John's Hospital. A year from now, at the age of fifty, he would be gone, this time for good. Together and separately, Dinah, Guy, and Shep would mourn the man they loved and do their best to keep him alive with stories and anecdotes and memories.

Dinah would never remarry. She and Flora would stay on in the bungalow, where Dinah would write and produce television shows, some with Juliet, some all her own. She would march in Washington, DC, with the National Organization for Women. She would write articles for *Ms.* magazine. She would visit the White House with Betty Friedan and Gloria Steinem, campaign for Shirley Chisholm when the congresswoman ran for president, speak out on behalf of the Equal Rights Amendment, and battle for women's rights.

Her sons brought their children to see her at the beach house whenever they could. Sydney came once and brought his fourth wife. Juliet and Nick would visit when they were in town from New York, where they lived and worked as investigative journalists for *The New York Times*. In 1967, they eloped after *Loving v. Virginia* legalized interracial marriage in every state.

Late at night, when she was alone, Dinah would sometimes turn on the television and watch reruns of the show. *It holds up better than expected*, she would think with pride. Yes, it was corny, but it was also sweet. Most important, they were all four there together—Del very much alive. As vivid and clear as if he were standing in front of her, thanks to the 60 mm film he had insisted on using.

Right now, though, years earlier, on this evening in 1969, the entire, extended Newman family sat at the dinner table—identical to the one on TV—and talked over each other as they ate.

Hours later, when Guy and Kelly and their kids, and Shep and Eileen and their kids, had spilled out the front door into the night in a blur of color and laughter and promises to see each other again soon,

Del and Dinah climbed the stairs to the bedroom they had shared for nearly thirty years.

Just before she closed her eyes, Dinah rolled over to look at her husband. "I was thinking," she began, "as we sat around that table tonight. *Meet the Newmans* hasn't been canceled. It's still going on, only there are more of us now. More Newmans. The only difference is that we're not on television."

Del looked up at the ceiling as he considered this. After a long moment, he said, "Not much pay, but the hours sure are better."

He smiled at her, his real smile, the one he reserved just for her.

With a single finger, Dinah traced his profile and then leaned over and kissed him. She felt his arms slip around her, the reassuring strength and warmth of her husband, of this body and this heart that she had loved for more than half her life. With everything she was, she kissed him back. And then she reached for the bedside lamp and switched off the light.

Acknowledgments

This book has been a journey of happy, boundless joy from start to finish. I wrote it as an ode to the magical medium of television and a love letter to my teenage self, who plastered her walls with the Shep Newmans of her era. I wrote it, in part, as a tribute to Ozzie and Harriet and David and Ricky, whom I discovered in all their black-and-white glory decades after they ruled the airwaves. And I wrote it because I'm fascinated by the behind-the-scenes of events and people. As Dinah says, we all have a behind-the-scenes. But what happens when we let others see it?

Thank you first and foremost to Kerry Sparks, who goes above and beyond the role of magnificent, crackerjack literary agent to be mentor, champion, sounding board, editor, creative partner, and friend. I couldn't do any of this without her, nor would I want to. Thank you to Tim Wojcik and Rebecca Rodd for all they are and do, and to the rest of the incredible team at Levine Greenberg Rostan. And to Sylvie Rabineau at WME for her enthusiasm, wisdom, and genius.

Thank you to Joe Kraemer, who befriended me in the tenth grade in Richmond, Indiana, and has been with me—my partner in crime, my kindred spirit—ever since. We spent many hours writing stories back and forth when we should have been paying attention in class, and so much of my love for writing comes from writing with him. In fact, we once came up with a TV spec script called *Meet the Newmans*, and he graciously allowed me to use that title for this story.

Thank you to Angelo Surmelis, my adopted brother, the Will to my

Grace, my family, who knows all my behind-the-scenes and loves me anyway.

Thank you to Caroline Bleeke, my extraordinary, brilliant editor, with whom it has been a complete and utter delight to work. And the extraordinary, brilliant Megan Lynch, who—with Caroline—saw in its earliest, incubator days what this book could be and helped me turn it into the thing I always envisioned. Their belief in me means more than I can express.

And to everyone at Flatiron Books for giving the Newmans and me the most wonderful book home—Mary Retta, Leah Carlson-Stanisic, Emily Walters, Frances Sayers, Eva Diaz, Maris Tasaka, Marlena Bittner, Katherine Turro, and Cat Kenney. And to Will Schwalbe and Bob Miller, who were not only with the Newmans from the start but published my very first book all those years ago.

And speaking of my very first book, Pan Macmillan was my first UK book home, and now I've returned to the roost with *Meet the Newmans*. Huge heartfelt thanks to my superb editor, Francesca Pathak, and to everyone there who has contributed in some way to bringing Dinah, Del, Guy, Shep, and Juliet to life: Melissa Bond, Daisy Bates, Emma Pidsley, Sian Chilvers, Emily Sumner, Natasha Tullett, Poppy North, Kimberley Nyamhondera, Stuart Dwyer, Leanne Williams, Poppy Morris, Lucy Grainger, Ellie Kyrke-Smith, and Claire Bush.

I'm indebted to my earliest readers—Kerry Sparks; my husband, Justin Conway; and fellow authors Angelo Surmelis and Kerry Kletter.

Dinah and Juliet's focus group wouldn't exist without the input of Amy Beashel, Ronni Davis, Kerry Kletter, Adriana Mather, Danielle Paige, Kelis Rowe, Kerry Sparks, and Beth Jennings White, eight powerhouse friends who took the time to talk to me about what it is to be a woman. And to the other strong women in my life—too many to list—who never cease to inspire me. Ansley Conway (my sweet, brilliant, beautiful Lady), Jennifer Koerner, Terrie Walker, Karen Prebble, Ashley Buchanan Williamson, Gay McGee Karlsson, Doris Knapp, Lynn Duval Clark, Krista Ramirez, Janet Geddis, Coddy Granum, Staci

Dawdry, Stacy Monticello, Holly Thomson, and the late Lucy Kroll, just to name a few.

Thank you to my parents, Penelope Niven and Jack F. McJunkin, who taught me to dream big, and who are proud of every book I write, even though they aren't here to read them. And to my mother in particular, who instilled in me the importance of loveliness, compassion, silliness, and unconditional love, and who—when I decided at nine that I wanted to be a writer—made sure I was fully stocked with paper, pens, books, and belief in myself.

When my grandmother Eleanor was alive, she would call up bookstores in the greater Charlotte, North Carolina, area and ask if they carried the latest books by Mom or me. If they didn't, she would say, "Well, you should!" and hang up. So thank you to Grandmama. And to my grandmama Cleo, for passing down her love of fashion, glamour, and all things Hollywood, as well as her sour cream cinnamon coffee cake recipe. And to my magical grandfathers, for being two of the greatest men I have ever known.

Thank you to my husband, Justin Conway, for picking up the baton that fell crashing to the earth when my mother died too soon. Not only is he the love of my life, he is my person and my best, the Clark Gable to my Claudette Colbert. I love you more than words. Always.

To my devoted (and, at times, highly disruptive) literary kitties—inside and outside—who sat on my desk, judged every line, and purred their little hearts out. Scout, Linus, Luna, Kevin, Zelda, Roo, Harriet, June, Angus, and Olly. Not to mention Ozzie, Tabs, Mr. Greenjeans, and Sue. And to Ashton Conway, who believes we have far too many but is always helpful and never disruptive of my work.

Endless gratitude to my friend family and my blood family, and to the booksellers, librarians, and educators who are on the front lines, placing our books in the hands of those who need them.

To my cherished readers, without whom I wouldn't be able to do what I do.

And to my great-aunt Sally, for never apologizing for being herself.

About the Author

Jennifer Niven is the #1 *New York Times* and internationally bestselling author of thirteen books, fiction and nonfiction, including the massive breakout *All the Bright Places*, which she also adapted for film. Her award-winning books have been translated into more than seventy-five languages and have sold upward of 3.5 million copies worldwide. Jennifer has loved television and film her whole life and has been lucky enough to develop projects with Netflix, Sony, ABC, and Warner Bros. She divides her time between coastal Georgia and Los Angeles with her husband and literary cats.